Jack had to grab Sara's shoulders to prevent her falling against him.

But it brought her close. Too close. Jack didn't pull her in, but he didn't push her away. A flood of sensual memories washed over him. The heady fragrance of ginger-lemon soap and the sound of the rain beating on the windows brought back vivid memories of burying his fingers in the frothy, scented strands of Sara's hair as he bathed her in the shower.

A heartbeat after the thought flashed in his mind, he found his tongue in her mouth. Hot, steamy water pounded his shoulders. Sara's slick, soapy, naked body pressed against his.

They kissed frantically until they were both panting and breathless.

Without warning, Sara ripped her mouth from beneath his, her breathing labored, her eyes flashing fire. "I'm going to *kill* you, Jackson Slater." She used both hands to shove him away. Hard.

"Hell—it wasn't—" The steaming water suddenly turned cold, just like her eyes before she vanished.

Braced by his arm, Jack thumped his forehead against the cool white tiles. To say he was in trouble didn't begin to cover it. Sara might be amping his powers, but she was messing with his head—and apparently with his ability to control his powers.

Turn the page for rave reviews of Cherry Adair's sensual thrillers!

Night Shadow

"Smoothly blends sensuality and espionage. . . ."
—*Publishers Weekly*

"Pulse-pounding . . . all the danger, treachery, and romance a reader could wish for. . . . Exceptional."
—*Romantic Times*

"Cherry Adair's intricately woven plot . . . will make your pulse race and your palms sweat."
—*Fresh Fiction*

Night Secrets

"Tremendous!"
—*Romantic Times*

"The night sizzles to new heights in these novels of romantic suspense."
—*Fresh Fiction*

White Heat

"A steamy fusion of romance and heart-stopping suspense."
—*Publishers Weekly*

"Heart-stopping adventure . . . spicy."
—*Library Journal*

Hot Ice

"A relentless page-turner with plenty of enticing plot twists and turns."
—*Seattle Post-Intelligencer*

"A very sexy adventure that offers nonstop, continent-hopping action from start to finish."

—*Library Journal*

Hide and Seek

"Cherry Adair stokes up the heat and intrigue in her adventurous thriller."

—*Romantic Times*

"Wow, it's gripping, sexy as all get out, and the characters will send you into orbit in steam heat . . . enough chills to keep you on an adrenaline high for the duration of the story."

—The Belles and Beaux of Romance

"Full of highly charged sensuality and violence."

—*Rendezvous*

"Outsize protagonists, super-nasty villains, and earthy sex scenes."

—*Publishers Weekly*

"A reason to stay up way too late."

—The Romance Journal

Kiss and Tell

"A sexy, snappy roller-coaster ride!"

—*New York Times* bestselling author Susan Andersen

"A true keeper."

—*Romantic Times*

CHERRY
ADAIR

BLACK
MAGIC

Pocket **STAR** Books

New York   London   Toronto   Sydney

Pocket Star Books
A Division of Simon & Schuster, Inc.
1230 Avenue of the Americas
New York, NY 10020

Copyright © 2010 by Cherry Adair

First Pocket Star Books paperback edition August 2010

POCKET STAR BOOKS and colophon are registered trademarks of Simon & Schuster, Inc.

For information about special discounts for bulk purchases, please contact Simon & Schuster Special Sales at 1-866-506-1949 or business@simonandschuster.com

The Simon & Schuster Speakers Bureau can bring authors to your live event. For more information or to book an event contact the Simon & Schuster Speakers Bureau at 1-866-248-3049 or visit our website at www.simonspeakers.com.

Text design by Jacquelynne
Design by

Manufactured in the United States of America

10 9 8 7 6 5 4 3 2 1

ISBN 978-1-4391-5381-9
ISBN 978-1-4391-6710-6 (ebook)

In memory of friends
I loved and admired for more than half my life:
Cynthia Reed and Kate Duffy.
Two extraordinary women who had had strength, humor,
and integrity, and whom I'll miss more than they could
have ever known.

Damn rude of you both to have left when things
were just getting interesting.

~ Prologue ~

Jackson? Get your ass in here."

Shit. Another minute and he'd've been upstairs. Sixteen-year-old Jackson Slater paused just inside the door to his father's study, fingers shoved into the back pockets of his jeans. "What's up?"

The log fire in the hearth cast flickering shadows on the walls of the dimly lit room, which was littered with untidy stacks of books and old newspapers. It smelled strongly of scotch fumes. Great. The old man had been boozing it up again. His father sold newspaper advertising space during the day, and spent his nights drinking.

Everything in the room looked the same, but an unfamiliar, electrically charged vibe made the hairs on the back of Jack's neck prickle.

Looking at his father was eerily like looking at himself in the mirror twenty-five years from now. Same dark hair, same piercing go-to-hell blue eyes, same strong jaw, but with deep lines of dissipation pulling downward around his father's mouth. His father hadn't smiled in the ten years since Jack's mom had died of lupus.

No excuse. He'd been a violent, unpredictable shit

as long as his son remembered. *Before* the drinking had started. There was no reason for his father to be the way he was. Jack figured some people just chose to be god-damned unhappy and shitty all the time. His father was one of them.

"How was school?" Sitting in his worn leather easy chair beside the fire, his father beckoned him into the room. He sounded tense. Not surprising. Verbal communicating wasn't his style. Give him a nice sturdy stick or a fist, and Jackson Slater Sr. was a happy guy.

Jack glanced at the bottle of scotch sitting within easy reach. Half empty. He could already predict what was coming. "Good," he muttered cautiously, trying to remember any infraction, minor or major, from the last couple of days. He could think of several right off the bat. But it was unlikely his father knew or gave a shit that he'd had sex with smoking-hot Rachel Thomason in the backseat of her car after school that afternoon.

Jack slouched against the doorjamb, neither in nor out. He had a date with Rachel later. She'd taught him the nuances of French-kissing, and he was an avid student. Tonight he'd teach *her* a thing or two when they weren't restricted by time and a gearshift.

"Come in," his father said impatiently. "There's something I have to give you." Irritation laced his words.

Have to? Today was Jack's birthday, but since his father wasn't into gift-giving, it was unlikely he was talking about the car Jack wanted. And he was pretty damned sure his father hadn't sent him the watch that had appeared hovering over his head in the early hours of that morning. Where it had come from, and why today, Jack had no idea. But it was a cool watch with a striated agate face and a gold bezel. He'd worn it to school.

"But first we have to talk," his father added belligerently.

Crap. "No need for a lecture," Jack said coolly. "I'm saving money for the car myself." The odd jobs he'd been doing for a construction company after school not only added to his savings, they kept him the hell out of the house.

His father's blue eyes flashed a warning. "This isn't about a damn car. *Sit.*"

Jack crossed the room to flop in the opposite chair. He might look relaxed, but he sure as hell wasn't. Sitting meant he was pinned and might not be able to move fast enough to block anything Dickwad threw at him. He braced himself to deliver some serious whup-ass if his father made a wrong move.

Jack's wizard skills weren't as honed as his father's, but he was working at them. Cold had been the Slater family's power to call for seven generations. For years, Jack had considered it a wussy power. His friends and fellow wizards had kick-ass superpowers, like Chad's ability to become amphibious, or Edelstein's ability to Mindwipe. But those were skills he could, and would, learn over time.

Still, once he'd mastered conjuring a hailstorm, he'd advanced to materializing razor-sharp shards of ice. Now Jack had an arsenal of cold powers that was just as serious as the superpowers of his friends.

This better not take long—he didn't want to keep

Rach waiting. *Bring it on, old man.* Jack shifted his center of gravity, ready to move. Fast. "Things to do, places to go," he told his father, glancing at the broad-banded agate face of his watch before looking up to meet his father's icy gaze. *And fuck you too.*

His father cleared his throat. Uh-oh. Throat-clearing indicated his father wasn't happy—and high stress for Jackson Slater Sr. equaled pain for Jack.

He was taller than his father by almost a foot now. Taller, and stronger. If the son of a bitch came at him, Jack would take him down. Hard. He was through having his father's point of view shoved down his throat. Never again. Today he was sixteen. A man. No one was ever— *ever*—going to use him as a punching bag again.

He leaned forward, bracing for a long lecture about . . . *something.* They rarely had a real conversation. It seemed to Jack that when they did, his father saved up every unused word, then strung them together in a monologue that could last hours. Jack felt a monologue coming and silently cursed.

"The Book has decreed that you have ownership of it from this day forward."

Holy shit! Stunned, Jack sat up, his heart pounding. He'd only glimpsed the Aequitas Book of Answers once, the day his mother died. His father, drunk and destroyed, had looked for answers. Jack, standing nearby, had too—any kind of damned answers to explain why a terrific mother had to die, while the shitbag she was married to lived. He'd seen the Book, but only the rightful owner could retrieve it from its invisible psionic safe.

It had been in the family, passed from father to son, for thousands of years, a mark of their family's leadership position within the wizard community. Being an Acquitas was far more important to his father than Jack himself had ever been. His father was a relatively young guy—forty-one—and Jack had always figured, if he'd thought about it at all, that he'd receive the Book when he was in his thirties or forties. "Isn't that a bit . . . premature?" he asked cautiously.

"Not my decision." His father cleared his throat. Twice. "The Book has spoken. Stand up."

Jack rose, but kept ten feet of carpet between them. The fireplace poker—a favorite nonmagic weapon—was right by his father's chair.

"Put out your hands, palms up, to receive it."

He extended flattened palms, ready to yank them out of the way if Dickhead struck. The fine hairs on Jack's body suddenly rose as magically charged air shifted and swirled around him in a current of cold air. Holy shit, it was *strong*. He braced his feet, holding his breath as he felt the power of the psionic safe hover nearby. Waiting for *him*.

"What do I do?" he whispered. He felt it, but still couldn't see anything. He had the odd sensation of being underwater as sounds muted and his vision pinpointed down to his outstretched hands.

"Call it to you."

Jack focused on bringing the invisible safe to him. His skin felt ice cold as if the psionic safe holding the Book hovered inches above his spread hands. He sucked in a breath that caught in his lungs as the safe instantly materialized. "Holy shit," he breathed, awestruck by the strength of the magic emanating from the glowing cube.

A twenty-three-inch square, the safe was an intricately carved, clear block of ice with a slightly convex top. A faint, pulsing green light revealed that nothing else was encased inside. Where was the book?

"Open it."

Jack swallowed against the dryness in his throat as he mentally repeated the spell he'd learned from his father when he'd been a small kid. Jesus. Did he even remember all the correct words?

Apparently so.

A hingeless door in the front of the cube opened with a distinct pop as the seal broke. A plume of acid-green smoke, smelling strongly of ozone, spiraled from inside, then hovered like a drape over the safe as if to protect it.

The cube disappeared, and the book fell into his hands. Unprepared for the sudden weight, Jack dropped it. As he lunged to catch it, his father shimmered in front of him, face red with fury, breath reeking of scotch. Jack closed his fingers around the heavy leather-bound book as it hovered inches off the floor.

"Clumsy idiot!" The poker swished upward, then slashed down. At the same instant, the Book jerked between Jack's hands, partially blunting the blow. It still hurt like hell as the cold metal rod bit into the side of his hand. More concerned for the safety of the impossibly heavy tome, Jack barely felt the pain, although he was pretty sure his thumb was broken.

Gently lifting the Book, he straightened with it

clutched firmly in both hands. Almost without thinking, he shot a powerful bolt of cold toward his father,
who was yelling as he swung the poker again. The noise
cut off abruptly. In his peripheral vision, Jack caught
his father's shocked expression as he was literally thrown
back, then pinned in his chair by thick ice restraints
across his chest, wrists, and ankles. His father cursed him
as he struggled uselessly against his bonds.

Awed, Jack hefted the Book. Little sucker must weigh
fifty pounds or more. Unlike the icy safe, the Book was
almost alive in his hands. Warming to the touch. Vibrating. It's magical power jolted up Jack's arms and traveled
pleasantly through his body.

Hundreds of Slaters had held it in their hands, just
like this. Felt the heartbeat of its power flow through
their veins. Felt the same surge of energy and strength
that Jack felt now. How was it possible for something so
small to exude so much power? he wondered, examining
the intricately embossed leather cover, brown and cracked
with age. The gilt-edged papyrus pages were warped with
a thousand years of careful study, the gold-leaf text on
the tooled cover flaking in places and hard to read.

Carefully supporting the weight on one hand, he
attempted to flip open the cover. No go. He tried again.
The Book was sealed shut. "How do I open it?" he
demanded, not taking his eyes off the Book. When his
father didn't answer, Jack glanced up, narrow-eyed. "Tell
me how to open it."

"You can't keep me pinned here forever," his father
snarled, livid. "You won't take me by surprise again,

you ungrateful little shit. I have powers you've never—"
His eyes opened wide as a dagger of ice nicked the skin
beneath his right eye. Jack kept it hovering there, a millimeter from his father's eyeball. He got a bloodthirsty
thrill from seeing a few red drops run down his father's
lean cheek.

"I'll kill you for this," his father snarled.

Not tonight, old man. "Answer the question."

"The Book will answer when you have a valid question."

Jack didn't know what the hell a valid question *was.*

As suddenly as the Book and safe had made their
appearance, he found himself empty-handed again.
"Damn it!" His heart sank. What had he done wrong?

A glance at his father told him no help would come
from that quarter. Bitterly disappointed, Jack turned to go.

"Release me from these damned restraints," his father
shouted. "I have to do my duty and tell you of your heri-
tage."

"No thanks. The subject was covered in school."

"There are things you can't learn at wizard school,
Jackson. If you want access to the Book, you *have* to listen. It's part and parcel of the transference."

Damned if he did, and damned if he didn't. Jack
paused at the door, then half-turned to pin his father
with a withering glance. "Make it fast, then."

His father glowered at him. "If you want the Book
and all that goes with it, sit your ass down and *listen.*
There's magic in the words of the ancient tale. They must
be repeated in the same way they've been repeated for

centuries as the Book passed from son to son. If you're too damn busy to listen, then I wipe my hands of you."

Jack didn't bother keeping his dislike out of his voice. "Thought you already had."

His father cocked his head. The ice dagger closely followed the movement. "The Book is no longer mine. Nothing I can do about that," he said bitterly. "If you don't listen to the tale, the Book will disintegrate within forty-eight hours. Think of that, Jackson, as you gallop off on your high horse. Hundreds of Slaters have drawn more power than you can even imagine from the pages of the Book. Willing to toss that away because you can't be bothered to hear me out?"

Jack returned to his chair and sat down. "Fine, start talking, but make it quick." He didn't want to talk to his father, but he was riveted. Intrigued. Hell, *excited*, to finally hear the legend of the Aequitas Book of Answers.

"Millions of years ago—remove these restraints, Jackson. Remove them now, or you'll curse the day you were born."

"Unless what you have to say is relevant, can it. Keep on track. Myth. Aequitas Book of Answers. Go."

His father's eyes narrowed. *Yeah*, Jack thought with satisfaction, *the worm has turned*. He was now magically as strong as his father—maybe stronger. Jackson senior had just met his match. More important, his father had no choice. The Book decreed who and when, and the transference wasn't up for negotiation. Jack thought it was hilarious that the Book had the answer to making his father toe the line. Sweet.

"The earth was populated by strange, enormous beasts," his father contrived and humans had yet to appear. There lived a giant, magical serpent named Ophidian. Ophidian drew his strength and rejuvenated his magical powers from the thousands of invisible ley-lines crisscrossing deep within the earth like arteries. He roamed the landmasses and oceans freely. The ley-lines' power was generated by the inner movement of the planet itself and was inexhaustible, and Ophidian was immortal."

"Tell me about the Book. I'm a hell of a lot more interested in the leys than I am in a giant mythical snake." He'd heard Ophidian stories since he was a toddler. None of them, as far as Jack was concerned, bore repeating.

"Yes, I remember. That experience when you were a child," his father said unsympathetically of Jack's near-death encounter with snakes as a kid. "Where the hell was I? Yes. As the only sentient being on the planet, he was the supreme and unchallenged god. Solitary for thousands of years, he searched for a mate.

"Year after year, Ophidian combed the planet, observing changes in the flora and fauna and waiting, always waiting, with the endless patience given to all serpents. At last, he found the goddess Aenari. Her strange and unfamiliar human form fascinated him. She was beautiful, delicate, mystical, and powerful in her own right. A goddess of the night. But she had no interest in a giant snake, no matter how handsome and charming he might be.

"Rebuffed, Ophidian kidnapped the beautiful Aenari from her home, returning with her to his lair—"

"High in the mystical and cloudy Pyrenees Mountains," Jack cut in. "It was a dark and sto—" It was just as well that looks couldn't kill. Well, actually, they could with some wizards; fortunately, that wasn't one of his father's gifts. The old man glared and spoke over him; nothing new there.

"There he loved Aenari in his own fashion, but he controlled her." His father repeated the tale in a flat monotone, his face slack now as if he were in some sort of trance; okay, something new after all. Jack began to really listen. "He kept her a prisoner until she bore him many wizard sons, each of whom inherited a unique mix of his parents' supernatural powers.

"Only sons?"

"No. There were females on both sides, but only the males could rule. This is how it's written. Now shut the hell up and don't interrupt again. All drew their powers from the leys, making their homes near the most potent lines, those closest to the surface. To the humans who had arisen to dominate the globe, they became known as wizards, shamans, mages; every culture had a different name for them and their powers, but the meaning was the same."

His father's eyes were glazed as he looked into the middle distance, barely aware that Jack was there. "Aenari prayed her sons would never know the dark heart of Ophidian, and she demanded they assist the mortal race, just as their father abused the mortals' friendship and trust. As humans evolved, turning away from magic, she taught her sons to conceal their powers so they could walk in tandem with man. Trapped and miserable within the mountains, she told her sons that only love would bring them happiness—without this tender human emotion, their very souls would wither and die."

Jack wondered savagely if his father had ever truly loved his mother.

"Aenari understood that with great power comes great responsibility," his father continued. "When the soil of the farmers' lands required nourishment, the wizards provided floods to blanket the earth with rich, dark nutrients. They oversaw the eruption of volcanoes to even the balance of overcrowded vegetation. Ecological balance was imperative, and she guided them well. The wizards also kept a careful watch on the duration of human wars and the natural order of plant and human life. Over the centuries, many of these wizard offspring became leaders, teachers. Men of thought and science."

Jack didn't believe his father had ever loved the frail woman he'd married. It was just something a guy did in those days. His father had told him flat-out that all he'd ever wanted was a son. But Jack had no idea why such a cold, impersonal man would desire a child. He was a shitty parent. Always had been.

"Not all of Aenari's offspring were good. Some were tainted by Ophidian's dark side, and instead of protectors, they became warriors. Mayhem and chaos erupted."

His father materialized a glass, magically tilted the bottle beside him to add two fingers of his preferred scotch, and brought the glass to his mouth while still firmly bound. He drank it all down, then the glass disappeared.

"What did Aenari do about that? Didn't she try to stop them?"

"Sometimes evil is just—evil. You can't change it."

Yeah. Jack got that. He looked at his father. "Go on."

"Aenari loved her sons and their sons too, but as time passed, some were filled with arrogance and a sense of entitlement, while others blended with humans, only using their magic for the good of mankind. Proud, Aenari named this group of sons Aequitas, Keepers of the Earth."

Jack's skin prickled, and he leaned forward in his chair. Wizard school taught the basics of wizardry. But what his father was telling him was the history of his own line. Jack was Aequitas through and through. If nothing else, his father had always been proud that he'd produced another Aequitas wizard. Kept the line alive. Of course, Jack had often wondered if his father could possibly be an Omnivatic since he was such a mean-spirited bully, but that bad-seed branch of the family had been killed off thousands of years ago, so it just came down to him being a bastard.

"Ophidian, not to be outdone, named his unholy faction Omnivatic—All-Powerful. Those sons were his pride and joy, and nothing they did was discouraged. The two factions fought night and day; months turned into years, and years into centuries as the brothers fought to the death—all for supremacy over mankind.

"Ophidian sat back, encouraging the Omnivatics to battle their brothers. No one else had matching wizard power; no one else had their magical strength. No one else wanted to rule the earth as much as they did. Over the millennia, each wizard developed extra magical powers. While teleportation, becoming invisible, and levitation were common, each generation developed superpowers possessed only by a select few. They used these unique superpowers to vanquish one another when the Omnivatics reverted to snake form, which was the only time when they were at all vulnerable to attack.

"Watching his sons' battles was fine entertainment, and Ophidian worked both sides, fueling the discords so that their wars would escalate.

"The Aequitas couldn't allow their brothers to rule, knowing the devastation this would cause. They appointed a governing council to oversee and resolve all disputes. The Aequitas Council of Twelve was called the Archon. Emulating their brothers the Omnivatics formed a council they called the Erebus, not to oversee but to instigate further chaos. The Omnivatics didn't just battle their Aequitas brothers; they battled one another for supremacy as well. There was only room for one ruler.

"Over thousands of years, Omnivatic brother killed brother, until their lair in the Pyrenees was littered with whitened bones. Each was determined to gain supremacy and become the leader of the Erebus.

"Eventually there were twelve brothers ruling on each side. "Those sons had sons, although it was hard to find human women who could survive bearing the Omnivatics' young, and their offspring became Half wizards. They were lesser wizards with weaker powers, but just as destructive as their more powerful fathers."

"Plenty of Halfs at school," Jack pointed out. "Most of them decent guys."

His father again used magic to materialize and refill his glass, draining it as if his son hadn't spoken. "As the wizard battles raged, their attacks on one another caused tidal waves, earthquakes, floods, and hurricanes. Earth was in chaos. Aenari and her Aequitas sons were stunned at the resilience of mortals as they rebuilt their world time after time. No amount of death or destruction defeated them.

"Aenari called a forum, fearing that one day humanity would lose the battle once and for all. Her Aequitas sons wanted peace—a chance to live normal lives with the women they loved. Her Omnivatic sons thrived on tragedy. Aenari cursed them—Ophidian's favorites. She made them sterile so that they couldn't breed more darkness. She cursed the Omnivatic females, causing them to become barren for a thousand years. Furious at his wife's meddling, Ophidian gave his favored sons the ability to assimilate the powers of all those they killed, as compensation for his mate's curse."

"What the hell does that mean?" Jack asked, intrigued. "They sucked the juice out of their enemies? That's pretty damned sick. What happened to the wizard who'd had all his powers—what? *Extracted?*"

"An Omnivatic entered an enemy's body to withdraw his power, causing his victim to temporarily have their joint powers. When he was done, the Omnivatic evacuated the shell. His prey eventually weakened and died. The attacking wizard gained not only his foe's magical strength, but all his superpowers as well."

"Scary shit." But damned cool, too.

"Not thwarted, Aenari cursed the Omnivatics again. Though they, like her good sons, were capable of walking unnoticed among men, she cursed these ancient wizards to return to their home high in the Pyrenees every thirty-three days, when they would return to their father's form. For twenty-four hours, they were to revert to their snake form and shed their skins and rejuvenate in the manner of snakes, to regain both their human form and their powers."

"If the Omnivatic did not return home at the specified time, he retained his powers but could not change back from snake to human form. Aenari knew their weakness was her Aequitas sons' strength."

His father upended the bottle to refill his glass. "Almost indestructible in human form, the Omnivatics were easier to kill in their original snake form. But since they were indistinguishable from other reptiles, they were almost impossible to identify. Only wizards with similar or stronger power levels could destroy them.

"The rejuvenation process gave the Aequitas an opportunity to kill them, and also time to aid the earth's healing."

"Ophidian retaliated by cursing his Aequitas sons. No longer immortal, they must live among the mortals they so admired. They could marry and have children, but their lives would be pitifully short, only a mortal's span.

His father fought briefly against his bonds, then gave up. He shot his son a vile look, which Jack barely noticed.

"After a thousand years of conflict, Aenari caught Ophidian when he was in his nest and at his most vulnerable. She flung his body into the firmament, using powerful magic to prevent him from returning to earth. Ophidian transmogrified into a powerful comet. Aenari's spell prevented him from making contact with the earth, but when he got close enough his magnetic powers pulled at the planet, increasing the Omnivatics' power a thousandfold.

"The Omnivatics had one chance at procreation. As Ophidian's comet orbited close to Earth every three hundred and thirty-three years, the Omnivatics had mere hours to find a fertility goddess to take their seed. The magnetic pull on his sons while they were shedding enabled a few—under the right circumstances—to sire offspring."

The sexual frenzy part of the story had always interested Jack. But now, as the history of the Aequitas unfolded as a whole, he was fascinated by the ancient hurling of curses, and by the ability of the Omnivatics to suck the powers from their enemies. He had a thousand questions, but he kept quiet. The Book was his now. When he needed answers, the book would supply them.

"Ophidian changed the comet's trajectory, causing massive volcanic eruptions, enormous tidal waves, and huge temperature fluctuations, keeping the Aequitas too busy helping humanity to search for their Omnivatic brothers. Throughout history, and despite these checks and balances, the Omnivatics became the scourge of the earth—despots and torturers, dictators and anarchists.

Their powers strongly linked to the invisible leylines and the land, they caused wholesale death and destruction by instigating 'natural disasters'—earthquakes, tsunamis, and volcanic eruptions.

"The Wizard Wars happened so far back in time that the stories passed into the realm of mythology. And with every passage of the comet, the Aequitas destroyed more of the known Omnivatics, until finally they became extinct."

When Jack was young, his father's stories about the snakelike wizards had been told to scare Jack straight. That had worked until he was about twelve. Then the fists had taken over, and that had scared him a hell of a lot more. Those days were now over. He'd physically restrained his father for the first time in his life. It wouldn't be the last.

"The Omnivatics are just a myth. A parable of good and evil," Jack pointed out flatly, getting to his feet. "I don't get what any of this has to do with the Book of Answers." He released his father's restraints when he reached the door, but put a binding spell on him to keep the older man in place. He didn't put it past him to attack when Jack's back was turned. "It's not like the Omnivatics were real."

"Be sure of that, Jack. Be very sure as you go through life with those high ideals of yours." His father's smile was pure evil as he leaned back and crossed his legs. "I'd watch out for snakes if I were you, son."

$\backsim$ One $\backsim$

Pilbara region, Western Australia
Present day

Jackson Slater lowered himself over the crumbling rim of the volcanic plug, then dropped into the cooler, shadowy dimness of a rust-colored soda trachyte rock tube. He didn't need the rope. He was a wizard, after all, and perfectly capable of drifting down the seemingly bottomless vertical tunnel, light as a feather, without it. But what the hell was the fun in *that*?

He was a wizard, but he was foremost a geologist. A field hand of earth science. Confined spaces, sweat, and the adrenaline rush of new discoveries fed his soul and fueled his imagination. The ley he was following originated south of Perth in Mandurah, south of Perth ran up through the mountains through small towns like Sandstone and Wiluna, and ended here in the Rudall River National Park.

Jack had climbed mountains, forded rivers, and slept on the hard ground for months to reach his conclusions before presenting his latest findings to the Archon

Council, which would in turn share that information with the Wizard Council.

How deep was this tunnel? he wondered, descending hand-over-hand. The plug, six feet across, didn't give him a lot of room to maneuver. He was a big guy. He'd been in darker, tighter plugs in other parts of the world, but rarely had he experienced this kind of intensity. Every twenty feet, he took out the meter to observe the happy dance of the gauge.

Jesus. *Look* at the thing jump. He couldn't wait to get back to his temporary lab in Perth and run his samples through the chromatograph.

The salt lakes characteristic of this desert region, part of a palaeodrainage system, indicated there was probably water far below. He could almost smell it, but what riveted his attention was the powerful force of the ley he was tracking. The leys, invisible force fields of magnetic energy deep within the earth's crust, were a source of power to wizards—millions of whom lived, worked, and thrived unnoticed along the leys, coexisting with the humans who had no idea magic was in their midst and beneath their feet.

The Archon, governing body of the Aequitas, had given him the enormous and delicate task of mapping and cataloging the thousands of leylines banding the globe. As keepers of the land, the Aquitas were charged with the safety and well-being of the mostly oblivious mortals around them.

"Oh, yeah. I feel you." His voice echoed slightly. The strong vibration of magic zinged through his body as though he were a tuning fork. Intense, alive, the ley pulsed around him harder and faster as he descended. Place smelled like dirt and sweat. Nah. *He* smelled of dirt and sweat; the tunnel had a slightly musty, damp clay smell, indicating water far below. "Better than citrus and ginger, and a hell of a lot more interesting."

Jack!

His head jerked up. What the. . . ? No one visible above.

Jaaaack!

Ignoring what honest to God sounded like a woman's voice shrieking in his ear, Jack took several soil samples one-handed. Maybe he should think about that beer and shower sooner than later if he was starting to hallucinate.

He continued downward, sweat oiling his skin, using his shoulder to swipe at the runnels on his face. He wondered if the leylines in the western deserts were the basis of stories told by the aborigines, who said the land was crisscrossed by a large number of mythical songlines or dreaming tracks associated with magical beings. One story involved the travels of two lizard-men known as the Wadi and Gudjara; another described an enormous snake who mystically disappeared beneath the earth and remained there to this day.

With the blue sky a small circle above him and a powerful ley beneath him, Jack felt at peace for perhaps the first time in several years. He was a loner by nature, more comfortable in a desert than a city. Better off identifying a leyline than what went on in a woman's illogical, convoluted brain. And while he enjoyed his fair share of the ladies, he always came back to what he loved most.

Geology. Leys. Solitude.

The Archon paid him. Paid him ridiculously well. But he'd be ley hunting if he were doing it for free. This was his life's work, his burning passion, what got him up in the morning and kept him going long past exhaustion. He *was* his job. All his eggs in one basket, and to hell with anyone who had a problem with that. There wasn't anyone he gave a damn about anyway. Not anymore.

A man knew exactly where he was with a leyline. There was no room for interpretation. Leys were logical. Honest. Reliable. And nonjudgmental.

He paused again to record the strength of the power surging up through the thick soles of his boots, then lowered himself another twenty feet. The meter in his breast pocket vibrated against his chest like a second heartbeat.

"And you—hell, *you* are the granddaddy of them all, aren't you, big fella?" And he should know; he'd mapped thousands of them all over the world. He slowly dropped another ten, using his booted feet to keep his body away from the walls, where he suspected snakes and poisonous spiders lurked to avoid the heat of the day.

Aboveground the sun-baked rocks were hot enough to fry an egg. The lower he dropped, the cooler it became—if one considered a hundred degrees cool. Jack grinned. He loved this shit. Loved the heat. The solitude. The high of discovery.

His meter was going off the charts, and he

methodically recorded into a small voice-activated tape recorder as he went. "Why isn't anyone living around here?" he mused aloud to keep himself company after he'd documented relevant data. It was too damned hot, of course. Only a madman would live—or work—out here in the middle of a desert, hundreds of miles from civilization.

The Rudall River National Park was one of the most remote wilderness areas in the world. Nothing but spiny pale green clumps of spinifex, a few stands of eucalyptus, and flat red earth as far as the eye could see.

His body ached pleasantly from long hours bent over his equipment in the broiling sun. But before he teleported back to camp and materialized an ice-cold beer and a cool shower, there were still several hours of daylight left to do what he loved—research the fascinating and complex leylines in this part of the world.

Exhilarated by his latest find, Jack had shoved aside the physical exhaustion, pushing himself long and hard for the last couple of weeks. South America was next on his list, but he'd been putting that trip off for a while now.

He unhooked his water bottle from his belt and chugged half of its contents down, relishing the warm wetness on his parched throat.

Jaaaack!

His head jerked up. There was, of course, no one there screaming down to him. He was alone. The only thing visible at the mouth of the tube was a small circle of blue sky. Ignoring the icy chill that had suddenly skittered across his nerve endings, Jack dropped another ten feet and paused to record the data.

San Cristóbal, Venezuela

SARA TEMPLE DROPPED ONTO a straight-backed chair beside her friend, when what she really wanted to do was pace like a caged lion. She hated feeling helpless. "Carmelita, we have to get help."

"You are all the help Alberto needs, *mija*." Carmelita's olive skin was gray with fear. Twisting her apron in her lap, she gave Sara a helplessly trusting look out of dark eyes. "You did good with him just now. He will get better soon. You will see."

"I didn't do any good at all," Sara said in a strained voice as they sat outside the closed bedroom door. The sound of furniture being thrown violently against the walls indicated that, far from settling down, Carmelita's husband was getting worse.

Sick with a fever, crazed and delirious, Alberto had tried to strangle his wife only moments before. He didn't know where he was. Didn't recognize either Carmelita or Sara. The only positive thing was that he wasn't using magic. God only knew what his distorted mind would conjure while he was in this state.

Damn it, how could any illness cause him to lose himself this fast? An hour ago he'd looked better than he had in a week, and been joking and laughing in his kitchen as he prepared the midday meal with his staff. Sara had gone in to let him know the head honcho, Grant Baltzer, wouldn't be home for lunch. Alberto was used to things changing at the last minute. He had been Grant's chef, and Carmelita had been Grant's housekeeper, as far back as Sara could remember. They and Sara had traveled all over the world with Grant and his business partner, William Roc, as Baltzer Enterprises built fabulous hotel properties in some of the most beautiful and affluent cities in the world. At present, they were constructing a string of luxury hotels down the west coast of South America and living in a sprawling hacienda a hundred miles from the nearest town.

Fifteen minutes later, after Sara delivered her message and shared an iced coffee with him, Alberto had thrown a carving knife at his assistant, then grabbed Carmelita by the throat when she'd come in.

Sara shuddered.

"We have locked him inside," Carmelita said resolutely, somehow managing to look as though she didn't hear the mayhem going on in the room behind them. "The fever will burn away. Can you not use your powers to make him sleep? The doctor, he will just give him medicine and tell him to rest. He needs rest, *mija*. You can make him sleep deeply and peacefully. You will see, my Alberto will be better by morning if you make him sleep now."

Carmelita had an unhealthy aversion to doctors. Sara had an unhealthy aversion to using her wizard powers. She suspected her foster father needed more than a good night's rest. Medication would surely help. Alberto's sudden psychotic and delusional behavior scared the living crap out of her. She had no idea if he'd picked up some horrific South American disease—they'd only lived here for a year—or if he'd been bitten by something.

Grant's inconveniently located, sprawling hacienda was surrounded by almost impenetrable jungle. It would take time to locate the doctor, time Sara feared they didn't have.

Sara looked at the determined and frightened face beside her. She had known Carmelita most of her life, and a picture of the woman belonged in the dictionary under *immovable*. If she wanted her husband to receive a magical sleeping spell, she would stick to her guns come hell or high water.

Finally giving in to her need to move, Sara got up to pace the corridor outside the master bedroom that Alberto was currently destroying. Her heart ached for him. He was a dignified man, and once he recovered, he was going to be humiliated that anyone had seen him behave this way.

The very mystery of what was wrong with him made her heart pound. She loved him without reservation. Alberto and Carmelita had held her together doing some of the worst times of her life. "He's really, *really* sick, Carmelita. He needs medical help. Possibly even a hospital—"

The other woman threw up her hands and began to wail, tears flooding her round cheeks. Oh no, oh no, oh freaking no. If Carmelita cried, in seconds Sara would join her. She wrapped her arms around her friend's plump shoulders and ran a soothing hand up and down her back. "You know I rarely use my power. And you know *why*," Sara reminded her, striving to keep the panic out of her own voice as she drew comfort from having Carmelita hug her in return. It had been a while since Sara had needed the comfort and security of her foster mother's strong arm about her.

Now their positions were reversed. Eventually she eased away, holding the other woman's work-roughened hands in hers. "I'm terrified my power will kill him," she admitted. "I'm not going to risk it. Please don't ask that of me, Carmelita. I can't. Even if I wanted to. You know my powers are unpredictable; you know what happened . . . before." She paused to regain control of her voice. "I won't use magic on anyone ever again."

"I would not ask that you use *fuego*, Saracita. Just to make him sleep a little while until he recovers."

Fire was Sara's power to call. Or had been. She hadn't used it since her parents were killed. And she never would.

Wood shattered in the bedroom, and Alberto started pounding on the heavy door with meaty fists, howling in Spanish to be let out. The four-inch-thick wood door shook, but held. The sound of his irrational fury sent a chill up the back of Sara's neck.

"I'm begging you, Saracita." The older woman's eyes were liquid misery, her grip all but cutting off the circulation in Sara's fingers. *"Por favor, mija."*

Sara squeezed her eyes closed. "You know I'd do anything to help Alberto. Anything but magic. You of all people know my powers never have worked the way they're supposed to—*especially* when I'm stressed. The fact that I teleported Alberto here, and not to his own bedroom—that wasn't magical skill, it was a fluke." And just proved how freaking wrong her powers could be. She'd teleported Alberto to *Grant's* master suite. Grant was going to freak out. No one went into his room uninvited. Ever.

"Please, let's call Dr. de Canizales before something"—*bad*—"happens." Magic was a skill Sara had never perfected. She hated using it, tried *never* to use it. She was an interior designer. Fabric and colors were her skill set, not her rusty magic powers.

She didn't want to make a seriously bad situation worse—and using her powers would undoubtedly make things worse in ways she couldn't predict. Alberto needed a doctor—a wizard doctor—who understood these kinds of things.

"Let me make a call. Then we can—"

Eyes flashing, Carmelita yanked her hands from Sara's. "Not the *médico*. He will report this to the *policía*. No, *mija*. No. Please do not call Dr. de Canizales."

Sara clutched her cell phone in a damp palm. *Jack* would've known exactly how to handle this. God. She so didn't want to think about Jack right now. Or ever. "I have a conference call with a fabric supplier in half an hour," she said evenly, scared by how agitated Carmelita was. "I'm just going to cancel, okay?"

Her friend plopped back onto her chair with a loud *umph*. "*Sí.* This is good. Cancel the call."

Grant would be annoyed. Every delay in the interior

finishes of the Lima hotel was money out of the company's pocket. Actually, Sara thought, he'd be more than pissed she was delaying the fabric order. Everything seemed to annoy Grant lately. God only knew his normally suave behavior had been somewhat erratic over the last few days. Obviously not as out of control as his chef's, but there was definitely *something* going on. Not that Grant would share his concerns with her. They were close, yes, but he never liked to bother Sara with his business problems.

She'd wrangle it out of him over dinner tomorrow.

Grant was going to be justifiably furious when he saw the havoc Alberto had wreaked on the kitchen and, worse, on his private sanctuary. As a nonwizard and a mortal, Grant was not a lover of anything involving magic. And while he knew she was a wizard, he also knew she was a nonpracticing wizard. Which was good enough for him.

Shaking her head, Sara made the call, speaking Spanish as she arranged to place the enormous fabric orders the next day.

"He is quiet," Carmelita whispered, pleased. "Poor Alberto, he wore himself out. Come, let us check to see he didn't harm himself. Then we will go to his kitchen and calm the staff with a nice cup of tea, *sí*?"

Sounded like an excellent plan to Sara. She removed the heavy key from the back pocket of her shorts. "Let me go first."

Alberto outweighed her by two hundred pounds. She'd *have* to use magic if he was lying in wait for them behind that door. She hoped he was sacked out on Grant's king-size four-poster bed, his feet on the red and gold silk spread, snoring away. Except that normally his snoring would wake a hibernating bear, and she didn't hear a sound from inside.

Holding Carmelita back with one arm, Sara cautiously opened the door. "Antoni—*shit!*"

The luxurious master suite was a shambles of broken wood, shredded burgundy silk, and shattered glass. Her eyes went wide. The last time she'd been in his room, more than a year ago, it had looked just as Grant had requested, like an expensive Victorian brothel. Sara had bought the bed and other furnishings in England at great expense. The sight of the *rest* of the décor made her suck in a shocked breath. A gigantic black metal cage, suspended in the center of the room, wasn't for any bird. Nor were the whips, chains, and various restraints bolted to the walls. *Holy crap!*

Carmelita pushed past her. "*Madre de Dios,*" she whispered, eyes impossibly huge as she surveyed the room. "Where is Alberto?"

With all the sex toys, Sara had barely noticed that the room was conspicuously empty.

Jack!

The woman's frantic voice echoed around Jack, ricocheting from side to side inside the lava tube. Annoyed by the persistence of the mental interruption, he muttered a pungent curse as one of his soil samples dropped from the precariously held core driller. He mentally grabbed it before it got too far and carefully placed it in the sample bag he'd already labeled.

That taken care of, he finally had to think about that voice. Was this incredibly powerful ley amping his connection to a woman he hadn't seen in two years? Damn it to hell, if he could ignore a damn phone ringing, why couldn't he ignore this?

Because this was a different kind of communication, in his gut, in his head. Visceral. *Insistent.*

The urgency demanded immediate attention. He shook his head as if he could shake away that mental SOS like an annoying insect, and tried to find another reason that he was hearing her, one that wouldn't require action. In his excitement over this leyline, he'd shoved aside exhaustion, pushing himself too long and hard for the last couple of weeks. Hell, he was probably dehydrated; maybe he was hallucinating. Yeah, that was it.

But even at the volume he imagined he heard, he recognized that voice.

Sara Temple.

He swore again. Too bad. He didn't want to know about it. Been there, done her.

"Get the hell out of my head, woman." He did not want to think about, see, or hear his ex-fiancée.

Not now. Not ever. Not even in a hallucination brought on by too little sleep and lousy eating habits.

Yet he *heard* her.

Sara.

Forget hanging on to the rope. Jack let go to manipulate his instruments. Magic had its moments. And right now, he needed the use of both hands. He jabbed the new data into his handheld, wiped some of the dust off the screen on the side of his pants so he could actually see what he was inputting, then added a few more numbers.

He was close, damn close. After a year of driving himself hard enough to obliterate thought of anything other than his job, he was almost done mapping Australia. He just needed a few more days, a week at the most. Fascinating as the new information was, though, it was impossible to ignore his racing heart; adrenaline flooded his system as if he were the one in danger.

He felt Sara's presence as if she stood right beside him. He smelled the soft lemony scent of her skin, the light fragrance as familiar to him as his own heartbeat— *No*, he corrected himself savagely. He *thought* he smelled her. "Get a grip." He pulled a rag from his pocket and swiped his sweaty face. His voice bounced off the curved, hard walls of the ancient tunnel.

"She isn't sending out a fucking all-points bulletin. How much trouble can an interior designer get into, for God's sake?" If he closed his eyes and concentrated, he could almost make out her words. Instead, he kept them open, trying to focus on what he was doing—

Jack!

"Fuck it!" Realizing that Sara would keep mentally yanking his chain until he *did* something, Jack sent his gear back to camp and followed her scream.

↝ Two ↜

The instant Jack materialized into an industrial-size kitchen, he felt the pulse of dark, malignant magic surround him. The pungent stink of burnt food didn't mask the distinctive metallic smell of blood. Under the circumstances, he chose to remain invisible until he knew what in God's name was going on.

The place was a shambles—cabinet doors ripped from hinges, shelves broken, drawers yanked out and upended. Beans, rice, and utensils were strewn across the stainless countertops and tiled floor as if some maniac had swept through, determined to wreak the most havoc possible.

Christ. Not seeing Sara the moment he'd teleported into the kitchen—when he'd been goddamned *braced* for it—struck him straight in the dead, hollow space that had once been his heart. The sensation was physical. He ruthlessly shoved it away. He never wanted to set eyes on her again. But he'd never wished her dead. *Keep looking, damn it.*

The counters and white walls of the L-shaped kitchen were splattered with a hell of a lot of red blood and brownish-gray brain matter. Someone had been seriously pissed off.

He glanced down the length of the room. A small group of shocked nonwizards—none of them Sara, and clearly household staff—pressed against the pantry shelves and huddled against the walls, the only sound their erratic breathing. Clearly they'd witnessed the events that had left the grisly scene but were too terrified to run.

Making a quick decision, Jack did a swift Mindwipe, replacing their memories of what they'd witnessed with the knowledge that today was their day off. Then he teleported them to safety outside and sealed the door. They'd go about their business unaffected. For now.

Despite the disorder, the kitchen was eerily quiet. Jack was über-alert, listening for even the smallest sound as he moved quietly through the chaos. He felt the traces of half a dozen wizards, but faintly, indicating they'd been and gone.

Circumventing one of the large islands, he stopped short, his heartbeat accelerating. Not gone. Dead. Five bloodied corpses were sprawled on the saltillo floor between the prep area and a giant industrial sink. Bile rose up the back of his throat.

They were all wizards. Jack knew because of their residual power traces—the signature a wizard left behind when he or she passed through a space. Through the gore, the bodies were almost impossible to ID, other than whether they were male or female.

Sara wasn't one of them. He let out his breath slowly, not even aware that he'd been holding it.

With a sense of relief, he moved down the long, narrow kitchen. A series of stainless steel-topped islands ran down the center between long expanses of counters and cabinets. Whatever prep work was being done at the time of the attack was now in disarray on the counters or dashed to the floor. Small appliances hung from their still plugged-in cords, and a brown bowl had strewn fresh lemons underfoot.

The miasma trace of evil lingered in the air-conditioned room. Nimbly bypassing a dozen pots and pans scattered on the tile floor beside a mangled wrought-iron pot rack, Jack had to consider that he might, in fact be too late. His heart skipped several beats at the thought.

Maintaining invisibility, he kept moving. But as far as he could see, whoever—*whatever*—had caused this was long gone.

He decided that as soon as he saw Sara, as soon as he was sure she was alive and relatively unharmed, he'd leave without her being any the wiser. Jack hoped like hell his optimism wasn't misplaced. Considering the state of the kitchen, she could very well be dead.

The clatter of metal—crashing against a hard surface broke the silence like a series of loud gunshots. Heart pounding, Jack raced around the corner of the L.

A burly man in a chef's coat screamed unintelligibly as he ripped plates from a shelf and dashed them by the handful to the floor among several cast-iron skillets.

Jack stopped in his tracks. *Shit!* It all came together. He knew the lunatic: Sara's father-figure Alberto Santos. And since Alberto and Sara both worked for Baltzer, and

Baltzer Enterprises was building hotels in South America, Jack knew *where* he was, even though he'd never been there before.

Baltzer's estate, in the jungles of South America.

Double shit.

There were few things Jack disliked more than Grant Baltzer. Jungles were right up there at number three.

Santos was shimmering in and out as though unable to maintain a teleport, his furious yells swelling and fading as he screamed at someone blocked from Jack's view by his rotund body. The guy stopped throwing things and was now waving around the bloody carving knife clutched in his other hand. He moved with superhuman speed.

Clearly deranged. Hopped up on drugs? Question was: Where the hell was *Sara*?

Jack shimmered the twenty feet separating them, coming up behind the knife-wielding chef, who had a hundred and fifty pounds on him and was a head shorter. Santos, his white chef jacket and pants saturated with scarlet, feinted and slashed, his apparent goal to fillet the two women he'd cornered. Which answered Jack's burning question.

Sara's location. Right in the damn thick of things. Six feet from an armed, deranged wizard-gone-bad.

Jack's heart double-clutched. With relief. With fear.

TERRIFIED, SARA STOOD FOURSQUARE in front of Carmelita, sheltering her with her own body. Alberto had killed *five* people. The thought made her sick to her stomach.

He'd been gone from Grant's room no more than a few minutes before they'd tracked him down to his kitchen. *Minutes.*

The crazy look in his black eyes as he advanced scared her to death. The madman in front of her was nothing like the gentle loving man she knew; it was as though he was possessed. She attempted yet again to magically restrain him, though it didn't work worth a damn. She tried to freeze him, trip him, snare him. . . . As a wizard, Sara thought furiously, she made a great interior designer.

Behind her, Carmelita sobbed, "Oh God, oh God, oh God." How the *hell* was Sara supposed to stop a homicidal man who outweighed her by two hundred pounds?

"Don't hurt the mother of your children, Alberto." The plea was bullshit since he'd already done just that, and appeals to his sense of decency and his rational side had already fallen on deaf ears.

Before Sara had managed to distract him, he'd stabbed his plump wife several times. Blood seeped sluggishly from several slices on Carmelita's forehead, her left arm hung limply at her side, and her right hand was pressed to her rib cage where blood swelled between her fingers—the price she'd paid when *she* tried to protect Sara earlier.

Unaffected by everything Sara was trying to do to stop him, Alberto started circling them, closing in. The long carving knife, professionally honed to a razor edge, glinted as he waved it wildly, babbling gibberish. Sara had never heard him speaking that language before, and didn't know what the hell he was saying, if anything.

She snatched up a meat cleaver from the floor and

braced her bare feet for balance. "Back off, Alberto," she said in a firm voice, bending her knees a little to steady her center of gravity. This was insane.

She couldn't hold him off forever. She'd *tried* magic. Of *course* it hadn't worked. But she kept trying. No choice. Alberto now had them cornered.

She tightened her grip until her knuckles shone white on the black handle of the cleaver. "You're sick, Alberto. I get it. But you aren't coming anywhere near Carmelita with that thing again. Put it down, and back off. *Now!*"

Brave words, but she knew he was way, way past the point of a negotiated peace. More like the point of no return. She'd felt this helpless twice before in her life. And both times someone had died. It didn't bear thinking about.

Behind her, Carmelita's sobs were interspersed with rapid Spanish as she prayed. Alberto was screaming at the top of his lungs, sweeping dishes, pans, and freshly picked vegetables onto the floor. He shouted unintelligibly before the knife slashed down in a gleaming arc. Sara pulled Carmelita out of the way just as Alberto suddenly stopped dead in his tracks.

He looked as though he'd been snagged and held back by . . . something. His red-rimmed eyes narrowed as he fought against an unseen adversary.

Imaginary? Or real? *Please be real!* Hope bloomed as the big man staggered backward, his arms windmilling as if fighting off an attacker. Was someone else in the room? She'd never been adept at tracing; if anyone was here, he must be a wizard, and invisible.

Whoever it was only managed to restrain Alberto for a heartbeat or two; then he was back lunging and jabbing at them.

Okay. Not real, Sara thought, bitterly disappointed, and annoyed that she'd pretended, even for a moment, that help had arrived. "*Talk* to him," she instructed, keeping her body in front of the older woman. Maybe hearing his wife's voice would snap him out of it. Unfortunately, Carmelita could barely string together two coherent words.

Backing up, Sara touched one of her sunstone earrings to amp her powers, then attempted another binding spell. Nothing. She tried a protective spell again. No dice. She attempted to teleport Alberto, and when that didn't work, herself and Carmelita. Everyone stayed just where they were.

Santos's next lunge elicited a sharp shriek followed by a babble of hysterical Spanish from his wife.

"That's it," Sara shouted, at the end of her rope. "Put the damn knife *down*, Alberto. I know you're not well. *Please* let me find someone to help you." Her voice broke as she struggled to stay calm. But she was pee-in-her-pants scared, her hands shaking so badly she was afraid she'd drop the cleaver.

"You *love* Carmelita," she reminded him, keeping her tone even with great effort. Sweat ran down her temples and into her eyes. Her fingers gripping the cleaver shook, but she held out the other hand, palm up. "Give me the knife, Alberto. *Por favor.*"

She turned her head, eyes still fixed on Santos, and

whispered to Carmelita. "I'm going to distract him. When he looks away, you *teleport*, do you hear me? Get help."

Who could possibly help them under these circumstances?

No one.

There was nowhere for them to go as Alberto backed them against the face of a giant Sub-Zero refrigerator. Sara knew unequivocally that in the next few seconds they were going to die.

Alberto sliced the enormous knife down. Heart practically jumping out of her chest, Sara yanked open the refrigerator door between them in the nick of time. The scrape of the blade cutting into the steel made her teeth ache.

He ripped the door of the Sub-Zero completely off its hinges, tossing it aside as easily as he'd done the skillets a few minutes earlier.

"This is absolute bullshit." A man's voice came out of nowhere. A second later, Jackson Slater materialized behind Alberto. "What the *fuck* is going on?"

Sara's eyes went wide. Jackson? Improbable. *Impossible.* Absolutely incredible.

She took in his ripped jeans and sweat-stained khaki shirt, which was covered with a thick layer of red dust. God. Was she hallucinating? He looked big and mean, and gloriously capable of subduing Alberto. If he wasn't a figment of her imagination. "Jack? What—"

"We'll catch up later. Yeah, you son of a bitch, look at me instead of the ladies." Alberto's bloodshot eyes tracked Jack. "Fill me in in five words or less," he barked

at her, pulling a giant knife out of the air and brandish-
ing it as Alberto followed him like a deranged zombie.

The two men circled each other.

"Sara?! Talk to me."

Her mind was blank. She absolutely could not com-
prehend how or why Jackson Slater was in San Cristóbal.

"Magic. Not working worth a damn," Jack pointed
out, feinting and parrying as he drew Alberto away from
her and Carmelita. "Some clues here—*fuck it*. There's
more than one way to skin a snake." He switched the big
hunting knife for a small black gun.

Sara pushed Carmelita into the nearby pantry, then
slammed and locked the door. "Don't *shoot* him, Jack! Use
magic. He's out of his mind and doesn't know what he's
doing," Sara yelled, eyes now fixed on the gun Jack was pointing at Alberto. "He might've been bitten by something,"

"By what—The devil? Why the hell isn't my power
working? Yours?"

Jack's magic didn't work either? "My magic rarely
works." Especially when she was scared out of her wits.
Instead of charging in to save the day, Jack was going
to be killed as well. Sara's stomach heaved and she swallowed bile.

Jack jumped over the refrigerator door as Alberto
sliced the air inches from his face. "Is that a no?"

"Yes, it's a n—" Sara shrieked as the sound of a gunshot ricocheted through the kitchen. The back of Alberto's pant leg bloomed red. He gave an unholy scream that
raised the hairs on the back of Sara's neck.

"Run! Get the hell out—oh no, you don't, you son

of a bitch." Jack grabbed the older man by the shoulder, trying to hold him back as Alberto turned toward Sara. "Come and fight like a man *with* a man."

Alberto's eyes gleamed as he stumbled back toward her. With nowhere to go, Sara pressed against the open cavity of the fridge; the shelves dug into her back, ice cold through her thin T-shirt.

Almost faster than the eye could see, the chef shimmered across the kitchen to within three feet of her, his beefy arm drawn back, his fist the size of a ham ready to strike.

It happened so fast Sara felt the rush of air before her brain perceived movement.

Suddenly Jack shimmered in front of her, blocking her with the solid warmth of his body. She smelled the clean sweat on his shirt, and the familiar Jack smell that used to make her hot and bothered. Then he said harshly, "You never did listen worth a damn, woman." And Sara remembered that two years wasn't long enough, and why she'd never wanted to see him again.

She flinched as he fired point-blank. This time the bullet knocked Alberto back several steps, leaving a monstrous red stain on the front of his white chef's coat. He howled in outrage and charged full-tilt, his enormous body practically levitating as he came toward them.

Reflexively, she grabbed Jack's wrist as he started to squeeze off another shot. *"Noooo—"*

"—oooo!"

Jack materialized in a long hallway, Sara's cry fading

in his ears. "Damn-fool woma——" He saw where he was and scowled. Familiar light gray walls, dark floor, bright lights. Great, just fucking great. He'd gone directly from the frying pan into the fire.

He was in the chilly hallway outside the chamber of the Wizard Council. The Wizard Council to which he'd been attempting to teleport Santos a second ago. He hadn't planned on coming here himself. He'd planned to report the details to the Archon later, and they could then follow up with the Wizard Council if necessary. Each governing body had a representative with the other Council.

No good deed went unpunished. He'd saved the girl. The crazy guy was supposed to have been delivered to the Wizard Council to deal with. He was supposed to pick up where he'd left off in the outback half an hour ago.

He scratched the stubble on his chin. Admittedly, this would save time. He'd report to the Archon and the members of the Wizard Council, and be done with it now. Then he'd return to the outback and that cold shower and colder beer. And the solitude he craved now more than ever.

"You promised you wouldn't shoot him," Sara's voice came from behind him.

Ah, hell. This just got better and better.

He turned around. She was leaning against the wall, looking ridiculously sexy and a complete mess, and glaring at him as though *he* were the one who had tried to carve her into freaking shish kebabs.

In the midst of Santos's rampage, Jack hadn't really

noticed that her pink shorts, and a mile of lightly tanned legs, were nearly as bloodstained as the skimpy tank top clinging wetly to the upper swell of her breasts. The cold air in the corridor caused her nipples to press against the wet cotton of her top. Her dishevelment and the splatters of blood, looked obscene. Jack felt a surge of . . . irritation. Yes. That's all it was.

She rubbed the goose bumps on her arms with both hands, her expression hard to read

"I never promised a damn thing," Jack told her, his voice cool. That was a hell of a lot of blood. Had she been cut? He tried to see without being overt about it. "It was him or you." He didn't see any cuts, and she didn't appear to be in pain. "Sorry, I should've asked if you'd prefer I just stand back while he fucking hacked you to pieces."

"Don't be a moron, Jack." Sara's silky, honey-brown hair was secured precariously on top of her head by a yellow pencil. Her skin was pale under her tan, and her velvety brown eyes blazed hot and pissed. "It was . . ." She swallowed hard, and pressed a hand to her middle. "It was overkill."

"I made the call. Live with it."

Her jaw clenched. "Is he dead?"

He shrugged and went to prop up the opposite wall, his fingers stuffed in the front pockets of his filthy jeans. He must stink like a bear. Sara, on the other hand, looked and smelled like some erotic, exotic fantasy. Jack knew he would recognize that combination of girl-next-door citrus coupled with the ginger flower of a siren if he were blindfolded and presented with a hundred women in a dark room.

He'd dreamed about the smell of her skin on so many lonely nights zipped into a freaking sleeping bag, fisting his cock; he was surprised he hadn't dislocated it. No other woman before or since smelled quite like Sara Temple.

"Where are we?" she demanded after a few moments of pulsing silence. In the too-bright overhead lights, her face looked drawn and strained, her big brown eyes shadowed. "Damn it, Jackson. You've got a freaking nerve, strolling back into my life thinking you can teleport me wherever you damn well please."

Jack hadn't meant her to teleport with them at all; she was a damned burr in his h—ass. Hell, he hadn't planned on making the trip here himself; he'd wanted to go straight back to his leylines and his solitary life. His fist was dependable. For the time being he was content with his love life, or lack thereof. When he was ready to do something about that, he'd do it—where, with whom, and as often as he liked.

Sara looked around curiously; the studs in her ears sparked orange fire as she moved. She turned back to shoot him an accusing glare. There'd been a time when her warm brown eyes had been soft and unfocused as she looked up at him with so much love it made his chest ache. A time when her soft lips curved with a loving smile when she looked at him.

Right now she was looking at him as if he were a particularly annoying stranger.

Strangers, he thought bitterly, was exactly what they were. He'd thought he knew her. Thought the love they shared was the real deal. He'd been wrong on every count. "I didn't bring us here. I didn't even bring myself here." He didn't like being teleported without his consent any more than she did. He kept his back to the wall so he could see down the length of the hallways on either side of him. No sign of the demented Santos.

"Apparently we've been summoned," Jack added.

"By whom?"

"The Wizard Council. Haven't you been here before?"

"Of course not." She raised both hands in questioning annoyance, then dropped them to her sides. "Why would they summon us?"

With an absent touch of her fingers to the sunstone stud sparkling in her earlobe, she instantly changed her clothes. Good. The skimpy shorts and tank top had revealed way too much smooth, tanned skin for his peace of mind. The blood had been disturbing as hell.

The severe cut of the chocolate-brown pantsuit almost disguised the slender, ultrafeminine body underneath. The severity was saved from looking masculine by a soft, frothy blouse thing in a greeny-turquoise color. All of the bloodstains were gone. Invisible pins replaced the pencil securing her hair, and gold hoops gleamed in her ears beside the sunstones.

She looked clean, fresh, and professional. She'd not only changed clothes, she'd freshened up and magically applied makeup and perfume. Magic suited her just fine when she needed it to. His gut twisted at the familiar, freshly showered, I'm-ready-to-go-out—or better yet, stay in—scent of her.

She smelled more strongly of sugared ginger and freshly picked lemons. Jack had to curl his hands into fists to stop himself from reaching out and pulling out those pins one by one and messing up her too-neat hair. Then burying his face between her breasts, in the curve of her neck, between her strong, silky thighs. *Oh, shit. Look somewhere else, pal.*

"Ours is not to reason why," he said sourly, dragging his gaze away from her soft mouth. He hoped like hell she couldn't see his reaction to her. A trace of panic welled up, which he told himself was ridiculous. So what if his body reacted to her closeness, to the smell of her, to the sight of her doe-brown eyes? So the fuck what?

His brain knew the score, even if his traitorous body didn't. He didn't have to love the woman to want to have sex with her. He wasn't dead.

"Fine," she said crossly. "I won't reason why. But I can damn well ask questions, can't I?"

"You can certainly give that your best shot." How and why had the events in South America triggered a summons to the Wizard Council? If Jack reported to anyone, it would be to the Aequitas Archon. Maybe they were here because Santos was a "regular" wizard?

"Maybe this has something to do with you," Sara said.

"It doesn't. It has to do with the fact that Santos is a member of the wizard community, and therefore has to explain his behavior to the Wizard Council. They probably want to hear what we have to say before they take action. And since I witnessed only the last few minutes of his rampage, I have nothing to add to whatever you tell them." Seeing Sara like this—beautiful, cool, un-fucking-changed—pissed him off. He squashed down the sudden surge of anger that had never gone away, just simmered under the surface waiting to explode again.

He remembered their last day, their last words, as if they were yesterday.

She had clearly forgotten.

Jack hadn't.

He didn't love her anymore. But, God, seeing her again didn't make him hate her any less.

"If you really need a reason, I suppose the Coun-cil might consider mass murder grounds for appearing before them," Jack added coldly. "Why? Do you have a more important appointment?"

"No, of course not." She chewed her lower lip, some-thing he'd enjoyed doing at one time.

There'd better be a damn good reason for him to be pulled into whatever the hell was going on, Jack thought savagely.

"If we're here, where's Alberto?" Both her tone and her body language were hostile. "Damn it, Jack, if you hurt him, I'll—I don't know what I'll do, but it won't be pretty."

"Hurt him? *Hurt* him?! Jesus, Sara, the man was a homicidal maniac with the kind of strength I can't even begin to explain. *Nothing* I did stopped him."

"Magic—"

"Well, hell, *that* didn't work, or didn't you notice?"

"Where is he?"

"The same people who didn't ask if I wanted to be here didn't stop to tell me what they were doing with Alberto. Oh, and don't bother thanking me for saving your ass," he said.

His discovery of the new leyline in Australia trumped this situation hands-down. Once he'd've rushed home to tell Sara what he'd found. Of course, the telling would have had to wait until his lips weren't glued to hers, but they'd both gotten used to that. Now it wasn't worth the effort; she didn't believe in the magical power of leylines any more than she'd believed in him. She was a wizard who didn't believe in magic of any kind. Except when it suited her.

Jack glanced at the sleek, striated agate face on his watch, then scanned the long corridor. A few black leather benches broke up the monotony of an endless ribbon of pale gray, doorless walls. How long were they going to keep him waiting?

This—whatever the hell this was—wasn't any of his business. He didn't want to be here. Didn't want to be within ten thousand miles of Sara. Since the Council had summarily hauled him in, he'd tell them what he knew—which wasn't much—then get back to his safe, scientific cocoon, out of reach.

With nothing to do but pace or look at Sara, Jack took his computer out of his pocket and turned it on. He started to press its buttons and tried to ignore just how many of *his* buttons had been pushed in the last fifteen minutes.

Good to have some-fucking-thing he could control.

❦ Three ❦

Sara strode down the corridor so she didn't have to look at Jack another second. She didn't know where she was going and didn't care. Sick to her stomach, she briefly pressed both hands to her midriff. She was damned if she'd humiliate herself by puking in front of him. Cold sweat bathed her body, and she picked up her pace trying to ward off the nausea.

Images from the past hour flashed through her mind. How in God's name had Alberto gone from weak as a baby to homicidal maniac in less than an hour? She shuddered, swallowing bile. None of it made sense. Not the business with Alberto, and certainly not Jack showing up in San Cristóbal.

He hadn't changed physically. His dark shaggy hair still needed cutting, he'd always needed a shave, and his clothes were more often than not just this dusty and disheveled. He smelled the same, too—a heady, sexy combination of soap, clean sweat, and whatever color dirt he'd been digging in that day.

What wasn't familiar was the coldness in his voice when he spoke to her, and the utter lack of warmth in his dark blue eyes. She'd only experienced that tone and look once, and once had been enough.

Not that she cared one way or the other. She had more immediate concerns. Where was Alberto? And had Carmelita gotten to her mother's house safely? Rubbing her arms, she lengthened her stride, her heels clicking on the smooth gray floor. She had a million things to do. Funerals to arrange, staff to comfort—

God. Grant would be back from his business trip tomorrow. This was going to take some explaining. She turned around and headed back, slowly. Why had the council brought them here if they were going to leave them cooling their heels in this soulless hallway?

Annoyingly, the wait didn't seem to bother Jack, who had one shoulder propped against the wall while he worked on his PDA. He was usually filled with restless energy and incapable of standing still. She used to find his mask of tranquility fascinating, knowing that it was his internal intensity that really drove him. He'd never been tranquil in the bedroom. On the contrary. Jack unleashed had been a force to be reckoned with in bed. There all bets of civility were off, and she'd liked it that way.

His dark hair almost brushed his rumpled collar, and Sara had a sudden, overpowering urge to go comb her fingers through the silky strands as she used to do. Then he'd cup her face, and his eyes would darken to a smoldering midnight blue as his mouth lowered, and he'd brush his dry lips over hers until her eyes fluttered shut. Then he'd take her offered mouth and kiss her as if nothing had changed between them.

And she'd knee him squarely in the family jewels, because she couldn't kick her own butt. What in God's name was she *thinking*? Had she lost her ever-loving mind? This was Jackson Slater, the man who'd single-handedly broken her heart, then stomped on it for good measure. He wasn't back for *her*, she reminded herself furiously. Why he was there was a mystery. But he wasn't there because of or for *her*.

The throbbing silence, chilly air, and creepy Repose Gray walls didn't contain a single freaking door. Anywhere. Despite the open, endless hall, she felt closed in, trapped.

What could he possibly be computing now? How could he be so completely . . . oblivious? Adrenaline still surged through Sara's body in sickening waves. She rubbed her arms again through her jacket. The last hour had been a terrifying nightmare; she wished to hell she had the opportunity to think this through before talking to the omnipotent Wizard Council. It was similar to being summoned to the headmistress's office at boarding school. Something she was also unfamiliar with. She'd been a good girl in school, but she'd watched other girls walk the long green mile to the principal's office.

How odd that the good girl had ended up—however briefly—with the bad boy. And Jack Slater would be considered a bad boy by any standards. She was lucky she'd come out of the relationship in one piece. She had Alberto, Carmelita, and Grant to thank for that.

Sara stopped a dozen feet away from him. Her heart did an annoying triple axel as she looked her fill while he was otherwise occupied. She felt the conflict of too many physical reactions to his presence. Anger was prominent. But the intense physical attraction she'd always felt for him was sending sparks of need jumping to every nerve in her body, and she was preternaturally aware of everything about him.

Jackson Slater: six feet and two inches of heartache.

He was a little leaner, a little tougher-looking than when she'd seen him last, two years ago. He wasn't a classically handsome man like her friend and partner Grant Baltzer. But it didn't matter. Jack had a rough-and-ready, primitive sexiness that had little to do with looks and everything to do with chemistry.

Shaggy dark brown hair, piercing read-your-mind blue eyes, and a stubborn chin. He would've had a perfectly straight nose if someone hadn't broken it when he was a kid. Sara had thought the bump was sexy until Jack admitted that the *someone* was his father. It was one of the few external scars the bastard had left on him.

She glanced at her watch—they'd been there seven interminable minutes—then looked up and down the corridor for the umpteenth time. Still empty. Tension was slowly being replaced by temper, and heaven help them all if she reached the end of her fuse. Council or no Council, she wasn't some lackey to be left to cool her heels this way.

Jack shifted his shoulder on the wall, drawing her gaze back to him. Every move he made was imbued with a masculine sensuality that called to every strand of female DNA in her body.

Had. *Had* called.

Not anymore. Now he was like a particularly attractive piece of artwork she'd purchase for the lobby of one of their hotels. One of a kind, maybe, but hardly the only appealing statue to be had. Sara wished with all her heart that looking at him didn't remind her of sweaty skin and tangled sheets. God. Sex with Jack had been life-changing. Earth-shattering.

That's how it had all started. How it had all ended.

He'd clearly been out in the field moments before he'd shown up in Grant's kitchen. His pants, faded khaki shirt, hiking boots, and deeply tanned skin were filmed with red dust.

For some stupid reason, her eyes filled with tears. She blinked them back before he could glance up and take them as a sign of weakness. "Are you going to change before they call us in?"

"I'm not dining with the pope." He didn't glance up from his computer. "They grabbed me, they can deal with me as I am."

He wasn't exactly a social animal, the fact that they'd met at a party notwithstanding. Jack had been a loner before he met her, and she'd bet her new Jimmy Choos that he'd reverted the second he walked away from her. Just like a captured animal released back into the wild, Jack would never be domesticated.

Yet here he was. Why? It was a hell of a coincidence for him to teleport from wherever he'd been to San Cristóbal at such a crucial moment. She admitted, if only to herself, that if he hadn't shown up, Alberto would probably have killed her just as he'd done the others. God only knew what had gotten into him. Mere hours before Alberto had gone berserk in his kitchen, Carmelita had called Sara to her husband's deathbed. Then he seemed okay for a while and well enough to go back to his kitchen.

In the space of an hour, he'd gone from ethereally pale and weak, asking for the priest, to a knife-wielding, gibberish-babbling psycho who was seemingly immune to her magic.

Admittedly, magic wasn't her forte, but even Jack had had a problem with Alberto.

None of it made any sense, least of all Jack's unexplained appearance.

Click-click-click. His finger tapped out whatever on his handheld. "Did you know Alberto did drugs?" he asked. Click-click-annoying click.

Did he have any idea how loud that sounded in the echoing hallway? "He didn't, doesn't, never has used any kind of drugs."

Jack met her gaze blandly. "Right." He looked back down. Click-click-click. "That was a bad reaction to the shrimp scampi he made for lunch."

Sara's blood pressure rose, adding to the throb behind her eyeballs. "As usual, you can believe whatever the hell you want to believe without checking facts or asking the right questions."

"Yeah?" He glanced up, his eyes unfathomable, his cynical mouth a hard line. "I'm not a mind reader."

Not her mind anyway. "Do you really want to go

back down this path?" she demanded tightly. "I believe we both said all there was to say on the subject."

She'd told him one thing, Jack had believed another. 'Nuff said.

"I don't recall being asked my opinion."

"Do you want to do this here, Jackson?" The anger surging through her was so strong Sara had to grit her teeth to control it. "Really?"

His face was blank, his eyes cold. "No." His voice was laced with boredom as he went back to his damn handheld. "I'd have to give a flying fuck." Click-click-click. "And I don't."

Raw inside, she materialized her favorite Coach purse, took out a lipstick and mirror, and turned away so he wouldn't notice how her hands shook. Jack Slater made her temper go from zero to a hundred faster than anyone she knew. Arguing with him used to be exhilarating. Now it was just annoying. He brought out the absolute worst in her. They were oil and water. She'd argue that black was white just because he infuriated her so much and she didn't want him to win. Stupid. Childish. It was a character flaw she thought she'd ironed out. Apparently not.

Lipstick applied, she got rid of the purse without giving it much thought. "You showed up without so much as a 'Hey there, haven't seen you in a while, thought I'd stop by and take over.'"

"Forgive me," he said insincerely, glancing up for a second. "My prime concern was preventing Alberto from adding you and Carmelita to his body count. Obviously,

I had my protocols wrong—I should have invited you to have coffee first. My bad." He went right back to work.

She took a deep breath. She'd loved him, and he'd turned on her when she'd needed him the most. She didn't want him anywhere near her. Ever. "I was handling him on my own." Which was a solar system away from reality, and she knew it. Two years spent regaining her equilibrium, of maturing—poof, shot to hell in a matter of minutes.

This time his head jerked up and he gave her a hot look that made her flinch. "Jesus, Sara. Listen to yourself. By the time I arrived he'd already murdered five people and almost killed his own wife. He was a heartbeat away from breaking your head open like a watermelon. Your pal's deranged. Tell me which part of that massacre you *handled*!"

Sara dropped down on one of the hard leather benches lining the wall, a safe distance from him. "Okay, I admit, the situation was completely beyond my ability to resolve. I've never seen Antonio like that. Not in all the years I've known him has he ever shown psychotic tendencies. To say that seeing him that—angry, that manic was terrifying is an understatement."

"Did you try using your powers?"

"Yes, Jack," she mimicked, lifting her head to shoot him a kiss-my-ass glare. "I actually did try using my powers." God, hating him was exhausting. Seeing him was ripping out her heart all over again. Sara wished for just a moment of peace. A moment when she could feel the strength of his arms holding her. Hear the steady beat of his heart. Know that she was loved. She'd do well to remember that Jack's love was conditional. "Clearly they didn't work any better than yours, did they?"

"You got that right. My powers were iffy, to say the least. I'd like to know why. Not in a gotta-know-right-now kinda way, you understand. It's more of a hmmm-wonder-why-not kinda way. Your buddy Santos obviously had a psychotic break. The mental health of Baltzer's staff is none of my business—you and the Council can figure it all out. I'm going back to work as soon as this meeting's over."

"Fine." More than fine. She couldn't wait to see the back of him. His front was bringing back disturbing memories, *muscle* memories. She inspected the gray flooring looking for a seam. There wasn't one. Maybe she could count the ceiling tiles next?

He glanced at his watch, using a thumb to clear the fine red dust off the multifunction face. "Five more minutes, then I'm out of here."

"Can you do that?"

"I can do anything I damn well please. I don't work for the Wizard Coun—"

An invisible door a few feet away snicked open to reveal a heavily made-up young woman dressed in black from her spiky magenta-streaked hair to her provocative thigh-high boots.

"Tsk, tsk." Little birds shouldna fight in the nest," she said in a lilting, accented voice. "Follow me, the Council is ready for you now."

A LITTLE CREEPED OUT, Sara followed her through the opening, then turned as the door closed silently behind her and Jack. There was no indication in the raised-panel wood that there'd been a door there at all. Another hall with no exit.

She braced herself as he passed, determined not to lean in his direction, not to reach out, to trace a fingertip across his lips as she used to do when she passed him. Casual touches that she still missed with a physical ache. She let out a soft, shaky breath. Once, they couldn't bear not to touch.

Fortunately, her willpower was now a hell of a lot stronger, because Jack, without making eye contact, strode past her to catch up with their guide, who was already several yards ahead.

"Don't lollygag," the woman admonished without turning around. Her black leather miniskirt exposed long legs encased in skintight patent boots with FM heels. "The Council doesna fancy being kept waiting."

Sara caught up and put the woman between herself and Jack. After this meeting, she never wanted to see him again. She didn't want him anywhere near the life she'd painstakingly reconstructed after he'd torn it apart.

The mahogany-paneled hallway was wide enough for the three of them to walk abreast with plenty of room to spare. Sara saw absolutely no reason for the Goth girl to walk that close to Jack, practically brushing at the hip. "I believe we were the ones kept waiting," she responded, her tone cool.

The other woman laughed lightly. "Now, you be sure to tell Duncan Edge that when you see him."

"He's the Head of Council," Jack clarified.

Sara ignored him. His actions in Alberto's kitchen had underscored how little she'd known him. This cold-eyed man who had efficiently disabled her friend wasn't the dusty, disheveled geologist she knew.

She'd be fair about it later, but right now she was annoyed that he'd popped in unannounced for no apparent reason other than to shoot someone she loved, even when she'd begged him not to.

The adrenaline was slowly seeping out of her body, leaving her exhausted and more confused than ever. Her spike of temper had subsided. She suspected that asking either of them a question would be a waste of time. She saved her breath and looked around with an appreciative, professional eye.

Unlike the bland waiting area, this long hallway had weight to it. The heavy antique furniture, gilded mirrors reflecting lush oil landscapes, and coats of arms all spoke of permanence. Of history. Of power.

The soft wool wall-to-wall carpet underfoot was museum-quality, the vegetable-dyed yarns aged to a glorious patina evident even in the subdued lighting of the wall sconces on the glossy wood walls. Antique Kerman Persian for sure, and several hundred years old, if she wasn't mistaken. An area rug of this quality would cost as much as a small house. Sara had never seen acres of it like this anywhere. She would've enjoyed getting down on her knees to inspect the stunning workmanship. The thought brought a faint smile at what the council would think of that.

"Where are we exactly?" She brushed her fingers reverently over a kingwood and ebony Louis XIV commode as she passed.

"The Wizard Council." The woman stated the obvious in her charming Scottish lilt. The ring in her arched black eyebrow glinted in the subdued lighting as she turned to Sara with a smile. "I'm Lark, by the by."

If one looked beyond the thick black eyeliner and white skin, Lark was really beautiful, Sara realized. Her appearance was jarringly at odds with her environment. The fuchsia streaks in her long black hair, the piercings, the black nail polish, and the Goth makeup were better suited to a groupie of a heavy-metal band than these august chambers.

"I'm—"

"Sara Jeannette Temple. I know, lovey." They came to the end of the hallway and stopped at a pair of intricately and exquisitely carved doors, easily twelve feet high. "In here with you then, they're waiting."

"That wasn't exactly what I meant—" The massive doors opened silently.

"Hell," Jack muttered under his breath.

Ditto, Sara thought, unconsciously moving closer to his side as they stepped into a large, dimly lit chamber filled with an elusive fragrance. Beeswax? The honeyed scent of the unseen candles coupled with the warm, earthy base note of balsam.

This was what pure magic must smell like. Magic wasn't for her. But here she could feel the resonance of magic pass through her body like the vibration of a tuning fork. Being here felt like being thrown in the ocean when you'd never been in water and told to swim.

"Go on with you, then," Lark murmured, giving Sara a little shove between the shoulder blades to get her moving.

The gloomy, hundred-foot-long room could easily have been the plush offices of a prosperous law firm, with its expensive carpeting, wood paneling, groupings of burgundy leather furniture, and, at the far end, an enormous William and Mary walnut desk with high-relief carvings across the front and sides. The only lighting appeared to be a spotlight over the desk that was bright enough to require sunglasses. Even without anyone seated there, it was the perfect focal point.

The designer in her was impressed. The Council Chamber was designed to intimidate. And God, it worked. She felt small and insignificant as she and Jack walked forward, their footsteps muffled by the thick carpet. She had an overwhelming urge to slip her hand into his, which she ruthlessly squashed.

She just wanted to get the questions over with and get back home. Was someone here taking care of Alberto's injuries? Was he still alive?

She knew Grant's staff would all be too terrified to go back into the house, let alone the kitchen. If for any reason Grant came home early—Lord, he'd completely freak out. He was one of the few people in her life who even knew wizards existed, and he accepted in a vague way what she was, but he'd be less tolerant when he saw his home torn apart by a wizard run amok.

Another twenty feet or so. Somebody better show up pretty darn soon, her nerves were starting to unravel. The heavy burgundy velvet drapes covering the twenty-five-foot-tall windows blocked all natural light, making her aware that she hadn't a clue where in the world they might be. Nerves flipped over and over like little goldfish in her stomach. What did she know about the Council anyway? Zip.

They were walking the longest mile. *Shimmer us closer and get this over with.* The desperate thought surfaced on its own. No. She did not want to shimmer.

"Keep your cool," Jack whispered as if he could read her mind. Mind-reading, she knew, was not one of his powers.

"Hot, cold, or tepid," she shot back under her breath, her attention caught by arcing balls of fire against a deep black background behind the desk. What the hell was that? "I'm none of your business."

"Hallelujah," Jack muttered.

"Couldn't have said it better my"—Sara sucked in a startled breath—"self." Seven shadowy figures had suddenly materialized on a raised dais behind the desk. The brilliant light just a few feet away cast no illumination on the figures shrouded in darkness. Even though their unexpected arrival had almost given her a freaking heart attack, Sara appreciated the theatrics of it all. She didn't sense any malevolence from the Council, but the power pulsing in the room made the hair on her arms and the nape of her neck rise. Her heart pounded in a fight-or-flight adrenaline rush.

"Take a seat." A tall man dressed in a black-and-silver ceremonial robe materialized behind the desk. Like the others, his face was deeply shadowed. Sara presumed this was Duncan Edge. Two tapestry-covered wingback chairs appeared a dozen feet in front of the antique desk. She and Jack sat down.

Edge might be head of the Wizard Council, but he was just a man, she told herself. A powerful, terrifying man, but a man nevertheless. Right. *You just keep telling yourself that,* Sara thought nervously. Which annoyed her, because it was rare that anyone intimidated her.

Senses sharpened, she noticed a loose silver thread on Edge's sleeve, heard the soft, sibilant breathing of the motionless majority, felt the utter stillness in the room before the head of council spoke.

"Slater," he said by way of greeting, then glanced at her. "Miss Temple, my name is Duncan Edge. We have a serious situation on our hands. The ramifications of what's happening in South America could very well be cataclysmic."

Cataclysmic? More theatrics? Sara wondered. But the goose bumps on her arms and the way her heart thudded in fear as the Edge spoke made her think that he wasn't exaggerating.

"With all due respect," Sara said, "how exactly do Alberto's actions translate into something 'cataclysmic'?"

"In a moment, Miss Temple," Edge murmured without looking at her. "Start with what happened when you arrived, Slater. Then Miss Temple can take us back to the beginning."

She didn't appreciate being dismissed. Yes, she got

that this—whatever it was—was serious. But Alberto was her priority. "First, can you tell me if Alberto's *gunshot wounds* are being treated?" Sara stressed the words for Jack's benefit.

A muscle jerked in Jack's strong jaw. "Maybe I should have let him finish you and his wife off and called it a day."

"Maybe you should—"

"Santos is recovering from his injuries," Edge interrupted, his voice tinged with annoyance and a trace of amusement. "He's in restraints and being monitored." He looked at Jack. "Slater?"

It took Jack only a few minutes to fill them in on what he knew. He was scientific and succinct. He didn't explain how he'd come to be there.

The Head of Council indicated it was Sara's turn. "I appreciate your concern for your friend, Miss Temple. But let me impress upon both of you that this situation has dire and far-reaching consequences. Consequences that far outweigh the life or death of a single wizard, or even six of them. Please proceed."

Sara's cheeks flamed at Edge's reprimand, and her mouth went bone-dry. She'd been smacked on the hand very firmly, but it was fear more than embarrassment that made her heart pound painfully against her rib cage. She had to swallow before she could make herself speak again.

"Alberto started getting sick about a week ago. He said his body ached from the inside out. After a few days, his temperature spiked and he had a very high fever. A cold or the flu, we thought. He got progressively weaker, and the fever didn't let up." She paused, trying to tell

Edge anything that might be relevant, that could help Alberto now that he was in the Council's care.

"Carmelita and I are extremely worried about him. Dr. Muller de Canizales, a wizard and a physician, has been coming every day—several times a day, in fact. But he couldn't find anything specifically wrong. The best he was able to do was treat the symptoms. Alberto refused to see him today because he suddenly felt better. But clearly that didn't last. We're all puzzled by his atypical behavior." *Try terrified out of our minds.*

"What about his powers?"

Sara frowned at the non sequitur. "His powers? He rarely used them."

"When last did you, or anyone else, observe Santos using his powers, Miss Temple?"

She bit her lip, trying to remember. "The sicker he became, the less he seemed capable of using them."

Edge pushed his robe's cowl off his dark head, exposing his strong, angular face to the merciless light. The silver threads in his robe caught the light like tiny zings of lightning as he moved. "All of them?"

Sara nodded. "Apparently. He collapsed in his kitchen and couldn't teleport to his casa. Nor could he do simple telekinesis when he was too weak to reach the glass of water at his bedside. We didn't think much of it. He rarely used magic."

"His power to call is the ability to walk on nonsolid surfaces, correct?"

She let out a tight breath. "Yes. I saw him do so a couple of years ago." He'd walked across a swimming pool to retrieve his favorite colander when Carmelita had tossed it there during an argument. He rarely teleported, claimed invisibility nauseated him, and, like herself, preferred living without magic.

It worked for both of them.

"You live together?" Duncan Edge asked her.

Sara glanced at Jack. For a moment she'd thought she felt his hot gaze on her, but he was focused on Edge.

"It's a large compound. We all live there. Alberto and Carmelita have a small house on the grounds, as do other members of the household staff. We all work for Grant Baltzer, who's building a string of luxury hotels and spas down the west coast. Grant's primary staff remain with him when he's in a place for any length of time."

"There are a hundred and twenty people living on Mr. Baltzer's estate in Venezuela," a man announced from behind Edge. His voice was thin and reedy. He sounded a hundred years old.

"Four wizards and one Half, Silas," added a woman with a light, silvery voice. "At least, there were."

"Thank you, Deborah," the Head of Council murmured dryly. "Anyone else in the compound have the same symptoms as Santos, Miss Temple?"

"Not that I'm aware of. I'm sure I would have been told had this happened to anyone else." Sara tried to ease the tension in her shoulders without actually fidgeting.

Another Council member spoke, his face shadowed by the black cowl covering his head. "Do you know where he might have gone or who he met on his last days off?"

"Alberto gets dizzy teleporting, and he takes the

company helicopter when he absolutely must go into town. But he rarely leaves the estate. His two passions are his wife, Carmelita, and cooking. He prefers staying at the hacienda even on his days off. . . . She trailed off, her palms damp. "Is this some sort of wizard pandemic? Do you think it's something he caught from someone else?"

"He's the ninth wizard this has happened to in the last three weeks." Edge paused. "That we know of."

Her gaze slid up Jack's long legs past his broad chest to his face. A longing so fierce it hurt rippled through her entire body as she let herself look her fill for just a moment.

What happened to us, Jack? How did we go from so right to so horribly, hideously wrong?

The bright lights showed the lines fanning out around Jack's eyes. He looked . . . older. Harder than when she'd last seen him. Sara felt older and a hell of a lot harder since they'd parted, too.

"Does this—whatever it is—only affect wizards?" Jack asked intently, rubbing a strong, elegant hand across his stubbled jaw.

In contrast, Duncan Edge's handsome face was clean-shaven, his hands covered by the long sleeves of his robe. "It appears so, yes," he told Jack, his demeanor somber. The glinting silver threads in his robe were the only indication that he wasn't completely motionless.

Jack dropped his hand from his face. "What happened to the other patients?"

"All dead."

Four

"Oh, my God." Sara went cold and prickly all over. Alberto's illness was as deadly as she'd feared. She bit her lip hard to quell the tears stinging beneath her lids.

"What else can you tell us?" Edge glanced from Sara to Jack.

"After several tries, I managed to disarm him. But it was tough," Jack admitted. "My magic seemed . . . slow. Hell, it was pretty much was useless."

"Are you saying that you were incapable of using your powers to subdue him?" Edge asked, his eyes dark and intense.

"Not incapable exactly. It was as though, I don't know—as though my powers were . . . muted. Leeched."

"Leeched is exactly how the lack of power felt." Sara agreed. "I was having just that problem before Jack showed up."

The Head of Council's gaze sharpened. "Then how did you get Mr. Santos here?"

"What is this, a trick question?" Jack gave him a puzzled glance. "*You* teleported us."

"No, we didn't. I ask again: How did you get here if your magic didn't work?"

Sara looked at Jack, then back at Edge. "I know this sounds insane, but I think it happened when I grabbed Jack's arm to stop him from shooting Alberto. I felt magic pulsing up and down my arm."

"Yeah," Jack admitted with reluctance. "So did I."

"So your magic worked—for both of you—when you touched. When you worked *together*."

Jackson glanced at Sara. "I suppose so."

Edge gave them a steady look, his eyes unreadable. "Excellent. There *is* a symbiotic connection between you."

Sara gritted her teeth. "There is no connection." Not anymore.

"You were in Australia." Edge didn't phrase it as a question, but Jack answered anyway.

"Right."

Sara had never seen Jack disconcerted, and she too waited for the explanation.

"Miss Temple was in San Cristóbal. How did you know she was in peril?"

"I sensed the urgency," Jack said tightly, again with obvious reluctance.

"The two of you have a telepathic bond, then?"

"No. But I sensed her this time, nevertheless."

"You're Lifemates."

Sara's jaw ached from gritting her teeth. "Absolutely not."

"Proven not true," Jack pointed out tersely.

"You knew when she was in danger. You're stronger together than apart. You are Lifemates," Duncan Edge said unequivocally. "And you were both positioned on leylines at the time. Your connection is both unique and uniquely suited to the Council's needs."

Sara and Jack stared at the head of the Wizard Council disbelievingly and, against their will, turned to look at one another. Sara didn't have to be telepathic to know that Jack was thinking exactly what she was: the hell with the Council's needs; what about their need never to set eyes on one another again?

"How is any of this relevant?" Jack asked too politely. Which meant that he was getting annoyed.

"We believe the Omnivatics are back."

"The Omnivatics? You've *got* to be kidding." Sara shot a quick glance at Jack and saw that he was unfazed by the ludicrous suggestion. "The Omnivatics are a myth," she said in the tone of someone pointing out the obvious. "My mother used to tell me stories about them. Boogeyman scary stories. But that sect of wizards was never real."

"Historical records suggest they were wiped out thousands of years ago." Duncan Edge's tone remained grim. A shiver of foreboding zinged down Sara's spine. Edge insisting she and Jack were Lifemates was ludicrous, but this line of conversation was scary.

"However," he continued, "we now believe that the Omnivatics were biding their time. Gathering strength."

Sara looked from Edge to Jack and back. Every hair on her body stood to attention. The boogeyman was *real*?

"If this is true"—Jack's voice was grim, his expression suddenly intent—"then this is a matter for Drakon Stark, your equivalent in the Aequitas Archon, to deal with, not the Wizard Council." He got to his feet.

"Stark and all eleven other members of the Archon were killed three weeks ago." Edge raised a hand as someone in the dark behind him started to speak. "Thank you, Lark. And also an undisclosed number of wizards who had formed a task force to look into the situation."

"The task force consisted of fifty or so Aequitas," a man interjected out of the darkness. "Ten of them Archon counting Daniel Thai, who served on our council."

"What the hell are you talking about, Edge?" Jack demanded, his lips a grim line. "You of all people know damn well that's fucking *impossible*."

"One would think." Edge's tone was as grim as Jack's.

Sara's mouth was dry, her rapid pulse spurred more by their seriousness than by her own knowledge about the governing body of Aequitas.

"However," Edge told Jack flatly, "it *did* happen. So far we've managed to keep it under wraps. The Aequitas chambers were breached while in session. They're all dead, Slater. And I don't need to remind you that the only faction capable of discovering their exact location, *and* killing such powerful wizards, is the Omnivatics."

Jack dropped back into his chair, clearly stunned. "Fifty of the top Aequitas and the *entire* Archon, dead? Jesus. *How?* That location was just as impenetrable and concealed as this."

"It's being looked into. Nothing we, in this chamber, can do about that situation right now. We have to put all our focus on the reappearance of the Omnivatics."

"They've been extinct for thousands of years—" he sucked in a breath. "Apparently not. Why now?" "Why now?" Jack leaned forward, his expression intent. "Why suddenly make an appearance after centuries—shit. *Ophidian's comet.*"

"Correct. Because of the impending advent of Ophidian's comet," Edge confirmed. He glanced at Sara, who'd been looking from one man to the other as if she were at a tennis match. "The comet passes near the Earth every three hundred thirty-three years."

Jack cursed under his breath. "I wasn't paying attention. Didn't realize it was this soon."

"And coming fast," the Head of Council reminded him. "We have just weeks to find the Omnivatics before that comet passes dangerously close to the Earth."

He swept his hand to one side, and a large screen hovered beside him. "This is Ophidian's comet." A bright ball of fire moved through the blackness of the sky on the monitor, seemingly in slow motion. "Its approaching speed is already thirty miles per second."

"The name Ophidian rings a vague bell," Sara murmured, eyes glued to the comet. Earth wasn't shown on the monitor. It seemed pretty far away. "But I don't remember who or what Ophidian was."

"A very powerful god, some say supreme. He mated with a goddess named Aenari," Edge told her. "Their children were born with wizard powers. They're the ancestors of all wizards, but the fight was between the Aequitas *and* the Omnivatic factions. Legend has it that for the Omnivatics to rule the earth, three things must happen: each must amass untold power by transferring of the magic of powerful wizards to themselves; they must return to their nest as the comet passes overhead; and they must mate with a female Omnivatic in the crystal cave."

"Drop a bomb on this crystal cave," Jack suggested pragmatically.

"Other than that it's somewhere in the Pyrenees, we have no idea where it is. We can't destroy three hundred miles of mountains in the hope that we strike the correct cave in the process."

Sara realized she was freezing and rubbed her arms through the soft fabric of her jacket. "So Trace-teleport and follow them," she pointed out. This was crazy. She tried to dredge up what her mother had told her, but it was so long ago. All she remembered was that it had something to do with snakes, and that the stories were deliciously scary. To this day she loved scary movies, and even scarier books. Her imagination filled in the blank spaces between the printed words. That kind of fear didn't come close to the chill she felt watching these two powerful wizards discuss the end of the world.

"The way an Omnivatic travels to his nest is through a portal, so Trace-teleporting isn't an option. And before you ask, Miss Temple, we don't know where or what such a portal might be, either." The Head of Council sat down in the chair behind him. "Nobody has seen an Omnivatic in hundreds of years."

"Are you telling us the world will end if you don't find a way to stop these Omnivatics in—"

"If *we*, Miss Temple"—he motioned to her and Jack—"if we don't stop them, and yes, that's what I'm telling you. They have the ability to speed the rotation of the Earth. Every earthquake the Omnivatics have caused over milliosn of years has permanently shortened the time it takes for the planet to complete one rotation, thereby shortening the length of a day. One of the Archon's jobs was to reverse, or at least slow down, that process. The advent of the comet will make the Earth rotate even faster, by nudging some of its mass closer to the planet's axis. They must be stopped. Especially now that their powers are increasing. A couple of weeks is how much time we have."

"How are they amassing power?" Jack asked.

"The first step would be to lethally infect their victims—powerful wizards—and drain their powers. With each transfer, they become exponentially stronger themselves. That's what happened to the wizards who died."

"There are wizards capable of doing power transference. Doesn't mean they're Omnivatics."

"True. But this is considerably more than a simple power transference. Apparently this 'sickness' is a slow, agonizingly painful process. Not only are the powers transferred to the Omnivatic, but so are the victims' thoughts and experiences. Their memories are assimilated with their powers."

"Hell."

"Yeah. It is for the poor bastards being targeted."

"But, according to Sara, Santos didn't *have* any

extraordinary powers. And his memories of being a chef don't exactly make him a prime target either."

"Clearly," said Edge flatly, "we don't have all the answers. Maybe we never will. What we *do* know is the trajectory and strength of the incoming comet. We know the devastation its proximity will cause."

"I get the magnitude of the situation, and I'll do what I can to help until another Archon is formed, but this has nothing to do with Sara or myself. Why call us in?"

"You two never had a telepathic connection, yet you heard her in Australia. Separately you couldn't use magic on Santos, yet when you touched and used your power together, you were able to teleport him. Didn't you ask yourselves why that should be?"

"No," Jack retorted mildly. "We haven't exactly had time to sit and reflect. But it's an interesting change of subject, Edge."

"Actually, it's not. Because you, Slater, are full Aequitas, and Miss Temple is half Aequitas. We're not sure why, perhaps because you are Lifemates as well as Aequitas, you have a unique connection. Your powers are amped because of this."

"It's never happened before."

"And we aren't Lifemates," Sara added, keeping her tone as even as possible. She wanted to leave now. The conversation scared her to death. She wanted to be far, far away from both the head of the Wizard Council and Jackson Slater. She wanted to go back to her normal life, where Jack was just a name and her biggest fear was matching two shades of blue.

"The Omnivatics weren't involved before. That changes everything." Edge paused, looking critically at both of them in a way that made Sara squirm. "Slater. Tell Miss Temple what the Omnivatics were known for."

"Geophysical realm," Jack said as if he were quoting from something, "earthquake, tsunami, and volcanic activity. Meteorological: storms. Hydrological: floods. Climatological: extreme temperature, drought, and wildfire." Far from sounding terrified, he actually sounded stoked. "Jesus . . ." Jack muttered, clearly as fascinated as he was appalled. "The snowstorms across a large part of North America? Worst in more than forty years. Hurricanes—"

"It took hurricanes Andrew and Katrina before we were alerted to the possibility that the Omnivatics were involved. Fortunately, with quick action, we were able to subdue Hurricane Ike before it made landfall. It hit at a Category Three in Cuba instead of the Five it was supposed to be. Still, it killed several hundred people and cost upward of thirty billion dollars in damages.

"Lest you dismiss all this as a string of coincidences, 2008 was a record year for natural disasters, as you know from your geological reports, Slater."

"More than two million fatalities worldwide from cyclones, earthquakes, floods, and other forces of nature. Yeah. Unprecedented.

Of course he'd known what was happening, but he'd never put it all together this way. Unprecedented wasn't the half of it. "This is Omnivatic interference on a grand scale."

"What do they want?" Sara asked, confused. She hadn't studied this as Jack had.

"World domination and the eradication of the Aequitas. And that can only happen if they eliminate wizards and drain their powers to amass the strength they need in time."

"I don't get it." She had fought back her fear—being irritated by the whole Lifemate issue helped considerably—and was, to say the least, skeptical. "They think they can dominate the world by killing wizards one at a time?"

"They're doing it to amass power. We don't know how many they've killed so far. What we do know is that before their deaths, at least nine wizards have had their magic stripped from them. All nine were from the South American continent."

"It's a big place," Jack pointed out. "Let me play devil's advocate here for a minute. A handful of wizards dying isn't that unusual, surely?"

"It is when they have their powers leeched. You were in Ecuador a couple of years ago, right, Slater?" Edge asked.

"Yeah. Quito. Guagua Pichincha erupted. I was also in Banjos just after Tungurahua erupted. But the country has almost three hundred volcanoes, twenty of them active. Do you believe these 'natural disasters' were caused by the Omnivatics?"

"We do. Unnatural 'natural' disasters are the Omnivatics' stock in trade. The Aequitas preserve the balance, Omnivatics destroy it."

Edge settled against the back of his chair, a greenish fire crackling between his fingertips, which he then turned into a sphere the size of a tennis ball that slowly rotated in his palm. "Can you imagine the chaos that would ensue if humans knew that in days a battle will be waged between good and evil?"

The tension in Jack's body made the fear in Sara's ratchet up another notch. He was a geologist. He spent his life studying such disasters, and he believed what Edge was telling him.

Jack started thinking out loud, analyzing information in the way he excelled at. "The bombardment of tropical cyclones, Hurricane Katrina, the tsunami in Southeast Asia." Jack rose and stood in front of his chair, too involved to stay still.

Sara, on the other hand, felt as though she'd been Krazy Glued right there. Icy cold filled her insides, making the conversation between the two men muted and surreal. She usually had an opinion on something, on everything—but today she was rendered practically speechless by the enormity of what she was hearing.

"Damn them to hell. That seven-point-nine-magnitude earthquake that hit China's Sichuan province could have been prevented."

The green fire snapped out, and Edge's eyes narrowed. "If we'd known about it in time, and if the Archon had intervened? Yes, it could have. The occurrences are escalating."

"If you'll give me what you have, I'll look into this for you."

"Investigate."

After a second, Jack nodded. "I have a couple of other geologists I can bring in to—"

"You're a man of science, Slater. Let's look at the facts. You and Miss Temple have a bond. The dead wizards have all been infected on the west coast of South America—where Miss Temple currently resides. You each have your powers amped by close proximity to the other. And together you have the strength to fight the Omnivatics because you're both Aequitas. I don't believe in coincidences. Do you?"

Sara found her voice. "Could it be something else? Anything else?" Was it really possible that all those horrific disasters were caused by the Omnivatics?

"You might wish it were, but it isn't. The Omnivatics are back. You are to work together investigating these events."

"No!" Sara and Jack said simultaneously, with exactly the same emphasis.

Jack kept going. "Out of the question. I won't work with her. You require that I use my skills as a geologist and an Aequitas to investigate a common thread in these natural disasters? Sure." He ran his hand over his face. "Sara's not qualified for this sort of investigation, Edge; you know that. You need a medical doctor—hell, you need a team from the CDC, more scientists, more geologists, not an interior designer who has made a point of not using what powers she has."

"And we're putting that team together. Unfortunately, our only member of the Aequitas Archon is dead, and this can only be done by an Aequitas. It's not as though every Aequitas in the country is registered with the Wizard Council. Going through the remaining records of the Archon will take time—time we don't have. In the meantime, you two are it." Orange and blue flames leapt across the fabric of Edge's robe close to his face. His eyes glowed demonically red.

Jack leaned forward, everything about him on the defensive from the line of his shoulders to the jut of his scruffy jaw. "My call."

He and Duncan Edge faced off.

The hair on Sara's nape and arms rose with the electrical power surging through the room. Her heart skipped a couple of beats.

"*Not* your call, Slater." Edge's grim expression was more eloquent than his words. "Until another Archon is formed and says differently, the two of you *will* work together. I don't want you out of each other's sight— literally—for the duration. Go back to San Cristóbal, and report back to us if this problem has spread. See if you can figure out how it's contracted. Until we understand what this is and how to contain it, you two will be our eyes and ears."

"Get someone else to team up with me," Jack suggested, his voice tight and hard. "What about the counterterrorist guys you used to work for? They have a psi division."

"I have no say over the psi division of T-FLAC. And since you're Aequitas, you're the only ones who can do the job—in this instance, even their paranormal division would be useless. Not to mention that we don't believe what's happening in South America has anything to do with terrorists," Duncan Edge pointed out dryly. "The counterbalance of the Omnivatics is Aequitas. You are both Aequitas. I can assure you that the Wizard Council will expedite the search for more Aequitas as swiftly as possible. That said, it's clear that you two have something I doubt we'll find in another Aequitas—your ability to amp one another's powers."

"You don't know that," Jack said baldly. "There could be any *number* of Aequitas out there who can perform the same power surge when they're together,"

"Possibly. Probably. But we don't know who or where they are. They aren't currently sitting in my council chambers. Look, Slater, Miss Temple—the Wizard Council doesn't exactly have a task force ready to be deployed at a moment's notice, not with the Archon gone."

"Then form another Archon," Sara told him flatly, standing up and leaning forward in unconscious imitation of Jack.

"Not possible in such a short time, Miss Temple."

"As much as he doesn't want to work with me, I don't want to work with him. I do agree with Jackson on something else: I'm not qualified for this. I didn't go to wizard school, and even though my parents were wizards, I was raised human."

"And have centuries of Aequitas blood flowing through your veins. You two don't get it." The Master Wizard rose, his robes flowing around him like black-and-silver liquid. Angry, spiked flames danced around his body and head as he braced both hands on the desk in front of him; Sara could feel his heat.

"Your powers are amped when you're together, and together you need to be for the duration. This is not a matter of national security. This is bigger. This is the *planet* we're talking about. If we don't stop the Omnivatics, the natural disasters will become bigger and more destructive. Civilization as we know it will be completely destroyed, leaving the field clear for absolute domination by the Omnivatics. You're Aequitas, the protectors of humans and of this world. Consider yourself deputized. End of discussion!"

"May I respectfully remind you," Sara said, raising her chin and looking straight into Edge's inscrutable eyes, "*I* do *not* work for you, or for the Wizard Council. I don't know anything *about* being an Aequitas. And I'm not comfortable with you invoking some arcane law that hasn't been used in hundreds of yea——"

Five

"—rs!" Sara finished on a high note, blinking to orient herself as they materialized.

They were no longer in the plush Wizard Council chamber, but in a sun-washed office. Jack knew it had to be Sara's, back at Baltzer's hacienda in San Cristóbal, because no matter where in the world she was, her offices were always identical. All of the furniture and accessories were creams, beiges, and black. There was an intentional lack of color in her primary work space.

She grabbed the high back of her black mesh desk chair to maintain her balance. "They're certainly theatrical."

But real. Fucking, horrifically real. And they both knew it. If she was hoping he'd tell her otherwise, Sara was in for a giant fucking disappointment. "If all twelve members of the Aequitas Archon were killed as Edge claims, then we're in deep, and I mean fucking *deep*, shit."

"I don't think he made that up," Sara said dryly, pressing her fingertips to the middle of her forehead.

Jack rested his butt on her desk and stretched out his legs, crossing his ankles in a relaxed posture that in no way reflected the myriad of facts flipping through his mind as he tried to come up with a cohesive plan. "No. No reason to lie."

Dropping her hand, she shot him a disbelieving look. "Everybody has reason to lie at some point. Although I tried to tell him he chose poorly. Oh, not in you—you can at least try to put some of the pieces together. But me? I don't even call myself a wizard."

"Doesn't matter what you call yourself. You are one. It's not as though you have no magic. It's your choice—always has been—not to use it."

"I don't *want* to do this, Jack. What does the Wizard Council gain by forcing *us* to deal with this?"

Jack shrugged. "Nothing, as far as I can see. I imagine we aren't the only people who've been deputized to look into this."

"Good," she sighed, clearly relieved they weren't on their own. "Then what are you going to do about their insane request?"

"Request? In case you didn't notice, that was an order. Go your merry way, Sara. Do whatever you were doing before. I'll do what I was told to do—look into the situation and report back. In the meantime, you have a houseguest for a few days." Jack maintained his temper by a hair. He didn't like this togetherness any more than she did.

"Grant hates you, and I'm perfectly aware that the feeling's mutual." She turned to give Jack a fix-this-damn-it glare. "He won't be happy playing host to you." Her tone implied she wouldn't either.

Jack raised a mocking brow. "A hotelier not willing to rent a room?"

"This is Grant's *home*. Damn it, Jackson, I'd almost prefer world catastrophe to living under the same roof as you." She closed her eyes wearily and shook her head. "Okay, that was ridiculous, but you know what I mean. Can't you stay at a hotel?"

"Like it or not, we're stuck with each other. At least until the Council pulls together a task force."

"Don't they care that I'm not qualified to do this?" Sara paced, ignoring the tempting view of a sparkling swimming pool outside her window. Her usually muted office was an explosion of color swatches and chaos. She'd clearly been in the middle of a large project when this business with Santos occurred. The mess had to be some sort of release valve to Sara's uptight nature. Jack scratched his chin, eying the wallpaper and fabric sample books littering every surface, a drafting table that held a blueprint, and several bulletin boards covered with paint and fabric swatches and notes. Sara skirted an enormous basket holding rolled blueprints and an umbrella; he'd lay ten-to-one odds that she'd completely forgotten putting the umbrella in there.

Jack leaned against her desk. "They think we are."

"They're wrong."

"Given what we know, yeah. Maybe. But I suspect that they didn't tell us everything."

"Great. So they throw two unprepared, unqualified, unwilling people into a life-or-death situation blind-folded. That's insane."

He was neither unprepared nor unqualified. "It's what Aequitas does."

"Too bad I didn't get the handbook."

"You chose not to learn, Sara. You can hardly blame the Council for that."

She stopped and glared at him. "They should respect that I have no interest in embracing my power. I resent being called to arms because of some archaic pledge and an accident of my bloodline. I don't want to do this. I particularly don't want to do it with you. I don't think I can be much plainer than that."

"As even fifty percent Aequitas, you don't have a choice. Suck it up and move on."

Sara bit her lower lip. His gut took a direct hit. Why in the hell did she have to have that annoying habit that fixated him on her mouth?

"Grant isn't going to like this one bit."

He hadn't seen the guy in two years and Jack was already sick of hearing his name. "Have him take it up with the Wizard Council."

"You know he isn't a wizard, Jack. How am I going to explain what you're doing hanging around?"

Jack turned away to stare sightlessly out the window where two blondes cavorted in the pool. He didn't like his reaction to seeing Sara again. He didn't like it a lot. This was exactly the reason he'd promised himself he'd never run into her again.

"Tell him I'm your bodyguard. Hell, tell him we're back together."

She cast him an exasperated look. "He's never going to believe that, he's not an idiot."

No, Grant Baltzer was anything but. Jack knew she

admired the guy and considered him handsome, charming, and brilliant. He was also loaded, which Jack knew she didn't care about one way or the other. Although she enjoyed the lifestyle and the perks.

While Sara's friend and boss was a playboy, he also worked hard. Jack had tried to be civil for Sara's sake, but it would be a leap to pretend that he'd ever liked the guy. "Tell him the truth then."

She thought about it for a second. "Maybe some of it. I have to explain Alberto's absence somehow." She looked none too happy about it. "Before I put on my Wonder Woman suit and save the world, I have to go take care of the kitchen and talk to the staff, then check on Carmelita." She leaned over her desk to depress a button on the phone. He held up a hand, and she paused.

"None of the staff have any memory of the slaughter they witnessed—I figured they could all do without it and Mindwiped them. So you might not want to comfort them for something they don't remember. You should think of a reason why the kitchen door is locked, though; I didn't want anyone coming in while I was trying to deal with Alberto, and I'm assuming it's still sealed, thanks to our hasty departure."

"I'm stunned."

"By my compassion? Jesus, Sara—"

"That too. I had no idea you knew how to do a Mindwipe." She put through her call, leaving the phone on speaker.

"Thank God," a woman's lightly accented voice said with obvious relief. "Are you okay, Sara? No one knew where you ran off to, all the cars are here and the chopper—"

"I'm fine, Pia." Thanks to Jack's quick thinking, Pia had no idea what had happened earlier. "We'll talk about it later. We have a houseguest. Jack Slater will be staying here for a few days—can you have a room prepared for him?"

"Did you say Jack—"

Sara picked up the receiver. "Yes. And I meant it. . . . No, I won't let Grant or the others kill him." She shot Jack a look meant to intimidate. He returned her glare with a bland smile.

"You're on speaker," Sara warned Pia, putting the receiver back in the cradle so she could continue pacing. She told Pia that Alberto and Carmelita would be gone for a while visiting Carmelita's mother.

"God, how long is a while, Sara? Grant won't be pleased, and William's going to have a fit if Alberto doesn't personally prep his meals." Her assistant sighed. "Want me to tell Héctor he'll have the honors?"

Sara's uninhibited laugh went straight to Jack's groin, and he tried to concentrate on the two practically naked women outside. How in God's name was he going to stick to his guns and keep his hands off Sara? *Liking* had zip to do with lust. Spending days, perhaps weeks in close proximity was going to take a hell of a lot more than willpower and fortitude. He was going to need superpowers.

Remember that last day.

Yeah, he thought bitterly. Good as a cold shower. He turned away from the window as Sara ended her call.

"Wait here," she told him briskly. "I'll be back in about half an hour."

He stiffened. If she thought she was calling the shots, she was sadly mistaken. Edge had instructed that they not be out of one another's sight. "I'll go with you."

"Fine." She changed into jeans and a crisp white shirt as she strode past him out of the room. A ripple of irritation scored him from head to toe. Sara could say all she wanted about being disinterested in magic, but when it suited her, she was all too ready to use her powers, if only to change her clothes. She was a hypocrite as well as a liar.

Good to remember.

Jack stayed in his sweat-stained, dusty clothes and followed her. "Nice place."

"Yes." She glanced back, the fall of her blond-streaked light-brown hair sliding over her shoulder. He stuffed his fingers into his front pockets before he did something stupid like reach out and touch the glossy strands. There was a time when he hadn't been able to keep his hands off her. A time when all it had taken was a look, and they were naked on any flat surface.

She'd killed that.

Hell. She'd almost killed him.

Jack looked out one of the wide windows to the backdrop of vegetation beyond the high walls of the estate. The sun was still shining, but it had started to rain, huge fat drops that turned to steam as they hit the thick vegetation. That impenetrable green wall of jungle, Jack noted, was held back by little more than a half-inch of plate glass. Made him appreciate the air-conditioning.

He rubbed a hand across his aching jaw—aching because, he realized, he was grinding his teeth. Hell, what man wouldn't be, stuck with the one woman he didn't want to be close to in the middle of a fucking jungle? God, what a clusterfuck.

There were a lot of windows, all barred and screened. All with views of dense foliage. Damn place was surrounded by jungle. "He's a pretty social guy. Why have a home so inaccessible?"

"It's logical to make a home base convenient to where we're working. And we're building seven new hotels down the west coast."

Rain beat a thunderous rhythm on the tiled roof and slashed at the windows. "We?"

"Grant made me a partner six months ago."

Yet another manipulation to keep Sara at his side, Jack bet. Baltzer did nothing that wasn't self-serving. "Congratulations."

She started to say something, then literally bit her tongue.

"What?"

Sara stopped walking and he almost bumped into her. She narrowed her eyes and glared at him. "Why does everything you say sound like a damned insult?"

"Maybe you're too sensitive?"

"You're an ass, Jack. You'd better be civilized to Grant. You're accepting his hospitality, and he's very important to me. Piss him off and you'll piss me off even more than I'm pissed off already."

She was damned appealing when she was annoyed.

Her brown eyes darkened and her cheeks got sweetly pink. He put up his hands in surrender. "I'll be on my best behavior."

"You'd better." She turned and started walking again. They went through the tiled entryway, through a great room, and down a side corridor. The single-story hacienda was enormous, the size of a small hotel. With any luck, he wouldn't have to see Baltzer for days. On the other hand, sticking close to Sara when there was this much room might prove to be problematic.

"What happened to Roe?" William Roe had been Baltzer's partner for years. About the same age as Jack, the guy gave him a serious case of the willies. The snake tattooed on his forearm, positioned so that it seemed to writhe and move forward whenever William shook hands, had a great deal to do with Jack's aversion to him.

"Still a partner, although of course Grant keeps the controlling interest in the company. William lives here as well."

God, this just got better and better. He'd have to sleep with one eye open and arm himself to the teeth. "One big happy family."

"You never told me you were Aequitas."

He stiffened, and crushed every soft feeling she'd been bringing out in him. "You didn't happen to mention you were mestizo Aequitas. So I guess we're even."

This time when she stopped, Jack had to grab her shoulders to prevent her falling against him, to stop at all costs making full-body contact. But it brought her close. Too close. He didn't pull her in, but he didn't push her away. He just stood there, enduring the torture of inhaling her soft citrus scent as a flood of sensual memories washed over him.

Their high-octane gazes caught, held. They froze.

There was nothing that revived the past quite like a smell associated with it. The heady fragrance of ginger-lemon soap and the sound of the rain beating on the windows brought back vivid memories of burying his fingers in the frothy, scented strands of her hair as he bathed her in the shower.

Jack had bathed all of her. Very slowly. And often. The shower was one of their favorite places to make—

A heartbeat after the thought flashed in his mind, Jack found his tongue in Sara's mouth, and his hands filled with her wet, naked ass cheeks. Hot, water pounded his shoulders. Sara's slick, soapy, naked body pressed against his. Her taste was still heady, the unexpected intimacy of her tongue curling against his shockingly sweet.

His erection was instantaneous, and hard enough to pole-vault him to Australia. He kissed her like a starving man at a feast. Her hungry mouth beneath his gave him jolts of intense pleasure, the sensation so powerful he went deaf and blind with it. He felt something give way inside him. Something hard and tight suddenly soared free.

Her lips were just as he remembered, firm, moist, delicious. Hunger fueled equal hunger as her mouth opened wider, and their slick tongues mated. He shoved her back against the tiled wall, pressing his erection to the soft curls between her legs, and held on to her as if she might suddenly disappear.

Skin flushed, Sara murmured low in her throat, angling her mouth against his, licking then biting his lower lip. Her entire body shuddered as he held her steady, one ass cheek cupped in his hand. He lifted her slightly and felt the erect pebbles of her aroused nipples through the hair on his chest. Her arms tightened around his neck as she curled one silky-smooth leg around his hips.

They kissed frantically. Jack pulled her tongue into his mouth, wanting to absorb the taste and feel of her as he worked his mouth over hers until they were both panting and breathless.

Without warning, Sara ripped her mouth from beneath his, her breathing labored, her eyes flashing fire.

Completely disoriented, Jack surfaced. "What's the matt—" It took him a moment to realize this wasn't where they'd been— either physically or emotionally— a few seconds ago. "What the f—" They were bare-ass naked in a steaming shower stall, their bodies glued together.

The tight vise of her leg dropped from its position across his ass. Water dripped from her lashes as she blinked up at him. "I'm going to *kill* you, Jackson Slater." She pounded a fist on his wet chest. "Get your damned hand off my ass." She used both hands to shove him away. Hard.

"Hell—it wasn't—" The steaming water suddenly turned cold, just like her eyes before she vanished.

"Crap!" Braced by his arm, Jack thumped his forehead against the cool white tiles. To say he was in trouble didn't begin to cover it. Sara might be amping his powers, but she was messing with his head—and apparently with his ability to control his powers.

He had to be cold-blooded around her. Unfortunately, Sara had always had a profound and disturbing ability to heat up his hemoglobin like no other woman before or since.

Good damned thing cold was his power to call.

He froze the droplets on his skin to glittering shards. Even so, it took a few moments to get rid of his erection. When he figured he was cooled off enough, he brushed the ice crystals off his skin, stepped out of the unfamiliar enclosure and materialized his clothes.

He needed armor. Body armor and brain armor. Head-to-toe-and-everything-in-between armor.

Jack closed his eyes for a long, pained moment.

He was so screwed.

JACK CAUGHT UP WITH Sara in the north wing. He must've traced her, damn it.

"Whoa! Don't go storming off in a huff. As interesting as that was, it was *not* my fault."

Sara hadn't had enough time—say, ten or fifteen years—to gather even a modicum of equilibrium after the shocker of finding herself pressed against Jack's wet, naked body without warning.

Interesting? She still felt the rasp of his calloused thumb stroking a light circle against the small of her back as he tugged her closer. *Stop it.* Walking faster, she bit her kiss-swollen lip until it hurt enough to bring her back to her senses.

"Whose fault was it, then?" she demanded, jaw aching from clenching her teeth. "Certainly not mine." She was not, absolutely *not* going to allow her rampaging hormones to erase the hurt and anger she felt toward him. She used to mainline her love and lust for Jackson Slater, and had been forced to cut off the addiction cold turkey. She wasn't going back down that dangerous path ever again. The withdrawal had almost killed her.

"Isn't it funny how *nothing* is ever your fault?" He let out an angry breath. "Do you ever take any responsibility for your actions, Sara? Or do you just blame your own bad choices on someone else because otherwise you'd have to acknowledge your own piss-poor judgment?"

Her blood pressure spiked, making her eyeballs throb. A hundred pithy, insulting responses came to the tip of her tongue. Sara ruthlessly suppressed them all. She knew what happened when her emotions were let loose. She dared not risk blasting Jack, angry as she was. Changing clothes was one thing; if that bit of magic went wrong, she could find herself in a red blouse instead of a black one. Serious spells going wrong had much more dire consequences.

There'd been enough death and destruction around for one day, but God, she was tempted. So freaking tempted. She settled for "Bite me."

"And get food poisoning? I don't think so."

She felt dizzy just imagining turning around and punching him. Hard. Somewhere. Anywhere. Words alone wouldn't relieve this tight band across her chest.

Breathe in. Breathe out. Do. Not. Respond. In. Out. In. Out. Stay calm. Immune.

"What the hell are you doing?" He peered into her face. "Having a seizure?" He didn't sound concerned, just rudely amused.

Sara closed her eyes and shook her head. *In. Out. In. Out.* "I'm ignoring you."

"Well, can you do that without sounding as though you're gearing up for a deep-sea dive?"

Her sensitized nipples rubbed annoyingly on the inside of her lacy bra as she moved, and the crotch of her panties was damp. Those few moments in the shower hadn't exactly been foreplay, but her body, deprived of Jack's for so long, didn't give a damn. She was primed and ready for sex. And she wasn't going to get any, not for the foreseeable future.

"No, Jack, I'm afraid I can't." Without looking at him, she kept moving.

They'd fought only toward the end. She'd hated it then and she hated it now. It gave her the same sick feeling, like putting on a favorite pair of jeans and realizing they not only didn't fit anymore, they pinched uncomfortably.

Jack was walking too close. Close enough for her to feel the heat emanating from his tall body. On him, her soap smelled nothing like it did on her. He smelled like clean male. A quick, surreptitious glance out of the corner of her eye showed he was back in his dusty, disheveled pants and shirt, but his dark hair was clean and slicked back off his forehead.

No more touching, she warned herself sternly. She could convince herself she was immune, as long as Jack didn't touch her. She unclenched her hands and took several calming breaths. If he smiled, if he even looked as though he might smile, she would smack him.

"If you ever do anything like that again, Jackson Slater," she snapped, picking up speed, eyes front, "I'm going to take great pleasure in using every ounce of my magic to emasculate you."

"Pull in your claws, Sara. It won't happen again. We're supposed to be working together here, remember? Let's just call a truce."

His heat—the hardness of his erection—had been shockingly familiar pressed to the tender juncture of her thighs. The encounter had been instantaneous—no buildup, no warning, no time to marshal her defenses. She'd literally melted into him before she remembered that this was now, not then.

Oh, God, Sara thought, adding jumpy and panicky to horny. *How am I going to handle seeing him every freaking day?* "Fine. But the truce doesn't extend to sex."

"Fine by me. And just as an FYI—I didn't do it," he reminded her flatly. "*We* did it. Next time you think of sex in the shower, make sure I'm not anywhere near you."

Oh, great, Sara thought, absolutely appalled. The sound of the rain on the roof, the smell of him after so long—how did *Jack* know she'd been thinking exactly that when he'd grabbed her? "I wasn't thinking about *you*," she fibbed. "Or a *shower*. Or anything el— hi ladies."

Thank God. Saved by the belles, Grant's latest vapid set of blue-eyed blond twins. The women, not even out of their teens, were identical. Both wore minuscule threads of black floss on their tanned, taut, oil-slicked bodies. Their combined IQ was close to their bra size.

"Inga and Ida Angstrom, meet Jackson Slater."

Inga had a livid bite-shaped bruise on her breast, and Ida had tried to cover the fresh marks on both wrists with makeup. Grant forgot his own strength sometimes, and if he wasn't careful, one day one of his playmates was going to report him to the police. None of her business, but hard not to notice. Sara sighed inwardly.

"Hi, Jackson," Inga cooed. The scent of coconut oil and hot sunshine mingled on her rain-wet skin with the smell of chlorine from the pool. The girl licked her lips like a porn queen, her hot blue gaze pinning Jack in place.

"We can't find Carmelita and it's way past lunchtime," Ida whined in the particularly annoying baby voice she used around men. Her big blue eyes were also locked on Jack like a tractor beam.

Jack had shirts older than these girls.

"Ladies," he said by way of greeting, a faint trace of amusement curving the grim line of his mouth. He didn't appear affected by so much nakedness up close and personal.

The girls, with no clue about personal space, crowded near him as if they were vaqueros herding a particularly interesting bull. If they got any closer, they'd leave oil slicks all over his dusty clothes. It would almost be worth seeing their reaction when copious amounts of Jack's red dust were transferred to them.

Disgust, and irritation sharpened Sara's tone. "Did you go into the kitchen?"

"No. Yumi came to get Harry out of the pool, and she told us the door was locked and to talk to you."

"Who's Yumi?" Jack turned to her, his dark blue eyes filled with amusement. Sara refused to be charmed by him.

"Grant's assistant. She and Pia both live here." She liked Grant's assistant very much. Because William's personal assistant stayed in town, Pia and Yumi had to pinch-hit for all three of them at times.

Jack had sealed the kitchen earlier to prevent any of the people he'd teleported outside from returning. Yumi was a Half wizard and would've known immediately that the seal on the door had nothing to do with a puny lock.

"Harry was in the pool again?" Sara asked. Honest to God, living here was like running a daycare center. Never a dull moment.

"Harry. Roe's giant snake, Harry?" Jack asked, amused changing to appalled in an instant. He looked around as if the boa constrictor might be napping nearby on the living-room sofa.

"Same old Harry." All ten feet of bad attitude usually stayed put in William's wing of the house. Unfortunately, every now and then the door was left open, and Harry decided to explore. He had a particular fondness for Sara's closet.

"Isn't bringing him here rather like smuggling a microchip into Microsoft?"

Of course it was. Just getting the darn snake through customs had been a logistical nightmare. As if William couldn't get his hands on any number of snakes by walking out the back door on any given day.

"I offered to buy him a parrot when we came to Venezuela," Sara said dryly, remembering that Jack had been less than fond of her partner's pet when they'd met at a Christmas party at William's house in San Francisco. "But he and Harry have been together for twenty years. Longer than some marriages. Don't worry, Harry usually sleeps most of the day in William's suite—you won't run into him."

"Good to know." Jack stuffed his hands into his front pockets. "Shouldn't we. . .?"

Get the kitchen out of the way. "Yes." She turned back to the girls, who were assessing Jack's attributes like accountants at tax time. "Carmelita and Alberto are both away," Sara informed Inga and Ida briskly. They went to stay with her mother in the village for a few days."

Sara dug inside the purse on her shoulder while she pondered this new and annoying wrinkle. She wasn't in charge of what, or whom, the girls did, but Grant was not a man who shared. And while she didn't want Jack, he couldn't be allowed to mess with Grant's girlfriends.

"Here." She took out her wallet and handed over a handful of notes, then removed a key from her key ring. "Go to dinner on me. Grant won't be back until late tonight or tomorrow, so go ahead and spend the night in town and have fun. Take the Aston Martin, if you like, or have Benito or Andres fly you in."

"Really? Wow, *tack*, Sara, you're the best." Inga snatched the key from her fingers. "We'll drive, *ja*?" They trotted off on ridiculously high heels, speaking excitedly in Swedish.

"An Aston Martin on these roads?" Jack asked as they headed to the kitchen.

San Cristóbal was modern and had good roads, but there were miles and miles of dirt road to get down the mountainous switch-backs and into the city proper.

Sara shrugged. She usually flew, but the three-hour drive into town would keep the girls out of her hair. "Grant enjoys fast cars. He's not going to be thrilled I let them drive the Martin, but I don't want them around while I clean up the kitchen and assess the situation." And figure out how to keep them away from Jack. "I hope I don't have to tell you to keep your hands off those two."

"Trust me, that'll be no problem. I like my women a little more seasoned. How old are they? Sixteen?"

Almost as bad. "Eighteen." They exchanged looks, on the same page for just a moment. Then the moment passed.

What women? Had he been dating since they broke up? Of course he had. Jack liked sex too much to be celibate.

"Maybe Grant's going for an age-appropriate total of thirty-six?"

"I'm serious, Jack. Don't even think about it."

"The fact that you think it necessary to warn me shows just how damn little you know me," he said with dangerous calm. "Don't worry, Sara, those kids are safe from me."

She believed him. Jack was a lot of things, but a cradle-robbing womanizer wasn't one of them.

"I see Baltzer's been his usual brutish self. Don't give me that look. I'm not blind. I saw the bruises on those two." When she didn't respond, he said instead, "Tell me more about this Yumi. Interesting name."

"Grant's new assistant, Yumi Kimura."

"He's got quite a harem here."

"Yumi's sleeping with William, as it happens. And Grant and I are friends. Always have been, always will be." There were so many conversations she didn't want to have with Jack again, it almost made her dizzy.

"Has he ever harmed you?"

Sara stared at him. "Of course not." *Only you did that.*

"No 'of course' about it. He likes hurting women."

"He likes rough sex. I am not having, nor have I ever had, sex with Grant. Not that it's any of your business. Let's move on. What's the plan of action?" she asked, straightening a watercolor on the wall as they passed. How dare he ask her anything about her life? He'd given up that right years ago. "The sooner we find out what the council wants to know, the sooner I can get on with my life."

"I'd like to talk to the local cops, see if anything out of the ordinary has happened. Crazies brought in, whatever."

"We should start with hospitals, then."

"We'll visit both." Jack put out his arm to stop her as they arrived at the kitchen door. Luckily for him he didn't touch her or that arm would be in a cast.

His lips twitched as though he knew what she'd been thinking, and he dropped his arm and turned to the closed door. "Like I told you, I did a down-and-dirty Protection spell so no one could get in."

Smart. Sara wished she'd thought of it first, but she'd been a little distracted at the time; large men wielding knives and screaming at her tended to have that effect. Jackson did something swift with his hands and she felt a subtle shift.

"Okay. It's lifted."

Sara pushed past him and turned the handle. The stench hit her before they opened the door. Even with air-conditioning, the bodies stank to high heaven. Jack materialized two face masks and handed her one.

"Wait out here, I'll take care of it."

She covered her mouth and nose with the mask, not wanting Jack's favors. "My home, my problem. I'll take care of it myself."

He stepped back and waved her in. "Have at it."

~ Six ~

The kitchen was just as they'd left it, but the smell was worse, sweet and sickly and redolent of violent death. Sara's stomach churned and she swallowed nausea.

"Council wants the bodies," he reminded her from the doorway.

"You do it," she told him tersely. The task was far too important to get wrong. The Wizard Council wanted the bodies, but *she* had the responsibility of telling their families. Between them it took only a few minutes to sanitize the kitchen. There were times when magic was necessary. As long as using it didn't involve emotion—hers—or anyone nearby, she'd do what had to be done, even if she preferred to go the nonmagical route. When they were done, one would never have guessed that there'd been wholesale murder done there just hours before.

"The Mindwipe I used on the kitchen staff is temporary and it won't last much longer. How do you want to handle that?"

She could only imagine how terrified the already superstitious staff would be if their memories started to return.

Most of them came from local villages, where myth and magic were an intrinsic part of their culture. "If I call them in, would you do a permanent Mindwipe?" She hated to ask him for help *again*, but she knew that since she was emotionally tied to these people, she'd screw up the wipe.

"Funny how you use magic when it suits you."

"Never mind, don't bother, Jack. I'll just talk to them."

"Talking to them isn't going to erase their memory of seeing their friends being butchered." He glanced at the agate-faced watch on his wrist. "They have about fifteen minutes of the temp Mindwipe left. Your call."

"Do it. Okay? Just damn well do it."

"Thank you, Jackson," he said sweetly. "I appreciate your help in a mess that has not a fucking thing to do with you!"

"Fine, Jackson. *Thank you.* Happy now?"

He gave her a sour look. "Not by a long shot."

She rubbed the Jack-induced pain in her temple with two fingers. Two Jack headaches in one day. A record. "This isn't going to work."

"Talk to the Council, Sara. Neither of us wants to do this. Not together, anyway. I suggest that for the duration, you embrace magic and use it to get this assignment done so we can go our separate ways."

If embracing magic would get rid of Jackson Slater once and for all, Sara would hug it with both arms. "I'll take that under advisement." He'd never understood her fear of her magic's backlash, and she wasn't about to get into it now. What would be the point? They'd finish the job and he'd be gone. Again.

They went back to her office, and she used the intercom to announce a staff meeting in her office immediately.

In less than ten minutes, the room was filled. As the workers gathered in tight groups, fear and suspicion surrounded the throng like noxious vapor.

Sara knew the moment Jack removed the memory and fear from their minds. Their body language changed instantly. Shoulders lowered. Creases of worry disappeared. Sara smoothly gave them mundane instructions for the rest of the week while the housekeeper and Alberto were away.

"Thanks," she told Jack after everyone had filed out. "Nobody should have to relive that hour."

"Want me to—"

"No." She didn't want him messing with her mind any more than his presence had already. "Now, about contacting the authorities. There are six different police forces here, but for our purposes I think we only need to talk to the Policía Técnica Judicial, the criminal police, and the Policía Metropolitana, the city cops."

"Do you have the coordinates?"

Sara picked up her tote and pulled off her sunglasses, then slung the strap of the bag over her shoulder. "Better. I have the addresses. We'll fly."

"Glad to hear you're coming to your senses."

"We're not teleporting, hotshot. We're taking the helicopter."

THE HEAT SLAMMED INTO them the moment they stepped outside. Jack materialized dark glasses and followed Sara around a gigantic, splashing five-tiered fountain in the center of a rustic courtyard filled with lush vegetation and enormous trees with vivid red flowers.

The rain had stopped. The scent of steaming jungle, verdant with an undertone of decay, saturated the muggy air. Jack matched his steps to Sara's and easily fell into her rhythm, getting a faint whiff of her citrus perfume as she moved.

Even in jeans and button-down shirt, she looked and walked like a woman wearing haute couture. She'd always loved clothes and, being tall and slender, wore anything well. Her stride was long and unhesitating, despite the combination of high heels and flagstones, as she headed toward the garage on the far side of the sprawling hacienda.

This was the take-charge side of Sara that had always surprised and delighted him, the more-than-competent woman who could take hours choosing between two fabrics and then handle a room full of businessmen as if they were friends.

The sunlight formed a circlet of light on the crown of her glossy, sun-streaked hair. The longer length suited her. He'd had a fondness for her nape, and the swirled-up hairstyle bared the pale, sensitive skin for anyone to see. He shot her a quick glance, hoping like hell Sara wasn't having that same thought right then. Clearly she wasn't, since they remained outside.

The concept of making a simultaneous thought a reality was intriguing. Annoying if it happened again, but fascinating because it had never occurred before today. On the other hand, it hadn't taken much to get them naked before now.

She used a remote to activate one of several double-size doors, revealing part of Baltzer's impressive fleet of luxury automobiles. *Garage* wasn't the word for the building they entered. The climate-controlled area held six vehicles and two top-of-the-line motorcycles and had what were probably servants' living quarters the size of a four-bedroom house above.

Jack had to admit, he had a pang of car envy. He usually teleported, but every now and then it was nice to drive a well-tooled machine just for the sheer joy of it. "Baltzer's doing well."

"He's a smart guy. This way." Sara walked between a late-model black Jeep and a bright red Audi convertible.

"I thought we were flying." Jack hadn't forgotten what a lousy driver she was, but he figured he'd strap himself into the passenger seat and teleport if an immovable obstacle loomed. Sara's claim to fame was that she'd never had an accident. He wasn't sure how many accidents her erratic driving might have caused over the years, however.

She shot him a look that told him she knew where that comment was going, and didn't appreciate it. "Relax, Jack. This is a shortcut. We have a small airfield and helipad out back."

She'd obtained her small planes and helicopter licenses before they'd met, but Jack had never flown with her. This was sure to prove interesting. On the plus side, there wasn't anything for her to bump into up there. Well, in theory, at least. It depended on whether the air-traffic controllers in San Cristóbal were taking siestas or not.

The helicopter looked damn small sitting out on the

helipad. "One of my favorite things about living in South America is that I get to fly almost every day," Sara told him, sounding more upbeat than she had for the last few hours. "This little beauty is a Bell 407. Smoothest ride in its class."

She opened the door and tossed in her bag. "I have to do a check. Climb in and buckle up. I won't be long." She gave the glossy red-and-white body of the chopper a fond pat.

While she circled the chopper, giving it a thorough check, Jack assessed the area behind the hacienda. There was another chopper nearby, and a small white plane with the Baltzer company red-and-black logo painted on the tail. A blacktop landing strip appeared to run directly into the solid green of the jungle and vanished there, along with so many other things.

Large snakes, for instance. Very, very large snakes. Crap, why the hell couldn't this situation be taking place in, say, the Arctic?

The estate's boundaries were marked by a twelve-foot-high stone wall. The place was a veritable fortress. High walls and the surrounding dense jungle ensured Baltzer's privacy. He suspected the guy had a top-of-the-line security system as well.

A damned odd and inconvenient place to live, no matter what Sara said about being close to the sites of the hotels they were building. And that was saying a lot, coming from a guy who spent the majority of his nights sleeping in a pup tent in some pretty inhospitable spots.

"All set." Sara climbed in, slamming her door shut. Jack did the same. The chopper was pretty spacious, with large expanses of Plexiglas for three-sixty views. It seated six or seven in comfort and had leather seats, stereo, AC. An absolute necessity, living way the hell and gone, so far from civilization.

"How far's this place from town?"

"By helicopter, half an hour. By car, three-ish hours."

Sara went through the engine checklist systematically, giving the task her undivided attention. He was impressed. She was completely professional and very thorough. Very Sara.

The engine started with a throaty roar and the chopper vibrated. "That's my girl," Sara crooned as the vibrations increased and the rotor started spinning. "Don't worry, Jack." She shot him a smile that made his chest hurt. "The computer does all the work."

His theory about teleporting still applied. "Good to know," he said affably, reaching for the headset she hadn't offered. He slipped it on as Sara informed the tower in San Cristóbal of their heading and ETA.

"We've got a few minutes to spare. Would you like an aerial view of the jungle before we head to San Cristóbal?"

"Maybe on the way back."

Sara took off, then turned left, flying low over the tree canopy. "As an Aequitas, did you know that you could be called in at any time?" she asked, her expressive eyes hidden by her sunglasses. "That you wouldn't be given a choice?"

"Yeah. It was certainly something I was instructed in. But it was purely theoretical. To be honest, I'm not sure the Wizard Council is accurate on this theory—but it's pretty hard to disprove that the hurricanes, tsunamis, et cetera, are the work of the Omnivatics. Although, the possibility that something other than nature produced all those disasters is fascinating."

"Fascinating? Now you want to do this crazy thing?" she asked incredulously, her voice crackling through his headset.

"Find an Omnivatic? Not particularly. But investigate the cause of all these seemingly natural disasters? Hell, yeah. I live for shit like this."

"I know you do. Did you ever track down the Australian ley you were researching . . . ?"

Before we broke up was the rest of *that* sentence. "Yeah. Matter of fact, I discovered its exact location this year. Even though it's an enormous power source and hundreds, even thousands, of miles long, it's unusually deep, and so far underground my equipment didn't pick up the incredible strength of it. I've still got a lot of work to do to finish my survey. I'll get back to it sooner than later, I hope."

"I'm glad for you, Jack. I know how passionate you are about documenting the leys. The Wizard Council should find you an *Aequitas* geologist to work with instead of an interior designer. Unlike you, I have no interest in either the existence of the Omnivatics or natural disasters. I have enough problems with my wallpaper suppliers."

Jack bit back a smile. "Funny."

"But true. Look down there, that's Inga and Ida in the Martin." On the snaking road below, a little red car followed the curves before being lost under the tree canopy again.

"What do we do for transportation when we get there?"

"We keep vehicles at a small private airport just outside of town. I'm really very annoyed with you for shooting Alberto, Jack," she said. Typical Sara. Out of left field, straight to the gut. "You're a powerful wizard—you should have been able to use one of your powers to subdue him."

"Want me to rewind that scenario for you? My powers didn't work worth shit. Neither did yours. I did what I had to do."

She was quiet for a minute; then her sigh came through the headset, rasping against the hardened edges he'd fortified around his heart. "I know. Damn it, I know. I hate, hate, hate that it happened. And I hate even more that a man I know and love was capable of doing what Alberto did today. It was as though he was . . . possessed."

"Maybe he was." Jack wanted to reach out and touch her, but resisted. The last time he'd done that, they'd ended up naked in a shower. Right then he liked her hands on the cyclic and the collective and her feet on the pedals. She had the sexiest feet of any woman he'd ever known, soft and pretty and very sensitive. He dragged his eyes away from her toes with their screaming red polish and little diamond pinkie ring. "Look, we have an opportunity here to gather some facts and present them to the Council. Maybe we can make a difference."

She made a rude noise. "Like saving the world? Come on, Jack, you didn't believe all the theatrical BS, did you?"

"Let's just say I don't disbelieve it. They have compelling data—even you can't deny that."

"Maybe it was the way it was presented. The setting was pretty impressive, certainly intimidating. All of them in black cowled robes, the Head of Council playing with fire, the call to arms . . ." She waved a hand.

"Make no mistake—they're the real deal. And don't forget it. Just because you attended a regular boarding school instead of wizard school doesn't mean that magic, and all that goes with it—the good, the bad, and the terrifying—isn't true."

She glanced at him, her eyes concealed by her sunglasses. "But a group of souped-up wizards out to take over the world?"

"Fifty Aequitas dead? The entire *Archon* dead? Yeah, I believe it." Jack glanced down at the trees below without really seeing all the green. "Omnivatics and Aequitas are both very real. Just because Omnivatics have been quiet for centuries doesn't mean they don't exist. The Omnivatics saw—hell, *see*—humans as a natural resource, to use and discard. The Aequitas believe in human rights.

"The Omnivatics always wanted to rule. Historically, it's been thought that their deadline, for want of a better team, is in 2012—the end of the world according to the Mayan calendar."

"I'm trying to remember what my dad told me about Omnivatics and Aequitas in one of our rare bedtime stories on the subject. Wasn't the deal that the Aequitas slowed down time until they could figure out how to stop them?"

"That was part of the myth, yeah." He tried to stop thinking about her feet, but then he fixated on her lip-stick-glossy mouth, with the full lower lip and the little dip in the upper—"A few minutes a day to literally buy time. But, yeah, our job in the beginning was to slow things down until the Omnivatics can be stopped."

She tapped her finger on the controls as she listened. She always had been a good listener—but stubborn, extremely damn stubborn.

"I'm not sure how Ophidian's comet plays into it, though," Jack continued. "A precursor to the end of the world? A necessary component? I don't know, and obviously neither does the Council. But somehow the Omnivahcs found their way inside the Archon and killed everyone. . . ." Jack didn't share how that thought scared the crap out of him. He liked to be the one in the know. Failing that, *someone* should have a fucking clue.

"Now, that is damn scary, Jack."

"Yeah." With any luck, all this had nothing to do with Ophidian's comet, and he could get back to the leyline in Australia. If he could stop looking at Sara's mouth and concentrate on the job at hand, not bring up anything inflammatory, and not think about sex at precisely the same second Sara did. He didn't think he could handle not having sex with her if he found himself naked with her in the shower again.

It didn't mean he was still in love with her. Shower sex could be as simple as scratching an itch. Right. Only if you planned to scratch an itch with a backhoe.

"We need to find out everything we can about the

Omnivatics. How can we do that?" She glanced at him, the jungle blurring beneath them. Except for the mountain range nearby, it was hard to get a bearing. The damn jungle looked all the same to him.

"I have access to ancient texts."

"Good. We need to study what we can. The more informed we are, the better chance we have of actually pulling this off."

"I agree. I'll teleport the stuff here once we get back to the hacienda. We can do some homework." It was an excellent idea. Sara was smart and organized. Where he preferred going by the seat of his pants, she was inclined to be meticulous. There was a place for both in this clusterfuck.

For the next ten minutes he let static and the occasional voice from the tower fill the silence, and tried not to imagine what was slithering among those trees below. As a ten-year-old, he'd had a run-in with a disgusting ball of mating snakes while on an "adventure" in Africa with his father, an avid hunter. Tumbling into a ravine and being swarmed with writhing bodies had been terrifying. Not to mention painful.

It would have been curtains for him if his father hadn't acted quickly and teleported him to a hospital for treatment. He still had vivid nightmares about that day.

After he recovered, he almost ended up back in the damn hospital. His father had beaten the shit out of him for being a pussy and stupid enough to fall among the snakes in the first place.

That experience, coupled with everything he'd learned

about the Omnivatics over the years, had given Jack a healthy resolve to keep the hell away from snakes of any kind. As the jungle below receded, giving way to asphalt, concrete, and steel, Jack—the man who liked country better than city any day of the week—breathed easier.

"THAT'S THE AIRPORT DOWN there. Grant's Cessna is the one next to the building." We have a pilot on call, but Grant likes to fly as much as I do," Sara told Jack absently. In fact, Grant himself had taught her to fly a single-engine plane. "He comes into town and spends the night at least once a week. Oh, hell—I hope he doesn't bump into the twins. I think he's got another girl-friend in town, and he won't be happy if he sees them when he thinks he's being discreet."

"Three girlfriends? The guy must eat Viagra like M&M's," Jack said dryly.

"Oh, I think he's got more than three girlfriends. We have a don't-ask policy, and believe me, I'm fine with that."

"Why? You don't want him nosing around after your lovers?"

"Exactly," Sara told him breezily. She hadn't had a lover since Jack. She was still working up to dating, let alone having another man touch her. She'd get there. Eventually. None of which was Jack's business.

"Who should we say we are when we go to the police?" She brought the helicopter down lightly beside Grant's plane, powered off, and removed her headset, lightly running her fingers over her hair. "The authorities aren't going to just give two people off the street information when we ask if anyone in their jurisdiction has gone insane in the last few months."

Jack put his headset with hers. "We're cops with the San Francisco PD. Here's your ID and badge." He materialized two small leather cases in his open palm, then handed one to Sara and slipped his own into his shirt pocket.

Sara opened the leather case. The ID card with her photo and the police badge looked like the real deal. She glanced up at him and couldn't help the grin she felt tugging at her mouth. "Wow. Ever thought of a life of crime?"

"Sure. It's the life behind bars part that deters me." He looked serious, except for the twinkle in his eyes.

She didn't want to be charmed by him. Thank God she was immune.

Broiling heat enveloped Sara the second she opened the chopper door and stepped onto the tarmac. By unspoken agreement, she and Jack picked up their pace and hurried to get into the marginally cooler shade of the Quonset hut.

"Unfortunately, this garage isn't climate-controlled. Brace yourself." She unlocked the side door, and Jack followed her into the dark, stifling heat of the enclosed space. Three late-model black Land Rovers were parked side by side with Grant's yellow Hummer. Sara frowned. "Grant must've gotten a ride with William."

She caught herself before she made some comment to Jack about Grant's increasingly odd behavior of late. It wasn't a big deal, she told herself. Financing pressure could account for frequent absences, but it didn't explain some of the other slightly off behaviors she'd started noticing in the past several months.

What was he hiding? She hoped to hell it wasn't a serious problem with any of the hotels—investors dropping out, strikes, union problems. Hell, in this part of the world, gang payoffs were a huge financial burden for business owners. Whatever it was, she hoped he trusted her enough to share the problem with her. She might not be able to fix whatever it was, but she had a right to know.

"What's the matter?" Jack asked.

Maybe Grant had a new and demanding girlfriend, and Sara was overreacting. She shook her head. "Not a thing."

She got into her Land Rover and opened the overhead door of the garage while cranking up the AC in the car. "Let's do a circle," she suggested, mentally mapping out a route that would take them to the police stations and hospitals with the least amount of doubling back. "The first precinct is on Compo de Carabo, which is only five minutes away." She left her door open as the air kicked in, and took out a lime-green hankie with palm trees printed on it to blot her forehead. Jack didn't seem the least bit affected by the heat. On the other hand, he'd started off the trip dusty and disheveled. Freshly showered and smelling altogether too good, but still in need of a Laundromat.

He adjusted his seat to give himself more legroom. "How many are there?"

"Four, and two hospitals." Sara slammed her door shut, and Jack followed suit. It was like being enveloped in damp cotton batting. "I think we can hit them all before it gets dark. I'm not crazy about flying at night." At one point in their past, he would have teased her about "hitting" them all. Now he didn't even crack a smile.

"The crime rate is astronomical here," he pointed out, fiddling with the air vent on his side. "I read that it's bad enough during daylight hours, but nobody in their right mind drives around here at night."

Jack was right. The crime rate—homicides, armed robbery, and kidnapping in and around the city—was legend, and the police presence made absolutely no difference. Sara rarely came into town on her own, and was quite prepared to use magic if she was in any danger. She preferred living as normal a life as possible, but when magic served her, she used it. Jack was right about that, but she was damned if she'd tell him.

"All of our company vehicles are bulletproof."

"That's great—until you have to get out of the car," he said dryly. "I'm surprised good old Grant doesn't supply you with a platoon of bodyguards, or at least a Kevlar suit."

She smiled. "He offered, and I do use guards if I have to come to any of the job sites alone. But I figured I'd be safe with you. In the car," she added. Because, of course, she knew she wasn't safe with Jack. Not even close.

"This shouldn't take long if we ask the right questions. How many hotels are you building?" He slouched back as she pulled out of the garage and crossed the private landing strip to head to the entrance to the *autopista*.

"Five to start, a total of seven by the time we're done. We're beginning with Cali, Guayaquil, Ica, and Punta

Arenas, as well as here. William procured amazing properties, and we're building luxury spa resorts, some with penthouse condos. We're already in phase four here in San Cristóbal—design and construction."

She ignored the way Jack rode the imaginary brake on his side as she drove defensively through the crowded streets. It was every man, woman, and flock of sheep for themselves. A year of driving here had given Sara a healthy appreciation of she-who-hesitates-gets-run-into.

"Must keep you busy."

"It does, but I love it." She adroitly avoided a collision with an aimlessly wandering cow crossing three lanes of cars. "Pia's terrific, and I have a great staff here. Even though this project is considerably bigger than the eight hundred rooms we built in Turkey, it's way more laid-back."

Talking about the project in Turkey brought back a rush of memories. She and Jack had met when she'd taken a rare vacation after the completion of that job almost three years ago.

They'd both been visiting friends in Lake Tahoe. She'd enjoyed the party given by his friends; he'd been bored out of his mind. She should have known right then that what they thought was instant love was nothing more than infatuation compounded by incredible sex.

Maybe the fact that they were so different had been part of the attraction, like polar ends of a magnet. Total attraction—but incompatible in every other way. Jack was solitary to her gregarious. She was Ms. Fullcharge; Jack was laid-back. She was walks in the rain; he was naps when it rained. Naps had usually turned to making drowsy love under their down comforter, the first household item they'd bought together when she'd moved into his house in Tahoe.

Sara wondered if Jack still had the house, or if he'd sold it.

"You like it here." He dragged his gaze away from the street—clearly believing he had to keep ever-vigilant—to shoot her a quick glance.

It wasn't a question, but she answered anyway, because she didn't want to remember making love while rain beat a tattoo on the roof that matched the syncopated beating of their hearts.

"I like the people here, and I love my work. I log a lot of flight time, which is a great bonus." In this sweltering heat, she could smell remnants of starch in his shirt. Who'd bothered to put starch on his work shirt? Was he seeing someone? The pain accompanying the thought shocked her. She was over him.

No, she wasn't, Sara thought with brutal honesty. And that was the problem with seeing him again. She'd loved Jackson Slater more than she thought she was capable of loving anyone. Half of her loved him still, and the other half remembered all the reasons why she hated him.

It was a razor-thin line, and she'd barely learned how to live life balanced on it. His unexpected reentrance into her life was throwing her off-kilter. "What about you, Jack?" she asked, keeping her tone casual. "After Australia, will you still be searching for the ever-elusive leys?" The search for the mysterious energy lines linking vortices of the earth had always been Jack's personal quest.

"Not—" He jerked upright. "Watch that kid on a bike on your left—shit! Christ, Sara. What's the penalty if you hit someone?"

"Not a whole hell of a lot," she told him cheerfully as the kid flipped her the finger and pedaled to safety. "You were saying?"

He shook his head. "That just took ten years off my life."

"Elusive leylines?"

"They're not elusive if you know what to look for. And I do. The power emanating from the one in Western Australia is off the charts when you go deep enough."

Jack was passionate about everything he was interested in. It was one of the things she'd loved about him. "Do you think that's what was responsible for you knowing I was in danger?"

"I suspect Edge was right and Baltzer's place is also on a ley—I'm going to look into it. And yeah, I think both of us being on powerful leylines at the same moment contributed to the unusually strong connection. What else could it be?"

"I don't know, but I prefer communicating via my cell phone." Although Sara doubted Jack would've picked up if he'd known she was the one calling. Oh, Lord. She wished he'd never come here. Looking at him made her stomach churn and her chest ache. She tightened her fingers around the leather-covered steering wheel because the urge to push his too-long hair off his face was driving her crazy. Old habits died hard.

"That's the police station across the street." She slowed to let several cars pass.

"You're not going to do a U-turn right here, are y—hmm. Okay."

She had to back up a couple of times to complete the turn, to the accompaniment of a few honking passersby, but she finally parked. The police precinct was housed in a crumbling old building that desperately needed a stonemason.

"You don't look like a cop," she pointed out as she pulled in at an angle under the shade of a giant African tulip tree. The dark leaves and vivid orangey-red blooms of the *Spathodea campanulata* were striking against the almost painfully bright blue sky. Sara loved the shockingly bright color of the flowers, and had had several of the graceful trees planted around the hacienda. Another reason she enjoyed living here—the wild profusion of brilliant flowers growing everywhere.

Jack magically switched the dusty pants and shirt for a clean white cotton shirt and jeans, and swapped out his hiking boots for his favorite cowboy boots. "Better?"

Her belly clenched. "Clean, anyway." She opened her door and got out. "We could split up, cover more ground."

"We stay together. Get your badge out."

∼ Seven ∼

Inside, the station smelled of urine and industrial cleaner, heavy on the ammonia, a combination that made Sara's eyes water. But the old, intricate blue-and-green mosaic tile on the floor was worth a second glance.

Jack rested his hand possessively on the small of her back. Electricity shot up through Sara's bones and lodged in her chest. Unaffected, he kept her walking forward. "You're not measuring the place for carpeting. You're a cop, remember?"

He dropped his hand as they reached the front desk. The guy behind the desk wasn't in the least bit reticent about telling the *norteamericano policía* about the last few weeks' worth of prisoner intakes. There'd been no reports of anyone losing his or her mind or behaving out of the ordinary. He suggested checking the hospitals.

Jack gave him his card and asked him to call if anyone meeting that description showed up. The man nodded vaguely and went back to his dog-eared girlie magazine, muttering under his breath that all Americans were *loco*.

The next two police stations had pretty much the

same smell, the same uninterested, overweight cop at the front desk, and the same answer. The trips to the hospitals were just as unproductive, and the smell wasn't much better. Sara hated hospitals and was glad to get out as quickly as possible.

Hot and thirsty, they stopped at a sidewalk café where she ordered a *papelón con limón*, a refreshing drink made from sugarcane juice and lemon, while Jack had one of the local beers.

There had been a small outdoor café near their house in Tahoe where they used to sit, holding hands, sipping coffee and talking about everything under the sun. Now they sat on opposite sides of the table. No hand-holding. No talking. In the last meaningful conversation they'd had, things were said that had forever driven a wedge between them. Nothing was going to change that.

Sara focused instead on her tart, icy drink and people-watched. Office workers were starting their commutes home, and the local bars and outdoor cafés were filling up. A young couple, clearly very much in love, sat at a nearby table with a tiny baby in a stroller tucked between their chairs.

Sara's heart slammed into her rib cage. The young mother lifted the infant out of the stroller and held her in her arms as she and the young man cooed to the baby.

Sara's chest hurt, and she couldn't drag in a breath. Seeing babies was always traumatic for her. Seeing an infant while she was with Jack was the equivalent of a body slam to her heart. She struggled to drag in a sip of air.

"We'll hit that last police station before heading home," Jack said, clearly unaffected by the happy tableau just feet away. He hadn't even noticed the baby. She was *all* Sara could see.

The late-afternoon sun beat down on the bright yellow umbrella over the table, but she didn't feel the warmth. Traffic passed within a few feet of them, but she didn't hear it. Pushing away from the small metal table on legs that barely held her, she snatched her purse off the chair next to her.

"Be right back." All she could think about was putting one foot in front of the other as she went through the open French doors and made her way between the mostly empty tables inside the café. Taking her sunglasses off with fingers that shook, she searched frantically for the sign to the restroom. The pain in her chest made breathing almost impossible.

"*Dónde está el baño, por favor?*" she demanded urgently of the bartender lazily wiping the counter.

Once inside the empty women's restroom, Sara braced her palms on the chipped tiles around the sink and struggled to choke back the dry sobs ripping up her throat. There were no tears. There never were tears. The grief was so vast, so intense that weeping was impossible. Sinking to her haunches, she squeezed her eyes closed and bowed her head. Pressing her folded arms against her waist, she rocked soundlessly as emotions twisted and clawed through her.

Through the blood pounding in her ears, she heard the echo of Jack's last words to her: "You selfish, coldhearted *bitch*. You didn't want him and you didn't give me the opportunity to have him. You killed our baby. I'll never fucking forgive you for this, Sara. Never." Through dazed eyes she'd caught a glimpse of the anguish on his face. Then he'd walked away without a backward glance.

She pressed her fists between her breasts. Would this pain never go away? She'd lost the baby and she'd lost Jack the same day. Nothing she'd said had convinced him that she hadn't had an abortion. He'd claimed he had proof. So she was not only a monster for killing her own child—she was a bald-faced liar as well.

Sara had been stunned, hurt to the depths of her soul that he would entertain for even a second the idea that she could— *would*—do such a thing. She'd only been pregnant for seven weeks. Then—not. Loved. Then—not.

She squeezed her eyes shut, remembering the arc of their relationship. They'd lived together—that had apparently been enough for Jack. They'd rarely argued at the start. But months before she discovered she was pregnant, they'd started bickering. Mostly about her long hours working for Grant. Her friendship with Grant. Grant, in any form, had pissed Jack off in small and large ways. They'd fought and made up, but soon they'd stayed mad longer, and the fights had become more and more hurtful.

She'd desperately wanted to fix it. She'd talked to Grant, who had—as usual—supported her. He'd even given her the number of a couples counselor he'd dated, so that she and Jack could try to work things out. But then, in quick succession, she'd realized she was pregnant and then lost the baby. She'd entered a waking nightmare. How could she ever, ever forget Jack's chilling accusation that she'd aborted their child? And how could she ever, ever forgive him for believing for even a *nanosecond* that she was capable of doing so?

Months after their breakup, when she'd recovered somewhat from the miscarriage and the horrific scene with Jack, she'd wanted to confront him about it, but Grant had talked her out of it. If Jack genuinely loved her, he would have known it was a miscarriage, Grant pointed out. Wouldn't a man in love trust that the woman he loved wouldn't intentionally do such a thing?

Grant had been right. He was an excellent judge of character, and he'd hinted gently for months beforehand that Jack wasn't the kind of man who'd settle down. It was all coming back to her now, whether she wanted it to or not, just like Jack.

"Don't g-go there," she warned herself brokenly. She wished she could cry. It might lessen the impossibly heavy weight she carried in her heart. Maybe one day she'd be able to. But even now, two years later, the pain of Jack's accusations made the relief of crying impossible. The grief was a hard pain lodged in her chest where her heart used to be.

When she was capable of breathing again, Sara pulled herself to her feet and looked in the mirror over the sink. It always shocked her to see how normal she looked when inside were only the broken remains of who she used to be. She ran some cold water onto a towel and held it to her dry, burning eyes for a few moments, then looked again.

Taking out her makeup bag, she quickly repaired her face, adding a little extra blush and a slick of glossy, fuck-you red lipstick to her mouth. A couple strokes with her comb and her hair was subdued, if only temporarily. If you didn't look closely enough to see the stark pain in her eyes, she was just fine. Just fine.

Stabbing on her sunglasses, she stood up straight, squared her shoulders as if she were heading into battle, and strode back outside.

"Parate o detente," THE police officer called as they turned to leave the last station.

"¿Sí?" Sara walked back to his desk. He spoke to her rapidly in Spanish, gesturing freely, but his attention kept flickering to Jack, directly behind her. She suspected that the officer didn't want her to understand what he was saying—sometimes these Latin men didn't take a woman seriously. She didn't have time to argue her case.

She hated to ask Jack for anything, but the local dialect frequently tripped her up, and Jack had always been terrific at languages. "Something about a girl. . . . Would you?"

"Sure."

It took a few minutes before Jack shook the guy's hand and ushered Sara out of the building into the afternoon heat. She looked up at him as they walked. "I got the part about a girl and not much else."

"Couple of local girls have disappeared in the last month. They suspect foul play."

"Nothing to do with what we're investigating, then."

"Nope. Here, give me the keys. I'll drive again."

Wordlessly Sara handed over the keys. It wasn't just Latin men who were overbearing in their maleness. Since she had the keys to the helicopter, she let him have the ones to the car.

"You're a better pilot than a driver."

"Gee, Jack. Thanks for the backhanded compliment." Her soft lips twitched, because the driving thing had always been a running gag with them. God, he missed the ease they used to have.

Jack missed a shitload of things, but he missed the friendship they'd shared almost as much as he missed the incredible sex.

He'd been raised by his father after his mother died. Jackson Slater Sr. had been a hard-ass, humorless asshole. Emotion was not tolerated. He didn't want to hear Jack's problems, large or small. They were Aequitas. Higher in stature than mere wizards. Superior in every way. The warriors of wizards.

As far back as he could remember, his father had expected his son to study and perfect magic as diligently as he did his other subjects, and brooked nothing less than straight As. There'd been no such thing as a pat on the back for a job well done. No such thing as fear. Jack had learned to suck it up. Hell, he'd learned to shut it out. To keep to himself, his nose down.

And then he'd met this woman who laughed and showed her joy without restraint. Sara had practically been an alien life form. And slowly, so slowly he barely noticed, he opened up. Shared himself with this amazing woman, until she held his life in her two small hands.

He should've fucking listened when she'd told him she wasn't ready to start a family. Should have heard.

Without discussion, she'd aborted their child and walked away.

"If you look down on your side, you'll see a village I think we should visit tomorrow," Sara said through the headset, oblivious to his train of thought.

If she could behave as if they'd never had anything between them, then so could he. "There are several small native villages within a fifty-mile radius of the compound. I think they all have wizards living in or near them. We should check to see if they've had any unusual events."

"Good idea." The last rays of the sun shone golden over the dense treetops below as they neared the hacienda. The house and outbuildings seemed to glow amber, the windows flashing like beacons. "And you'll be happy to know we'll have to teleport to most of them, becau— tighten your seat belt, Jack." Sara's voice was completely calm, but her hand was white-knuckled as she pulled up on the collective lever.

Wind buffeted the helicopter as they flew directly into the misty white of a cloud. They went from clear, sunset skies to zero visibility between one breath and the next.

"This normal?"

"Not even close."

He didn't miss the faint thread of fear in her voice. "We in trouble?"

"Nothing I can't handle."

"What do you need?" Jack said into his mike.

"What does the wind gauge read?"

"Head wind. Fifty knots, gusting at almost sixty," he read off the indicators on the dash. "Five hundred feet. Visibility—obvious." He glanced at the gyrostabilizer. The little plane there danced about sickeningly. Gale-force winds buffeted the small chopper, tossing it about like a leaf in a high wind while enormous drops of rain hit the Plexi with the force and percussion of hail.

As Sara fought for control, Jack took a nanosecond debating teleporting them both to safety.

"Don't! I mean it, Jack. I can do this. If you want to teleport—go for it. I'm not leaving my three-million-dollar baby without a—hang on!" The chopper bounced violently, then threw them sideways. "Fight!"

The rock and roll of the chopper had nothing to do with Sara's ability to handle her craft. She was fighting it for all she was worth. Jack magically tightened their shoulder and lap harnesses, and braced himself as the torque of both engines dropped simultaneously to near zero. They started spiraling toward the tree canopy—fast.

It was fucking poetic justice that she would literally kill him after all.

"Can you do an instrument landing?"

Sara's muscles flexed as she struggled to bring the nose of the chopper up, fighting the downward pull of the spiral.

"Only if I see something to land *on*. And finding that right about now would make me very, very happy. Damn this fog. Open your window a crack," Sara instructed, "and tell me if you can see anything." By pure willpower, it seemed, she pulled the chopper almost level. "Why aren't you dissipating this mess, Jack?"

"Because it's not fog. Try burning it off." Sara's power to call, when she chose to do so, was fire.

"I tried that a second ago. If it isn't a cloud, then what is it?"

Not fog. Not liquid in any form. Just . . . white. "I have no fucking idea," Jack said grimly.

After a moment's hesitation, Sara said tightly, "Find me somewhere flat. Now."

He heard the hint of desperation in her voice. "I can't see any better than you can," he answered over his own rising concern.

He considered the options. Teleport them the hell out of the helicopter and leave it to crash? That would give Sara—what? —seconds before she fell to the jungle several hundred feet below. Did he have time to check out where they were and get back to her? Or did he stay where he was, waiting for the split second when she realized they had to teleport or die?

The woman always was stubborn.

Wind howled through the cabin the moment the window slid down. He thrust a hand out the window: nothing but the updraft. Cloud, a light rain, fog would be wet. But the air felt warm and completely dry. Yet only moments before it had rained.

He wouldn't teleport until the last second, if that's what she wanted, but he reserved the right not to have to kiss either of their asses good-bye. In the meantime, Jack cast a protective shield around her, his eyes on the dials. "Four hundred feet."

Sara increased the collective again, but the chopper convinced its rapid descent.

"Three-fifty. Twenty. Three hundred . . ." Heart in his throat, Jack saw the red transmission oil light blink on. "Engine/rotor rpm below one hundred." Time to take charge of this clusterfuck and teleport—

"What's that?" He leaned forward, eyes narrowed as a red blur shimmered just beyond the veil of white. "Sara! Two o'clock. Aren't those the red trees beside the house?"

"Yes!" Her voice was filled with relief as she battled for control, turning the chopper's nose toward the compound. She increased the collective, fighting to maintain a normal approach profile, her arms shaking with the strain of keeping the craft airborne.

He reached over and lightly touched the back of her neck. "You can do this."

Jack braced for the inevitable crash landing and the split-second timing he'd need to avert a tragedy.

The sprawling hacienda emerged from the mist and trees, bathed in the amber glow of the sunset and approaching much too fast. The thick, blinding whiteness vanished as if it had never been.

"Hang on. We're in for a bumpy ride. And do not freaking teleport me, Jackson."

He made no promises.

〰️

GRANT YANKED HER DOOR open, his fair hair blowing in the vortex of the still-moving blades overhead. "Sara, Jesus, sweetheart, are you all right?" He was shouting to be heard over the noise, but Sara had to lip-read since she still had on her headset. Taking it off, she unclipped her belt, then sucked in a shaky breath.

William, Pia, and half the household staff clustered behind Grant on the edge of the helipad. They'd all witnessed the hard landing.

By some miracle, nothing was broken, not herself, Jack, or the Bell. But it had been damn close. Sara's heart was still galloping, and her entire body felt clammy as Grant reached up and lifted her out before she realized what he intended. He set her down on wobbly legs, an arm around her shoulders.

"My God, that was the most amazing piece of flying I've ever witnessed." Still in a crouch to dodge the buffeting of the spinning blades, he led her out of the way, then grabbed her in a bear hug. After a few seconds, he held her at arm's length, his pale blue eyes filled with worry. "Are you hurt, baby? Any bumps and bruises?"

"No. I'm fine." Other than her knees feeling like rubber, and her stomach still anticipating trashing three million dollars' worth of beautiful machinery. Even though Sara had known she and Jack wouldn't die—they'd have teleported before a crash landing—adrenaline still coursed through her body at the speed of terror. "The chopper's fine, too."

"I don't give a shit about the damned helicopter! I'm

going to have José's ass. He signed off on the maintenance two days ago. What happened?"

"Engine cut out. I do—"

"How about if she goes inside and takes a breath before she gets the third degree?" Jack suggested, coming up behind her. He slid his arm around her waist, and Sara somehow found herself in Jack's arms instead of Grant's.

Grant slung his arm around her shoulders and gave a little tug. She was the filling in a testosterone cookie. Deftly, Sara stepped out from between the two men. She was no dog bone.

Grant held on a second longer than Jack did. She threw him a warning look. She loved him for being protective, but she didn't need help with Jack.

"Slater." Grant's smile revealed his dimples as his attention transferred to Jack. "Good to see you. Pia told me you were visiting. You okay, pal? You must be almost as shook up as my girl here."

"She's an astonishing pilot," Jack told him. "I wouldn't have trusted anyone else to get us down in one piece."

Sara tried not to get warm and fuzzy about Jack's apparent sincerity—probably just adrenaline mixed with appreciation for getting him on the ground without mishap. Still, his admiration went a long way to stilling her thundering heartbeat. She didn't care whether the two men were genuinely prepared to tolerate each other, or whether this was all for show. As long as no blood was shed while Jack lived under Grant's roof, she was happy.

It was quite interesting to see the two men side by side. Other than a similarity in height, they had absolutely nothing in common. Grant was almost shockingly good-looking, the poster child for male beauty: clear blue eyes, lightly tanned skin, dimples, and thick, lightly curling natural blond hair. He was gorgeous.

Jack, on the other hand, looked like a movie villain, with his dark hair and brows, tanned skin, and deep blue eyes. There was nothing pretty or soft about Jack.

Pia came up and gave her a tight hug. "*Madre de Dios,* woman. That was some landing. Let's go inside and I'll pour you a giant glass of wine and you can tell mamma all about him."

"Her," Sara said absently, observing the power play as Grant shook Jack's hand with his right, using his left to hold Jack's forearm.

"Not the helicopter, *mujer tonta,* Jackson of the smoldering eyes and rock-hard abs."

Sara's lips twitched. "You can't see his abs."

"Trust me, *amiga,* when a guy looks like that, he has abs of steel, and a *pene* to match."

"Holy crap, Pia," Sara half-groaned, half-laughed. "He's standing right there."

"So we go inside and you tell me all about your trip into town with the bad boy, *sí*?"

"*Negativa,* but nice try. There's nothing to tell."

"Have you seen the way that man looks at you? *Caliente. Muy muy caliente. Ese hombre es muy sexy.*"

"He just saw his life flash before his eyes. That's fear you see."

Pia hooked her arm through Sara's and they started walking toward the house, leaving the men to follow. "I know *hombres*," Pia said with a knowing grin. "And that man isn't afraid of anything."

"Hurt her again, and I'll wipe the floor with your ass. Then I'll kill you," Grant Baltzer said so quietly that only Jack heard him.

Taken aback by the vehemence of Baltzer's tone, Jack gritted his teeth instead of replying with a punch to Grant's perfect nose. Despite his expensive, well-cut summer-weight linen suit, Baltzer looked more like an easygoing surfer dude or a model than a tough, insanely successful business tycoon used to being in charge. Sara would never forgive him for knocking the shit out of her pal.

He stuffed his hands in his pockets. There was something about the man he didn't like. He still felt that same weird hair-standing-up-on-the back-of-his-neck thing that he'd experienced on the few occasions when he and Sara had met up with Baltzer in the past. It seemed obvious to Jack that Baltzer had a more than avuncular interest in Sara.

Too bad Baltzer wasn't a wizard. Jack's old-fashioned code of honor required a fight to be on a level playing field. Baltzer was human, and therefore doubly off limits.

"I'm not going to hurt her," Jack assured the other man coldly. "Sara's tougher than you think." Despite her chic prettiness and soft voice, the woman had granite where her heart should be and balls of tungsten steel.

"No." There was no dimple action when Baltzer gave

Jack an ice-blue glare. There was a lot going on behind the guy's eyes. Taking Jack's measure. Sizing up the enemy. Drawing a line in the sand.

That was cool with Jack. He was doing the same thing. Not that he considered the older man competition, but there was such a thing as being overprotective. Sara didn't need protection. Not from him anyway.

"Sara's not as tough as *you* like to think, Slater. And make no mistake, I'll do whatever I must to protect her." Baltzer strode after the rest of the group across the tarmac back toward the house.

Jack fell into step. Jesus, this was going to be a hellishly long week. If he hadn't figured out what was causing the deaths of local wizards within a week, he'd hand the whole thing back to the Council, and go on a little geological expedition of his own. With any luck, Edge and the Council would find replacements for himself and Sara, and he could go on to do something for which he was qualified.

Like investigating the clustering of natural disasters.

"I'll pretend to welcome you into my home because apparently that's what Sara wants right now." Baltzer stopped outside an arched back door and turned to look at him. Jack looked back squarely, not batting an eyelash as Baltzer stepped into his personal space. "But do anything to so much as make her look like she's going to cry, and so help me God, they won't find your body out there"—he indicated the jungle—"until the next fucking ice age, *comprende?*" Without waiting for a reply, he opened the door, and they entered the house.

Jack remembered Sara's assistant, Pia, from when he and Sara had lived together. A stunning pocket Venus, the petite brunette had creamy olive skin and black eyes that danced with amusement. Jack wondered now if she knew the truth about why he and Sara had split. He and Pia had always gotten along just fine; still, he was on Sara's turf. He figured he'd keep his back to the wall and the Ka-Bar under his pillow for the duration.

"Sara requested that you be in her wing," Pia told him in her lightly accented voice. She'd been born in Mexico City and raised in El Paso, and had been Sara's right hand for half a dozen years. "I figured right next door would meet all the requirements of propriety. Here you go." She pushed open a door and ushered him inside a spacious Spanish-style bedroom. "There's a connecting door. With a lock on both sides."

Not "Sara wanted you close by," but rather, "Sara requested." Since Pia hadn't given him a cot in the garage, he figured she wasn't an enemy. "Thanks, Pia."

"*No hay de que.*" She paused at the open door. "Don't hurt her again, Jackson. She wants you here. And I always liked you. Don't prove me wrong."

"I've already been warned. Unnecessarily. Sara has nothing to fear from me."

She smiled. "Drinks in the pub at eight. Dinner's at nine-thirty."

With a flick of his fingers, Jack locked the door behind her. Not that he expected anyone to stroll in unannounced, but he'd rather be safe than sorry. Obviously, he had no luggage; he'd take care of that wrinkle in a bit. No luggage, but Jack felt the weight of the psionic safe as it hovered nearby, invisible. Waiting for him.

Wanting Sara was a physical ache that wasn't going to go away anytime soon. The more he was with her, the more Jack wanted her. The smell of her skin, the sound of her voice—hell, everything that made up of the hills and valleys of Sara called to him on a basic level he was helpless to resist.

"Maybe the Book has the answers to *that* age-old question as well," he said softly, bringing the safe down. It materialized as it drifted gently to hover inches off the colorful spread at the foot of the bed. The twenty-three-inch-square ice safe pushed with a faint green light from within.

Cold had been the Slaters' power to call for seven generations. Jack was the last of his line. Thanks to Sara, there would be no sons or daughters to pass this amazing secret to before he was gone. No one other than himself knew of the existence of the psionic safe. And if they had, they wouldn't be capable of summoning or opening it. He brushed his fingers lightly over the slightly convex top, felt the burn of the frigid surface as he whispered the spell he'd learned from his father, an inheritance passed from father to son for generations.

The last time he'd seen it had also been to ask a question about Sara. His chest ached and he savagely shoved that thought aside as the hingeless door open, emitting a plume of acid-green smoke that spread and hovered protectively over the safe.

Jack reached inside the glacial interior with both hands and carefully withdrew the thick leather-covered journal. Warm to the touch, the Book seemed to give a hum of pleasure as he stroked his thumb across the scar on the edge. He hadn't been prepared for the weight of it when he'd first taken it out on his sixteenth birthday; that frigging fireplace poker his father had used had not only marred the ancient Book but had broken Jack's thumb.

The size of a hardbound novel, the arcane Aequitas *Book of Answers* weighed about fifty pounds. He'd last held the Book two years ago. And the question he'd asked was: "Why did she do it?" The answer: SEARCH YOUR HEART. Which was a stupid fucking answer, all things considered.

He hadn't seen the book since.

Until tonight.

It looked and felt exactly the same.

It had better give him a better answer than last time.

The Book was warm to the touch. Magic and power flowed from it and through Jack's very veins and arteries, through his organs and his brain. The sensation was intoxicating.

The gilt-edged papyrus pages were a little warped, the gold-leaf text on the tooled, dark brown leather cover almost impossible to read. He could barely make out the word *Aequitas* and the letters *n, w, r* and *s*.

Cradling the heavy tome in both hands, he carried it to a chair beside the window and sat down. The sun had set, but the sky was still light enough to read by. A feeling of calm came over him as he rested the book on his lap, waiting for it to open to the page he needed to read.

The heavy cover dropped open. Instantly, the thin pages rapidly flipped in a blur of gold edging and black text, emitting the musty herbal smell of ancient papyns and thousands of years of Aequitas secrets.

Jack's heart pounded. After several moments, the movement stopped. Anticipation welled, instantly followed by disappointment. Both creased yellowed pages were blank. "Well, hell."

The text had obviously faded over time. Perhaps there was a way to refresh it digitally. He'd have to find out right away, he thought—then realized that, with all the members of the Archon dead, he had no one to ask. "Shit."

He attempted to close the cover. It resisted, heavier than it had been just moments before. Apparently it didn't want to be shut yet. "Okay, then. What do you have for me?"

After what felt like an eternity, an image slowly materialized. The jumbled letters, two inches high in a heavy black font, shimmered six inches above the pages and cast their own shadows.

"Cool," he whispered under his breath as the words shifted and rolled, then strung together to form a sentence:

ALL THAT YOU SEEK IS HERE.

Eight

A week at the most," Sara told Grant as he poured her a glass of wine. He had asked her to join him a few minutes before everyone else arrived for drinks in the pub in the north wing of the house. Sipping the pinot grigio, she slid up onto a barstool.

She'd changed into a strapless, flame-red silk charmeuse Betsey Johnson dress and strappy bone-colored Christian Louboutin sandals. The color of the short dress looked good with her light tan and flattered her figure. Not that she was trying to look sexier than usual; she just wanted Jack to think she didn't give a damn what he thought, and that she looked this good all the time.

Basically, Sara thought, *I want him to see what he threw away, and then I want to see some regret.* Petty, but true.

Grant liked playing bartender, and Sara had found him an insanely expensive solid-oak bar counter in an Irish pub on a business-related shopping trip a few years before. Grant had loved it so much he'd bought the entire pub, ceiling and floor and everything in between, and had it dismantled and shipped to San Cristóbal. He'd then had the house remodeled to accommodate it.

He'd changed into cream linen slacks and a pale blue silk shirt the exact color of his eyes. His honey-colored hair was artfully tousled. Probably in his early fifties, he admitted to forty-two. Grant Baltzer looked young and fit, and Sara's heart swelled with love for him. He'd been a good friend to her parents, and an even better friend to her. There was nothing she would not do for him. Grant had saved her sanity twice, and she'd always love him for his unflagging affection and support.

"I don't want to have to pick up the pieces again, babe," he told her sincerely. Sara was sure that if he could have frowned, he would be doing so. No lines marred his forehead. Botox, she suspected; he was quite vain about his appearance. She thought it was sweet since he always addressed his vanity with a droll sense of humor, inviting her to laugh along.

"You know me." His smile was gently loving as he reached over to brush cool fingers across her cheek. Sara adored Grant, but for some odd reason, she'd never liked him to touch her. Something he enjoyed doing frequently. She tolerated it because she couldn't bear to hurt his feelings by rebuffing his innocent caresses. But she always managed to ease just out of reach before she shuddered.

"I'm all for giving a person a second chance." His dimples flashed. "But I wasn't sure you were going to bounce back after what he did to you last time."

He didn't know the half of it. Sara had been afraid that if she told Grant everything, he'd set a hit man on Jack's tail. She'd hated Jack, but she'd never wanted him dead. Just dead to her.

She knew Grant loved her and would do anything, up to and including wiping out the man who'd broken her heart. Grant had saved her life when he'd managed to extract her from the house fire that had killed her parents.

He'd taken care of her and practically raised her. He and his friend William had been the only visitors on alternate weekends while she'd attended the British boarding school Grant had paid for. William was a few years older than Sara, and for a while she'd wondered if the two men were lovers, but Grant had so many girl-friends that thought had dissipated over time.

He'd taken her on amazing summer vacations, tutored her in Spanish in Spain and French in Paris. He'd taught her to fly and watched proudly when she'd received her pilot's license. He'd sent her to college in London, then hired her to do the interiors of all of his hotels when she'd earned degrees in business administration and interior design.

Six months ago he'd made her a partner. Grant was friend, brother, father, and mentor to her, all rolled into one.

"I'm fine," she told him, going for nonchalant. "His being here isn't a big deal."

She decided that lying to Grant about what was going on wasn't a good idea. First of all, she was a crappy liar, and second, she didn't want anyone to misunderstand Jack's presence at the hacienda. She couldn't pretend to be lovey-dovey, given that her physical response to Jack hadn't changed along with her emotional attachment. She had to have a no-hands policy for the duration.

Seated on the other side of the wide oak counter,

Grant took a sip of his red wine. "I always told you William is the guy for you. He's nuts about you, babe. You could do a lot worse than a multimillionaire who adores you." He nudged over a platter of duck liver pâté canapés.

She shook her head, and Grant pushed the platter aside. Ultra careful about what he ate, Grant was a health nut, and had the gym body to prove it.

Jack didn't need a gym, Sara thought disloyally. His body was rock-hard muscle from working outside day in and day out. "I adore William back, but that isn't romantic love."

"Respect and mutual interests might be enough. Love will grow. You know what Mencken said—love is the delusion that one man is different from another."

"Did he now?" Sara said, amused. "You know you're flogging a dead horse, right?" She smiled to take the sting out of her words. "Besides, I have this business with Jack to deal with before anything else."

"Business?" Grant asked skeptically. "What kind of business?"

"Let's just say it's got something to do with that which we don't discuss, and leave it at that."

He rolled his eyes. "Oh, hell, babe. This is *wizard* business?"

"We never talk about wizard business, because I never have wizard business *to* talk about. And if I did, you'd ask me not to."

"True. Especially when it involves having your ex-lover as a houseguest. I'll brace myself. What kind of wizard business?"

"Alberto had a psychotic meltdown this morning. Nobody knows why, or if anyone else has been infected. But the Wizard Council asked Jack and me to look into it."

"Jesus, Sara! There's a diseased wizard running rampant, and instead of being concerned for your safety, your fucking wizard hierarchy told *you* to look into it? That's preposterous. Tell them to bugger off and find someone else to do their dirty work."

She noticed he didn't ask about Alberto's or Carmelita's well-being or whereabouts. "It's complicated."

"Which is why, my darling, you don't have anything to do with all that mumbo-jumbo wizard crap, remember?"

"Right. A week or so. Then I'm done."

He looked as if he were about to say something, then gave her a resigned look that spoke volumes. "Tell me the symptoms in case you start going psycho, too."

She laughed. "I'll let you know if I feel insanity coming on, I promise."

"Not funny, babe. Just the fact that you have Slater in the house makes me question your sanity." Grant leaned over and took her hand. "He abandoned you when you were at your most vulnerable, when you needed the people who loved you to support you in your grief. If you've forgotten what a mess you were right afterward, I sure as shit haven't."

"Thank you. I love you too."

He gave her fingers a light squeeze. "I worry about you."

Sara squeezed back, then let go to pick up her drink. "I know. But this is okay. Really."

"Were you and Jack arguing in the chopper?" he asked carefully, eyes filled with concern. "Is that what caused the engine to stall?"

She had no idea why the engine had malfunctioned. Grant hadn't wanted her to go back out to check the chopper, but she'd do an engine check with José tomorrow. Jack could figure out what the white stuff had been. "We weren't arguing exactly."

"You were remembering. The engine cut out, and you thought about teleporting back home, right?" Grant pointed out the obvious very gently. "You know what happens to your magic when you're upset, sweetheart. It goes haywire and causes accidents. That's going to happen a great deal with Slater underfoot."

Suddenly chilly in the warm room, Sara rubbed a hand briskly up her bare arm. Impossible to forget that she was a magical misfit. "I'll be careful. I promise."

"A week?"

"More or less."

"Let's try to make it less." Grant's mobile lips twitched. "If there's anything I can do to expedite this investigation of yours, let me know. I'll put all my resources behind you."

"Considering that your resources are a bottomless well, I might take you up on that generous offer."

"I'm doing it for you, not Slater or the Wizard Council."

Sara grinned. "Got it. More wine, please."

A few moments later the twins came in, wearing identical ice-blue minidresses that barely covered their girly bits. Grant had run into them in town and brought them back in the Cessna, leaving the Martin at his garage near the landing strip. William had gone to Lima for the week.

Sara wondered if the girls were capable of sitting down without doing a Britney Spears and exposing themselves. Grant encouraged the skanky way they dressed, which always amazed Sara because Grant, like herself, was an absolute clotheshorse and spent a fortune on his wardrobe.

The girls went behind the bar to drape themselves over him. They had not an ounce of modesty. Grant's disregard for privacy with his women was one of the few things he and Sara argued about; his PDAs embarrassed her most of the time and frequently grossed her out. Especially since most of the girls were young enough to be his daughters. It had the same ick factor as seeing one's parents having sex.

Sara swirled her stool around to give them privacy while she sipped the crisp, slightly fruity wine. She'd had the antique lighting retrofitted with timers and light sensors, and as the sky outside the enormous picture windows darkened, the small sconces along the walls flickered on.

She savored the dark, interesting room that smelled of countless pints of spilled beer and ignored the kissing sounds behind her. She always imagined young couples falling in love at the scarred tables, tipsy wedding receptions held there with lots of singing and laughter.

The pub had a happy, warm ambiance. She'd been delighted to give Grant something he hadn't expected for his birthday a couple of years ago. He loved the small, dark pub as much as she did, and they had drinks there most evenings before dinner.

She always teased Grant about his age, which he refused to tell anyone. Judged solely by his looks, he could be any-where between thirty-five and fifty. Sara knew he was older than she by at least twenty years, since he'd taken unofficial guardianship of her following her parents' deaths and had already been a successful businessman then.

If he'd had work done, he had a damn good plastic surgeon.

Suddenly a little shiver ran down her spine. She didn't have to see him to know that Jack had just walked into the room; the air seemed to crackle with electricity. She took the last sip of wine, not turning as she listened to his footfalls on the worn plank floor.

His warm palms slid over her bare shoulders. Jack's hands weren't smooth and pampered like Grant's; they were large and slightly abrasive, like a cat's tongue glid-ing over her skin. His dark hair brushed her cheek as he leaned down. "I missed you," he murmured, not that softly, against her ear.

Missed her from where? Sara thought indignantly, about to turn and give him the evil eye, if not a sharp nudge with her knee. What was he playing at now?

Her breath caught as his lips skimmed her cheek. His fingers closed around the sensitive skin on the nape of her neck, bared by her upswept hair. She made a small sound of protest, a little moan of need. Damn it.

He'd showered, and smelled of oatmeal soap. His hair

drifted damply against Sara's throat, causing a delicious shiver to race up her spine. "Jack, do—"

Her words choked off as he exerted pressure on the back of her neck, just enough to turn her head in his direction. He tilted her head back with his thumb under her chin and looked down, his eyes dark, his cheekbones flushed. Sara felt waves of heat and cold shudder through her body.

"Do n—" she tried again, but no sound came out. Their eyes locked.

"Let's go."

"Dinner . . ."

"Not hungry," Jack murmured, running his hand up the side of her neck, then tracing the curve of her ear with an incredibly gentle finger. "You?"

Little shudders of pleasure raced across her nerve endings as she shook her head. She was starving. But not for food. "Grant—"

"Doing what we're too polite to do in company." He took her hand, tugging her off the stool. "Come on."

Nobody noticed them leave the pub. As soon as they closed the door behind them, Jack backed her into a small restroom close by. He kicked the door shut, closing them in the darkness. He backed her against the wall, imprisoning her hands on either side of her shoulders as he bent his head.

"Jack! What on earth's got into you?!"

"*This* hasn't changed." His mouth grazed hers, a bare skimming touch, more the promise of what was to come than a kiss. "Has it? I'm sick of resisting. How about you?"

Sara's mind went blank; her nipples hardened beneath the silk charmeuse of her dress. She felt a few pins fall out of her hair and didn't care. "I—"

He had her slightly off balance and she grabbed his broad shoulders so she didn't fall. He anchored her with the weight of his body.

His mouth crushed down on hers, this time with a damn-the-torpedoes kiss that made her deaf to anything or anyone. His tongue delved deeper, and Sara met it with a mindless sweep of her own.

He turned her, unerringly hoisting her up onto the counter. She felt the cold marble through the thin fabric of her dress, then the heat of Jack's hard body pressed between her legs, hauntingly familiar, sparking a lust so swift, so intense Sara could barely breathe. He took her mouth again, longer, deeper, while she fumbled then found the buttons on his shirt, ripping them off in her haste to get to bare skin.

Jack's breath was ragged, his fingers tightening on the back of her neck. His other hand slid down the swell of her breasts, then slipped beneath the strapless bodice. His fingertips brushed her hard and painful nipples, and Sara moaned.

He chuckled, laying a line of kisses down the sensitive cords of her neck to the rapid pulse at the base of her throat. Panting, Sara slid both hands into his thick, silky hair, tugging on the damp strands to bring him closer.

She had to stop this. Now.

In a minute.

No. Now.

Hard fingers cupped her ass as he kissed her again—hot, openmouthed kisses that went on and on and on. He was fully aroused as he leaned into her. Sara wanted to touch him there. Wanted to curl her fingers around the hot silk of his penis. Wanted to—

The room instantly felt . . . different. There was the faint tang of smoke from an applewood fire, the scent of sun-dried sheets, the feel of Jack's naked skin against hers. A sense of disorientation, swiftly followed by outrage, washed over her as she forced her eyes open and used both hands to shove—hard—at Jack's chest.

They were no longer in the guest bathroom at Grant's house.

"Where are we?" She sounded breathless instead of appalled. She would have struggled to sit up, but Jack was firmly between her thighs and *this* close to penetration.

Sprawled on top of her, he pushed himself up, his arms caging her beneath him as he glanced around. "Looks like that little ski cabin in Switzerland where we didn't do any skiing over Christmas three years ago." Hunger burned in his eyes as he looked down at her. "We spent the entire week in this very bed, if I remember correctly."

"Impossible," Sara whispered thickly, then arched her back as Jack drove into her to the hilt.

He started to pull out, and her body shuddered in denial. Sara pressed her bent knees against his hipbones, holding him in place. "Don't."

"You sure?"

She wrapped her bare legs around his narrow hips.

"No. Yes. Don't leave me hanging on the edge like this. Finish it, damn you."

"That a yes?"

"Yes. I w——" What she was going to say was forgotten as Jack slid his hand under her hair, fingers hard and cool as he cupped the back of her neck. "Jack——"

The gentle brush of his lips on hers made Sara's breath catch. He lifted his mouth a fraction of an inch, his eyes asking again: *Do you want this?*

Her choice.

She didn't want him to give her a choice, damn it. She wanted to keep hating him. She wanted to grab him and drag his mouth back to hers.

He brushed her hair out of her eyes, his body still when she desperately needed the thrust and parry of hard, juicy, sweaty, mind-blowing sex. "Remember——"

"No." *Just do me. No memories. No sweet talk. No promises.* Like he'd said—why resist?

His smile tore through the wall around her heart. "You don't know what I was going to ask."

Sara's eyes fluttered shut. She remembered everything. Every touch, every word, every nuance. She remembered the love. And the hate. "Doesn't matter. I don't remember any of it."

"Liar."

And there they were, exactly where they'd been two years ago. Love was greedy and demanding. Loving Jack had almost killed her. She wasn't prepared to put that much of herself back on any line.

With a little moan, Sara surrendered to the erotic

temptation. This had never been a problem for them. Sex with Jack had always been intense and all-consuming.

She missed it. She missed this. She missed him.

They were perfectly matched in bed. It was out of bed that they weren't compatible. She sank into a hot swell of pleasure as he took her mouth with all the gusto of a buccaneer boarding a treasure ship. His tongue dove deep, and she savored the heady taste of Jack flavored with minty toothpaste.

The hint of danger she felt in his arms was seductive. Want and need vibrated between them. Jack couldn't hide his desire from her, and she wondered how she'd ever imagined she could hide hers from him. She squeezed her eyes shut, in an agony of need. The warning bells seemed to be getting fainter and fainter.

She'd had a deep, untapped reservoir of love to give a man when she'd first met Jack. She'd known instantly that he was the one for her. She hadn't hesitated, had given him everything she had. Now she knew better. Never again was she going to lay her heart out for any man to destroy. Especially this man.

Their passions had run hot enough to melt steel, and gentle enough to make her heart ache with love for him. Those feelings were gone now. Her heart was as hard and cold as a lump of ice. With lips and tongue she claimed him because her body, unlike her heart, was whole, and needy, and greedy for his touch.

Jack lifted his damp mouth from hers, his breathing ragged, his eyes hot. She remembered that the more aroused he was, the deeper and gentle his voice became.

"Love me." Her voice was husky, an invitation when she knew she should push him away. But she wanted him as she'd never wanted another man. Everything inside her yearned to go back two years. Before . . .

The climax rolled over her in an tidal wave so intense she went deaf and blind. Another swept in right behind it, and another right after that. She couldn't catch her breath for several minutes after Jack's body went slack as he shuddered against her.

Small delicious aftershocks made her body quiver as sweat beaded her skin and her breathing resumed in erratic gasps.

Oh, God. It was worse than she'd feared. Making love with Jack again was like coming home.

Damn. I can't stop wanting him, no matter how hard I try, no matter how far away I hide myself. She shifted beneath him, bringing him in even deeper.

She might have slept, or perhaps fallen off the edge of the world. Sara's eyes fluttered open to find Jack propped up on his elbow, silhouetted by the window of night behind him. Drifts of snow gleamed white in the moonlight. Midnight in Switzerland, dinnertime in San Cristóbal.

She shoved her hair out of her face, feeling exposed and strangely vulnerable. "Grant will wonder where we are."

"No he won't." Jack traced a finger between her breasts, then followed with his mouth, taking his sweet time. "He was getting a blow job when we left," he murmured against her hip.

Sara punched his shoulder. "He was not."

His gaze—so blue, so warm—connected with hers. "Yeah. One of the blondes was out of sight behind the bar, and very busy."

"That's dis—ohhhh! Disgusting."

"Your pal is a perv."

She opened her eyes wide in exaggerated shock. "Oral sex is perverted?" Sara shifted her hips to give him better access. "You never mentioned that hang-up to me before."

"It's only perverted when performed by a kid and in full view of several disinterested parties." He nuzzled the underside of a breast, his hands moving down to cup her cheeks in both palms. He trailed his lips down the center of her body, and Sara's skin quivered with anticipation. "Stop me if this feels too perverted for you."

She ran her fingers up the indents of his spine as his damp mouth moved down her body. His skin felt like warm satin under her hands as he paid particular attention to first her left nipple, then the right.

"Do you have any idea how soft and delicate you are just here?" Jack stroked his tongue along the underside of her breast. "Softer than silk. Smoother than satin."

Sara brought both hands up to grip the corded muscles of his shoulders, which were keeping her knees spread wide. The blazing heat of his mouth moved to the juncture of her thighs. Her body arched as his hot breath fanned her damp curls.

With a moan she slid her fingers through his hair, drawing him hard against where she really needed him.

His tongue found her swollen clitoris; then she felt the gentle scrape of his teeth. "Jack . . ."

His fingers tightened under her ass as her body bucked and strained to get closer. Heart manic, sweat gleaming on her skin, Sara fisted his hair at the tormenting slip and slide of his agile tongue. Panting, she stiffened with the imminent approach of a climax. Jack held her there—at the top of a mountain—for what felt like eternity. Then he plunged his stiff tongue deep inside her and bit down on her mons at the same time.

Sara's body arched, and she cried out as intense pleasure spread through her in multiple rolling waves.

Limp and replete, she waited for Jack to kiss a damp path up her body. She tasted herself on his mouth when he kissed her lightly. She was too spent to give the kiss much enthusiasm, and he laughed as he tucked her against his side.

"God. That was. . ."

"Amazing? Excellent?"

"Yeah. All of the above." Sara snuggled against him. She could hear the slightly unsteady beat of his heart beneath her ear. "I missed this," she said softly, her voice still a little breathy. *I missed you.*

"Yeah. Me too."

She closed her eyes as she trailed lazy fingers through the crisp hair on his chest. "We lost so much. Can we ever even hope to get some of that back?"

"I don't know, Sara. There was a lot said and done that can't be mended."

Her chest hurt. "But yo—*we* can try, can't we, Jack?"

She wanted him to apologize and really mean it. Needed him to explain how he could possibly have imagined she was capable of doing something so underhanded and final as aborting their baby.

Discussing what had happened two years ago would go a long way toward healing the festering wound, getting it all out in the open where they could sort out where they'd gone so horribly wrong. Over the ensuing years, Sara had tried to figure out why Jack had believed what he had. She'd honest to God thought he knew her better than that. The fact that he hadn't had hurt just as much as his words that day. It had all boiled down to trust—or lack thereof.

Was it possible to go back to the time before that last fight? She wasn't sure. But she desperately wanted to try.

She lifted her head to look at him. "We have an opportunity to start over. Clean slate. New page."

Eyes closed, Jack let the silence drag on for an eternity. "We have to find the time for a real conversation, Sara. You did something I just can't wrap my brain around."

She started to speak, but he put a finger over her lips. "Shh. Not now. We're in the middle of a fight that's bigger than both of us. Let's just call a truce until this is done. *Then* we'll talk, okay?"

How damn long would it take him to say "I'm sorry, Sara, I was an insensitive ass?"

~ Nine ~

Walking through the leafy sauna of the jungle with Sara early the next morning, Jack thought the night before seemed more like a fantasy than a reality. Or the better part of it did. After the spectacular sex and, more important, the closeness they'd shared, he hadn't wanted to hear Sara's explanations or her apology for what she'd done. There really was nothing she could say or do that would fix that. He would eventually forgive her, he supposed. But he would never forget. And that memory would forever be the wedge between them

No amount of *I'm sorry*s would make the pain go away.

He hadn't planned on ma—on having *sex* with Sara last night. Not by a long shot. Yet he'd walked into the pub, already redolent with the smell of sex, and all he'd seen was her. All he'd wanted—all he had to *have*—was her. Jesus. The primitive need had been impossible to resist, all reason turned off. Good thing she'd been swept up along with him. It made him damned uncomfortable to wonder what he would have done if Sara had said no.

Barely an hour had passed between their departure

and their return to Sara's suite at the hacienda. They'd made it to dinner with minutes to spare. A few glances were all their absence warranted, and if anyone noticed a certain air about them, no one commented on it.

After dinner, Sara had claimed a headache and gone to bed. Jack had hit the pool for two hours, then gone to his own room. *Eventually* he'd managed to fall asleep.

"Been here before?" he asked, swatting at an iridescent insect the size of his fist as it buzzed past his nose. While his arm was up there, he wiped it across his face. Small insects clung to the sweat on his skin, making him itch. If he never saw green foliage again, he'd be a happy guy.

"Several times," Sara told him cheerfully. "This is where Carmelita's mother, Inez Armato, lives. It's a small village. Maybe twenty-five, thirty people."

"So this is where Baltzer met Carmelita?"

"About twenty years ago. She—and later Alberto—has traveled with him, managing his household, ever since."

"Very loyal."

She frowned as she wiped away a rivulet of sweat running down her throat. "Yes."

"What did he have to say about what happened to his chef?" Jack asked curiously. He'd bet Baltzer's concern had been for his own comfort. He'd never given Jack the impression that he gave a damn about anyone but himself. And Sara. In that order.

"There wasn't really time for him to say much of anything. He's very concerned, of course. And I'm sure he'll pay for any medical treatment they need."

"I'm sure he will." *If you tell him to.*

Their two Indian guides were about twenty yards ahead, hacking through the jungle with razor-sharp machetes to reclear the path to the village. The rain forest kept covering the scars made by man. All he and Sara had to do was follow the trail.

He took his handheld out of his back pocket and started tracking the magnetic field as they walked. An accurate reading would require objective-prism spectra of the major sources of light visible from the stars. No interference from cities or major civilization way the hell out here to mess up his readings, which would make it somewhat easier.

"Don't tell me—you're testing to see if the village is on a leyline."

He ignored the light mockery. "Yeah. And it is. I'll need my theodolite and other equipment to confirm it. Can't you feel the energy pulsing up through your feet?" He'd teleport his equipment from Australia when they got back to the house. He didn't like leaving it in the middle of the bush even with a protective spell over it.

"I'm not sure," Sara said cautiously. "What's it supposed to feel like?"

"A low-pitched hum, a buzz almost. Goes up through my feet and travels through my entire body. I like it. It's like a low-amp power surge."

"God, I hate to say this, but yes. I do feel exactly that. But then, I have that same feeling at the house."

"That's because Baltzer's place is on the same ley."

"Jack . . ."

"What?"

"I know you don't like Grant, but don't pull him into any of this."

"I don't believe in coincidences, do you?"

"Well, I assure you, Grant didn't buy a house on a leyline intentionally, because he would have no idea what a ley *is*."

She'd never put much store in his research into leylines. He'd never convinced her of their reality. She hadn't believed in leys, but she'd believed in him. Or so he'd thought at the time.

"The hacienda couldn't be more than, what? Maybe seventy-five years old? Maybe This ley goes back thousands of years—so no, but his house is definitely on a ley. Fascinating that out of all the choices he had, he went for this place."

"I can pretty much guarantee you the ley had nothing to do with it," she told him dryly. "I think he bought it from some long-lost uncle a long time ago."

He'd have to come back at night, which he didn't relish. Fortunately, Jack wouldn't have to walk in; he could teleport and take aerial readings. This was a ley, without a doubt. And a strong one. He couldn't wait to see just how strong. How far did it run? And more important—what was the point of origin?

He'd need an objective series of soil samples, of course, and an accurate reading from his version of a surveyor's wheel. He'd built his own specifically for the measuring of leys. Electronic, it calculated the energy emitted from the earth as well as distance between major points.

Baltzer's sprawling estate was definitely built on a leyline, and so was the village they were about to visit. Fascinating. If he couldn't combine his research with the job he was doing for the Council, he'd come back later—if there *was* a later—and do a thorough job mapping this one. He wouldn't have to interact with Sara if he returned; hell, she wouldn't even have to know he was there.

His shirt clung unpleasantly to his back in the stifling hothouse atmosphere, but he was able to ignore it as he input more numbers and saw preliminary data compute on the screen. His heart thumped with excitement. God—a new leyline, confirmed.

Every surface either oozed or dripped water. Thick and hard to breathe, the humid air felt like a living presence, and smelled exactly like rotting vegetation in a compost heap.

Sara's long legs matched his strides. Wearing khaki pants, a long-sleeved black T-shirt, and a black baseball cap, she looked like a fashion plate in heavy hiking boots. With a sheen of perspiration on her golden skin, she could have been the girl in some commercial for clean living and beautiful people. Small hoops and the sunstones studs in her ears caught stray rays of sun and glinted gold and orange as she walked. He closed his eyes briefly as he inhaled the soft lemon fragrance of her skin.

He wanted her naked under him again.

Jesus. Talk about making one hell of a bad call—he wished he hadn't made love to her. It had been too amazing. Too fantastic.

Loving Sara had been so damn *easy*.

Recovering from Sara had taken much, much longer.

Their physicality had the same undeniable magic. *That* had never been the problem.

The thick carpet of dead leaves underfoot was spongy and dank, the undergrowth littered with man-size ferns and knots of leafy vines. He heard the shrill, tortured cry of a bird, the rustle as a small animal rushed unseen through the trees.

"How many wizards in this village?" he asked, keeping the conversation casual because he wanted to ask her what she'd been thinking that day, the day everything had ended. He wanted to resolve the two-year-old conflict *now*. But that conversation would take more than a few minutes. They'd both been furious, both been hurt by the words flung like weapons at one another.

She'd changed since they'd broken up—now, wasn't *that* a fucking apropos expression? *Broken up*. Yeah. That's how his heart had felt at the time.

He'd mended, of course. His father had done a bang-up job of teaching him to suck it up and move on, to be a man. No complaining, no whining. But the experience had sure as hell inoculated him against ever falling in love again.

Seeing her played havoc with his libido, however. He could, and had, switched off brain and heart; his dick was another matter. It had a mind of its own, and its mind was on Sara. On all of her.

Idiot.

One of the character traits they shared was a strong sense of self-preservation—Sara because of the early death of her parents, Jack because of his father. They'd opened up to each other in a way Jack had never experienced before or since. But he'd never imagined that Sara would take matters into her own hands and make the decision to abort their child.

He knew, that unlike himself, she'd been ambivalent about having kids. But once she discovered she was pregnant, he'd been sure she was becoming increasingly excited about it. Man. Had he been wrong.

She had a thousand great qualities, but quick decision-making wasn't one of them. She considered. She meditated on things. She waffled. There, they were different. But she hadn't taken time to weigh *anything*. She'd made up her mind and acted on it without a word, without input. Without *his* input.

Fire was Sara's power to call, but that last day she'd been colder than an arctic winter.

Water under the bridge, he reminded himself. Nothing he could do about it now. Or ever, for that matter. He doubted he could ever forgive her for what she'd done.

He'd moved on, and so had she.

He'd do well to remember that.

A little black snake—okay, possibly a worm— dropped from a twig right in front of his eyes and landed on his shirtfront, then arched, flicked back and forth, and fell to the dirt at his feet. His heart pounded, jolting him out of his memories.

Christ, he loathed all this green and the things it hid. The soil was black and rich and alive with creatures large and small. Jack didn't mind bugs, didn't mind spiders, not even creatures with sharp teeth. But his eyes moved carefully in search of fucking snakes.

In a rain forest, they hung lazily from branches, tauntingly slithered over his boots, and generally made their presence felt, their beady little eyes tracking his every move, their forked tongues flicking.

He realized Sara hadn't answered his question. "Any wizards?" he repeated.

Sara wiped her damp face with a swatch of blue fabric dotted with pink rosebuds. Her ponytail, pulled through the back of the ball cap, bounced as she walked. "About half of them are, including the village elder, Enrique Rojas."

"Uh-huh," Jack muttered, keeping his attention on a long, slimy, brown . . . *log* as they passed it. There was a good reason why he'd left the plotting of South America's leylines until dead last. "And the thought of *teleporting* didn't enter your mind?"

"It's only three miles, Jack."

"Three miles of snake- and bug-infested rain forest."

"You've been in worse places." She smiled. "Quite a switch, huh? Usually I'm the one who wants to call a cab, and *you're* the one who wants to hike all over hell and gone."

He felt them then—wizard signatures. Perhaps twelve or fourteen full wizards, most with medium- to low-level powers. They were perhaps a mile off. *Yay*, he thought sourly. *Civilization.* He, the man who reveled in sleeping under the stars six months out of the year, longed for sidewalks and the stink of diesel fuel. "I'm not partial to green."

She shot him a querying glance. "Uh-huh. You liked the green dress I wore to the awards ceremony when you won the Wollaston Medal in London."

The award for proving the existence of British ley-lines had been nothing compared to seeing Sara wearing a dress made of paper-thin fabric that hugged her curves—light, *soft* green like one of those party mints, as opposed to dark, dangerous, verdant, *jungle* green.

He'd barely made it through the speeches before he'd had her back at their hotel, and the dress in a heap on the floor. They'd never made it to the bed.

Music drifted faintly through the trees—a rhythmic drumming reminiscent of Africa, a little Spanish-inspired guitar, and the indigenous contribution of maracas. Two black-striped snakes with golden bodies dangled threateningly on Sara's side of the path, their bodies arching toward the path as they reached for another branch.

He would have warned her of the danger, but his tongue was stuck to the roof of his mouth. Pissed him off that he was afraid of anything, especially something he could make disappear with a thought.

Gritting his teeth, Jack stepped in front of Sara and used the machete he carried to sweep them out of the way. They dropped to the ground in a twined knot and vanished into the undergrowth.

"That was very gallant of you, but those were striped queen snakes and not poisonous."

"I didn't want them falling on you. Know what I remember about that green dress? Rug burns."

Sara gave him a faint smile. "They didn't bother me."

"No, because they were on my ass," Jack reminded her dryly. Best rug burns he'd ever had.

The music got louder for a few minutes, then abruptly cut off. Their guides disappeared up ahead, leaving them alone in a forest devoid of the chatter of birds or animals. Humans lived close by, and the animals kept out of the way.

Sara offered him a drink from the water bottle she'd just unsnapped from her belt. Jack shook his head.

"We're almost there. I'll visit Carmelita and see how she's doing. Inez can introduce you to the head honcho. He's ancient, but spry and pretty alert. He seems to know everything that goes on within a hundred-mile radius. Interesting guy. I think you'll like him." She cast him a curious look.

She had amazing eyes. Big, beautiful, velvet-brown eyes that could read a man's soul—if he let her.

Jack tore his eyes from the movement of her damp throat as she lifted the bottle and drank. God, he'd like to put his mouth there. Sara's skin tasted like no other woman's—he could do a blindfolded taste test, and know whose skin he was licking.

"Where were you in Australia before you showed up in Alberto's kitchen?" she asked after she'd drunk half the bottle down.

"Rudall River National Park, Western Australia." He looked forward, seeing glimpses of small whitewashed houses and smelling the cooking fires. "Nice and dry and hotter than hell."

She snapped the bottle back on her belt. "Did you follow your ley?"

"I was in the middle of mapping before you screamed your mental SOS and almost dropped me down a volcanic plug," he said dryly. "I'd heard myths and legends about that particular ley for years, if you remember. Pretty damned amazing. At least a thousand miles long and incredibly powerful."

"We were never able to communicate that way before," Sara pointed out. "Any idea why it happened *this* time? Don't get me wrong, I was very glad to see you. But I question *why* you think you heard me. Or not why, necessarily, but *how*."

"You must've been thinking of me swooping in like a superhero and saving the day."

"Actually, I was just trying to keep myself and Carmelita alive. I wasn't thinking about you at all, Jack."

JACK WASN'T SURE WHAT he'd expected of the mother of plump, motherly Carmelita. But he sure as hell hadn't expected Sophia Loren. Inez's *café au lait* skin was smooth and practically unlined, her voluptuous body was a knockout in blue jeans and a form-fitting T-shirt, and her curling dark hair brushed her shoulders with nary a gray hair in sight. She must have been at least seventy, but she didn't look a day older than a very hot fifty.

While Sara visited with Carmelita, Inez escorted Jack to the home of the elder. "You can find your way back to my house, *si?*" Inez asked with a smile after introducing him to Enrique Rojas, a slight man who looked every one of his hundred-plus years.

"Sure. *Gracias*, Inez."

Rojas offered him a seat on a worn-smooth wooden bench outside his house in the shade of several thickly leafed trees. Removing a Coke can from his jacket pocket, he offered it in a gnarled hand with dirt-encrusted nails.

Jack accepted it with thanks and watched, amused, as the old man pulled a bottle of beer from his other pocket and wrenched off the cap. The man's skin was nut dark, with so many folds and wrinkles it was hard to make out his features. His black eyes were alight with life, and he smiled often, showing all three of his black teeth.

"You have heard of Inez's son-in-law's illness?" Jack asked in Spanish, popping the tab on his soda. Jack could tell from his signature the man was the highest-powered wizard in the area, but that wasn't saying much. His powers were earth-aligned, so perhaps he could get a garden to sprout easily, but he wasn't going to be causing any earthquakes or volcanoes.

The old man nodded. *"Sí."*

"Is anyone else in your village afflicted with Alberto's terrible disease?" He took a swig of warm, too sweet, fizzy cola. Hit the spot. "Anyone acting loco in the last few weeks?"

The dialect was a little tricky, but Jack got the gist of Roja's response. Yes. Two wizards had become ill. Both men had died within twelve days of complaining of the fever. Their bodies had been burned by the superstitious villagers. Probably a good thing.

"What were the symptoms?"

"High fever. Tingling in their feet. Paralysis."

"*Tingling in their feet?!* Perhaps I misunderstood?"

Rojas repeated it.

The feet thing really threw him. "Insanity? Violent behavior?"

Rojas nodded, but his crepey lids fluttered as he glanced away. "*Sí.* They also had a very bad fear of water."

"*Agua?* Water?" Jack asked carefully, not knowing what to make of this new information. Sara hadn't mentioned a fear of water when describing Alberto's symptoms. "Do you know what this sickness might be?"

"*Sí,*" Rojas assured him, indicating the almost impenetrable wall of green on the outskirts of his village. "*Murciélago vampiro.*"

"Vampire *bats* are biting the villagers?"

The old man chugged down half his warm beer before he nodded vigorously. With a lot of hand waving, or rather one hand and the bottle, he indicated how the bats came out at night from the cave outside the village. They came down and bit people on the feet. The young girls in the village were protected by their amulets, which they wore on leather strings around their necks. None of them had been bitten, but three had been taken.

Jack wasn't sure they were having the same conversation. Itchy feet. Girls. Amulets. Taken. How did that relate to vampire bats and wizards dying?

"Do the girls come back?"

"*Sí. Algunas de las muchachas vuelen.*" Yes, some of them. "*Pero no todas.*" But not always.

"The girls who came back . . . where have they been?"

"Sarulu." Rojas glanced fearfully over his shoulder, then got awkwardly to his feet. He stood there for a moment, irresolute—then shook his head, waved his hands in a never-mind motion, and wandered into his house without looking back.

Jack didn't know what the hell to make of any of that. Who or what was Sarulu, and how did it relate to the wizards, the vampire bats, or the missing girls?

It wasn't funny hearing that several people had died from what sounded like rabies. Jack walked down the stony street between the small houses, back to Inez's. But if the bat thing was true, the deaths had nothing to do with the Omnivatics or Ophidian's comet.

He shook his head. Christ. Bats?

Sara was waiting for him outside Inez's tiny one-room house. As soon as Jack saw her, he moved faster. She wasn't a crier, but when she did cry, her nose got pink and her cheeks very pale. "What's the matter?"

"Alberto died two hours ago. The Council just notified Carmelita." She looked up, her big brown eyes swimming with tears. "They won't release his—damn it, Jack, they won't release his body for burial until they know definitely what killed him."

He wanted to fold her in his arms. He wanted to have the right to comfort her. He didn't, and he didn't. "I think I know what killed him."

"You do?" She swiped at her cheeks with her fingertips.

Jack produced a Kleenex out of thin air and handed it to

her. "I'll tell you when I tell the Council." "Are you ready to go, or do you want to stay here while I go tell Edge?"

"Carmelita has Inez. I'll go with you."

THIS TIME WHEN THEY appeared in the Council Chamber, they teleported directly to Duncan Edge. He sat at the big desk under the spotlight writing in an enormous leather-bound ledger, and glanced up as Sara and Jack materialized before him. "What do you have for me?"

Sara cleared her throat. Her chest felt tight, her throat raw with grief. "Would it be possible for me to see Alberto before—before?"

"No," the Head of Council told her impatiently; then his gaze softened as he got a look at her. She hadn't had a chance to fix her makeup, and it must be pretty obvious she'd been crying. "Yeah, all right," he said less harshly. "I'll make sure you're protected before you're taken in to where his body is being held."

"Thank you," Sara said with utmost sincerity. She wanted a moment to say good-bye to a man who'd treated her like a daughter for almost twenty years. Plus, she'd be able to tell Carmelita that Alberto was being well taken care of. Sara hoped that the Council would release him for burial soon. Carmelita would need closure. And so would she.

Edge materialized two chairs in front of his desk and indicated they be seated. "Okay. What do we have?"

"Two villagers died, both within twelve days of onset of their symptoms. The village elder believes both victims were bitten by local vampire bats."

"Vamp—Silas?" Duncan Edge said quietly.

"Yes, sir?" The man's voice came from the pitch darkness behind the bright light. Did he sit there in the darkness all day and night just waiting for an order from Duncan Edge? Sara wondered. What a boring and crappy job that must be.

"Have Santos's body tested immediately for any trace of anticoagulant." A ball of fire appeared between his fingers, and Edge rotated it absently while he considered this new possibility. "While vampire bats are sanguivorous, they usually feed on the blood of cattle, horses, pigs," he mused, adding two more balls of fire to the one already leaping between the fingers of his right hand. "Pretty damned rare for them to feed on humans unless there's absolutely nothing else around. And that rain forest is filled with mammals. Let's see what the tests tell us. Anything else?"

"We were returning from San Cristóbal—Sara was piloting Baltzer's helicopter—when we experienced a whiteout. This was no ordinary whiteout," Jack told Edge. "Cold is my power to call, Sara's is fire, yet neither of us could get rid of it."

"Because your powers didn't function?" Edge demanded.

"Because," Jack told him flatly, "there was nothing there."

Edge's dark brow rose. "An illusion?"

"Yeah."

"The engine stalling wasn't an illusion," Sara pointed out.

Jack glanced from Sara to Edge. "Maybe. Maybe not."

"You believe it was *all* an illusion?" she asked him. "That doesn't make any sense. To what purpose?"

"Hell if I know," Jack responded. "What I do know is that chopper could easily have crashed with a less capable pilot. But if, as I suspect, a wizard caused the illusion, he or she must also know that we wouldn't have been harmed in a crash. We would obviously have teleported out in time."

"Maybe someone wanted to crash Grant's three-million-dollar chopper."

"Maybe."

"Keep track of all these anomalies." The fireballs between Edge's fingers sparked white-hot, and jagged bits of lightning snap-crack-popped along the silver threads in his robe as he shifted. "They might or might not be connected. But everything should be taken into account. What did you find out in the village?"

"Apparently, young girls keep going missing. Some return. Similar story to what we heard at one of the police stations in downtown San Cristóbal. I'm not sure how missing and exploited young women tie in with wizards dying after being bitten by vampire bats in the jungle."

"What else?"

"Something about a cave just outside the village that everyone is terrified of."

"If it's filled with biting bats, I'd be terrified too," Sara muttered.

"The young women apparently wear some sort of amulet to ward off evil. Some of them have come back, although apparently they could show up miles from where they were abducted. The girls who do return are ostracized and held in contempt because they allowed themselves to be caught by—Sarulu? Yeah, Sarulu, and—"

"Is that what Rojas told you?" Sara asked with a small smile. "The girls were taken by Sarulu?"

Jack leaned forward. "Yeah. Know who he is?"

"He's not real," Sara told the two men. "Sarulu is a myth. Not to be unsympathetic, but I suspect the girls ran off with their boyfriends, then changed their minds and came home. They're using the myth to their advantage."

Edge's eyes glowed as the balls of fire passed between his bare hands. "What kind of myth?"

"Legend says that without Kasipoluin, the rainbow, it would rain without end. But the rainbow goes to Juya, the rain, and tells it to stop. The story goes that the rainbow is really the tongue of a rainbow-colored snake that lives in the earth like a root, deep inside a cave—Sarulu. His tongue is rainbow-colored and three-pronged. Since snakes are the enemy of the rain, and rain is the enemy of the snake, the rain strikes the snake with lightning bolts when the it comes out of its cave. Legend claims that rainbows always come from the boa."

"Either of you see any large, rainbow-colored snakes hanging around the village?" Edge asked wryly.

"Ah, man," Jack squeezed the bridge of his nose. "Why the hell does all this shit keep coming back to snakes?"

∽ Ten ∽

It was a relief to teleport out of the Council, away from Duncan's sharp eyes, to her suite at the hacienda. The scond they'd materialized, Jack toed off his dirty boots and his socks, leaving a dark pile on the white wool flokati area rug. Then, with a grunt of satisfaction, he flung himself backward in an overtly male pose on her snowy duvet, his hands stacked beneath his head against the pile of pillows, looking for all the world like some pasha of old. If pashas lounged in art-deco boudoirs. She'd designed the white-on-white room to suit the tropical surroundings. Sara hadn't envisioned Jackson Slater in it.

Jack defined sexy—his hooded gaze, his kissable mouth, the dark fall of hair over his forehead. She swallowed, unable to look away. He looked completely relaxed and ridiculously *male*.

"Go to your own room, Jack. I want to take a shower."

She was hot and sticky and longing to immerse herself under cool jets with mounds of her favorite ginger-citron soap. Without him hovering nearby. Unfortunately, Jack seemed in no great hurry to leave.

He gave her a lazy grin. "Go ahead. I won't look through your things while you're in there."

It wasn't her things she was worried about. "You can look at whatever you like. There's nothing in here I don't want you to see." *Except me naked in the shower.* She didn't feel safe with him a mere door's-width away when she was naked and vulnerable.

His lips twitched as if he knew exactly what she was thinking. "Really?"

"Yes." She removed her shoes and opened the louvered closet doors to put them away, enjoying the coolness of the aged Brazilian walnut floor under her bare feet. "Rea—oh, hell. *Harry.*"

"Harry? Shit." Jack pulled his feet up onto the bed, suddenly wide awake. He wasn't smiling now. "You mean that damn monster snake is in here?"

The boa was stretched sinuously atop a row of Jimmy Choos. "He likes my shoes." Harry's forked tongue darted out and in, tasting the air as he turned his triangular head to look at her. Sometimes she swore Harry had a brain. She gave him a little stroke between his eyes.

"I'm guessing none of them are made out of any of his relatives."

"He hasn't said. Shoo, Harry." Sara waved her hands. Harry blinked yellow eyes, and kept flickering his skinny black tongue at her. Sara turned her head, her gaze settling on Jack. "Will you—"

"Not just no," Jack told her shortly, his attention focused like a laser level on Harry. "*Hell* no. I'm not touching it. Lock the damned thing in there and throw away the key."

"I don't like him watching me. Come on, Jack. Harry weighs almost seventy pounds. I'm not sure I can pull him out of there myself."

Jack shuddered. "I wouldn't touch him if he weighed seven *ounces*. Trust me, I'm not your snake go-to guy."

"All right, buddy." Sara bent and hefted Harry up with both hands, then gave a little grunt as his weight dropped onto her shoulder. He hung down almost to her feet front and back like a scarf. His smooth skin against her neck felt cool and dry and not in the least unpleasant. "You can't stay in here, big boy, you know that's a no-no."

"Christ almighty. You talk to it like it's a cute, fluffy puppy. Get that thing off your neck before he decides to start squeezing you to death."

"He's a sweetheart." Sara stroked Harry's head with her fingertip. "You're just not giving him a chance."

Jack made a rude noise behind her.

"I'm guessing you don't like snakes," she said with a smile. She'd noticed as much when they were in the jungle. It was odd knowing he had a little chink in his machismo. She carried the boa across the room. He curled his back half around her hips as she walked, and raised his front half so he could flick at her face with his tongue. "See? He's kissing me."

"He's tasting you to see if you need more salt."

She huffed a laugh as she opened the door and stepped into the tiled hallway. Unwinding Harry from the complicated knot he'd made around her body, Sara set him on the floor. "Go look for a rat or something." After a moment's hesitation, Harry silently slithered away over the cool tiles.

Stepping back into the room, she closed the door. "He's harmless."

"He's a wild animal. And a predator. Harmless he's not. Not only does he have freaking *teeth*, he could squeeze all the air out of your lungs in a second flat."

Sara smiled. "That's a slight exaggeration. But Harry's really used to people. He wouldn't hurt a fly. I've known him since he was a baby."

"Well, I haven't, and I don't like the way he looks at me."

"He's not looking at you now. Go away, Jack. I really want that shower."

He lay back, hands under his head again. "Take your time. We need to talk about that whiteout."

He wasn't leaving. Sara straightened her brush on her mirrored art-deco dressing table, then pushed a silver dish holding hairpins a few inches over. She debated telling him something she couldn't stop thinking about. At least if she said it out loud, she could hear how ridiculous it sounded, and then she could stop wondering if it could even be a possibility.

"I think you know that I'm responsible for the whiteout," Sara said flatly, removing the diamond-studded gold hoops from her ears and placing them in a crystal bowl. "I was too embarrassed to admit my deficiency to Duncan Edge."

Jack took up a great deal of space. The room was

predominantly white, making him appear larger and darker and a lot more dangerous to her peace of mind. Oh, hell. He'd be dangerous to her peace of mind if he were in the middle of the Grand Canyon.

"It's not a deficiency, Sara. It's lack of practice or the willingness to try." He lifted his head an inch so he could peer at her over the well-defined muscles of his chest and abs.

Sara closed her eyes briefly, regretting her confession. "I can't risk *trying*. When I'm—" Damn. She shouldn't have brought this up. It had nothing to do with their assignment, and she'd promised herself to keep things impersonal.

"Because when you're . . . ?"

She sat down on her padded dressing-table stool facing him. "When my emotions are high, my powers tend to go on the fritz," she reminded him. "I've told you about this, Jack. Don't you remember?"

The unpredictability of her powers was just one of the reasons she didn't like to use magic for anything other than fun, simple things, like changing clothes with a thought, or shimmering short distances for expediency. She tried never to teleport, the longer version of shimmering. Too much could go wrong.

His eyes kindled. "Practice would certainly help with that. But *this* wasn't your doing. None of the examples you gave me bore out the theory that your powers are affected by strong emotion." He sat up on one elbow. "However, I do believe that something, or someone, caused that whiteout. It's the why of it we need to figure out. And, like Edge said, we need to determine whether that has any relevance to what we're looking for."

Sara rose from the stool. "I don't see how it could possibly be related to dead wizards, or rainbows, for that matter," she told him, walking to the window. She held the filmy white sheers out of the way. The ever-present sunshine bathed the garden in the incredible hues of Technicolor. Backed by the lush green of the jungle only a few hundred yards away, the manicured garden filled with almost fluorescent-hued flowers was a view she never tired of.

A small flock of scarlet macaws swooped in, their rainbow-colored wing and tail feathers spectacular in the sunlight.

She turned away. Rainbow-colored snakes. Rainbow-colored birds. Myth and reality. "The one incident alone is enough evidence to support my theory."

He pushed himself up, shoving several pillows into the small of his back. "Hell, sweetheart. You can't still believe you caused the fire that killed your parents? We got copies of all the police and insurance reports. Pored over every page, every notation, every photograph for days. And you and Baltzer had done it before me. I thought we proved to you conclusively that it was an accident. Nobody caused the fire. Especially not you."

Sara hadn't forgotten that day. It had turned from shit to sunshine because Jack had been with her. He'd obtained every report he could get his hands on. They'd read and reread them one rainy day at home in Tahoe. He was right. They hadn't found anything any of the investigators had missed. They'd ended up naked in front of the living room fire, making love as though their lives depended on it.

He'd proposed to her the next day. Sara hadn't believed her own capacity for love until she'd fallen for this scruffy geologist who'd claimed to love her more than he'd ever loved another human being. Six months later, they'd hated each other's guts. Thank God they hadn't gone through with the wedding; the divorce would have been brutal.

"It was due to faulty wiring," Jack insisted. "An accident—a hideous, life-changing accident. Nothing more nefarious than that."

Still, she knew there was something missing from those official reports. Something that none of the investigators could have seen or known: her attempt to teleport her parents to Timbuktu because she—at that moment in her life—hated them as only a teenage girl could.

"I could read ten times as much paperwork, and I'm telling you—I had a monster of a fight with my mother before school that day. I refused to speak to her all afternoon, refused to eat dinner with them, and sulked in my room until I went to bed. If it wasn't for Grant, I would have died in the fire with them."

"Maybe you're mistaking regret that you and your mother didn't make up for guilt. Do you even remember what the fight was about?"

Sara rubbed her temples with her fingertips. "I think I've just blocked it out because that day was so horrendous."

"It was a terrible thing to happen, but it's totally changed who and what you are." He was sitting up now, completely focused on her, his voice the gentle, comforting sound she'd come to depend on, the voice she still missed.

"Of course it did! I was barely thirteen. My entire life was turned around by their deaths."

"And because of that, because you think that emotion adversely affects your magic, you ignore half of who you are."

She glared at him. This part, she didn't miss. At all. "I'm one-hundred percent who I am. I just choose not to use magic."

"Even though half of you is Aequitas?"

"The other half of me isn't." Her father had been a wizard, but he wasn't Aequitas. She pressed her temples with her fingers again as a sharp, insistent pain made her bite her lower lip.

"Come over here. Let me see what I can do about that headache."

She hesitated. In the old days, his hands were all that could stop the hideous headaches that developed whenever she thought about her past. Torn between wanting to safeguard her heart and wanting Jack to work his magic, she walked over to the bed, sat down, and presented her back to him. Dropping her head, she closed her eyes as Jack moved behind her, his hard thighs bracketing her hips. The brush of his fingers against her nape made her tense her shoulders in anticipation. "Relax," he murmured, stroking his palm soothingly around her nape. A deep shiver traveled down her spine as he brushed her hair aside.

"This is what always happens when you try too hard to think about it and make sense of what happened." His thumbs moved with firm, gentle pressure up the sides of her neck.

Sara wanted to hum with pleasure as his strong fingers kneaded the tight tendons. The delicious sensation shivered all the way to her bare toes. "It's frustrating not to have all the . . . pieces." God, that felt good. She allowed herself to sink into the sensation of Jack's hands on her for just a few more moments.

She smelled him. The starch in his shirt, and a subtle male smell that was all Jack. Her toes curled against the fluffy texture of the flokati. She found the smell of Jack's perspiration an aphrodisiac. His pheromones didn't just call softly to her pheromones; they stood on a mountain-top and yelled her name.

And even now, when she least wanted to be attracted to him, she was turned on by the familiar scent of his skin and the arousing slide of his hands on her bare nape. "Yeah," he murmured, his fingers moving to her shoulders, manipulating the trapezius muscles, searching and destroying knots of tension, gently but firmly. He knew her body so well, Sara thought, taking a deep, shaky breath. "It must be frustrating," he told her, his breath warm on her neck. She imagined his lips following his fingers, warm and tender, trailing soft kisses across her throat. He'd turn her face up to his—

"But fighting to remember something you've

obviously blocked out is counterproductive. Baltzer was there, right? Maybe there's something he knows that he might feel you're ready to hear now. It's been twenty years." He shifted her head to one side and drew long, deep strokes along the length of her neck.

"He says not," Sara murmured, eyes closed. In a moment she'd get up and walk away. Both mentally and physically. What had happened last night was an aberration. She knew it, he knew it. As long as they didn't both think of the same highly charged sexual moment in their shared past, they wouldn't find themselves unwilling participants in duplicating the experience now.

They were no longer lovers. They weren't even friends.

She felt the pull of his touch deep inside her womb. Her nipples ached for his touch. It would be so easy to turn in his arms. To push him onto his back. To imagine them naked, and to position herself over him . . .

"I asked him about it a couple of weeks ago," she said too quickly. Think about the wallpaper for the lobby of the Cali property. Think rainbow snakes. Think Jack's skin rubbing against hers . . .

Think of my dead parents. That was an effective bucket of ice water on her lusty thoughts. "He just repeated what I already know." She lifted her head and looked toward the window, trying to focus on the blurs of greens and crimson through the sheers, and not on the tactile torture and bliss of his hands. "My parents had a dinner party. Grant and his girlfriend were just back from Paris and spent the night. The fire started in the living room. The gas jet beside the fireplace malfunctioned and exploded.

Grant managed to get his friend and me out. His girl-friend had third-degree burns. My parents died. My dog died. The house was a total loss. Everything I loved was gone in the blink of an eye. End of story."

She didn't want to think about it anymore. Fire was her power to call. Fire had taken away everything she cared about. The guilt she felt was staggering to this day. Not only did thinking about it always give her a hellish headache, but thinking and not remembering was frustrating. And scary.

"Grant thinks my powers go crazy because I didn't go to wizard school and didn't learn how to control them." Jack's fingers traveled down either side of her spine with exactly the right pressure. "Instead he sent me to boarding school in London."

"He doesn't like that you have powers."

"He knows I'm not properly trained and that some-times when I use my powers, things don't go exactly as planned. And, yes, I know he feels uncomfortable when I use them. Big difference."

His breath was soft on the back of her neck. Goose bumps rose on her skin. She jumped to her feet. "That felt great," she told him brightly, striding to the open closet. "Thanks." She unhooked a baby pink toweling robe from behind the door and bundled it in her arms to conceal that her nipples were hard and erect. Her knees felt like overcooked spaghetti. "I'm going in to take my shower. When I come out, you'd better be gone."

He leaned back again and quirked a dark eyebrow. "Why don't we talk about what just happened instead?"

He saw too much. "Why don't we—*not*."

Her cell rang.

"Ignore it."

She skewered him with a look, then picked up her phone from the dressing table. The mirrored surface showed that her hand was shaking. "I have regular business hours, Jack."

"They'll leave a message."

Sara ignored his high-handed order. "Hi, Carmelita, how are y—"

Jack rose from the rumpled bed and stalked toward her, barefoot. Beneath his khaki pants, his erection was unmistakable. "Tell her you'll call her back," he instructed thickly.

Sara backed into the table and braced a hand on the shiny surface for balance. She looked away from the heat in Jack's eyes so she could concentrate on Carmelita's hysterical words. "When? . . . Teleport. . . . Yes, right now! Get out of the house. I'll be right there. I'll find you. Go!"

Jack's voice changed as he halted a few feet away. "What is it?"

"There's an earthquake in the village. My God, I don't feel a thing—do you?"

"Localized." He grabbed her hand. "Stay here. I'll find her."

"She and Inez won't teleport and leave their friends behind."

"Shoes."

⁂

THE SECOND SARA SHIMMERED hiking boots onto her feet, Jack teleported them directly to the center of the village. A great rumbling, like a subway train shooting past beneath their feet, shook the ground just before they were flung against each other as the earth buckled and heaved. Towering jungle trees swayed, monkeys screamed and chattered, and, with a cacophony of shrill cries, birds shot into the air like buckshot. Then, just as suddenly, there was a moment of eerie silence, as if every animal had at the same moment been wiped out of existence.

Jack grabbed Sara's arms to steady her as he tried to assess the situation in a sweeping glance. Blocking out the shrieks of animals and people, the grind of falling rocks, the creak of trees ripped from their moorings, he concentrated on the visual of the disaster.

Without a Mercalli intensity scale, he guestimated the intensity of this second shock as close to six on the Richter scale. "Brace yourself," he told Sara, releasing her arm. "Earthquakes come in clusters. The main shock was probably a six-point-five or a seven, so the aftershocks are going to be strong. And the animals just went quiet, so an aftershock is coming. Stay the hell away from the buildings."

The words were barely out of his mouth when another roll of the ground sent them to their knees. A wall of the mud brick house closest to them began to wave, then buckled, sending down a shower of mud bricks. He moved to cover Sara, casting a shield over them both. The bricks bounced off with dull thuds, but he sensed every one of them as they tried to punch through the shield.

The earth roared and bucked like a living animal fighting to get something off its back as it shot upward, sending Jack flying backward and knocking the breath from him. Sara piled into him, landing an elbow square in his gut.

Screams pierced the air, drowned out by the deafening grind of rock against rock and falling debris. But loudest by far was Sara's scream of terror in his ear, making his heart nearly stop.

He held on to her as though his entire existence depended on it. "Stay with me! Just stay with me. It's almost over," he yelled over the noise.

Sara burrowed closer to him. Jack strengthened the shield. Goddamn. Why couldn't she be thinking about Switzerland right now? Or Tahoe? Even Greece? Anywhere but the epicenter of an earthquake.

And just as suddenly as it had begun, the aftershock stopped. Rolling Sara on top of him to protect her back from the hard ground, he wrapped his arms around her, pulling her head down to his chest.

"Stay put." He waited, counting off five minutes, then six, seven. Just to be sure.

Macaws began to squawk, monkeys whooped, and he heard the groans and hysterical chatter of dozens of people. At last Jack released her, and they got to their feet slowly. He glanced around. The houses—fortunately all one-story—on the left side of the dirt road were now fifteen feet down a crevasse where the ground had opened, a giant split seam in the earth, and swallowed them whole.

"*Carmelitaaaaa!*" Sara amplified her voice to be heard over the cracking of branches and the thuds of falling bricks. "*Ineeez?*"

"*Sara! Gracias a Dios! Estás bien?*" The two women came charging out of the jungle, flinging themselves at Sara in a flurry of arms and voices as they talked over one another.

"I'm going to do a void space search," Jack told her when the women broke apart. "Look around and see what you can do to help."

Sara spoke rapidly in Spanish to the two women, then turned back to him. "They think just about everyone ran for the jungle when the earth started moving."

Jack had understood the conversation just fine. "Yeah, but there are some people down in that pit. I heard screams when the fault cracked open. Look, let's teleport everyone we can off the fault line, then look for any injured. How far is the next village?" he asked Inez.

"Seven or eight miles. They will welcome us there."

"All right." Jack's voice was grim. "It's going to take a hell of a lot of juice." He took Sara's hand. "Ready?"

Her hand felt small in his. He'd always thought of Sara as an Amazon, never vulnerable or weak. Never afraid of anything. For Christ's sake, she manhandled a giant boa like it was an evening wrap. Her hand was clammy and cold in his. He squeezed her fingers.

Her eyes were huge and dark as she glanced up at him. "People, livestock, houses?"

"In that order." His fingers tightened around hers. He imagined the villagers materializing in the larger village. He visualized everyone safe and whole. Then he poured all his power into combining his magic with hers. It was different this time from when they had spontaneously teleported Alberto. Maybe it was the conscious effort, but the fusion felt stronger, and he got a fleeting sense of untapped reserves of power in Sara. Then it was over.

"It worked."

The sudden quiet made the remaining buildings seem like a jungle ghost town, except for the snort and squeal of a few pigs and the clucking of chickens.

"Great," she said briskly, trying to tug free of his hold. Jack tightened his fingers around hers, making her frown up at him. "Let's get their livestock and homes to them, then go and check on everyone."

"Whoa." "What's going on in that head of yours?"

She disengaged her fingers from his and stepped out of reach. Her agitation set off warning sirens in his head. "Nothing. I want to check on—"

"You think this happened because we had the hots for each other back at the hacienda?" *Hots* was like saying a plinian volcanic eruption was a freaking campfire.

"I don't know. Maybe." She wouldn't meet his eyes.

"Not maybe at all. This was purely scientific. The release of stored energy deep inside the earth radiates in seismic waves," he explained calmly. He tilted her head up and waited until she looked at him, his gaze holding steady with hers. "The lithosphere—that's the outer layer above the earth's asthenosphere—is a patchwork of slow, constantly moving plates that push and rub against each other. That stress causes movement in the weaker, overlying crust. It's as simple as that."

"TMI, Jack. I don't care what caused it right now. I just want to see that my friends are all right. Let me go."

He wasn't going to change her mind, at least not now. He released her. Watching her stride off and pick her way around the debris, he shook his head. Where the hell had she gotten this idea that her powers were, a. malfunctioning and, b. responsible for a fire and an earthquake, plus whatever other natural disasters she ran up against?

Sara's powers appeared to be fully operational. And she seemed to have control. He was somewhat surprised to realize that, once again, their magic worked better when they were physically connected than when they were apart. Granted, they were still on the leyline he'd discovered running through the hacienda and the village, but he felt it was more than that, something deeper.

Edge might be right about them being Lifemates. *Might* be. Jack wasn't sold on the idea. They'd tried being together. It hadn't worked. Hell, it had been a fucking disaster.

Jack wondered what happened to Lifemates who chose *not* to be together. And realized he hadn't heard one single story about that. Not one. Then he wondered why not.

～ Eleven ～

Carrying a lost, sleepy toddler on her hip, Sara watched Jack help an elderly couple draw water from the well in the town square, then carry it away down the street. The meager light cast three long, eerie shadows on the cobbled road. Dark came quickly in the rain forest, and while the sky above the tree canopy was a deep navy, beneath the thick leaves it was fully dark.

A few lamps along the rough stone street burned little circles of pale yellow, but almost everyone was safely inside. The villagers, many of whom had friends or relatives among the people rocked by the quake, had opened their homes to the evacuees.

Sara, Jack, Carmelita, Inez, and several of their friends had worked tirelessly, helping families reunite in the chaotic aftermath. The hours had passed in a blur of activity—finding lost goats, helping get food and water, and doing basic first aid for minor injuries.

Sara couldn't remember having eaten anything. Carmelita had brought her coffee what felt like years ago. She'd taken a sip, then left the cup somewhere when she'd responded to a call for help.

Now, other than the little one who was wilted against her body, her damp little head buried against Sara's throat, everyone seemed to be okay.

It felt good to be needed.

The shower Sara had desperately wanted hours ago was now a necessity. She was sweaty and filthy, and her clothes were ready to walk themselves into a laundry hamper.

Sara scanned the road for Jack. He'd first caught up with her as she'd helped set up a triage area for the people who'd been hurt. Fortunately, the doctor who'd been treating Alberto was in the village visiting his grandmother. Dr. de Canizales had indicated with a flip of his chin who required basic first aid and who needed the hospital. He and Jack had quietly teleported those people to San Cristóbal without fanfare.

She and Jack had worked for hours, sometimes together, sometimes apart, always aware of one another. Between them they'd helped everyone make a connection, get a meal, and find a place for the night. But they hadn't spoken in hours.

She'd been grateful when he'd ambushed her to spray her with insect repellent, his small grin acknowledging that she had totally forgotten her own needs while taking care of everyone else. She couldn't stop an answering smile. He'd winked and gone on to hose down the next person.

How did Jack manage to remain so damn charming in the midst of a crisis? She tended to retreat behind a wall of feigned indifference that Jack had once described as cold. It wasn't that she didn't care, but that she was frightened of what might happen if she cared too much.

Where was he?

The little girl, probably two or three years old, wrapped her arms tighter around Sara's neck.

"We're going to find your family, honey." Someone in a village this size would surely know who the child belonged to. Sara's heart melted as she thought of the child she'd never gotten to hold. "I promise."

The little wizard in Sara's arms didn't seem to be afraid, but she didn't know where she lived. Sara presumed she'd wandered away with the influx of new people into the village. As soon as the girl was returned to her family, Sara planned on going home. She was exhausted and starving, and that cool, refreshing shower was starting to feel like the Holy Grail.

Insects swarmed around the lights, blocking what little illumination they emitted. The savory fragrance of roasting meat and fried *arepas* made her stomach grumble and almost blocked the fetid smell of the jungle. Keeping the vegetation from encroaching on the small settlements nestled in the rain forest was a constant battle, but these people had been doing it for hundreds of years.

"*Dónde está tu mamá, niña?*" Sara asked the little girl softly. The child hiccuped and gripped Sara's neck so hard it almost cut off her air. Poor baby. Sara dropped a kiss on her dark, matted hair and ran a soothing hand up and down the child's back.

"*Hay mi mamá!*" The child suddenly jerked upright with an excited shriek. "*Mamá!*"

"Dónde, niña?" Sara looked around. "Where, baby?"

The little girl wiggled to get down, but Sara wasn't putting the barefoot child anywhere but in her mother's arms. "Shh. Shh. Show me where, okay?" The child pointed across the street where the jungle had overtaken what might once have been a house. Sara doubted anyone lived there now. The stone walls sagged and most of the roof tiles were missing, although that could be a trick of the iffy light.

Still clutching the suddenly energized child, she crossed the street and eyed the small, dark house dubiously. It didn't look in any better repair up close. "How about if we go and talk to Tia Inez first?"

With a shriek, the little girl tried to launch herself over Sara's bracing arm. *"Mamá! Mamá! Mamá!"*

Sara kept her grip with difficulty, afraid the wriggling child would catapult onto the hard ground. "We'll go and look, okay?" *I am absolutely not going inside this death trap.* Six feet from the doorless opening, Sara stopped. A pile of firewood had been dumped against the crumbling wall; the spiderwebs covering the rough logs caught the light and appeared to have been there for ages. Three out of four support beams for the porch overhang were missing.

"Hola?" Sara called, her arms tight around the squirming child in her arms. *"Hay alguien en casa?"*

She leaped back as a small object came zooming out of the window opening and over her head, her heart knocking, praying it had been a bird and not one of the damned vampire bats in the area. The cave where they supposedly hung out was closer to this village than to the other one. She grimaced as she edged closer to the house.

"Mamá!" The excited child pointed to the left of the derelict house, into the darkness of the jungle.

"No, there isn't—*oh.*" A small beam of light, possibly from a flashlight, moved between the trees. "I don't think that's your ma—"

With a shriek of frustration, the child finally wrenched out of Sara's arms and landed with a little thud and a puff of dirt, taking off toward the blackness.

Sara was hard on her heels. She had never had much interaction with children, certainly not wizard children, and the little girl's freefall just about stopped her heart.

The toddler moved fast on chubby little legs, and Sara put on a burst of speed to catch up just as she slipped into the thick undergrowth behind the small house. She reached down to grab the escapee, only to find her hands empty. The child just disappeared.

"Oh, sweetheart. *Now* what do I do?" Teleport to Jack or Carmelita and get help? Follow her through the shrubbery? She couldn't even call the child's name because she didn't know what it was.

Teleport, Sara decided. The more eyes there were, the better chance they had of finding her. Jack could trace the child faster than she could find her in the dark. Touching the sunstone in her right ear, she cast a protective net over a hundred-square-yard area. That should contain her, wherever she was. Those baby legs couldn't go much farther than that.

Just as she was about to shimmer to Inez's sister's

house, Sara noticed the light again—closer and brighter this time. Was the little girl right? Was her mother out there looking for her?

Sara projected her voice toward the light. Behind the beam she could just make out a pale figure moving rapidly several hundred yards away. *"Hola? Está buscando a una niña?"*

No reply other than the sound of a few restless birds shifting in the branches overhead. Sara hesitated, narrowing her eyes to focus on the figure dodging between the trees as if being chased by the hounds of hell.

Definitely a woman. A *naked* woman. Her pale skin caught the beam of her flashlight as her arms and legs pumped furiously, her long blond hair streaming out behind her. Mouth dry, heart palpitating furiously, Sara teleported to get Jack.

"Thank you, Jackson." Carmelita poured Jack a second cup of coffee. Several women were gathering towels and blankets for friends, leaving the two of them alone for a few moments in the small kitchen.

Jack liked Carmelita, but he was damned hungry, and while food had been offered several times, he didn't want to deplete what already had to stretch to feed all the evacuees. It was time to go.

More urgent than hunger was the nagging feeling that Sara needed help. Foolish, really. They were in a tiny village of fewer than a hundred people, all of whom knew each other. Discreet inquiries as he worked side by side with the people had netted him the information that one wizard had died the same way Alberto had. There were no more sick people in the village.

"You are a good boy," Carmelita told him, her plump, lined face sweet and gentle as she patted his shoulder. He could see why Sara loved this woman. Carmelita Santos was the epitome of motherhood, soft, kind, and unrelentingly maternal. "We could not have moved so many people without you and Sara helping us. *Gracias, gracias por lo mucho.*"

It had been a while since he'd been called a boy. Jack covered Carmelita's work-worn hand on his shoulder with his own and gave her fingers a squeeze. "Glad to do it. Will you be all right here in this village?"

Okay, Sara. Where the hell are you? I'm not a hundred yards from where you could possibly be. Come and get me.

"*Claro. Esto no es un problema. Está es mi familia.*" Sitting down opposite him, Carmelita poured herself a cup of coffee, wrapping her hands around the chipped mug. "You have no family, my Sara told me."

Dangerous ground. Jack drank his coffee, then set the cup, covered with parrots, down on the oilcloth cover on the table. "My mother died when I was six. Lupus. My father, a heart attack, when I was twenty-three." He glanced surreptitiously at his watch.

She crossed herself. "Not a good man." Carmelita patted his hand affectionately. "Sara did not tell me everything," she assured him hurriedly.

"He wasn't a particularly good father," Jack said diplomatically. Jackson Slater Sr. had been a militant perfectionist. Unkind, to say the least, and frequently brutal.

No, he hadn't been a good father—but he'd been determined to make Jack a damn good Aequitas. Even if it meant practically killing his only son in the process.

"He was probably a good man," Jack told her, stretching the truth like a rubber band. His father had been harsh, overbearing, and emotionally bankrupt. The only thing that his father had been good at was training him for the day that the Aequitas would be called into service.

Slater senior hadn't wanted a *geologist* for a son. He'd wanted a high-ranking member of the Aequitas Archon to live through vicariously. If it had been possible, he'd've snatched the Slater watch off Jack's arm and been in the front lines himself. "Or at least, he tried to be," Jack murmured, wondering what the hell was taking Sara so long.

"He had no patience with children. I don't think he ever wanted kids. Now my mother"—his lips smiled, but his gut wrenched—"my *mother* wanted to fill the house with children. But, unfortunately—or fortunately for my father—I was an only child."

The other women came back into the kitchen before Carmelita could turn on the interrogation lights and stick bamboo shoots under Jack's fingernails. He got to his feet, carrying his mug to the sink. "I'd better look for Sara."

"She knows to come here," Inez told him, taking the mug out of his hand before he could rinse it himself. "Go sit. I'll give you some supper."

"Thank you. Another time. Sara should've been here by now. I'm going to go find her and take her home."

After hugs good-bye, which Jack tolerated with admirable patience, he went back to the town square. No Sara. He frowned. Where was she?

EVENING CHANGED TO BROAD daylight between one heartbeat and the next. "What the—" Sara stopped dead in her tracks, blinking into the unexpected brightness, and shaded her eyes with her hand.

How had she walked so deep into the forest without realizing it? She turned in a circle to orient herself. She couldn't see the broken-down little house or the village.

The heat-released fragrances of foliage and ginger flower saturated the heavy air. Filtered sunlight streamed through the leafy canopy, catching in droplets of moisture on the leaves and blades of grass underfoot. Birds chattered in the branches, and the musical hum and buzz of the ever-present insect life made a backdrop to the quiet music of the rain forest.

A few moments ago the air had been relatively cool, but now it was hot, humid, and still. The drenched heat pressed down on her like a wet electric blanket.

Run! a voice in her head shouted. *Don't stop!*

Go. Go. Go.

Keep running!

Disoriented, Sara followed the primitive directive screaming inside her. She started to run. From whom or what, she had no idea. Where was the child? Where was the mother?

Sharp branches slashed her bare legs and snagged in her hair, yanking until her eyes watered with pain.

Don't stop. Don't stop. Don't stop.

Something bounced on her chest. A cord. A thin leather cord. *"Madre de Dios. Ayudame. Por favor. Ayudame."* Her voice sounded high-pitched, scared, young.

Run.

Faster. Oh, God, he was going to catch her. Couldn't let him catch her.

Where was her amulet? Had he stolen it before he cornered her? She *needed* her amulet. She had no protection without it. She wrapped her fingers around the empty cord as she ran.

"What amulet?" Sara panted, feeling as though she were in an alternate universe. She shouldn't be this winded, shouldn't be huffing and puffing like this. It was hard to pull the thick, damp air into her heaving lungs. Several gangly, long-haired spider monkeys swung hand-over-hand from branch to branch above her, their curious pink faces observing her every step like spectators to a marathon.

Run. Faster.

Iridescent birds were flushed from their hiding places as she passed through the understory, squawking in a flurry of wings as they fled.

Faster.

Her bare foot slammed down on a sharp rock. Pain radiated up her leg. She stumbled, grabbed a tree trunk to prevent herself from sprawling face-first, then righted herself and hauled ass. Sara considered herself in pretty good shape—*gym* shape, not jungle-running among tree trunks, head-high ferns, and leaves the size of a car shape. Heart pounding hard enough to explode, Sara ran, her breath sawing frantically from her overburdened lungs. Sweat dripped and stung her eyes.

A branch slashed across her left hip, sharp as a whip. "Ow, hell!" No sound came out, her mouth was too dry. Slapping her palm over the cut, she kept going, glancing down at the injury as her legs pumped and her bare feet flew over the ground.

She was naked.

Her lacerated skin burned from hundreds of small slices; the cut on her hip oozed a thin line of blood. Coffee-colored skin. Not *her* skin. More meat on her bones. Bigger breasts. No polish on her fingers or toes. Bottle-blond hair whipping around her arms and shoulders.

Not her. But her.

She *was* in a damn parallel universe. The question was: whose?

Magic.

Not her own.

Touching both earlobes, Sara realized that for the first time in memory she was *not* wearing the small sunstone studs her father had given her for her fifth birthday. Her magic could work without them, she supposed, but the crystals in her ears were used for one thing, to amp her powers when necessary. Just like Jack used that big-ass watch to amp his.

She tried to teleport, the most basic magic a wizard could perform. She stayed exactly where she was, running through the jungle for her life. Foe unknown.

Her heart hurt inside her chest as she exerted herself

beyond her endurance. This was crazy. She didn't want to be naked, and she sure as hell didn't want to be running as if her life depended on it.

Whoever the woman was, she was running without purpose, without direction. Blindly terrified. Possibly with cause.

Sara tried to think. For the first time she heard whatever it was directly behind her. It was loud and large as it crashed through the foliage. It was perhaps a hundred feet behind her, and closing in fast.

Man or beast?

The woman was petrified. Sara was pissed.

What was the plan? For her to run until she couldn't run another step? Until her heart gave out? Then what? She'd be raped? Killed? This chase seemed like overkill. If a man was bent on rape, this seemed like a hell of a lot of work. Surely there was easier prey to be had?

If, as she suspected, it was an animal, she should probably scale a tree. Easier said than done. Because of the scarcity of sunlight in the understory, branches tended to be high up. And she wasn't sure this was the appropriate time to learn to climb a tree.

Screw this. No more running. She stopped, her breath harsh in her ears. Panting like a freight train, she turned around. No luck in her attempt to materialize some clothing. Fine. Whoever the hell it was out there wanted her naked. She'd pretend to be fully dressed. The emperor's new clothes.

It, he, wasn't getting within arm's length of her. Or this body.

The ground was littered with fallen branches and debris. She scanned her surroundings until she saw a small log, easily four feet long, crooked in the middle, but nice and solid. She bent and snatched it up, gripping one end in both hands, holding it over her shoulder like a baseball bat. It was heavy, and she gave it a couple of experimental swings. She wouldn't have to be accurate to inflict some damage.

"Come out, asshole, whoever the hell you are." She hoped she sounded a lot more confident than she felt. Spreading her bare feet in the spongy ground for balance, she waited. "Let's see you." Some of the delivery was lost because she still couldn't quite catch her breath.

And because she was scared. Really scared.

Something crashed through the undergrowth, making her flinch. A strange, unrecognizable sound—something between a sibilant hiss and a hoarse roar—made goose bumps rise all over her body. Branches lashed and snapped overhead, causing the sunlight to ebb and flow over the area where she stood; it felt as if she were underwater. Leaves dropped around her like green butterflies.

She held her ground. But right then her conviction that she needed to bring this to a head sooner than later didn't sound like such a good idea.

She was naked and, other than a big branch, defenseless in a rain forest filled with dangers of every kind— animals, human predators, snakes, insects, poisonous vegetation.

She needed help, and she needed it fast.

If Jack had heard her all the way in Australia when she *hadn't* called him, surely he'd hear her now when they were in the same country and she *was* yelling his name.

"Jaaaa—"Her voice died and her eyes went wide.

OhmyGodohmyGodohmyGod.

Impossible—

The snake's upright body blocked the trees as its back end slithered to catch up, coiling behind it. At first it looked an almost iridescent black, but as the sun's rays struck it Sara saw its true colors: red, blue, green, yellow. *Rainbow*-colored markings. Her eyes went wide and her heart seemed to stutter to a terrified stop.

Sarulu.

The snake's scales, each bigger across than a dinner plate, glistened in the filtered light pouring through the canopy. At first all Sara saw was the enormous body, easily six or seven feet across, curved upright in front of her like a vast, smooth tree trunk reaching for the sky.

She took a faltering step backward, feeling the rough bark of a strangler fig tree against her naked butt. She couldn't take her eyes off what must surely be the biggest snake known to man.

How long is it? she wondered wildly, noticing the fat *mountain* of coils behind its body. Two hundred feet? Three? She couldn't see its head, but she figured it was up there somewhere. This was one hell of an anaconda.

With barely a thought at the how and what of using magic, she blasted the snake with an enormous ball of fire, ten feet across and blazing hot. She felt the vibration and blast-furnace whoosh of superheated air as it shot from her toward the snake, felt the burn all the way down her naked body.

Her eyes stung and her nostrils burned. But the damn snake just hissed and swayed. The flames didn't appear to have any impact on it. She shot another ball of energy-charged fire at the silky body in front of her. Faster. Hotter.

The snake didn't so much as flinch.

Using the fingertips of one hand, keeping a firm grip on her weapon with the other, Sara felt her way around the wide tree, just as the triangular head curved down from twenty or thirty feet above her head. She froze as it came closer and closer.

Ssssaraaaaa. Yellow eyes the size of platters with elliptical pupils gleamed metallic gold as it ducked its head lower to look right at her.

She barely breathed when it stopped a dozen feet away. Eye to eye with the monstrous reptile, Sara screamed inside her head, *Move! Move, damn it!*

With a sound of flapping wet leather, the snake opened its enormous mouth, exposing needle-sharp, curved yellow teeth lining the shiny, pinkish-white interior. A spiral of red, sulfurous smoke drifted from the giant mouth to hang over the snake's head in a diaphanous red haze.

Ssssaraaaaasaraaaaa.

Lord. It sounded as if the damn thing was calling her name. Its mouth was big enough for a person to stand in. Sara voted not to be that person. It would swallow her whole with no problem at all. The snake was so grotesque, so pee-in-your-pants freaking *huge* that if it did swallow her, her carcass wouldn't even leave a bump in its enormous body. Like the missing girls, she'd be another statistic.

Its guttural, hissing roar froze her marrow.

Move! Gogogogogo.

The snake's three-pronged, rainbow-colored tongue lashed out, all ten feet of it, licking Sara's bare skin from ankle to chin. *Sssssssaraaaa.*

Cold. Heat. Ice. Fire.

The rough bark of the fig tree pressed into her spine. She flung her head to the side as one prong of the snake's triple-forked tongue slithered across her throat. At the same time, another prong circled her breast, teasing her nipple.

She gagged, as a prong slid between her legs, her skin creeping in a vain attempt to distance herself. *Do something! Anything.* What, for God's sake?

Fire was her power to call. She hadn't even *tried* to use it in years. Yet those fireballs had appeared without effort, and really—how much worse could the situation possibly be?

She shot a couple of lightning bolts; the first one went wide, but the second struck right between its eyes. Its head reared back as the pure white zigzag of electricity struck, but it didn't release its hold.

Sara went stone cold as nausea welled inside her. She knew it wasn't sexual—it couldn't be. But it *felt* like an invasion of her body.

Run.

She couldn't breathe. Couldn't move. Couldn't think beyond blind terror.

Snap the hell out of it, Sara Jeannette Temple!! she screamed in her head, eyes riveted to the golden elliptical pupils of the snake as it watched her.

The branch. She still had the heavy branch. *Hit the damn thing!* With a howl of rage, Sara swung the branch with all her strength. Incapable of aiming, she just put her weight behind the swing and whacked whatever she could reach as hard as she could. The hell with clothes, what she wouldn't give right now for a nice sharp machete.

A lucky blow caught it where its tongue forked. Sarulu reared back its head, making an unimaginable noise, and blurring her vision with another cloud of foul-smelling red smoke.

Coughing, eyes burning and tearing, Sara hit out blindly. Half the time she didn't even connect, but half the time she did. Sarulu uncoiled and slithered closer, seemingly unaffected.

Terror-induced adrenaline flooded her body. Sara turned and ran blindly. All that mattered was that she put as much distance as possible between herself and Sarulu.

The snapping and cracking of tree trunks and branches meant the monolithic snake was right behind her and closing fast.

Sssssssarasarassssara.

Lungs exploding, sweat blurring her vision, Sara felt more than the intense primitive urgency to elude her predator. Hundreds of tiny hummingbirds catapulted out of hiding, missing her by inches.

Zigging and zagging through the understory, she squeezed her body through the narrowest of spaces, between the thickest tree trunks, the most impenetrable vegetation. Anything to slow the snake's progress. Branches cracked and fell behind her as monkeys shrieked and birds and insects added their noisy fear of being eaten to her own. Everything raced to get the hell out of the way.

She saw the mouth of what looked like a small cave up ahead. Oh, God. Was she being herded there intentionally? Dare she risk running inside for shelter only to find herself trapped?

Or was the opening too small for the monster snake? Did she have a chance of hiding until she could manage to extricate herself somehow? Surely she was smarter than a freaking snake. Or maybe Jack would hear her call.

It was her only option.

With all the energy she could muster, Sara screamed Jack's name as she plunged into the dark maw of the cave.

⌒Twelve⌒

Jaaaack!

Sara. Not his imagination. She *was* screaming his name. Worried, Jack realized he hadn't seen her in hours. *No one* had seen her in hours. She wouldn't have left without telling him first.

Hell, maybe she would, he thought as he stood in the middle of the quiet street and did a slow circle, looking for a clue to her whereabouts. The thick ozone-scented air was preternaturally still, heavy with the promise of rain. What little air movement there was touched his skin with hot fingers and barely ruffled his hair.

A sky full of stars was visible here and there through chinks in the canopy, and a waxing gibbous moon flooded sections of the cobbled street, leaving other areas in darkness. The streetlights were nothing more than bug-covered yellow blobs, useless for visibility.

"Where did you run off to, Sara?" Jack closed his eyes, feeling the press of the night jungle surround him. The only sound was the musical flutter of leaves stirring in the humid breeze that had finally picked up a little. No cheeps or growls from the birds or animals.

Too quiet.

Something was out there on the hunt.

Jaaaaaaaack!

In his head, but as clear as if Sara were shouting directly into his ear. "I hear you," Jack murmured, his voice grim as he Trace-teleported, following Sara's wizard signature, as unique as the scent of her skin.

He materialized somewhere darker than night, and instantly produced a high-beam flashlight. Caught by the beam, flakes of mica winked from the surrounding rock face like stars in the night sky.

The crystals were due to the porous limestone, Venezuela was riddled with thousands of similar caves; he'd explored several of them over the years. The small crystal cave, was a domed room, no more than twenty feet by about thirty.

He bisected the area with the light cone, and saw Sara's crumpled form near the back of the cave. Racing over to her, he shimmered the flashlight to a rocky outcropping nearby and crouched by her side.

Lifting her upper body, Jack gently cradled her in his arms. He hated that she felt small and insubstantial. This was Sara, Amazon Woman Supreme; she wasn't supposed to be vulnerable.

She was deathly pale, but that could be attributed to the artificial light. Her eyes were closed, her face sweat- and tearstained. Her clothing was a little dirty and rumpled, but he didn't see any blood anywhere. Jack stroked her damp hair off her face, searching for any evidence of injury, his heart pounding. "Sara?"

Her long lashes fluttered. "Jack?"

"What happened, honey? Are you hurt? Did you get lost?"

Her body jerked in his arms. "Did you see it?" she asked, clearly on the verge of hysteria, which was totally unlike Sara.

He stroked her cold cheek with the back of his finger. "See what? Bats?" More than likely this was one of the caves where the vampire bats roosted, although he didn't smell them.

Her gaze darted behind him, her pupils huge, her expression terrified. "Sarulu."

Sarulu? The penny dropped. "The rainbow snake?" He searched her face again, looking for a head wound, an injury of some kind. He didn't see any blood. Thinking the light closer, he checked her pupils. They dilated just fine, and when she shoved the Maglite out of her face, he put it aside.

Supporting her shoulders on his bent leg, he tenderly probed through her hair for a lump or contusion of some kind. "Do you have a headache?" Had she fallen? Had someone hit her? He found no injuries, much to his relief. "Did you fall asleep and have a nightmare?" he asked gently. That made sense. She must be exhausted after the day they'd had. Hell, he was ready for a shower, a meal, and a comfortable bed himself. But how the hell had she gotten herself to this cave, somewhere out in jungle, in the dark?

"I did *not* fall asleep." She struggled to extricate her-self from his hold. He wasn't about to let her go. She was shaking, her eyes wild. "And I can assure you firsthand—Sarulu is *not* a freaking myth." She shuddered violently, then pulled away to sit up. "Look at the cuts on my . . ."

Jack grabbed her shoulders as all the color drained from her face. He thought she was going to pass out. "Look at what, honey?"

Using both hands, Sara touched her arms, her breasts, her hip, then her legs, searching for—what, Jack had no idea. "I had cuts all over me."

"We'll check in better light, okay?" he murmured soothingly.

Her eyes were huge when she looked up at him. "Are you real?"

"Jesus, honey—" Jack yanked her into his lap and wrapped his arms around her. "I'm very real, and so are you. You had some kind of nightmare or something. A bad one, apparently. But I'm right here, and I won't let you go."

Sara wrapped her arms around his waist, clutching his shirt with both hands. "I'm totally freaked out, Jack."

"Yeah, I see that." He rocked her slightly, feeling the frantic pounding of her heart against his chest and the sweaty dampness of her shirt under his soothing hand. "Shh. I've got you, honey. Shh."

"Take me home," she whispered against his throat. "Please, Jackson. Take me home. *Now*."

Since he was thinking exactly that, at exactly the same moment, they ended up on a wide bed in a cool, dark room.

Sara struggled to sit up, trying to shove his weight

off her. But even if Jack had wanted to, he could barely move. While she shoved with one hand, her other arm was around his neck, and her legs were locked around his waist. He wasn't going anywhere.

"I have to shower, right this *second*."

"Magic or water?"

"Magic now." She shuddered, lying back and tightening her arms about his neck as she buried her face against his throat. "Water later. Lots and lots of lovely hot water. Later."

Jack magically stripped off their clothes, leaving both of them shower-fresh without either of them leaving the bed.

His head lowered, and with a small sigh Sara closed her eyes, parting her lips to welcome him.

He gently cupped her face in both hands, studying her soft mouth, the lush sweep of her dark lashes on her lightly flushed cheeks. Emotion welled up inside him. God, he'd missed her. Missed this. He wanted to deny it, and failed completely.

Sara curled her fingers around his wrist. "Don't . . ." Her voice shook, just enough for him to know she wasn't as sanguine as she wanted him to believe. He wanted to devour her, but for now, a taste would sustain him.

Drawing her up, Jack bent his head, covering her mouth with his. Her lips parted and he tilted her head back a little so he could slant his lips against hers and deepen the kiss, tapping into the deep, passionate core he remembered with every beat of his heart.

He brushed her lips with his in a light, tantalizing

caress, then cupped the warm, silky weight of her breast in his palm, rediscovering the lush curves he'd never forgotten. His thumb moved over her nipple, slowly rousing it to a hard nub.

Sara felt a low hum vibrate deep in her throat. His gentle, rough-skinned hand on her breast felt absolutely perfect. The purr morphed into a small whimper as he kept stroking her sensitive nipple. She wanted him with a desperation that should have set alarm bells ringing in her head. Instead she relished the hungry exploration of his mouth on hers. He nibbled and teased, catching lightly at her lower lip with his teeth, then played over the little sting with a hot sweep of his tongue.

Her breath hitched, but his lips drifted away to stroke a burning path across her cheek, paused over her closed lids, then returned to her eagerly waiting mouth.

She welcomed his tongue, silky-smooth and wet against hers as he tasted her, the subtle strokes and forays made more thrilling by his control. Jack had always been a masterful lover. He didn't plunder. He didn't grab. He savored. And he took his sweet time. Her temperature spiked and her pulse raced with anticipation.

Fine tremors rode through his body as Jack buried both hands in her hair, cupping the back of her head in one palm as he gently teased her mouth. She reciprocated by combing her fingers through the cool strands of his dark hair. She scored her nails gently against his scalp, causing him to draw in an out-of-rhythm breath, but he didn't stop what he was doing.

Jack's body, sprawled half over hers, burned with a

furnace heat. His arms were like steel bands surrounding her. A haven.

He lowered his lips to her throat and whispered, "I want you more than my next breath."

And that breath was gratifyingly ragged. A shudder ran through her body as his mouth crushed down on hers. She slid her open palms up his chest, enjoying the sensation of smooth, hot skin and crisp hair, then rubbed her face against him like a cat. She felt like purring. "Make me forget. Help me, Jack."

His eyes glittered as he stared down, and he murmured thickly, "Beautiful."

Sara cradled his head in her hands. She wished she could pull him around her like a magic cape of protection and safety. Bringing his mouth down to hers, she met his tongue thrust for thrust. His warm fingers closed around the cool globe of her breast. Gliding his palm down to span her rib cage, Jack lowered his head.

The silk of his hair brushed her breasts as he opened his mouth, drawing a peak deep into the hot, wet cavern of his mouth. She let out a cry as he sank his teeth delicately around the tight bud, then stroked it with his tongue. He paused to look up at her. "Don't think of anything but this. Us. Now." His voice was soft, thick with desire. His hands were everywhere. "Lift up. . . ."

He kissed his way back up her exquisitely sensitive skin until his lips were against her throat, and his hand slid purposefully up the back of her thigh. Her legs were still wrapped around his waist, and she lifted her hips in entreaty.

"Now, Jack!"

He brushed his lips around the curve of her ear, setting every nerve in her skin tingling as his mouth traveled to the pulse beating in her temple, then skimmed across her cheek. "Is that an all systems go?" he asked hoarsely against her lips.

She wanted to say something clever and witty, but barely had enough breath to demand, "I want you inside me." And just in case her urgency wasn't coming through loud and clear, she slid her hand down his hip, then wrapped her fingers around his penis.

He was hot, silky, and hard. She stroked her thumb over the head until he groaned, then closed her fingers around him.

"Wait," he murmured.

Jack was a big guy. He had big . . . hands. He slid two fingers inside her, moving them in intense circles, massaging and testing her readiness. Sara shuddered, moving her hips against his hand in jerky, involuntary motions. She was wet, swollen, and desperate, and several stages beyond ready. "Talk about chatty. . . ."

With a huff of laughter, Jack withdrew his hand to position his narrow hips between her spread knees. She had a moment's pause to feel the sheer size of him—there—before he pushed inside.

He hissed out a shuddering breath as he buried himself to the hilt in one powerful thrust, then lay still. And Sara was grateful. The sensation of him inside her was so piercingly sweet, so monumental, that she couldn't move herself.

"Okay?" he asked, voice rough against her ear.

All of her senses were tuned to him; she was absolutely aware of everywhere their bodies touched. Everywhere. She smiled against his throat. "Better than."

"Tighten your legs around me."

"I was getting there," she said thickly as he pushed himself impossibly deeper. She walked her heels up his back, feeling gloriously invaded, and kissed his jaw as he started to move.

Pinned down by his weight, she tightened her legs as he moved his big, powerful body inside hers. She felt alive, supernaturally so as she ached and burned and shuddered in his arms.

The beauty of their lovemaking had always astonished her. Every time it transcended anything Sara could imagine even in her wildest dreams, anything they'd shared before. It always felt new. Their bodies were perfectly matched. Yin and yang. Waves of pleasure crashed and churned until she went blind and deaf, her entire being focused on where they were joined. She was being helplessly urged higher and higher, impossibly higher, as the earth shifted, rocked, trembled, with her at the very epicenter. Her entire body clenched as she came hard.

It might have been minutes or hours, Sara didn't care. Their bodies were glued together, and somehow she had wound up on top, her head on his broad shoulder. His fingers trailed lazily up and down her back.

The drapes were drawn, and it was cool and dark in the room. Jack played with her hair. "Ready to talk about what happened earlier?"

Sara told him what she'd experienced, attempting not to sound insanely melodramatic. But there was no way to make a gargantuan iridescent snake sound even remotely everyday.

"Not that there could possibly be such as thing as a two-hundred-foot snake with a psychedelic triple-forked tongue," she finished. "But however it was done—illusion or hypnosis—I saw what I saw. Hell, I *felt* it."

"I don't know about two hundred feet," Jack said doubtfully. "But the fossilized vertebrae of a forty-five-foot-long snake were discovered last year in Colombia. It's *possible* your snake were one of Titanoboa's great-great-great-grandchildren." He brushed a kiss on the bridge of her nose. "Possible, but not likely. *Titanoboa cerrejonesis* might be related to present-day anacondas and boas, but it lived fifty-eight to sixty *million* years ago. The temperature has changed in those millions of years. A snake can only become so large before its metabolic rate becomes too low to support its bulk. It's almost impossible for a snake as big as you're talking about to live in the current temperature of the rain forest."

"It stood upright"—Sara shivered hard, and Jack tightened his arm around her—"or rather, half of it did. Its head went above the tree canopy. At least fifty if not seventy-five feet. I'm telling you, that thing was at least two hundred feet. It smelled *gross*—sulfur and, I don't know, dead things." She rubbed the hair on his chest absently. "And I didn't imagine the colors. God. I'll never look at a rainbow the same way again."

She dragged in a breath. "Truthfully, now that I'm

home, I'm really not sure if it happened or if, like the whiteout when we almost crashed, it was an illusion."

"It was another illusion," Jack assured her. "Do you hurt anywhere? You said it lashed you with its tongue. Perhaps you crashed into a tree branch and it knocked you out?"

"It did more than lash me with its tongue," she told him grimly.

"More? Like what?"

Now she felt ridiculous, and her skin felt hot, then cold, then hot again. "It . . . felt me up."

"Felt you up?"

"Like this." She took his hand and slid it up between her legs.

"Christ—"

Something heavy crashed to the floor in another room and shattered. Sara actually managed to ignore Jack and listened; who, or what, was out there? She'd had more than enough mysteries for one night.

"Shhh," a woman hissed drunkenly.

"I bought the damn vase. Don't tell me to hush. Who's going to hear us?"

Sara frowned. Who'd come to her wing of the house at this time of night? She bet it was friends of Inga and Ida. She'd have a little chat with them tomorrow.

"Everyone in the neighborhood, if you keep yelling like a damn crack whore," the man shouted. "Didn't you think I might be embarrassed by your behavior tonight? People already think we're a joke. Why'd you let Babs lay one on you like that? Isn't it bad enough that people think you married a guy young enough to be your son? Now they'll think I can't satisfy . . ."

Sara sat up, getting more annoyed by the second. She didn't recognize the voices, and she sure as hell didn't want to hear their marital problems.

"Jack?!" She nudged him with her foot.

"I hear them."

"I so did not let her kish me, kiss me, Malcolm, honey, sweetie, lover," the woman's voice said drunkenly over the unsteady click-click-click of high heels on hardwood flooring. "It was a friendly peck between neighbors. *Everrryy*-body at the partay wanted to kiss her."

"They're coming this way! Hurry. We have to—" Sara whispered, yanking the sheet up.

"Nobody is going to come into your quarters. Door's locked." Jack attempted to strip the sheet off her with his teeth. "Mmm. I love the smell of your skin after sex, you know that?" he said against the curve of her breast, his breath warm on her skin. He always snuggled after sex, and usually fell asleep in her arms. But right now she needed him wide awake.

"Listen," she hissed, prodding him in the ribs with her elbow.

"You were the fucking floor show, Christina," the man yelled. Something metallic clattered to the floor, followed by the high-pitched noise of chair legs scraping across tile, then the tinkle of breaking glass. "You can't even stand up," he snapped, clearly disgusted and at the end of his rope. "Go to bed. We'll talk in the morning."

"Aw, don't be mad," the woman slurred. "Aren't you coming?"

"I don't do sloppy seconds. Or thirds." Something thumped. "Bitch." Something else thumped—Sara suspected the woman's other shoe.

"Fine," the woman shrieked loud enough to wake the dead. "I don't need you. I'll finish myself off with BOB."

"Damn it, Jack," Sara whispered, appalled. "Those people are right downstairs—*downstairs*?" There *was* no downstairs. "Where *are* we?"

"Oh, shit." His voice was laced with amusement as he sat up beside her, scratching his chest.

"Jack?"

"You said to take you home."

"And?"

"Tahoe."

"Oh. My. God," Sara gasped as giggles welled up inside her.

Unsteady, muffled footsteps shuffled down the carpeted landing outside the bedroom. There was a thump, more broken glass—probably a picture off the wall, followed by the woman's quiet, slurred, "Shit, I liked that one."

"You sold the house, didn't you?"

"Yeah." Jack laughed. "You going to teleport like that, or put on some clothes? We have about a nanosecond to decide."

The door handle rattled.

STILL LAUGHING, THEY LANDED in a naked tangle of arms and legs on her bed at the hacienda. With a grin, Jack cupped her face in one large hand and kissed her lingeringly on the mouth. "That was close."

Sara wound her arms around his neck, her heart aching with love for him. "I can't believe we were in someone else's house." *I can't believe you sold the house where we were so happy.*

"In their bed," he corrected, nibbling her bare shoulder.

She cradled his head as he kissed a damp trail down her throat. The house, of course, was his to sell—they'd lived in it together for less than five months—but Sara knew he'd loved it, and done a lot of the renovations himself over the years. She'd loved the house too. Loved Jack.

He drew her nipple into the hot cavern of his mouth, laving the hard bud with his tongue. The sensation shot to every cell in her body, and she hummed low in her throat, eliciting a throaty chuckle from Jack. "I see I still have work to do," he murmured, sliding his mouth to her other breast.

Sara tangled her fingers in his hair, loving the roughness of his chin and the smoothness of his lips against her soft skin.

One moment Sara was ridiculously happy, filled with renewed lust, laughter still fizzing inside her like bubbles of champagne; she didn't want to be anywhere else but right where she was.

Then, as if a curtain had dropped over the sun, her mood shifted. Suddenly and inexplicably, her chest ached, and she felt as though her heart would break. Eyes stinging with unshed tears, she buried her face against Jack's warm shoulder.

She resisted the inexorable tug of despair. Just a few more minutes of happiness was all she wanted. She tried to retrieve the laughter, the lightness, the love, but it was gone. Vanished.

Maybe it was the knowledge that with the sale of the house, her last tenuous connection with the baby was gone forever. When Jack had found out that she was pregnant, he'd been so thrilled, that he'd rushed out and bought a crib the same day. As terrified as Sara had been about her pregnancy, she'd loved teasing him as he put the thing together.

But *she'd* barely done more than choose the color of the paint.

Just because they'd made love in the house they'd once shared didn't mean anything, she reminded herself as Jack's mouth moved down her body. Detached, she felt the stroke and glide of his hands and mouth as if it was happening to someone else

This was a posttrauma sex session. A crazy rush of adrenaline and the very basic need to feel safe. That was all. She couldn't read any more into it than that.

She shifted restively as he started delving his tongue into her sex. "I have to take that shower, Jack."

He looked up, his eyes hot and filled with lust. "Later."

As much as she wanted to stay where she was, Sara forced herself to roll away from him, taking a large, ruffled pillow with her. "No. Sorry." She wished she could shut off her thoughts and just enjoy the moment. But the past hung like a veil of darkness over any future they might have, spoiling the mood.

"I have a business meeting in Lima this afternoon, so I'd better get cracking, or I'll be really late." Only if the shower ran more than five hours, since it was barely dawn. But Jack didn't need to know that.

Jack smiled, but she could tell he couldn't figure out why she'd gone from sizzling to arctic in two seconds flat.

"I'll speed up the process and shower with you." He was gloriously, unashamedly naked. She wondered what he'd do if he knew Harry was sleeping under her bed. She could just see a few inches of the boa's tail under the bed skirt.

Harry was, unfortunately, going to suffer the fallout of her Sarulu experience, because the thought of touching him now gave her the willies. Poor Harry.

"No, relax. It'll be quicker if I shower by myself." Before Jack could respond, she closed the bathroom door.

Showering was one of Sara's favorite things to do, especially when she was stressed. Lots of hot water, mounds of scented bubbles. . . and, once upon a time, Jack.

She showered in record time, then pulled on the apple-green satin robe hanging behind the door on a quilted hanger. Tying the sash, she strolled back into the bedroom.

"That's cheating," Jack said huskily, shoulders

propped up ag[ainst] the headboard. Now he wore jeans, but nothing el[se.] [S]ara wanted to throw herself at him and kiss her wa[y do]wn his broad, tanned chest. She went to sit at her dre[ssing] table instead. Back in the day, they'd been known to [spen]d an entire weekend in bed.

Jack's eyes s[mold]ered. "That robe is clinging to your damp skin, yo[u kno]w."

She picked [up he]r comb and ran it through her wet hair. "You're [na]ked," she pointed out, watching him in the mirror. [He wa]s going through the motions of the game, but she [could] tell his heart wasn't in it. What was going on in his [head?]

God. What [the h]ell was going on in hers? Her mood was flickering [like a] switch. High. Low. On. Off. Hot. Cold.

Narrow-ey[ed, Jac]k leaned forward. "So fair's fair?"

She shrug[ged, th]en gave a little scream, half surprise, half laughter, [as he]r robe disappeared, leaving her sitting there damp and naked. "Now who's cheating?" she demanded, magically removing his jeans at the same time she shimmered onto the bed. Onto him.

Knees on either side of his hips, she held him down with her hands on his chest. "You were saying?" Just as she leaned down to nibble at his lips, Jack grasped her shoulders. Suddenly his expression was anything but loverlike. He looked haggard and beaten.

"Where the fuck did we go wrong, Sara?" he asked, his voice raw. He plucked her hand off his chest and held it in both of his, over his heart. "How the hell did we go from this to shit?"

Sara's heart clutched. "God, Jack . . ."

His fingers tightened around her hand. "Just one moment of honesty in all this, Sara. Please?"

She rubbed her suddenly throbbing temple. "Not naked."

"Fine." He was back in his jeans and added a black T-shirt.

Sara materialized jeans and T-shirt as well, then had to put some distance between them and went to sit on the other side of the bed.

"No." Jack snatched up her hand and tugged her back into the middle of the bed facing him. "You wanna go first?" When she shook her pounding head, he said, "Okay. I loved you, Sara. I've never felt that way about another woman—ever."

"Right." She tried to extricate her hand, but he just tightened his hold. Rather than arm-wrestle him, Sara left her hand in his. "You loved me so much you didn't believe me when I told you what happened. My heart had just been wrenched out, I was a physical and emotional wreck. I *needed* you, Jack. You chose to believe the worst and threw me away. *That's* how we went from this to shit."

❧ Thirteen ❧

I didn't throw—damn it, Sara. You told me flat out that you weren't ready for children."

"Right. I wasn't. But that changed when we found out I was pregnant. It *changed*, Jack. I was scared, but I was also excited."

"You never told me you were anything other than ambivalent."

"That wasn't ambivalence. It was *terror*. I was working through my fear, and I needed time to adjust. People I loved *died*. My parents, my dog . . . I was *scared*. I already had nightmares that I'd be doing some stupid bit of magic and I'd kill *you*, and suddenly I was responsible for a tiny little being." Tears stung her eyes. "I was terrified."

He squeezed her hand, shaking his head, his eyes bleak. "I thought you were pissed off," he said, voice raw. "You should have come to me, told me how scared you were. Hell, the thought of bringing a baby into this world was pretty damned freaking scary for me, too. We could have worked it out. Together." He must've read her expression, because he said, "Take a breath, and don't pull away. We have to sort through this, one way or the other."

Why? They'd said what needed to be said. "I went to see you. Afterward. You told me to go to hell. And I went."

He frowned. "Afterward *when?*"

"Grant finally changed his mind,and persuaded me to give you another chance. I went to Barrow Creek. I couldn't stand that you believed I'd had an abortion."

"Are you saying you tried to find me in the Northern Territory eighteen months ago?" he demanded, incredulous.

"I didn't *try*. I Trace-teleported, and found your camp—why am I telling you this? You were *there*."

"Pretend that I wasn't."

Sara sighed. "Fine. I waited for you all day." Hurting. Emotionally in pain. Alone with nothing but her thoughts and fears for six long, lonely hours. "The second you saw me, you told me to fuck off."

He shook his head. "Never happened."

Sara tugged at her hand. Again, he kept an implacable hold on it. "Are you calling me a liar? Again?" The headache behind her eyes ballooned into a sharp rhythm in time with her heartbeat.

"No." Jack's eyes were narrowed as if he were thinking something through. "But I am seeing a damn pattern of illusions."

She blinked at the non sequitur, rubbing one temple with her fingers. "Illusions?"

"Headache?"

What illusions? Damn it, she needed some aspirin. "I'm fine. Carry on so we can get this over with."

"Tell me about the abortion. I'm not going to say a word until you're done. Then it'll be my turn, all right?"

She shook her head and tried again to pull away. "I can't do this. I really can't."

"Tell me what happened that day, Sara."

She took a deep, unsteady breath. "You were in Australia that week."

"I remember. Setting up to start—sorry. Go on."

"It wasn't a damn *abortion*, Jack. I had a miscarriage. I lost the baby, and you were thousands o-of m-miles away." She was furious to find herself crying, something she hadn't been able to do since that god-awful day. She punched Jack's chest with her free hand.

He captured that hand too. "I saw the doctor's report, Sara. It said abortion."

"*S-spontaneous* abortion. It was an ectopic p-pregnancy—the egg implanted itself in my fallopian tube. I was only thirteen weeks, and I started having contractions an hour after you left." Tears splashed on their joined hands. "My ob-gyn told me to go lie down. But the cramps and pain got worse. When the bleeding started, I teleported to the nearest h-hospital and called you again."

His hands tightened over hers and he held her gaze, his eyes almost black with emotion. "Jesus, Sara—"

"The most common procedure performed to stop bleeding and prevent infection after a miscarriage is a dilation and curettage. I had a D&C, Jack. Not an abortion."

She sucked in a lungful of air to steady herself. "I *wanted* our baby. You made an assumption, Jack. You didn't *ask*. If you loved me, you would have given me the benefit of the doubt."

She looked at him, expecting to see a look of skepticism or doubt on his face. All she saw was pain. After another controlled breath, she continued, "I still couldn't reach you, couldn't even pick up a trace of you, and I called Grant. He came to Tahoe and took care of me. It was hideous, Jack. I was devastated. We tried to call you, but your phone didn't even ring. We couldn't even leave a damn message."

"I believe you. I do. But the paperwork from the hospital didn't say a fucking thing about a D&C or miscarriage, or anything like it."

She shrugged, and the movement made her cry out as her headache intensified. Jack picked her up, turned her around, and started massaging her neck and shoulders. "Tell me about these headaches."

"Headaches . . . why? What do they have to do with a-anything?"

"You get these severe headaches—when?"

"Not that often."

"When you're stressed?"

"No."

"When you think about your parents?"

"Yes. Always."

"When you think about the miscarriage?"

"Yes."

"When you think about me?"

She turned around. "Sometimes."

"Hear me out for a second, okay? I trusted you as I'd never trusted or loved another human being in my life.

Why would I suddenly believe the worst of you, without proof? Without talking about it?"

"Clearly you *didn't* trust me. I don't understand where you're going with this. What are you getting at?"

"I think that Grant wanted us apart. He never liked me, was never happy for your happiness. He did everything, in a very subtle way, to break us apart. And when that didn't work, he used some kind of a mind illusion to drive a wedge between us."

"Oh, for goodness' sake, Jack!" Sara jumped off the bed. Folding her arms tightly against her midriff, she glared at him, the tears drying stiffly on her cheeks. "You *always* do this, use Grant to deflect our arguments. Don't bring him into this again. For the umpteenth time: he is *not* a freaking wizard! So even if he wanted to, he couldn't use mind control over me. Unless he's a secret hypnotist or something."

"What if he's the Omnivatic we're looking for?"

"What?! Sara stared at him incredulously. "What's *wrong* with you, Jack? Why not Pia, or Inga, or William? None of *them* give off a wizard trace—does that mean they're Omnivatics too?"

"He was there when your parents died. He kept you in an exclusive boarding school in England—and away from the wizard community—half your life. You work for him, live with him—"

"You're *jealous*."

Jack leaned forward, intent. "He manipulates you. Preys on your feelings. Keeps you dependent. I believe he used your miscarriage to his advantage. Something that he knew we'd believe like nothing else. Our emotions were high. It was the perfect time to draw from each other's strength. Instead, with a little help from your friend Grant, we turned on one another. He effectively hammered that wedge home."

"He protects me. Too much sometimes. But whatever he does, he does because he loves me and doesn't want to see me hurt."

"Why doesn't he like you to use your magic?"

"Because it has a tendency to go haywire and hurt people." Her voice was tight, her emotions in turmoil. Poor Harry, about to slither from under the bed, made a U-turn and went back into hiding.

Jack stood beside the bed, now wearing his heavy boots. He had a huge knife in a scabbard on his thigh, and a gun in a belt holster. It was a good thing the boa was undetectable, Sara thought bitterly. If Jack would shoot Alberto, he'd sure as hell shoot a snake.

"Grant tell you that?" he demanded sarcastically, tucking in his shirt with force.

"*I'm* living this life, Jackson." She scooped her hair up into a low ponytail. "*I* tell me that. Facts are facts."

"I think Baltzer seeded that idea in your head the moment that fire killed your folks." He walked to the connecting door, and paused. "Convenient to make you believe that your magic killed your parents. It would make you feel like shit, not to mention guilty and dependent. His to manipulate."

"So Grant killed my parents? Destroyed my entire family?" Sara raised one eyebrow. "Stuck me in a fabulous boarding school and paid for an amazing education when he didn't have to? Made me his business partner, with a fat paycheck and spectacular benefits, to do a job I adore? Okay, I'll bite. To what purpose? What does he want?"

"You," Jack said grimly, opening the door between their rooms. "He wants you, Sara."

PISSED, JACK SHUT THE door behind him. How the hell had something so good turned to shit in the blink of a god-damned eye? Again! He leaned against the cool wood and closed his eyes as he went back over his new line of reasoning.

Fact: When they were anywhere other than in Baltzer's fucking orbit, things between them were, if not perfect, then workable.

Fact: The minute they were anywhere near Baltzer, the shit hit the fan. Feelings were inflamed, reason went out the window.

Fact: Whenever Sara started to think about some-thing that might not be good for Baltzer, she got a split-ting headache.

Fact: Sara had been the victim of entirely too many illusions, and all of them somehow connected to Baltzer.

Was he making connections that didn't exist? Jack asked himself. Was he using a man he didn't like to explain away the arguments he and Sara had where nei-ther seemed to win? He shoved away from the door. Damn it to hell. He had no idea.

Knowing that Sara was in the other room, hurting as bad as he was, ripped out his heart. Why was it that he heard her words, believed what she'd told him, yet his emotions insisted that what she told him was a lie? And what about her claiming she'd gone to see him his first week in Australia?

Hadn't happened.

But she *insisted* she'd been there.

Was it possible they were both right?

Were their emotions and reactions being manipulated? Jesus. Seemed farfetched as hell to think Baltzer was as evil as Jack was painting him. But what if . . . ?

He took a deep breath. He had to go back in there. Whether she—or he, for that matter—liked it or not. They'd been instructed to stay together, which meant she was going to have company at her meeting in Lima.

He suddenly noticed a faint buzzing sound, just under the noise of the air conditioner, and glanced around.

The psionic safe was visible when it shouldn't have been without a summons, hovering over the chair beside the window. With a sense of urgency, Jack said the words, and opened it, retrieving the Book from the icy interior.

He was prepared for the weight of it, but not the unexpected blazing heat. "Ow, shit!" He dropped into the chair and let the book rest on his knees, his fingers stinging as if he'd touched a hot stove.

The book opened without fanfare, the pages flipping almost faster than Jack's eyes could see them. "Got it," he muttered, intrigued. "Something big. Something urgent."

The pages stopped moving, and he waited for the words to form. But instead of text, a face hovered half a foot above the papyrus.

Enrique Rojas.

"Sara?!" he yelled, yanking open the connecting door. "We've gotta go to the village. Now! Move it!"

THE MOMENT THEY MATERIALIZED in the village, Sara and Jack saw the crowd clustered nervously outside one of the small houses.

Inez Armato saw them first, rushing to meet them halfway. Her usually neatly braided hair was a wild mess, and she had aged ten years. "Jackson. Sara." She snatched up Sara's hand, then turned and tugged her along. "How did you know—never mind. It is Enrique. He has the *enfermedad*—" She waved her hand as if to erase the word. "The sickness. I was just about to come and fetch you to his bedside."

"He seemed fine when I saw him yesterday," Jack told her, sensing the woman's urgency and fear. The people gathered outside the house parted like the Red Sea to let them through.

Jack didn't want Sara within a freaking mile of the place. "Stay out here," he told her flatly when they stood on the narrow front porch. "Let me go in first and see if—"

"No. I'm coming in with you."

"Jackson? Please, take this inside. And you, Sara." Inez handed them each a small item. Without looking at it, Jack stuck his in his back pocket, and saw that Sara did the same.

He opened the door, then took Sara's hand rather than argue with her and waste time. "Safer together than apart."

They stepped inside the dimly lit interior. "From your lips," she said quietly.

Her fingers felt small and slightly damp in his. *Ah, Jesus, Sara. Please don't catch whatever the fuck this is.*

The one-room house was filled with acrid smoke that hung in a smelly haze about six feet off the floor. Jack coughed as his lungs filled with the putrid stench. The predominant smell was garlic mingled with a dozen unrecognizable herbs and plants, making breathing and visibility tricky. He materialized a paper mask for Sara, and heard her grunt of surprise as it fitted over her nose and mouth.

There was no wizard trace in the room. Not a whiff. Ah, hell. "Señor Rojas?"

"*Ven aquí. Sé rápido,*" the old man's voice trembled, and he hacked a cough that hurt Jack's lungs. "You must hurry."

It took only a few steps to reach the high, old-fashioned bed on the other side of the room. The village elder hardly made a bump under the mountain of covers. Enough light filtered through the closed drapes for Jack to see the elder's flushed face and too-bright eyes.

"Is there anything we can get for you?" Sara asked softly, standing too damn close to the old man for Jack's peace of mind. "Anything we can do?"

The man reached out a gnarled hand. "Jackson Slater?"

Jack took his hand. It felt like nothing more than papery flesh over brittle bones.

"You are Aequitas, *sí?*"

"I am, *señor, sí.* And so is Sara."

"Omnivatics are—" He coughed for several moments. Sara let go of Jack's hand, picked up a bottle of water from the table beside the bed, then leaned in and lifted the old man's head. She held the plastic bottle to his mouth until he'd drunk his fill. Rojas waved her away, his glazed black eyes all for Jack.

"You know of this, *sí?* You know of the great Ophidian's *cometa? Sí,* you would know the date of this event."

"I do." Jack said evenly. "What can you tell me to help me—"

Agitated, Rojas gripped his hand, hard enough to hurt. He started babbling in a combo of Spanish and Latin, so fast that Jack could only catch a word here and there.

"*No entiendo, lo siento.*" Like not a fucking clue what he was saying. "*Ralentizar.* Slow down, all right? Sara and I aren't going anywhere." Although Jack wished Sara would take a walk, or go to her damn meeting, or something. Anything other than stand here beside a wizard about to go ballistic at any minute.

"Open the first *cajón* in the chest over there." Since he was still attached to Jack's hand, Sara gave him an inquiring look, and Jack nodded for her to open the drawer. "Yes. That one, Miss Sara. Please to remove the—" He coughed and gagged. Jack helped him drink more water. "Bring me the two boxes inside."

Sara withdrew two boxes covered in a crystallized fabric that picked up the dim light and threw tiny rainbows of color all over the room. She brought them over and placed them by Rojas's side on the bright quilt. One was less than twelve inches long and about three inches high. The other, covered in the same shiny material, was small, the size of a pillbox.

The old man palmed the small box in his free hand, then nudged the larger one forward. "This one. This one is for the Aequitas. You must take it and go."

Whatever was in the box wasn't a gift, Jack knew. "What do I do with this?" he asked softly.

"*Usted sabrá cuando lo necesite.*"

When you need it, you will know. Great.

"They are working to find a cure for this illness," Jack told him in Spanish.

"And they will be too late for me."

"No," Sara said, also in Spanish, bringing the water back to him. "This sickness takes at least twelve days." "You've just become sick. We still have time."

Rojas wiped his dry mouth, then motioned for her to bring the water closer. Very gently she tilted the bottle so the old man could drink. When he was done, he patted her hand, then closed his eyes and released his grip on Jack's fingers. The open pillbox lay beside his lax hand.

Jack knew he was dead. Whatever Enrique Rojas had just ingested had killed him instantly.

"WHAT WAS IT ROJAS whispered to you back there?" Sara asked as soon as they materialized just outside the entrance to the cave. Jack had insisted that they come back for "just a few minutes."

Against her better judgment, she'd agreed. Thank God the cave wasn't very big. It would take them only a few minutes to walk around the entire chamber.

"They've made a shrine out of this place; check this out." Jack was trailing his fingers over the rock face. "He said he was too old and too weak to be the keeper of the portal."

"*The* portal? Or *a* portal?"

"I think he meant exactly what we think he meant. But we'll soon find out."

Sara stayed where she was beside the cave entrance. She didn't find rock as interesting as he did. "Are you telling me that Señor Rojas claims that *this* little cave is the Omnivatic's portal? The one it travels through to reach their nest in the Pyrenees? My God, Jack. Do you think he's *right*?" It sounded unbelievably farfetched. But then, so had a two-hundred-foot freaking snake.

"Won't know until we check it out, will we?"

"How will we know?" She glanced around the entrance, debating which would be safer, inside or out. "Looks like any other cave to me. Why don't we go and report what we know to the Council? Let *them* handle it."

"I have to check it out and see where it goes, if anywhere."

Sara grabbed his arm. "You're *not* going to follow some freaking tunnel/portal/snake path, are you?"

"Relax. I'm just going to reconnoiter. It's a small cave, shouldn't take more than fifteen minutes. Then we'll go and tell the Wizard Council what we find."

"Okay. But I don't want to be long. I have a lunch meeting in Lima. I don't want you to follow the trail of the snake if it'll take you through some terrifying portal to God only knows *where*. Let the Wizard Council deal with it."

~ Fourteen ~

The entrance wasn't huge, a couple of feet above Jack's head and about ten feet wide when he stepped inside. Big enough for a two-hundred-foot snake to slither into? He shook his head. "There's just no way a snake that huge could fit in here. Which is good. Really good."

While he didn't completely believe that Sara had actually seen a two-hundred-foot-long snake, the thought of one that size was enough to put him into a cold sweat in the middle of a sweltering jungle.

Still, she'd been terrified of *something*. Just to be on the safe side, he'd brought the Sig Sauer and the Ka-Bar hunting knife. He wasn't taking any chances if his powers went on the fritz again. They'd been talking about the myth of the rainbow snake with Duncan Edge; Sara must've fallen asleep, and her subconscious had filled in more details than Jack really wanted to hear about.

He didn't want to have the same freaking nightmare.

The hothouse jungle, alive with noise and movement, grew right to the cave opening. As he stepped outside, the chattering of monkeys, the squeaks of rodents, and the slithering, chirping, and rustling of other creatures assaulted his senses.

Rocks had been placed in an untidy pile six or seven feet high against the outside wall, almost like a religious shrine. To the god Sarulu? Jack stepped up for a closer look. "Come and take a look at all the stuff people have left."

Sara had her back to the cave wall, her gaze shifting across the foliage in front of her. "I can see it just fine from over here, thanks."

Jack turned to inspect the offerings. Among the baskets of brightly colored fruit were candles of various sizes and boxes of matches. So Sarulu could light a candle or two when necessary? Seriously, did a snake need to light up? Jack thought wryly.

The fruit was fresh, as were the gourds of water and small plates of *arepas,* half-eaten by the animals and already covered with insects happily finishing the job. He ignored the buzz of the small bugs close to his face. They were everywhere, and swatting them away didn't make a jot of difference.

"What did Rojas give you?" Sara asked curiously, leaning against the sun-warmed rock face.

"I'll check it out when we get back. I don't want to open it here. In fact, let me send it somewhere for safe-keeping. Whatever it is was clearly important to Rojas." He pulled the box from his back pocket and sent it to the psionic safe, then took a closer look at the display. "This is . . . interesting."

Hundreds of thin leather cords hung from the limestone rock. From each one dangled a shiny amulet, moving slightly in the hot breeze, refracting the sunlight into a kaleidoscope of colors.

"What is it, a mobile of some sort? Look how the prisms make little rainbows on the leaves over there." She pointed. "Pretty but, under the circumstances, creepy."

No shit. Jack lifted a braided cord on his finger, holding the six-inch amulet on his palm. His lip curled with distaste, and he wished he hadn't touched it: while not the real deal, the good-luck charm looked unnervingly like a shed snakeskin. Made of crystal, it had heft to it and was an intricate work of art. Why anyone would find shed snakeskin interesting or beautiful, he had no idea.

"Ah, hell." He reached into the pocket where he'd stuffed Inez's gift and pulled out an identical amulet, sans the leather cord.

She swiveled her attention from the prisms. "What?"

"Inez generously gave us each the same crystal snake-skin amulet."

"Keep it in your pocket." Her lips twitched. "It might ward off bad juju."

"Who gives a fuck about juju? Let's hope it wards off snakes." For a moment their eyes met, and they were in complete agreement.

He returned the amulet on the cord to the rough rocky wall. If these things warded off snakes, he was all for them staying right where they were, blocking the entrance to the cave.

"Let's go in. Keep your eyes open for anything that slithers, large or small." Jack grasped Sara's hand in his and moved toward the entrance.

"Wouldn't you prefer to have someone else, someone more powerful, check this out with you? I bet the Council would send someone," she suggested hopefully, and digging in her heels right inside the entrance.

She cast a nervous glance outside. Bracing herself to see those freaky elliptical eyes watching her? Nightmare or illusion, whatever it was, it had scared her to death.

"I don't have time to call in reinforcements, and I don't have anyone else right now. Who am I supposed to take with me? My butler?" Jack asked, trying to keep things light.

"If he can use magic, shoot a gun, *and* iron your shirt, go for it."

His lips twitched. "I've never considered an ironed shirt a weapon."

Sara bit her bottom lip. "Do you really want me to go with you?"

"Considering my relationship with snakes, and that you think you saw one bigger than a city bus, I think it might be a good idea. I might need you to protect me."

"Don't even joke about it." She shuddered. "Although . . . I *did* blast that damn snake with some pretty powerful fireballs."

"See? Your fire power, my cold powers—we can take down just about anything, right?"

"If you say so. And, FYI—I didn't *think* I saw a gigantic snake chasing me. I *did* see the damn thing. Felt it. And looked into its beady eyes." Her phone rang. Schubert's Unfinished Symphony. Baltzer's ring tone. Just hearing it made Jack want to grab the phone and stomp it to pieces. Hardly mature, but satisfying on many levels.

Grinning, he pulled her closer and kissed her lingeringly on the mouth. "Beady eyes? A *snake*?"

"Yes. Observe." She indicated her body from head to toe. "Full-body shudder, Jackson." His lips came back down, lingering on hers for a few more seconds. When he lifted his head, she touched her fingertips to his mouth.

Her phone was still ringing, but she didn't pull away to answer it, even though they both knew who was on the line.

"Catch up," Jack said softly, then stepped aside.

She dredged up a smile. "Hi, Grant."

She'd put the phone on speaker. "Hi, babe," Baltzer said smoothly. "I'm at the Lima project, want to meet me for a drink later?"

Her eyes met Jack's, and he thought, *Here we go again.* The two men had a tendency to compete for her attention, making her the prize in their unspoken macho rivalry. It was ridiculous, Jack knew. She considered Baltzer more of an uncle than anything romantic. But he'd never been able to suppress a little bit of jealousy when Sara spent so much damn time with the man.

"How crazy is it that we live in the same house and have to make an appointment to see each other in another freaking country?" Sara said with a small laugh.

Baltzer made a sympathetic sound that grated on Jack's nerves. It was all posturing. Had Baltzer ever had a genuine emotion that wasn't self-serving? Jack doubted it. "I don't want to intrude on your reunion with Slater." The older man sounded sincerely apologetic. "But I do miss you, babe. If Jack doesn't object, I'd love to spend some alone time with you."

"Don't be silly," she said, her tone a little sharp. "Jack doesn't dictate who my friends are."

"Where are you? You sound as if you're in a tunnel."

"Just a bad connection."

If he only knew, Jack thought, turning his back to give her some space. She didn't turn the phone off speaker, and there was no way he was going farther into that wall of green to give her real privacy.

"I'd love to get together with you later," she said cheerfully. "I'm coming into town for a late lunch with William and Aarón Guerrero. Do you want in on the meeting?"

"I'll have to pass. I have a videoconference call with the money people in Geneva. Are you taking the Cessna or teleporting?"

"Teleporting is a lot faster, and I have some things I want to clear off my desk before lunch."

"Are you sure that's wise?" Grant asked gently. "With Slater back in the picture, I'm sure your emotions are all over the place. Do you really want to risk teleporting now?"

Sara's emotions were all over the place? Interesting way of tying her emotions to him in a negative-reinforcement kinda way, Jack thought. Baltzer had always had the ability to point out, and emphasize, Sara's limitations. Jack's point exactly. Unfortunately, Sara just didn't get it.

"I'll be careful," she told Baltzer. "I really don't have eight hours to spare to fly there and back."

"Maybe you can meet with William and the architect another time, my dear. Sometime when you *do* have eight hours to spare to travel to a *business* meeting."

"I prefer," she said mildly, "in this instance anyway, not to waste time. Not when there's no need to do so."

"This is *business*, Sara. Slater will have to amuse himself while you work. He does know that you have a job, right?"

Sara rubbed her temple with two fingers. "I'll come to your office at, what? About seven?"

Baltzer switched gears, the annoyance gone from his voice. "I love you, baby, and I'd never forgive myself if something happened to you because I didn't remind you to consider things carefully before you use your powers. Just promise you'll be careful."

"Of cour—"

Baltzer had already disconnected. "And have a nice day," she muttered wryly.

Jack started walking back to her just as an enormous antique lantern, almost as large as Sara, materialized beside her. She sighed.

"Heads up? That's *supposed* to be a freaking flashlight. Still want me to go in with you?"

Jack's lips twitched. "Get rid of it and try again."

A camera flashbulb appeared in her hand next.

"Three tries and you're golden," he promised as she shot him a see-I-told-you-so look.

A large Maglite materialized in her hand. "Eureka!" She brandished it, looking very pleased with herself. "Have weapon, will travel."

They turned to walk side by side through the opening into the cave. "Baltzer was pulling your chain, you know."

She heaved a lugubrious sigh. "Can we *please* agree to disagree? I really don't want to hear any more of this crap about Grant. Leave him out of it. Please, Jack?"

Same song, different chorus, Jack thought bitterly. "Sure." For now. He leaned over and kissed her, because he hadn't in a while. He had to touch her—in case she disappeared again. But he had to be damn careful he didn't get hooked.

What had the Book meant? *All that you seek is here. Here* meaning here inside the Book? Pretty frigging cryptic. Here, as in the hacienda? That could mean he was seeking Sara. Or the truth. Or Grant fucking Baltzer.

All very mysterious. But in the meantime, he had a cave to explore and a beautiful woman, his beautiful woman, to keep him company. Barring the appearance of a snake, Jack was in geologist heaven.

"Listen," he said, pausing for a moment. The cave was much deeper than it had first appeared as they'd turned a little jog and continued on.

"What? I don't hear anything unusual."

He smiled. "That's the good news. No roosting guacharo. That'll make getting back in there much easier, not to mention quieter." The pigeon-size oilbirds usually colonized by the thousands in caves, coming out at night to feed on the abundant fruit in the rain forest. If they were in *this* cave, the noise at their intrusion would be deafening.

"How do you know about oilbirds?"

"I went spelunking with friends a few years back at the Guacharo Caves in the Caripe Mountains in Monagas. The most remarkable sight was at dusk, when thousands of guacharo flew out into the night, screaming overhead in a frantic flurry of wings and unholy noise. They navigate the dark using a primitive echolocation system, like bats."

"Excellent. No birds and, more important, no foul-smelling bird crap to deal with. Hey, you don't see any bats, do you?" Sara pulled her ball cap down tighter over her head.

"Nope." Materializing his own large Maglite, he turned it on, aiming it into the darkness ahead. He pulled out a few toys he'd retrieved from Australia. Time to explore.

Under the optical microscope and SEM, he could see that the masses in the limestone formation were perfectly formed needles of small crystals in en echelon patterns.

He motioned to Sara. "Look at this. See here? These speleothems originated by water condensation and very slow seepage from wall fractures."

"Uh-huh."

"All mineral species form at normal environmental temperature and pressure, but—" He stopped and looked at her, the tone of her reply having finally registered. "You don't give a shit about bedrock constituents, carbonates, or trace minerals, do you?"

Her teeth were very white in the glow from his Mag. "Not so much, no. But it's fun to see you in your natural habitat." She pointed at the wall where the crystals were clustered. "That's pretty, but hardly the find of the century. Unless they're diamonds?" she teased.

His wrist vibrated, and he glanced down. The bezel

on his watch was rotating—confirmation from his own crystal that the small crystal cave was on the same leyline as the village and Baltzer's hacienda. It was a miracle that it hadn't imploded during the recent earthquake, since the fault ran so close to this particular leyline.

The hair on the back of his neck rose. On a hunch, he took his handheld out of his back pocket. "Where did you say Baltzer's new hotels are, Sara? There's one in San Cristóbal, right?"

"Yes. But what—" She stopped talking as he punched in the coordinates for San Cristóbal.

With a rush of anticipation, he glanced up. "How about Colombia? Where was that one again? Cali?"

"No. Santa Marta."

"Can you hold this?" He handed her his Mag so he could use both hands. "Okay. Where else?"

"Guayaquil, Ecuador."

He stared at the string of numbers running across the screen as they kept walking deeper, the two flashlights shining a path into the darkness. "Holy shit. Peru . . . Chile." Jack stared at the stats. If he did the rest of the construction locations Sara had been listing off, he'd bet his last clean shirt they'd fit, too.

"What?"

"They're all on the same leyline."

She paused for several beats. "And we're back to Grant, aren't we?"

"In a roundabout way, yeah. It is all about fucking Baltzer. Because he's always right here between us," Jack pointed out. "He's *always* been an issue between us,

Sara, and you know it. He does everything in his power to keep us apart. I know I've said it before, but now I really mean it: when this is all over, you're going to have to make a choice. Him or me."

"Right now, there is no *you*, Jackson. Or did you forget that? And for the record, giving me an ultimatum like that is patently unfair. It wasn't before, and it sure as hell isn't now. I've known him longer, *loved* him longer, than I have you."

She took a few steps back. "You're asking me to give up my past, my only family, even if it's just a surrogate family. Other people have their families *and* the people they love; why can't I?"

"Because he's constantly driving a wedge between us in an underhanded, insidious way. Because he and I dislike each other intensely. Because, goddamn it, I'm asking you—hell, *begging* you—to choose."

"I'll give you the same answer I did the last time we had this conversation. No. You can't have all the crayons in the box just because you don't want to share."

"I hope to hell that you come to your senses before Baltzer forces everything you give a damn about out of your life so he can have you all to himself."

"Get your mind out of the gutter. My God, Jackson. Grant is like an uncle to me."

"Then you haven't seen his damned eyes when he looks at you. All he needs is chocolate sauce, and he'd eat you with a spoon."

"Shut up, Jack." Her voice shook with anger. "Just shut up."

He was so pissed he didn't notice the steep ledge ahead until his foot went over.

"Jack!" Sara grabbed his arm. "Watch out!"

He corrected his balance, squinting against the beam of light from Sara's Mag. "Put that damned thing away, would you plea—"

The floor at his feet fell away into a drop he hadn't seen. Across the gap, the cave ended at a solid rock face. The mountain was plenty deep enough to support a cave a hundred times this size beyond that blank wall. All he had to do was find a way in.

Christ, he thought suddenly. Was he going nuts connecting dots that really had nothing to do with one another? But what if he was right? Was Sarulu linked to Ophidian? Had he stumbled across the Omnivatic's portal? His heartbeat did double time. He *had* to find a way across the gap. He stepped back and peered down, focusing his flashlight into the deep darkness to see just how far down the drop extended.

Below, the floor seemed to undulate and move. "What the hell is that?"

Sara moved her light to look. He wished she hadn't. She sucked in a scream. "Snakes—hundreds of snakes."

An icy flash of fear froze Jack solid.

The ledge he was standing on gave way.

He tumbled down the rocky, crystal-strewn slope and landed in something soft. And it was moving. Jack yelled. Snakes, dozens of them, writhed and twisted around him, on him, over him, under him. He fought to breathe. Struggled to think.

Above his head, Sara screamed, "Jack! Teleport!"

He was immobilized by fear. As the fucking snakes slithered around him, he sank deeper and deeper; they wiggled over his chest and coiled about his arms and legs.

Fuckfuckfuckfuck!

Sara! Jesus. Sara. The thought of her in danger freed him from the spell, and he tossed a handful of snakes aside. "Get back. Move away from the edge. You aren't going to do me any good if you're down here too." He attempted to shimmer. Nothing. He tried again. Nada.

Damn it to hell. He wasn't going to stick around while he kept trying. He fought his way up from the moving snakes, pulling them off and ignoring the painful bites. Crawling up the slope, he was shaking and sweating, not from mere exertion but from gut-deep fear. It was every bit as terrifying as he remembered from his childhood. Down in the darkness of the ravine, he'd thought he'd die. Now he knew better, but it still scared the hell out of him, and he didn't want Sara anywhere close to it.

He focused on Sara, homed in on the pulsing beat of her heart, her unique wizard signature, and dug into the slope with his bare hands until he managed to get his shit together and teleport back to where she was.

He lay there panting, his feet still dangling over the edge of the cliff and the pit full of snakes.

Sara fell to her knees beside him. "Oh, my God. Jack, speak to me. Are you okay?"

He rolled over. He wanted to puke. "Did I mention I *hate* snakes?"

∞

Sara and William Roe, the company's project manager, sat in a small restaurant across the street from the Lima construction site. Though shorter than Grant, William had warm brownish-topaz eyes and well-groomed light brown hair. Like Grant, he dressed well, but wasn't quite as conservative. His great smile was bracketed by dimples that made him look boyish and trustworthy, both of which he was.

But as fond as Sara was of him, William didn't light any of the fires Grant kept trying to add fuel to.

"Want a drink while we wait?"

She shook her head. "Water's fine for now." She glanced out of the picture window beside their table and people-watched.

Wearing a black-and-white fitted raw-silk jacket, a short white skirt, and a black scoop-neck silk shell, she felt cool, professional, and girded to deal with the architect.

She couldn't stop thinking about Jack falling into those damned snakes right in the middle of their argument. That was no coincidence. *Nobody* would consider that a coincidence. Her temper had caused both the accident and his fall into what he feared most. He'd been so terrified he'd been incapable of teleportation.

Her temper had almost gotten Jack killed.

She rubbed the pain in her temple. Despite the sun shining through the window, she shivered, ice cold all over.

The fourteen-story, two-hundred-room Lima Resort Hotel was almost complete. The area was frequently covered with coastal fog, but today the hotel's gleaming bronze-marble façade looked simply stunning in the sunlight. It gave her a thrill of accomplishment, knowing she'd had a hand in creating such beauty.

The four penthouse condos had been sold before they poured the foundation of the hotel, and they already had 70 percent occupancy for the opening week.

But her mind wasn't there. It was back at the hacienda where she'd left Jack. He'd tumbled into the shower and then fallen onto her bed and nearly passed out. She'd called Dr. de Canizales to come and check on him, then treated what she could of his cuts, bruises, and bites before the doctor arrived.

The doctor had assured her Jack would be fine. The snakes had not been poisonous, and Jack was a fast healer.

It had been hard kissing him good-bye as he slept.

Jack didn't just dislike snakes; he was genuinely terrified of them. And God only knew, after her firsthand experience, she didn't blame him one bit.

She'd asked both Carmelita and Pia to check on him every hour or so while she was gone, and to make *absolutely*, *positively sure* that Harry didn't manage to get into her room.

"Penny for your thoughts, beautiful?"

Sara smiled at William. "They're worth at least a dollar. I was just deciding how to handle this situation with Aarón."

"I could—"

"Thanks. But I need to deal with him. You just sit there as my moral support."

"I feel very decorative," he teased, and Sara smiled, then took a sip of her water.

This project had gone surprisingly smoothly. It was the hotel in Chile that was causing them all sorts of headaches. Hence the meeting with the project architect, Aarón Guerrero. He didn't take suggestions well, but since Sara had worked with Grant and William for twelve years, she knew what they liked and what they didn't.

She was also confident in her own abilities as a designer. Unfortunately for Aarón, the buck stopped with her. The partners each had their own divisions and responsibilities with the company. The architecture and design of the hotels, inside and out, was her baby.

Aarón didn't like working for a woman, and his chauvinism showed. He balked at requests, flat out refused to compromise once he'd decided on something, and was an aesthetic pain in Sara's butt. He was also brilliant and worth every penny of his exorbitant paycheck, and the only architect she wanted for their hotels.

Stalemate.

"You think treating him to a nice lunch is going to convince Guerrero to place your spa on the roof?" William asked.

The rooftop spa was a pet project of Sara's. The architect insisted that the lavish spa be placed discreetly at the rear of the hotel with a view of the sumptuous gardens and waterfalls. Sara wanted it to take up the entire rooftop, and envisioned lush tropical foliage, outdoor massage tables, and a small, exclusive restaurant— all of which would serve as a nightclub after hours.

"I think telling him that checks don't write themselves and that I'm not feeling inclined to write one if he's not inclined to put my spa on the roof might work better," Sara said dryly, taking a sip of her water. Sometimes she found being diplomatic exhausting. "Of course, given how he feels about having to work with a *mujer*, he likely won't take the threat seriously unless it comes from one of you."

William looked at his Patek Philippe with annoyance. "He's unconscionably late."

Sara had known William almost as long as she'd known Grant, but not as well. He was younger than Grant by about a decade.

Grant had tried to play matchmaker between them on numerous occasions, and while William was pleasant in a stiff, British sort of way, he wasn't Jack. Jack had a healthy glow from being out of doors, whereas William's pale skin had a tendency to turn very pink when he was annoyed, which he was now.

"If he isn't here in five minutes, let's order," Sara told him. She was starving, and equally annoyed that the architect had already kept them waiting for forty-five minutes.

"Perhaps he rang," William offered in his mild British-accented voice. "You should check again."

Sara glanced at her phone, which she'd left on the table the last time she checked. "No message."

"Bugger it." He hailed the waiter, and they placed their orders.

"Will you have time to do a walk-through this

afternoon?" William asked, tearing a roll into pieces on his side plate. "The bathroom fittings have all been installed, and the spa is being plumbed this week. You were spot-on about that bronze wallpaper in the lobby bar, by the way. Worth every bloody penny, now I see it installed."

Sara smiled. "Can I have that in writing for the next time you threaten to have a heart attack when I show you an invoice?"

"Show me results like that, and I assure you, you won't have another battle next time you exceed your budget by forty-six percent." William's lips stretched into a sly smile. When he reached out and covered Sara's hand with his, she wasn't surprised. Grant must have been encouraging him to pursue her again. "You've become a remarkable asset to us, Sara. I hope you're happy and content in your work."

She tried to extricate her hand, but although he wasn't gripping her fingers, he wasn't letting go either. He was nothing if not persistent. "I love what I do, you know that." She pointedly glanced at his hand on hers. His skin was smooth, his nails well-manicured. His blunt fingers began swirling a pattern on her wrist.

"I love the bread here. How are the rolls today?" *And could you let go of my hand so I can—* Sara looked up into William's face and saw not the unusual topaz eyes staring back at her, but yellow eyes with elliptical pupils focused so intently on her she knew he was reading her soul.

Hot and cold prickles flooded her body, and she let out a low gasp of distress, shoving her chair back.

Fifteen

"Sara? What's the matter? Are you all right, my dear?"
She blinked, and William's concerned topaz eyes looked back at her. God. She'd had a flashback to Sarulu. Sara rubbed her temples with shaking fingers.

"Sorry. I'm fine, really. I just thought of something I need to take care of before I leave today. I wish Aarón would either call to cancel or show up."

"Well, at least we're making very good progress here," William said smoothly, unaware that he'd freaked her out on several levels. "I wish I could say the same for the Punta Arenas property," he told Sara with a deep frown as he buttered his roll. "The labor strike there has already delayed the pouring of the concrete three weeks, and put us behind on the entire project by a good month."

They talked business as their meals were served. The Lima hotel across the street opened in ninety days. William did an amazing job keeping everything and everyone moving. How he juggled seven projects at once astounded Sara. It was no wonder he'd never married. He was constantly traveling and lived out of a suitcase most of the time.

At a tap on the window beside their table, Sara glanced up.

"Just in time for dessert," William said dryly, nodding at the architect standing outside.

In his mid-forties, Aarón Guerrero was already a legend in his industry. The fact that the Chilean architect was barely five-two in his lifts didn't stop him from emanating power. His thick hair was jet black and hung artistically to his padded shoulders. He was as vain as he was talented, and was dating a famous older Hollywood actress who was a good foot taller than he was. He didn't have much cause for his personal vanity, but Sara didn't care. He earned his pride in his work a hundredfold. And for that, she'd tolerate his arrogance.

She waved to him as the waiter removed her plate.

He came inside, pausing to place his lunch order with their waiter on the way over to their table. Full of meaningless apologies, he shook hands with each of them, then pulled out his chair and sat down.

He'd ordered the restaurant's specialty, ceviche, a dish both Sara and William had just finished. She'd thoroughly enjoyed the succulent raw fish marinated in lemon juice. But now the smell of Aarón's spicy meal seasoned with chili, onions, and cilantro made her stomach churn and her head throb.

While he talked and ate, Sara subtly downed a couple of aspirin, drank two cups of coffee, and tried to concentrate on the very important conversation. But all she could think about was those eerie yellow damned snake eyes on William.

While Aarón went into a lengthy monologue on the pros of his desired location for the Chilean spa, Sara tried to control her breathing and the insanely rapid thundering of her heart. Her entire body was still bathed in a mist of terror-induced perspiration, which she hoped neither man noticed.

Even though she knew she'd imagined the yellow eyes, she couldn't stop glancing at William to check his eyes surreptitiously.

"I think Sara's location for the spa will be far more profitable, a crown on the most auspicious building in Punta Arenas," William said smoothly.

Aarón slapped his napkin down on the table, letting loose a spate of Spanish curses. "No. It is no crown, it is an abomination. The spa will be inside or I will not finish this building."

Good God, Sara thought. He was refusing only because it was her idea. No woman could possibly be more astute than the great Aarón. One of these days he was going to choke on that stupid male pride of his.

In the middle of a heated exchange with William, Aarón suddenly made a hideous wheezing noise, his face flushing a deep red as he tried to take a breath.

Stunned at how quickly the situation turned critical, she started to her feet. "Aarón, do you need the Heimlich?"

His eyes watering profusely, struggling to suck in air, he waved his hand. *Yes.*

Sara shot a frantic glance at the wide-eyed patrons and the wait staff gathered across the room. Surely a waiter would know something this basic? But while everyone was watching, no one rushed forward.

With one hand braced on the table, Aarón clawed at his throat. Sara didn't hesitate. Basic first aid had been a mandatory course at her boarding school, and she knew how to do the Heimlich maneuver, even though she'd only practiced it on other students at school what seemed like a lifetime ago.

She reached between the chair and Aarón's back. Grabbing him around the middle, she hauled him out of his chair. "I can help you, okay? Just try to stay calm. You'll be breathing in a second. Just hang on." The chair fell over unnoticed as she positioned her fist above his belly-button as she'd been taught, grabbed it with her other hand, and did five hard squeeze-thrusts against his abdomen.

The sound he made put the fear of God into her. Was she doing this wrong? Obviously the obstruction was still in there.

Breathe, damn it.

Sara kept squeezing, but Aarón was almost a dead weight and just about pulling her arms from their sockets. His knees sagged, and both he and Sara went down.

Shitshitshit.

"William," she said grimly, still squeezing as she tried frantically to remember how to clear his airway. "Call one-one-six." The emergency number for the local *bomberos*. The fire brigade could traverse the insane city traffic faster than any other emergency vehicle.

Vaguely she heard the susurrus of voices surrounding her, but she was completely focused on the unconscious man.

Sara prayed the paramedics would get there in time.

"COME ON! WHAT'S TAKING SO long?" Sara paced the worn linoleum floor of the waiting room at Clínica San Pedro. The noises and smells associated with any hospital were the same, Lima or London. Despair. Industrial-strength cleaners. They always gave Sara the same welling of nausea, trepidation, and uncertainty.

She hated everything about hospitals. She'd been admitted on two occasions, and both were indelibly engraved in her brain: once when she was treated after the fire that killed her parents, and the second time when she'd miscarried.

You're not helpless or frightened now, she reminded herself. And this wasn't about her. *Put the past in the past, and concentrate on Aarón.*

"This is Lima, darling, not the States. They probably have one doctor for this entire floor. It could be hours. Are you sure you want to stay?" William asked.

God, she hated not knowing if Aarón was going to be all right. Both of the extremely young-looking nurses at the desk had assured her that as soon as the doctor had a moment, he'd come out and give her an update on her friend's condition. They'd admired her Manolo Blahniks, and the conversation had killed five minutes.

It already felt like an eternity ago to Sara.

She was worried about Aarón, but she was also

worried about Jack. She wanted to call and check on him, but he'd been so white-faced and exhausted, she didn't want to wake him.

She should call Dr. de Canizales and ask him about Jack's condition. Thank God none of those snakes had been poisonous. If Aarón's doctor didn't come out and talk to her in the next fifteen minutes, she'd let the nurses know she was going outside, and she'd make that call.

Sara absently fiddled with her string of large freshwater pearls, running them through her fingers like worry beads as she walked from the door to the window and back again, her heels clicking impatiently on the tiled floor.

"Bloody hell, Sara, sit down. You pacing isn't going to speed up the doctor."

"They'd cleared his airway, and he was breathing when they took him." The paramedics had managed to dislodge the piece of fish blocking Guerrero's windpipe while he was at the restaurant, but by then he was unconscious.

"If we'd driven rather than walked, we could have gone and come back by now," William said, tapping his bottom lip with his thumb.

A frisson of annoyance raced along Sara's skin. She'd refused William's offer of a ride because walking was quicker than fighting the traffic.

William glanced at his watch, then stood up and caught her hand. "Unfortunately, I can't stay. My flight leaves in an hour, and I have an appointment in Chile I can't miss. I need to go get my car. I'll let Grant know you're here and about Aarón's incident. Are you certain you'll be okay here alone?"

She pulled her hand from his and walked back across the empty waiting room, sat down in a chair, and picked up a handful of magazines. "I'll be fine, I'll just look at these." She waved them at William.

"Call Grant as soon as you know about Aarón's condition. He'll want to know you're on your way home."

Sara nodded. "You'd better hurry or you'll miss your flight."

William winked. "It would be for a good cause, since I got to spend time with you."

"Flirting with me isn't going to hold your plane."

He kissed the tips of his fingers, then waved them at her as he walked down the hall to the elevators. The two pretty nurses at the desk watched his progress.

Sara checked the clock on the waiting room wall. How could it have been only fifteen minutes? A cursory glance at the magazine covers caused a familiar pain that made her hastily replace the parenting publications on the table.

Every picture, every advertisement, commercial, or flesh-and-blood baby she saw was like a knife to her heart. She wondered if that would ever ease, if she'd ever be able to look at another woman's child and not think of the baby she'd lost.

It always struck her as ironic that she'd already mourned the child for longer than she'd had time to love him. Was that "accident" on her shoulders too? The idea had been running around inside her head for months, ad infinitum.

Was Aarón Guerrero's accident, like Jack's, her fault? She'd been annoyed that he'd been running late, and by his flat refusal to consider her ideas; had her anger transferred to him, causing him to choke? Absently she rubbed the pain in her temple.

It seemed she'd spent half her life controlling her temper, and the other half compensating for what her temper did to her powers.

She hadn't been attempting to use magic this time, though. Perhaps Aarón's situation *was* purely an accident? God, she hoped so. She'd never forgive herself if she'd caused Aarón harm, even inadvertently. The thoughts went around and around in her brain like gerbils on a wheel.

Going to the nurses' station, she told the young brunette she was stepping outside to make a phone call and would be right back. Outside, she called Grant's Lima office, and ended up talking to Yumi. She asked her to let Grant know she was still at the hospital, and that she had to postpone their drinks date. That done, Sara called Dr. de Canizales, but had to be content to leave a message with his service.

She went back inside the too-cold building, back to the waiting room. Back to wait.

She wasn't used to sitting around doing nothing. She had her briefcase with her, but she had no interest in looking at color swatches for the bar and grill at the Santa Marta project, nor did she want to go over the figures Pia had put together for her from the San Cristóbal pool bar.

Forcing herself to sit down, Sara flipped through a two-year-old fashion magazine, then got up to pace. She went to the machine and bought a thin cardboard cup of coffee-flavored lukewarm water, then placed it on a table and forgot to drink it.

Finally, after almost an hour, she went back to the nurses' station. "Are you certain the doctor has no update?"

"The doctor will come to you as soon as he can."

"He's a busy man." And she understood that she wasn't a priority. But a quick "Your friend is going to make it" would go a long way toward lowering her guilt factor.

"Sí."

"I've heard some wild stories about some kind of sickness in San Cristóbal that makes people go loco, and then they die. The sickness hasn't traveled down here to Lima, has it?"

The brunette's eyes widened. "Sí. Do you know that in the last month alone, we've had four men and a woman brought in?"

Not to be outdone, the redheaded nurse chimed in, "My brother-in-law who is with the policía, he says people they go loco up and down the west coast. The doctors don't know what it is, but they are concerned it might be contagious."

Asking as many casual questions as she thought would get answered, Sara was afraid to push her luck too far. She and Jack were going to have to make another trip to the council to report all these developments. She hoped they'd put together a task force of people who knew what they were doing. Jack was better at this than she was.

It was starting to get dark out, and the nurses' shift was almost over. "Be careful on your way home tonight. Have you been reading the papers about all the missing girls?" Sara asked. "I have to tell you"—she didn't really have to fake the shudder— "they freaked me out. I haven't gone anywhere alone at night for weeks now. Does the hospital give you any protection when you go to your cars?"

The two nurses glanced at one another, then looked around to see if a supervisor was within earshot. "We know," the red-haired nurse said conspiratorially. "There's a woman on the second floor, she was brought in yesterday. Her brother-in-law is with the *policía* too and said she'd been missing from her home in Colombia for a week. Then she turns up wandering the streets of Lima in rags."

Sara felt a surge of hope. Was it possible that this young woman could give her any clues to what was happening in San Cristóbal? She leaned over the counter, lowering her voice. "Can I see her?" She had no idea if, or how, the missing women were connected, but it was worth asking.

"She is—how you say?" The little brunette looked at the other nurse for help.

The redhead lowered her voice. "*Una locura.* Loco."

The dark-haired woman nodded, eyes darting down the corridor again to assure that no one else overhead her. "She say to the police, to the doctor, to her family, she is *violada*—raped, yes? *Por una serpiente muy grande*," she whispered with relish.

Sara's knees buckled, and she had to grab the edge of the wooden counter so she didn't fall. "She said she was raped by a *snake*?" It took everything in her to sound incredulous instead of stunned.

"*Sí.*" The two nurses tried to conceal their amusement. They didn't imagine that what they'd heard could be true. The girl was out of her mind, babbling about rape and a giant snake, and no one believed her.

"Take me to her," Sara begged urgently. But the nurses, perhaps realizing that revealing so much about a patient could get them fired, suddenly clammed up. And before Sara could push, the doctor arrived with an update on Aarón's condition.

JACK FROWNED DOWN AT the information on his monitor. He'd set up his laptop on Sara's desk in her office a couple of hours ago. The twins, who'd been playing naked in the floodlit pool right outside the window, had been shrieking and giggling for a solid hour. They must be damned good in the sack, because they were as annoying as hell out of it.

The fragrance of ginger and lemon drifted into the room, and a second later Sara materialized near the door. She looked good enough to eat in a tight, deliciously short skirt, a figure-hugging jacket, and very high heels that made her legs look a mile long.

"Hey," he said softly.

"You're up," she said, surprised to see him there. She removed the sunglasses she'd pushed up on top of her head, then deposited them with her briefcase on a fabric-covered table. The slim, cherry-red leather briefcase he'd given her for her thirtieth birthday.

Jack raked his fingers through his hair. "Dr. de Canizales gave me a clean bill of health."

She turned to look at him, expressive eyes opened wide. "Really?"

"Really." Jack dragged his attention away from her exceptional legs to look at her face. She was beautiful there, too. "How'd your meeting go?" He had plenty to digest before he shared what he'd learned in his research. In the meantime, just looking at Sara was enough to give him a hard-on.

"Dramatic," she said ruefully, peeling off her jacket and going to a narrow closet, where she hung it on a padded hanger. Very Sara. The thin black top she wore did very nice things to her breasts. Jack relaxed back in her very comfortable office chair and enjoyed just looking at her.

"But before I go into *that* particular drama, I have other news. Five people with symptoms matching the description of the wizard 'sickness' were brought into Clínica San Pedro in Lima in the past week. *Five*, Jack."

Five in one hospital. How many more that they *didn't* know about? "I'll call Edge and let him know."

"You have the Wizard Council on speed-dial?"

He took out his phone. "As a matter of fact, yeah."

"Wait! There's *more*."

His lips twitched at her delivery. "A Ginsu knife?"

"Another woman claiming to have been raped by a snake, just like the village grills. They have her in the psych ward at the same hospital."

He gave her a look of concern. "What were you doing in a hospital? Are you okay?"

"I'm fine. I *didn't* imagine what happened to me."

"I never thought you did."

She rubbed her arms. "*I* thought I did."

"I repeat, what were you doing at the hospital?"

"Our architect, Aarón Guerrero, nearly choked to death at lunch." She sounded strained.

"Let me talk to Edge, then you can fill me i—Duncan? Slater." Jack gave the Head of Council as much information as he could. "No, I didn't get that. Where did you . . . I'll ask Sara. But I don't think so." He listened with dawning horror. "Jesus! No shit? Christ, that's bad. . . . Yeah. Yeah, I hear you. . . . That would be excellent, yeah. Thanks. . . . Right, we will. See you then."

He disconnected, shoving the phone back in his pocket. "Edge sent people to every hospital up and down this coast. He knew about the five in your hospital in Lima—actually, there were seventeen throughout that city alone. He has reports of more than a hundred and forty wizards either dead or dying within a two-thousand-mile area. They have an infirmary set up in—hell, wherever the Council is. He says the council has been sending us an updated list every day."

Sara frowned. "I haven't seen anything. Where did he say he's been sending it?"

"Here."

"Hang on, let me check with Pia." She leaned over the desk to pick up the phone. "Pia? Hey, did I receive any communications with a list of names and hospitals? . . . Oh. Okay. Thanks. . . . Just a project I'm working on with Jack. . . . No problem. Shoot that to my personal e-mail, will you, please?" She disconnected. "They sent the updates to my business e-mail. Pia had no idea what the lists were. Odd. That's not like her to get something and not tell me about it. Anyway, she's forwarding them to me. We should have them in a minute."

"Good. Tell me about your architect. How's he doing?"

"Still in the hospital in a coma. They think he suffered brain damage from lack of oxygen. God, Jack. I was so freaking pissed at him for being late, and then his arrogance—I think my temper's to blame for what happened to him."

She pressed a hand across her mouth, her eyes dark with concern. She dropped her hand and bit her lower lip. "I tried doing the Heimlich on him, but it didn't work. *Nothing* I did worked. How the hell can a restaurant not have anyone trained to do something so basic?"

Jack got up and went to her. He wrapped her in his arms, saying softly against her hair, "Clearly, you did everything you could. You can't blame yourself."

"Yes, I can." She stepped out of his arms and started pacing. "Because it *is* my fault," she said bitterly, pressing two fingers to each temple.

The nervous pacing was something new. He'd noticed

it when he'd first arrived, too. "Don't you see what's happening?" Jack said evenly, going back to the chair he'd vacated. Apparently she needed a lot of pacing room. "Every time something happens, you start connecting dots that don't exist. This was clearly an accident, honey. Chances are, if you hadn't done what you did, your architect would be dead now instead of in a coma."

She did a U-turn and headed back his way. He took a nanosecond to admire the flashing length of her silky, tanned legs in that short white skirt and the sexy FM heels, before he looked back at her face. Her eyes flashed; she knew he'd been sidetracked.

"What about you falling into a pit of snakes right in the middle of an argument?" she demanded pugnaciously. "Was *that* also just one of those things? Because I have to tell you, Jack, I'm *sick* of those things constantly happening around me. This is why . . ."

"Why you were afraid when you got pregnant?"

"*Yes*. I'm a jinx. I'm Typhoid Mary. I'm the freaking *Hindenburg*. I'm the iceberg that sank the *Titanic!*"

Jack's lips twitched. "No, you're not."

"I am. One moment I'm happy and relaxed; the next my head is spinning, and I'm spewing frigging pea soup!"

He snagged her around the waist as she passed, pulling her into his lap. Wrapping his arms around her, he rested his chin on the top of her head. "I love pea soup."

"Don't come running to me complaining when I kill you, Jack."

"I'll stick by you, and haunt you for the rest of my days."

"I'm not joking. This jinx thing scares me to death. My temper scares me even more."

"Well, you don't scare *me* to death. We'll figure this out together, okay?"

"Okay." She turned in his arms and cupped his face in both hands. "Why do we fight, Jackson?"

He inhaled the heady citrus fragrance of her skin. "Because it's so much fun to make up?"

"Hmm. Kiss me. Let's see."

He took his time, tracing her lower lip with his thumb, and she sucked it into the warm, wet cavern of her mouth, her eyes wicked above his hand. Jack closed his eyes as Sara's slick tongue slid around his finger. The sensation lodged in his groin.

Removing his thumb from her mouth, he replaced it with an open-mouthed kiss. He loved kissing her, loved her taste and the texture of the inside of her mouth. He loved the way her eyes fluttered shut, and how she put everything into the mating of their tongues. He cupped the back of her head, his fingers tangling in the sun-streaked strands that felt like silk against the roughness of his fingers. God, he'd missed her.

He nibbled lightly at her lower lip until she shuddered and her arms tightened around his neck. Breathing in her sigh, Jack slanted his mouth across hers, deepening the kiss, feeling his heart rock back into the empty place.

His pleasure rose like a tide, and he wanted to pull up her short skirt and take her there, on her office chair, in front of the window.

He chased her tongue, reaching deeper, kisses harder. The pleasure was intense, almost painfully so. Drunk with loving her, he wanted to inhale her essence, to lie with her on a field of new grass.

Unless the world ended before then.

Reluctantly Jack lifted his head. Sara murmured a soft protest, taking several seconds to open glazed eyes.

"Hey, I wasn't done with you yet," she protested, sounding a little slurred, as though she'd had a few too many appletinis.

He gave her a quick kiss because he couldn't not. "Keep that up, woman, and that little skirt you're wearing is going to be a belt." He gave her a nudge, and she slid off his lap. Slowly.

Tucking her shirt into her waistband, she gave him a sloe-eyed look. "You're a hard man, Jackson Slater."

"That too." He ran both fingers through his hair, then spun the chair to follow her progress across the room. Snapping open her briefcase, she removed several sheets of paper.

"Sara," Jack said cautiously, feeling like a complete moron. "You saw those snakes, right?"

She turned to face him, resting her butt on the table, her hands braced behind her. "Why?" Clearly his expression telegraphed his thoughts. "Yes, I saw them. Hundreds of skinny black snakes. I also saw the bites all over you. Why?" she repeated.

"There's not a mark on me now."

"None?" When he shook his head, she said flatly, "Like me after Sarulu chased me. Another hallucination."

Jack pushed out of the chair and shoved his hands in the front pockets of his jeans. "My job takes me to some of the most inhospitable, dangerous places in the world. Nothing I've seen or done in any of those places has fazed me. There are two things in this world that scare the shit out of me. Know what they are?"

She shook her head.

"Losing you, and snakes. *Two* things, that's it. I lost you once, and I'm still not sure that I survived that. But this snake thing . . ."

"Do you think your feeling about snakes is something like a self-fulfilling prophecy? That you hallucinated that pit of snakes because you subconsciously expected to come across them in a cave?"

"Maybe. Hell, I don't know. The bites felt and looked real enough, even if they healed fast."

She walked toward him, her luscious, tanned legs exposed by her short skirt. But it wasn't her legs Jack focused on this time; it was the soft compassion in her velvety brown eyes. Eyes he could drown in.

"Then I hallucinated them, too. I was never particularly afraid of snakes before being chased by an improbably large one," she said softly, standing right in front of him. She cupped his cheek in her cool, soft hand and stroked her fingers gently over his skin.

"I practically grew up with Harry." She combed her fingers through the hair over his ear, her nails gently scoring his scalp. "So being almost sexually assaulted by Sarulu was a shocker because it wasn't exactly on *my* greatest fears list. Now I can barely stand the sight of my favorite Christian Louboutin python stilettos." Her trailing fingers curled around the base of his skull.

"Here's the interesting thing," he told her. "Practically every culture on the planet has some sort of snake myth. The beginning of Omnivatics and Aequitas: Ophidian. Venezuela, Africa, and Australia all have tales about a rainbow-colored snake; Sarulu? Hopi Indians, East Indians—hell, Greek cosmological myths, Egyptian myths—they *all* have these freaking snake-related stories. And you wanna know what I think? I think every single one of those damned snakes was an Omnivatic, hiding in plain sight."

"Jack?" she murmured, her soft mouth an inch from his.

His breath tangled in his lungs as she brushed her mouth against his ear. "What?"

"Remember where you took me as a surprise three years ago?"

"Yeah. What does the Icehotel in Jukkasjärvi have to do—"

And there they were, in a candlelit ice room, tucked into an insulated sleeping bag spread over reindeer hides.

Bare-ass naked.

~Sixteen~

N o snakes two hundred miles north of the Arctic Circle," Sara assured him. "Not at this time of year, anyway." Beneath the sleeping bag, she slid her bare leg across the smooth skin of Jack's naked hip. His fingers tightened in her hair, and she sighed low in her throat at the feel of his hot skin against hers.

"The perfect place," he murmured, touching his mouth to the pulse at her temple.

Anywhere she was with him was perfect. But Sara didn't articulate that. "Oh, my God." She laughed, burrowing into his warm arms as goose bumps pebbled her shoulders and arms. A single candle on a nearby clear ledge flickered with her movement. "It's *freezing*."

The ice walls glowed an eerie pale blue around them as if they were in the center of a very large ice cube. Which basically they were. The entire hotel was carved from tons of ice and snow. Jack had brought her here on their one-month anniversary. The icy room had been bathed in flickering candlelight, the air perfumed by hundreds of deep red roses. He'd loved her then. . . .

"I forgot how freaking bitterly cold it was—*is*." Her

breath hung in front of her lips, each word a little puff of condensation in the frigid air. She snuggled her cheek against the warmth of his chest and heard the steady beat of his heart.

"I'm a professional," Jack assured her, tightening his arms around her, enveloping her in the furnace heat of his body as he pulled her the last millimeter against him. Stroking a large hand down her back, he dropped a lingering kiss on top of her head.

"As much as I want to be here with you, we have to resolve our problems back at the hacienda. You know— damn, it's freezing!"

"Trust me, *vacker, flicka*, I know *just* how to keep you hot."

Oh, yes, he certainly did. And clearly he wasn't going to take her back until . . . later. She ran her fingers through the hair on his chest, loving the springiness and crispness of it under the pads of her fingertips, then buried her cold nose in the prickly hair. God, he smelled good. Inhaling the musky, all-male fragrance of his skin made her feel hot and sizzling all over. "Brr. I barely noticed how cold it was when we were here last time."

They'd been so in love, so totally focused on one another that Sara had noticed very little around them when they were together. It was only when she was back at home, alone, that the fear and uncertainties set in.

She pushed the thought away. Right here, right now, there was neither fear nor uncertainty. Just Jack.

"You won't notice this time either, *min kära*," he assured her in an intentionally terrible accent. He was actually an accomplished mimic and really good with languages, but it wasn't his facility for verbal communicating Sara needed right then. He twirled an imaginary mustache when she lifted her gaze to his face. Hunger burned in his eyes.

Her heart ached. Running her fingers through his hair, she savored the feel of the heavy, satiny strands. Foolishly, her eyes stung with intense emotion.

Her nipples were hard and peaked, happily nestled in his chest hair. Gently she shifted her upper body so that both she and Jack were teased by the hard little points and gentle friction. "Are you a Swede now?"

She loved the little lines beside his eyes as he smiled wickedly. "When in Lapland. . ."

She tugged his head closer, brushing her nose against his Eskimo-style. "Lap?"

He grinned, sliding his hand up her thigh to settle on the flare of her hip "Quite so. Come into my lair, *älskling.*" With a combination of magic and strength, he tugged her body deep inside the large sleeping bag, where it was dim and marginally warmer.

Heat unfurled in Sara's belly as Jack trailed his mouth over her closed lids while his hand slid across her hip and slowly up her midriff. His calloused fingers abraded her skin as he savored the silky texture of her breast. She shuddered with pleasure as the sensation traveled through her body like sheet lightning.

His tongue traced the line of her lashes, gentle as a butterfly wing, at the same time he took her nipple between his fingers, rolling the hard nub until her back arched with need. Moisture pooled between her legs, and it took every vestige of willpower she could muster not to impale herself on him right that second. Her breathing was becoming more ragged, and they were barely moving.

His erection, hard and silken, brushed her wet heat. With her knee over his hip, she was open to him anytime he wanted to take her. But Jack loved the anticipation of slow and deliberate. *She* loved the throbbing, breathless anticipation of leisurely lovemaking—too, if she could manage to outwait him. She could smell the heat of her own arousal combined with the scent of her lotion, the sharp tang of lemon and the spicy sweetness of ginger, heady in the warm, cocooned darkness.

"Feel what you do to me, Sara-mine," he murmured against the unsteady pulse at her temple. His penis moved against her, seeking, searching. Waiting. "The smell of your skin makes me so horny I can't think straight, do you know that? This—God, I've missed this. I want to wait, draw out this sweet torture. But I want to fuck you till neither of us can walk. Then I want to start all over again."

"Yes. To both," Sara murmured languidly. "Any and all of the above. In any order you like. You—hmmm, right there—don't even have to give me a heads-up. Surprise me."

The hard muscles of his belly contracted as she lazily trailed her fingertips down his side. She loved touching him. He didn't have an ounce of fat on him. His skin there was blazing hot and incredibly smooth. She knew that when her hand trailed lower, the silk would turn rough with crisp hair. He shuddered in reaction as her finger glided into the crease between his torso and his leg.

"Slow torture it is."

She hummed her approval, tilting her face as he trailed more kisses across her eyelids, brushing his lips across her cheek, then nibbled lightly on her nose, making her smile. Back across her cheek. Her need climbed another notch as he swirled his tongue in the shell of her ear. The sensation shimmied all the way down to her toes. His lips drifted down until he lazily traced her smile, his mouth soft and pliant against hers.

I love you, Jack. But she didn't say it, just met his wet, slick tongue with her own. He tasted dark and seductive, and so familiar and dear that her chest hurt. The kiss was delicious, hot enough to make her heart gallop, and tender enough to make her eyes sting.

Rolling her onto her back, Jack slid his large hands up the insides of her arms, drawing her hands above her head as he settled into the cradle of her thighs. "This is . . ."

"Yes," she breathed against his warm skin. Bombarded by intense physical desire and tangled emotions, Sara had to remain perfectly still for a moment, listening to their syncopated breathing as she teetered on the razor-sharp edge of an orgasm before they'd done much more than kiss.

Jack dropped his forehead to hers. "You are so damn beautiful," he whispered. "And you *smell*—you smell like heaven. Horny woman drenched in flowers. I'm drunk with wanting you."

Maybe I should tell him, she thought. *Maybe I should try one more time.* But what if he didn't feel the same? What if it was just passion, the relief from danger translated into a need for physical release? Better not to break this spell, she decided; better to seize the moment and accept that that was all it was—a moment. And oh, what a moment.

The small swell passed, and she restlessly moved her smooth legs against the roughness of his. He shifted his hips just enough to anchor her legs with one of his. Her fingers flexed in his hold in a wordless plea.

"Give me a minute," he said thickly, then brushed his lips down her throat, and bit the side of her neck.

"Ow!"

It wasn't a gentle nip; Sara felt the sharp edge of his teeth on the tense cords of her throat. The fine tremors became a shudder that shook her whole body. He kissed the sting, succulent, wet kisses.

He trailed kisses along her collarbone as he shaped her breast with his fingers, and down the inner swell of her breast. He licked her skin to cool it, then heated her flesh with more sharp, hot nibbles. He found her nipple, brushed it with his thumb, then pinched the hard nub between his fingers. "Too tender for gentle," he murmured against her throat. "I remember."

His open mouth moved across the plump swell and he took her nipple into the wet heat of his mouth, his teeth gently clamping down until Sara whimpered with need. He sucked hard, and her back arched, her fingers fisting in his hair, holding his head in place.

She moaned in protest when he moved on, his mouth starting a familiar journey south. He paid attention to her midriff, counting her ribs with flicks of his tongue. Down her belly, taking tiny nips and soothing her sensitized skin with small kisses meant to calm; they incited her even more, though. Maybe they weren't meant to calm, at that.

A thrill of excitement ran chased through her veins, as Jack kissed his way down her body. Her abs fluttered as he dipped his tongue into the indentation of her navel, and her hands came down to grip his broad shoulders.

She hissed in a breath when he touched his mouth to her mound. "God . . ." he breathed hoarsely against the damp curls. She shuddered as his fingers dipped into her silky wet heat. He slid two fingers deep inside her, manipulating the tight bud until Sara arched against him.

Please, please, please, she chanted in her head as his fingers worked her body into a mindless symphony of sensation. He pushed her higher, higher, and still it wasn't enough. She wanted more than his fingers inside her. Damn it, she wanted him inside her *now.*

And just when she thought she'd go mad wanting him, he put his mouth on her. Air tangled in her chest. A pulse throbbed a jungle beat in her ears. The universe around them bled into soft focus, leaving Jack's mouth in sharp relief and everything else a hazy blur. *Jack. Jack. Jack.*

Her entire body throbbed and pulsed. Her goose

bumps had goose bumps. Everything inside her turned to churning, seething, molten liquid.

His breath harsh, he returned his fingers to her slick heat, bringing her close, so close—

"Let go," he whispered. "Come for me, sweetheart."

Sara didn't have a choice. The climax crashed over her with such force everything went dark. Her body bucked as she came hard and fast, her body arching against his mouth. He anchored her hips, his fingers digging into the cheeks of her ass.

The tremors were still peaking through her as he surged up her body, then made a raw, primitive sound as he filled her, moving until she swore she felt him touch the bottom of her heart. And still, it wasn't enough. She wanted more. Wanted him to be so deep that he'd never find his way out again. In that wild half-second when all she could feel was his length pumping inside her, she knew that she'd always loved this man. Would always love him. No tragedy, no misunderstanding would ever change that.

He gripped her hips and held her still. The sensation of their joining was so intense, so sharp, neither dared move. His head swooped down the few inches separating them, and he took her mouth savagely, as if he couldn't get enough of her.

She wanted to scream. To beg him to stop moving inside her. She needed a moment to catch her breath, a few minutes for her body to calm down. She wanted to make him stop. She wanted it to last forever.

Too much. She was going to shatter and break apart.

He continued to rock his body into hers. His fingers continued to work that small nubbin that was now over-sensitized. He prolonged her multiple orgasm beyond endurance. Sara's body shuddered and quaked under the onslaught as he let one climax roll into the next and then the next.

She didn't know where his body ended and hers began. Any second now she was going to shatter into a gazillion pieces.

"Finish," Sara begged, her nails digging into his back.

"I'll never be finished with you," Jack muttered, "Come again."

"N—" *Yes!* Sparklers and rainbows. Shooting stars and fiery waterfalls. He could still make her earth move.

She came again, riding that last blast of sensation along with Jack, who finally surrendered and gave himself up to the climax that had been clawing at him all night.

She smelled the roses as soon as they breached the edge of the sleeping bag and came up for air. The shimmering glow of a thousand candles reflected off the ice walls, turning frosty blue into molten gold. The freezing surfaces were softened by hundreds of cut-crystal vases filled with deep, claret-colored roses in full, magnificent bloom. The entire room wavered. "Oh, damn it, Jack."

"Wrong color?"

"Perfect," she whispered, turning back to face him. "In every way." As close as they were lying, she still had to touch him. Sara brushed his hair out of his eyes, then trailed her fingertips down the side of his face, from smooth to rough. His jaw was bristly under her fingers, and she could still feel the delicious, faint abrasions on her skin from her forehead to her toes where he'd thoroughly rediscovered her body. She traced a finger down the slightly crooked bump on his nose where his father had hit him, and over the scar on the underside of his chin that he'd gotten when he was eight and had fallen off his skateboard.

Kissing him lightly on the lips, she snuggled against him. "I forgot to ask." She combed her fingers between his, palm to palm. They used to lie like this after making love, touching all the time, even if it was just holding hands. "What else was in the box Rojas gave you?"

"Wanna see it?"

She gave him a naughty smile. "The box?"

"Well, yeah." He laughed. "You've just spent considerable time looking at *other* things, maybe a break is in order?"

She tweaked his nipple gently, and he mock-growled. "You have this box on you? You feel pretty naked to me."

"I put it in the psionic safe. I can call it." He shifted when she shivered with cold. Moments later she was sitting up between his spread knees, her back warmed by his chest. Wrapping his arms around her, he rested his chin on her hair. She smiled as he tucked the sleeping bag around her shoulders, protecting her from the biting cold.

Jack, his arms and shoulders exposed, seemed impervious to the several-degrees-below-freezing air. Their breath hung in front of their faces as they spoke.

"Stop feeling me up." She elbowed his belly, her voice husky, as his penis did the happy dance against the curve of her ass. "Call it."

"You have a one-track mind, woman. Look. It's here."

A two-foot-square box shimmered and glowed as it hovered a few feet above her lap. "Is it always ice, or is that just because it's thirty below in here?"

"Always ice." He murmured unintelligible words softly, and the front of the cube opened.

"Because cold is your power to ca—" She coughed. "Good grief." She waved her hand to dissipate the almost fluorescent lime-green smoke eddying out of the icy safe to hover over it, almost protectively.

Jack reached inside and removed the long, thin box given to him by the village elder.

"This isn't fabric." Sara reached out and lightly ran her fingers over the hard surface of the box as Jack held it on the flat of his palm. Tipping her head back against his shoulder, she stroked the slightly textured top "It is the same crystallized snakeskin that the amulets at the cave are made of."

"Looks like. Yeah, let's hope it opens. There's no clasp or sign of a lock on this thing." He turned it this way and that. The surface caught the candlelight and refracted the golden luminosity into thousands of brilliant pinpoint prisms on the translucent blue-white ice walls. The tiny rainbows reflected in the icy sides of the hovering psionic safe.

"There isn't even a seam. Maybe it's not supposed to open," she suggested, smiling her thanks as Jack adjusted the warm sleeping bag higher to cover her bare shoulder.

Instantly, the top half of the box snapped open. "Wow. I'm impressed," she said.

"I touched you."

In every way that counts. "Yeah. I got that. Turn it around, let's see what's—oh, Jack," she whispered with awe. "It's exquisite. Look at the incredibly detailed workmanship on this." A slim, clear dagger rested on a bed of lush black velvet. The fabric ate the light, but the sharp double edges of the blade glinted and glistened, throwing off giant prisms, filling the entire room with dancing rainbows. "Beautiful. Is it made of ice?"

Jack reached into the narrow box and reverently lifted out the twelve-inch dagger, balancing it across his palm. "Not ice—crystal. Hell. Touch it."

"Is that like saying, 'This tastes gross, *you* try it?'"

He smiled. "It's almost . . . alive."

"It's not going to turn into a freaking snake, is it? Because, seriously, Jackson, if it does, you're toast."

"I'm not going to bring a snake into bed with us. No guts, no glory. Go on, I double-dare you to touch it."

Sara grinned. She never had been able to refuse a double dare. She ran a cautious finger along the dagger, then yanked her hand away as a sharp shock buzzed all the way from her finger through her shoulder. She turned her head to frown at him. "Thanks for the heads-up," she said dryly. "Electricity?"

"No idea. The sensation's unlike anything I've experienced before when touching crystals. And I've worked with endless varieties in the course of my career. Nothing has ever had this kind of punch."

She touched it again, this time prepared for the energy. "I can feel the power running through it."

"Yeah. Feel familiar?"

"No, not really." She closed her eyes, letting the soft vibrating current flow through her. "*Yes*. It's the same power as the leyline in the jungle when we were on the way to the village yesterday."

"Yeah. It's as if a ley has been transformed into a tangible object." She felt the rapid pounding of his heart against her back. Jack loved this stuff, lived for it. Another connection to leylines must be music to his ears.

Taking her finger off the dagger, she rested her head in the curve of his shoulder. A perfect fit. "What's it for?"

He stroked the blade again. "Primarily, daggers are used for stabbing or thrusting. See the razor-sharp double-edged blade?"

"It's ceremonial, though, right? Look at all the intricate carvings along the blade and hilt." She knew she didn't need to point out the obvious. Jack wasn't blind. The almost transparent surface was covered with intricate carvings, all right—of snakes. They twined around the handle and slithered down both sides of the blade, eerily realistic despite being carved in crystal.

The dagger was a fascinating study in triangulation. The eight-inch blade contained a triangular void, and was itself shaped like a long triangle, coming to a pinpoint tip. The hilt was a pair of twined snakes in an intricate triangle of spikes emanating perpendicularly outward from the eye sockets of an open-mouthed snake skull. As incredible as the workmanship was, just looking at it gave Sara the willies. Her shudder had nothing to do with being naked in a room made of ice.

"The longer I hold it, the more I'm convinced that it's an ancient power source. It's practically vibrating in my hand. Rojas knew we're Aequitas. So, no," he said against her hair, "I don't think he gave us a ceremonial dagger. Though I wish to hell that were so. I think we're supposed to kill something or someone with it."

Her heartbeat picked up speed, galloping uncomfortably against her breastbone. She had to swallow several time before she managed to push out a word. "Who?"

"More like *what*. Rojas said it was the guardian of the crystal cave. Just a guess, but based on these carvings, I think it might have something to do with killing that giant snake you saw."

"Now you believe me?"

"Yeah. But, trust me, I tried damned hard *not* to."

A shudder of revulsion traveled up and down her spine. Visions of the enormous yellow eyes and rainbow tongue flickered behind her eyelids, somehow making the refractions of rainbow light against the ice walls malevolent rather than beautiful. She turned away from the dagger.

"I'm putting it away now." Understanding, laced with a pinch of amusement, filled his voice. Carefully he laid the dagger back into its case. The lid immediately snapped shut, and it floated to the open psionic safe, then hovered just outside the opening.

"Uh-oh. Why can't it go back inside?"

"The way is blocked."

Sara sat up a bit straighter to peer inside the ice safe. "I don't see anything—" A small leather-bound book floated out over the box holding the dagger. "Where did *that* come from?"

"It was inside. Put out your hands, see if it'll come to you," Jack said softly against her ear. "It weighs about fifty pounds, so brace yourself."

"How can a little book weigh fifty—yikes. No kidding!" The weight of the book made her hands drop to the sleeping bag.

"Jesus. It came to you."

Sara stared at it in fascination. It looked hundreds, if not thousands, of years old, the leather cover dark with age and wear. Although there were no air currents in the room, the pages started flipping over, creating their own breeze. "You told me to hold it."

"Yeah, but I honest to God didn't think it would allow you to. It's been in my family for thousands of years."

The pages were turning in a blur of papyrus and gold leaf. "Ah . . . Jack. Is it supposed to be doing this?"

"It'll stop in a minute."

It was a long minute. More pages than the book seemed to contain kept turning. Suddenly they stopped, and she remembered to breathe. Black letters floated randomly from the pages of the open book, settling a few inches above the papyrus surface. They rotated and righted themselves to form a sentence.

"'EREBUS NOVEM TWO ARE ONE TO INFINITY IF NOT STOPPED.' What the hell does it *mean*?" She jumped when the book slammed shut, then watched it narrow-eyed as it drifted over to the floating psionic safe. The book led the way inside, followed by the box. Spatially, neither should be able to fit inside. The door clicked shut, and the safe vanished.

"Erebus is the name of the Omnivatic equivalent of the Wizard Council, or the Aequitas Archon. Unless it's someone's name. Novem is the number nine in Latin."

"Okay. And?"

Jack kissed the side of her neck. "Don't have a clue. But whatever it means will be revealed when we need to know."

"I want to know *now*."

"Yeah. I hear you. But experience has taught me to have patience. That said, can't let the candles and roses go to waste." Jack turned her in his arms, kissing her gently on the mouth as he stretched out beside her. "Where did we leave off?"

↞ Seventeen ↠

They were back in her office at the hacienda, having spent the rest of the night in the Icehotel, alternately making love and sleeping. By silent agreement, they hadn't talked about anything inflammatory—not the crystal dagger, or snakes, or Baltzer, or the cryptic message.

And especially not the other elephant in the room. The baby.

It was cowardly, but Sara wanted to keep the détente and their fragile status quo for a little while longer.

Minutes after they materialized, her cell phone rang. Thank God it wasn't Grant. She wasn't ready to deal with him right now. She let out a little sigh of relief when she heard the senior nurse at one of the hospitals in San Cristóbal asking for Detective Temple. Sara perched on the edge of her desk to talk to her.

Jack nibbling on her neck made concentrating on the conversation a little difficult. After a few minutes, she closed her phone, and gave him a gentle shove. "That was the hospital. The woman who was in a coma woke up. I'd like to go into San Cristóbal to talk to her. Want to come?"

"Yeah, sure," he said easily, dropping into her desk chair and grinning wickedly. "We'll stop and see Duncan on our way back."

"Okay." Sara slid her freezing hand into his, receiving a boost of comfort as his warm fingers closed around hers. She met his deep blue eyes. "Is the world going to hell?" she whispered, her voice cracking.

"Not if we can help it, honey. Not if we can fucking well help it."

She hoped he was right. Spotting several feet of Harry across the room, Sara let go of Jack's hand and strolled in his general direction. She picked up several wallpaper books, ostensibly to put them away. She'd never been bothered by Harry, but now she didn't want to be anywhere near him. She contained a shudder of distaste.

God, why did the damn snake have to be waiting for her in her office when she was with Jack? It was almost as though the blasted boa knew Jack—and now Sara—didn't like snakes, and was determined to freak him out at every turn. A snake, Sara reminded herself, was a snake was just a snake. Even Harry. And while it wasn't his fault she'd suddenly developed this phobia, he still had to go.

"How do you feel?" Jack stretched out his legs, crossed his ankles, and stacked his hands behind his head, the picture of a content man.

Sliding the large books into place, she willed the boa to slither all the way under the table out of sight. "Perfect." She stretched her arms above her head and gave him a feline smile. "Fantastic. Well loved. How do you feel?" She tried to nudge Harry beneath the table skirt with her toe. She really was going to have to talk to William about his pet running loose all over the house.

"Same." Jack grinned, standing up and coming over to her. "All that. Headache?"

"Not at all." She loved how he slid his big hands around her waist when she wrapped her arms around his neck. "Why?" she asked, nibbling his lower lip. "Do I look like I have a headache?" Actually, she felt as though she could leap tall buildings in a single bound, and fly to the moon and back.

"No, just the opposite. You look sexy, and like a well-loved woman. That said, I hate like hell to spoil this, but . . . do something for me, would you please? Think about your folks and the fire for a minute."

She disengaged her arms and sighed. "Oh, Jack, I hate to—" She pressed two fingers to her temple, where an instantaneous spearing headache pulsed. "I have that headache now. Thanks."

"We're back at the hacienda. Sara, that damned headache only comes when we're anywhere around Baltzer."

"He's nowhere near here, Jack." Harry's tail vanished completely under the tablecloth. "He's in Lima." In Lima, where another young woman claimed she'd been raped by a giant snake. He'd been in Colombia when three young women there had disappeared. He'd been in San Cristóbal when—

God! Don't go there. Grant can get any woman he wants. And he does. And how could he possibly be a giant snake anyway? Besides, hadn't William been in those places too? William had Harry and the tattoo, the whole weird fascination with snakes.

"How about William, Jack? Yesterday at lunch, I'd swear his eyes turned yellow and had elliptical pupils."

"What?!"

"It was my *imagination*, Jackson. Just my imagination."

"I'm not going to fucking well discount anything about either of them. What happened with Roe?"

"I told you. That whole thing with Sarulu freaked me out, and I had a flashback or something."

"What you mean is you just tried to use sleight of hand to distract me from Baltzer."

It was disloyal, but she was going to have to tell Jack her suspicions. Even while she hoped and prayed she was wrong. Not only did she have to tell him, she was bound as an Aequitas—even a half Aequitas—to report this to the Wizard Council.

She hoped like hell she was wrong.

"As a matter of fact, I'm leaning that way."

"You're leaning . . . what way?"

Her headache pulsed, and the brilliant morning sunlight streaming into her office made it even worse. She'd also gone from almost euphoric to irritable and cranky in just a few minutes. "I think you're right. I think there's somethi—ow, God, that hurts." She pressed the heels of both hands hard against her temples. "I want to change. Come with me?" She started for the door, then turned when Jack stayed where he was. "Are you coming?"

"It's Baltzer or me, Sara. Your call."

God, he was infuriating. She'd been about to tell

him . . . whatever the hell it was that had now been completely obliterated by the pain. "We've *had* this damned conversation, Jack." But why were they rehashing it again? Why now? Sara rubbed her palm over her aching forehead, where the headache was like a tightening vise.

"Well, you'll be happy to know that this is the last fucking time we'll do so." His body language had changed completely. The languid, sensual lover had vanished, replaced by an angry stranger whose entire body radiated animosity. "Choose," he told her coldly. "Decide this, once and for all. Him or me."

She gripped the doorjamb with one hand. "Why do I have to give up the only family I know for you, Jack? Why does it have to be all or nothing? If my parents were alive, would you be irrationally jealous of them too?

"Is it just *Grant* you don't want me to have contact with, or is it Carmelita and Pia and William as well? How far do you want me to go to weed out anybody I care for and who cares for me? Everybody? All of them? Why does it have to be you and only you in my life?"

"Baltzer's a tool." Jack scrubbed a hand across his mouth, his eyes glittering with anger and frustration. Good. Let the bastard be angry. "Fuck," he snarled. "He has something—"

"What?" Sara tried to modulate her voice, but she was getting more and more furious, and she knew she was almost shouting. The angrier Jack got, the colder he became. The angrier she got, the more her temper flared. "What, Jackson? A penis? A brain? A shitload of money? *What* does Grant have that pisses you off so much?"

"You get headaches when he's around. He—"

This was about her *headaches*? She wanted to scream. "God, that's lame, even for you. Look around." She flung her arm out to encompass the sun-filled office. "Who's in the freaking room? I get headaches when *you're* around, Jack. *You're* the one who hurts me. *Not* Grant."

Turning on her heel, Sara stalked out of her office. Tears of anger blurred her vision. How in God's name had everything changed so quickly?

Bastardassholedickshithead.

The line between love and hate was insanely thin. And right now she hated Jackson Slater, she really did. What was worse, she was starting to hate herself. What was *wrong* with her? She couldn't put her finger on why she was almost schizophrenic around Jack. She didn't know herself anymore. Her damned moods swings were starting to worry her big-time. One minute she was ready to forgive him anything; the next, she wanted to make him as miserable as she was.

She had to get out of there. Had to think this through logically and calmly. She was so angry with him. The fury pulsed behind her eyes and made her skin feel clammy.

"Don't walk out on me again- Damn it, Sara!" Jack chased her out into the corridor.

Foolishly, Sara ran.

His fingers closed around her upper arm. "We can't keep doing this. Get back in there and let's *finish* this conversation once and for—" Her phone cheeped. "Do *not* fucking answer that!"

~~~

UNFORTUNATELY, WHEN THEY ARRIVED at the hospital in San Cristóbal, the girl already had visitors. The police were interrogating her. He and Sara headed to the hospital cafeteria to wait.

It was lunchtime, and the place was packed with hospital personnel and visitors. The noise level made conversation difficult; he should probably have taken Sara to one of the waiting areas, but those had people coming and going as well. The large cafeteria smelled like fake cheese, corn *arepas* fried in old oil, and industrial-strength cleaner. Zero ambience.

But he doubted Sara could be seduced by ambience right now. Every line of her body showed how annoyed she was. "There's a free table in back, come on."

He shimmered, leaving her to make her way between the tables, chairs, and people moving through the line to pay for their food. Nobody even noticed him traveling a hundred yards in next to no time. Jack kicked a chair out from the table and sat with his back to the wall, watching Sara.

She wore straight-legged, faded jeans, a white T-shirt, and a form-fitting, short red jacket. Her hair—he was sure she'd swept it up, baring her nape, just to make him insane—was a just-got-out-of-bed fashionable mess on top of her head. Enormous gold hoops swung from her ears, and above the hoops her sunstones sparkled orange in the fluorescent lighting.

She looked elegant, and sexy as hell as her long legs closed the gap between them.

If only, he thought bitterly.

"We could've waited outside," she said, velvety brown eyes critical as she took stock of the table filled with dirty plastic plates and cutlery. The table magically bussed itself, and all the crap disappeared.

Jack raised a brow as she again used magic to clean the sticky residue off her chair and the table before sitting down. Neither commented on it. Things between them were inflammatory enough.

"The cops are in with her now," Jack reminded her. "We have a few minutes. Let's grab a soda or something, and you can tell me what's going on." His temper had cooled some since they'd teleported to the hospital.

"I don't want a drink. Get one if you—"

"I don't either."

She lifted her attention from the table surface to his face, her eyes large and dull with pain. "What happened to us?" she asked roughly. "How did we go from who we were last night back to this?"

He held her gaze. The answer was obvious, to him anyway.

She closed her eyes briefly, then looked at him again, her eyes narrowed. "Do *not* blame Grant."

"Fine. I won't. But you'd better start connecting the dots soon, before he destroys everything."

"I'm so damned confused, I don't know what the hell's going on." Removing the large gold hoop from one ear, she reinserted the post in an atypically nervous gesture. Five inches of thin gold bracelets jangled on her arm with the movement. "What does 'Erebus Novem two are one to infinity if not stopped' mean?"

He presumed that was a rhetorical question.

"Okay. We shelve that puzzle for later." Sucking in a deep breath, she met his eyes and said baldly, "Can you keep an open mind while I tell you something?"

"Must be about Baltzer. Sure. Go ahead."

"I have no idea how this whole snake things ties in with—oh, hell. You're right, Jack. I think Grant has something to do with all these girls. Am I crazy? He can have any woman he wants. He's rich, good-looking. . . . Why would he have to hypnotize them and make them believe he's a snake, or a snake god, or whatever?"

Jack paused. "He wouldn't." He'd resisted touching her since the scene at the hacienda, but she looked pretty calm right now. Despite his misgivings, Jack picked up her hand and laced his fingers through hers.

She didn't pull away. Heartened, he ran his thumb over the back of her hand. Here was a perfect example of their mercurial change in mood from one location to another. All the anger, mistrust, and animosity he'd felt at the hacienda was lifted, gone as if it had never been.

He knew exactly what Sara had been talking about earlier when she'd claimed she was losing her mind with her mood swings.

"Look," he said calmly, "I'll be the first person to say I don't like the guy. And I don't. Big-time. But I'm not sure how you jumped from point G to point S."

She took a deep breath, and her fingers tightened in his. "I did some research when I was at my office in Lima yesterday. Every single place where a woman has been reported missing, every place that the women have shown up after an attack—*if* they've returned—is somewhere that Grant visited on that exact day. Same place. Same location."

"I don't know, sweetheart. I'd love to think that Baltzer's the guy, but even for me it seems farfetched." Jack certainly blamed him for a whole shitload of other things, but he doubted Baltzer was the rapist.

Her fingers squeezed his. "There's more. Jack, I think Sarulu said my name when he had me cornered. No, I don't think it—he *did* say my name." She put up her hand to stop him from speaking. "I *know* a hiss could sound like *Sara*. And yeah, I was scared out of my mind and adrenaline was zooming through my system at the speed of light. But the more I've replayed that moment in my mind, the more I'm positive that he called me by name."

Christ. "It was a hypnotic state. Your mind could've interpreted it—"

Her gaze locked with his. "That damned snake called me by name, Jackson."

"Okay. Okay. I believe you. It makes a sick kind of sense. Everything we've seen and heard so far comes back to snakes."

"Yes, it does." The color suddenly drained from her face, leaving her eyes huge and very dark. "Oh. My. God."

Worried, Jack half-rose, reaching out for her. "What's the matter?"

She shook her head vehemently. "No. Impossible."

"Tell me."

Sara bit her lower lip. "We were happy at the Icehotel.

We were happy in Tahoe, and in Switzerland. But the second we got back to the hacienda, we were angry, and fighting. . . ."

Jack shut the hell up, because she was going where he'd gone and come back. It all circled around Baltzer.

"I thought you were *jealous* of Grant. But that's not it, is it?"

He shook his head.

"*Harry* was always in the room with us when we fought, Jack. Under the table today, in my closet, hiding behind the drapes. We keep going from fabulous to crap in two seconds flat. No wonder I feel like my head has been spinning and I'm spewing pea soup! You were right." She folded her arms on the table and leaned forward. "We *are* being manipulated."

"I think we have been all along." Jack could practically hear her wheels turning as she reviewed their recent history and calculated how it all added up. He kept his voice level and calm, while inside he was shouting hallelujah that she *finally* believed him. "I told you there's a weird pattern to our behavior depending where we are. The farther away we are from Baltzer, the more intensely we care about each other; the closer we get to him, the more we distrust one another and the more we fight."

"Do you think he's somehow harnessing whatever connection there is to the leyline to call the giant snake?"

"It's possible. Hell, it's *probable*. Anything else to tie him to the women?"

"I—God, Jack. I feel so disloyal even thinking this, let alone discussing it out loud. *Especially* with *you*."

"Get over it. *Fast*," Jack said unsympathetically.

"I adore Grant, and he's been nothing but kind and loving to me for all these years. . . ."

Jack tried to compute this rational, calm Sara with the woman who'd practically ripped his balls through his nose less than an hour ago. "But?"

"But he's been behaving very strangely lately. For one thing, he's been more insistent on fixing me up with William. And while I like William, I don't in any way like him romantically."

"Good to know."

"Shut up," she said without heat. "At first I thought perhaps he was having financial problems—investors pulling out, the strike. . . . But there have been other things." She chewed her bottom lip, clearly torn. Her eyes met his, and a slight blush rode her perfectly made-up cheeks.

"He's—*kinky*. God knows I'm no prude, but it's more than the obvious displays of public affection, which he *knows* embarrass and gross me out. The girls always have weird welts and bruises on them. Not just Inga and Ida, other women he's brought to the house. I don't even want to go into the fact that I've seen William going into Grant's room and staying there for hours, or Grant coming out of William's room. I don't care if he's gay or bi or whatever, but he's got some—stuff in there that's really sick and twisted."

Sick and twisted? As much as Jack wanted Baltzer to be the bad guy in all this, that wasn't enough proof. "Like?"

"You mean other than all the S and M equipment like

chains, harnesses, whips, and metal collars with spikes on them?" She shuddered, then blushed as a young orderly walked right behind her chair, clearly having heard what she'd just said.

"So he's into BDSM. That doesn't make him a snake charmer or a rapist." Lips twitching, Jack shook his head. "Christ, I can't believe I'm *defending* the guy."

She lowered her voice as a couple slid their trays onto the table next to them. "He has a steel cage in there."

"Anyone in it?" he whispered back, his heart swelling with love for her. God, this mess between them had to be resolved one way or the other before it killed them.

Sara reached over and punched his arm. "Be serious."

"So the guy plays games. That still doesn't make him the rapist." A sick fuck, but not necessarily a rapist.

Sara frowned. "My gut tells me, as much as I hate to say it, that Grant has something to do with this snake stuff."

"I trust your gut. And while I hate to condemn anyone without solid evidence, I agree with you. Baltzer's up to his bleached-blond hair in all this."

"The whole giant snake hallucination, Ophidian, Sarulu—*all* of it is connected. Right?"

"Yeah. I agree." Jack frowned, drumming the fingers of his free hand on the table impatiently. "Still, we're missing a key ingredient."

With a jangle of bracelets, she covered his hand to stop the drumming. "What?" Jack turned his so he could twine their fingers together. Old times.

"No idea. But we need to join all these maybes into

a solid 'we have it' before approaching the Council with our suspicions."

"Is *Harry* the Omnivatic?" Her lips twitched. "Harry who loves to sleep on my Choos is the all-powerful bogeyman supernatural Omnivatic? Seems a bit of a stretch, don't you think?"

"Baltzer, Roe, and the boa are the only constants since we started seeing each other. It makes more sense that either Baltzer or Roe has the ability to turn into a boa."

She wrapped her arms around her waist. "So the Omnivatic we've been looking for is either Grant or William? Maybe Harry?"

"That's my take."

"Grant's taken care of me most of my life. He loves me. William's been a friend almost as long. Why would either of them want me to be unhappy? That just doesn't make any sense. Both of them knew how much I loved you. They *knew*. They also knew how devastated I was that you didn't believe me about the baby—God, Jack. Did *they* somehow cause the miscarriage?" Tears of anger filled her eyes. "Was it due to one of them that you didn't believe me, didn't care enough to stay?"

Jack scooted his chair around the table right next to hers, close enough so that he could wrap an arm around her. She didn't pull away, just rested her head on his shoulder for a moment.

He brushed a strand of hair out of her eyes. "I don't know. But it was hard for me to wrap my brain around what I believed you'd done. I know you, Sara. I know that if that's what you chose to do, you would have confronted me, told me. And, yeah, I would've been upset by your decision. Pissed for sure. Yet, even knowing all that, knowing *you*, I still believed the worst of you."

He kissed the top of her hair. He'd lost her once; he damn fucking well wasn't losing her again. Not because of Baltzer, or Roe, or a snake—any damned snake. "I hate to use Baltzer as a cop-out for my shitty behavior. But I know you. And I know myself. And neither of us behaved in character when you miscarried."

"I never could figure out why I didn't confront you and force you to see the truth. Why I *allowed* you to believe what you did." Sara materialized two sodas, drank greedily, then set her can back on the table. "And when I thought about *that*, I got a massive, debilitating headache. We *were* influenced. When we were at our most vulnerable, someone controlled our emotions. God, who would be so cruel?"

Grant Baltzer was the only answer. Roe fit into this somewhere. But at the heart of it all, Jack was convinced, it was Baltzer pulling Sara's string. "And why?"

"Yes. *Why*? What purpose would it serve?"

Jack pulled his handheld out of his back pocket and starting punching in the locations of all the missing girls.

"What are you doing?"

"Putting together the pieces of the puzzle. Everything that we've seen and heard comes right back to the Omnivatic. At first I didn't think the missing women had anything to do with wizards being infected. I didn't consider that the leyline had much to do with anything but

Baltzer. Let's see what happens when we enter all the data and layer facts on top of each other."

"Can you do it with one hand? I need this one."

He shot her a smile, and tightened his fingers around hers. "Yeah. One hand's good. Let's see what we have."

He felt a rise of excitement as he keyed information into his computer with his thumb. "Both the abduction points and the reappearance locations are on the same leyline that runs beneath Baltzer's home, the hotels, and the village."

"And the cave. I was chased to by Snakus Giganticus." She released his hand, obviously realizing that she was hindering his access to the small keyboard. "But, just to play devil's advocate here for a minute, that's the same house *I* live in," she pointed out. "The same hotels *I'm* a partner in and work in every day. The same earthquake that I experienced. *I'm* not our Omnivatic."

The snake was a rapist as well as a killer. "You're a woman."

"And Grant isn't a snake."

"A matter of opinion," Jack muttered. "We have to give this info to the council right away."

"Agreed. But how about if we figure out a way to blow up that cave first, just in case it is the portal?"

God, he loved how her mind worked. That was *exactly* what he'd been thinking. "We can stop there on our way to see the council."

Jack glanced up and smiled; the young nurse who'd informed them the police were interviewing the patient stood beside their table.

"¿Perdón? You may go in now."

Sara got to her feet in a musical jangle of bracelets. "Have the *policía* finished questioning her?"

"*Sí.* I will escort you to her room. Please to follow me."

"I hope she'll talk to us," Sara said quietly as they accompanied the nurse down a series of long corridors to the patient's room. "If her story is anything like that of the girl in Lima, she must still be terrified."

The young girl looked awfully small in the hospital bed, her soft cocoa-colored skin marred by livid bruises crisscrossing her arms and neck. The whites of her wary eyes were still bloodshot, her lips swollen and scabbed as though she'd bitten them until they bled.

Sara approached her bed while Jack remained farther back, but the girl was clearly skittish having a strange man in the room.

"Maybe you'd better wait outside," Sara suggested.

She heard him move behind her, his shoes squeaking on the linoleum. "I'll be right outside the door."

Listening, she knew. She nodded and gave him a grateful smile. The girl's face noticeably softened.

"*Hola,* Valentina, my name is Sara Temple. They say you are having bad dreams," Sara started in slow Spanish, pulling up a green molded plastic chair beside the bed. "Will you talk to me? I think I might be able to help you."

"The nurses think I am loco," the girl replied in broken English. "So do the *policía*. They think I am—*que la component*—making it up to hide a boyfriend who was too rough with me. I do not have such a boyfriend."

"Will you tell me what happened?" Sara considered

revealing that she too had been chased—*assaulted*—by Sarulu, but decided to play it by ear. This child hadn't just been *chased*. She'd been whipped and brutally raped.

The girl, only about fifteen, stared out the window, as if she couldn't bear to look at Sara while she spoke. "Sarulu came to our village seeking payment. Each family must sacrifice one of their daughters to appease the snake god. It was my family's turn.

"He comes as a man. A young, *handsome* man, with hair and eyes of gold. He laughed and told me to run, to run fast. And for a moment I thought that I would be the one who got away." The girl lifted dull brown eyes to Sara's.

"Some girls get away. Raped. Hurt, *sí*, but they get away. *Algunas veces*. I know the jungle near my home. I have lived there all my fifteen years. Who would know it better? But then he came behind me, *tan rápido como el relámpago*, very fast, his feet barely touching the ground."

Sara shuddered. "He turned into a giant snake, with eyes of gold and a three-forked rainbow-colored tongue."

"*Sí*." The girl touched the welts on her neck—lacerations, Sara knew, from Sarulu's damned tongue. The whip marks that cut and scored flesh until it split open in agonizing streaks that burned like fire.

"The snake—*Madre de Dios*—it licked and—and *tasted me*, then held me with sharp claws around here, and here."

Sara noticed the stark white bandages wrapped around the girl's ribs beneath her thin green hospital gown. Sunlight poured through the window and the room was warm, but Sara was freezing cold.

"He squeezed and squeezed. I could no longer scream. I could no longer breathe."

"Shh. Shh," Sara soothed as the girl's breathing became labored and hurried. "You're safe here. No one can hurt you now, Valentina."

"The more I—*luchó?*"

"Struggled?"

The girl nodded. Her long, dark hair was probably pretty when it was clean and brushed, but she looked exactly what she was: a girl on the brink of womanhood who'd been terrorized by something freaking, *unbelievably* frightening.

"The more I fight, the more Sarulu laughed." She twisted the sheets, her breathing becoming erratic. Tears ran down her face and throat. The monitors beside the bed began to beep with the frenetic beat of the girl's pulse.

"Okay. That's enough. You don't have to tell me any more. Shh. Shh." Sara sat on the side of the bed and gathered the girl in her arms. "Shh. You're safe. You're safe." Rubbing the thin back, she rocked the girl in her arms, feeling helpless and absolutely furious. She and Jack were going to find this—whatever it was. Snake, man, whatever. And kill it stone dead.

"He was inside me everywhere at once." Valentina's arms tightened around Sara and she spoke against her shoulder. Sara kept rocking, not sure if she was giving comfort to this young woman or herself. "Sarulu went inside me. The pain . . . He was inside all m-my—inside my body." She lifted her head and met Sara's eyes. "Inside down there." Crimson, she buried her hot face back against her neck as Sara continued rocking her, murmuring soothing nonsense when she wanted to scream and cry just like Valentina.

The girl wailed harder, her voice rising to a crescendo as she flung herself away from Sara, almost falling out of the narrow bed. The clatter of the metal headboard slamming against the brick wall added to the chaos.

Jack raced in, taking in the scene in a glance, followed closely by the nurse. The middle-aged woman glared at Sara and spoke in rapid Spanish to Valentina as she readied a syringe of sedative.

"Can you do a Mindwipe," Sara begged Jack as, behind her, the girl continued sobbing hysterically. "Leave her with the facts, but not the emotion?"

"Yeah." He glanced at Valentina, and a second later the girl's sobbing stopped.

Sara reached out and squeezed his hand. "Thank you. Hang on a sec." She went over to the bed. The nurse gave her a hostile look. "I just want to tell her good-bye." When the woman stood back to give her access, Sara leaned down and smoothed the girl's sweat-dampened hair off her face. "Thank you for telling me what happened, that was very brave of you. You are *not* loco. It happened to me as well, Valentina. And I swear to you, we're going to figure out what's going on near your village, and we'll stop it."

"You promise?"

"I promise."

The girl wearily closed her eyes, then opened them

and grabbed Sara's hand, tugging her down so she could whisper in her ear. "What if I am *embarazada—pregnant*—yes?" Tears welled. *"My bebé—serpiente o humanos?"*

Wrapping her arms about the girl's thin shoulders, Sara hugged her tightly, murmuring words of comfort.

If Grant or William really was responsible for this, she'd kill him herself.

Eighteen

Sunlight filtered through the trees and the air shimmered with the drone of insects and the oppressive, sultry hothouse heat. A curious capuchin monkey, its inquisitive face capped with a tuft of black hair, sat on a nearby branch watching them.

To Jack, the whole damn jungle smelled like a rotting compost heap. Even in broad daylight, this particular chunk of rain forest had an evil feel to it that kept making him want to look over his shoulder. Both the cave and the jungle real estate surrounding it needed to be blown to hell, and he was ready to do just that.

"The sacrifice business seems to be thriving," Sara said dryly, pointing to some new offerings that had been left at the mouth of the cave since they'd been there last. Flies buzzed around the rotting fruit, and the crystal snakeskin amulets strung around the entrance swayed and tinkled in the muggy breeze like macabre wind chimes.

She put a hand on his arm. "Jack, I don't think I *should* help you with magic after all. My emotions are all over the place, and you know what could—I don't want to hurt you."

Jack took her in his arms. "You can do this. Concentrate, shove everything else out of your mind. Our strength is that our powers are stronger, more focused when used together. Even more so when we're touching. Concentrate."

She squared her shoulders and sucked in a fortifying breath. "You're right. I'll do my best."

"That's my girl. Besides"—he shot her a grin—"what's the worst that can happen? The place will blow up?"

She smiled. "Good point. Okay. Let's see how much of an explosion we can make together." She turned to face the cave.

"Ready, Sara-mine?" Jack asked, standing beside her.

Sara's bracelets caught the sun and jangled as she touched her fingers to the sunstones in her ears to amp her powers. "Ready as I'll ever be."

"On three. One. Two. *Three.*"

A faint echoing pop came from inside. No explosion. Damn. "No cigar. Let's try that again, but this time I'll hold you to see if that amplifies the effect." He felt the tension in her body as his arms went around her. "God knows that holding you makes *me* blow up. Let's see what the two of us combined do to the portal."

Sara gave him a real grin, leaned into him, and nodded to indicate she was ready to try again.

No luck. No *nothing*. Not even a tremor. Hell, the little monkey still sat right there watching them with big, curious eyes, nibbling on a leaf, blissfully unconcerned.

"Now what?"

"Now we use C-4," Jack told her grimly.

"And you just happen to have some in your back pocket?" Sara asked, casting a nervous glance over her shoulder as the leaves rustled.

There were plenty of unthreatening reasons for there to be noises in the bushes, Jack knew. And several threatening reasons, too. "Funny you should ask. I don't, but I will."

He called the psionic safe, spoke to it, and removed the C-4. He'd obtained the brick of explosive earlier from a friend in Montana and stuck it away as an insurance policy. He wasn't proficient at blowing shit up, but Jack was perfectly capable of following instructions.

"That thing's like a clown car," Sara observed with dry irreverence as the ice cube closed and disappeared. "Oh, freaking hell." She turned to look at him. "We don't have to go inside, do we?"

He hefted the gray brick of explosive material. "I'm not leaving you out here alone."

"Guess that answers the question." She slipped off her bright red jacket and looked around for somewhere to put it. After a moment, a padded satin hanger materialized; Sara hung up the jacket, and a second later they disappeared.

"Better get rid of those shoes too, while you're at it."

She held out a foot clad in a strappy red high heel; her toenails were painted the same sexy red as the sandals. She pulled a face. "Jimmy does *not* make appropriate footwear, but—" An instant later she wore heavy, bright red hiking boots, and her white T-shirt had changed to the same sunny yellow as the shoelaces. She gave him a smart salute. "Ready, Captain."

He knew how vivid and terrifying her experience had been in this very spot, yet here she was with him, because he needed her to do this. Not only was Sara present physically, she was willing to do whatever was necessary. He was as impressed as hell.

Brave. Beautiful. And so sexy that just looking at her made his heart ache.

"Good little soldier," he said thickly as he swooped down and captured her mouth, holding her with his free arm. The kiss was hot enough to compete with the temperature, but over too fast.

Reluctantly breaking away, he held out the brick of C-4. "This is a plastic bonded explosive. It's like putty. We'll squeeze off chunks and fill as many crevicees as we can, then get back out here, and you can use your firepower as detonation. We'll bring down the cave and everything in it. That'll shut the portal down, if this *is* the damn portal."

Blinking her eyes into focus, Sara tucked her yellow T-shirt back into her jeans. He hadn't realized that in the nanosecond he'd been kissing her, he'd been trying to undress her right there. The idea had merit, but he'd rather their lovemaking in the great outdoors took place in a field of clover rather than in the rotting vegetation of a snake-infested rain forest. He'd work on that. Later. If there *was* a fucking later.

She secured a pin in her hair. "I don't doubt it for a moment, do you?"

"No," he said grimly. "Here's the drill. We teleport in as far as we can, apply this stuff, and teleport directly to the Council. Do not pass Go. Do not collect two hundred dollars."

"Don't you want to stay and see the fireworks?"

"Just knowing there *are* fireworks is good enough for me. Ready?" He took her hand.

Her fingers felt cool and trusting in his as she tightened her grip. "As I'll ever be. Let's do it."

Dim as it was inside the cave, he saw well enough and didn't need the flashlight. Chunks of crystal sparkled around them like brilliant stars in a dusk sky.

Sara's fingers tightened in his as she glanced around. "This place gives me the heebie-jeebies."

Thinking about the pit of snakes at the other end of the cave wasn't doing wonders for him either. But there was something that scared him more. "My powers don't work in here, Sara." That gave *him* the freaking heebie-jeebies.

She stopped, her eyes wide. "What do you mean, your powers don't work in here? Mine are just fine."

"Yeah. I know, I can feel yours."

Sara took out a square of linen with little yellow happy faces on it and mopped her glowing face. The smell of her hot skin made him hot, and he had to tamp down his lust and concentrate on what they were there for.

Later.

She shot him a puzzled glance as she tucked the hankie in her hip pocket. "Why do mine work and yours don't?"

Damn good question. And he bet Duncan Edge had the answer. Finding out the answer was next on his agenda, after they blew this place to hell. "Doesn't matter. Let's get this job done and get out of here."

"Doesn't matter?" Her eyes widened. "Oh, God. Do you feel okay ?" She scanned his face, eyes anxious, then put the back of her hand against his brow.

Jack grasped her hand. "What are you doing?"

"What if your powers aren't working because you're getting sick, just like those other wizards?"

"I'm perfectly fine. My powers aren't on the fritz except in this cave. I'd bet my degree it has something to do with these unusual crystal formations." Which apparently had no effect on *Sara's* powers.

She twisted the sunstone stud in her ear. "You're sure? Absolutely sure?"

"We teleported here, didn't we?"

"I'd just hate for—"

He grabbed her and kissed her hard. "Yeah. I felt the same way when you told me about that giant snake attacking you. So let's stick together, blow this place, and get the hell away from here."

"You'd tell me if you felt sick, right?"

Hell, no. "Of course."

She narrowed her pretty eyes at him. "Okay."

The good news was that the pit he'd fallen into was no longer there. The bad news was that the dead end was. There had to be another way around this wall of rock, Jack was damn sure. But blowing the cave, entrance and all, was even more rewarding than seeing where it might lead. Cutting off the Omnivatic's route would work, either coming or going. With any luck, the son of a bitch had traveled through the portal to his nest. In a few minutes he'd be trapped there, unable to return.

With any luck.

Jack didn't set a whole helluva lot of store by luck.

He showed Sara how to break off smaller pieces of the explosive, then demonstrated how to insert the malleable material into nooks and crannies in the rock face. He didn't plan to stand around doing any crimping or inserting of detonator caps. It would've taken more than an hour to set them. Fortunately, one good blast of Sara's firepower, from a safe distance, and the portal would be nothing more than a pile of rubble.

It took twenty minutes for them to pack the C-4 in the walls and ceiling at the back of the cave. It was hot going. He hadn't noticed how warm it was inside the cave the last time. Maybe it was the time of day? Perhaps a hot spring somewhere? He was used to working in the heat, yet sweat beaded his forehead. He used the hem of his shirt to wipe his face.

"Looks good."

Pale gray lumps of compound stood out against the dark rock and diamond-bright glints of crystal, forming an arch across the walls and ceiling. Enough C-4 to blow up ten caves this size. But with one shot, he wasn't taking any chances.

Sara grabbed his upper arm. "I really want to see this place blown to hell."

Jack grinned at her fierce expression. "Why not? The

Council can wait another few minutes. Let's get outside and watch the show."

She smiled back. He swung her flush against his body, dipping his head to kiss her. Lifting his head after a few moments, he cupped her face in one hand. "When I walked away from you that day, it was as though I put on dark glasses. Being with you again is like walking into the sun."

He kissed her again, short and unbearably sweet. Breaking away reluctantly, he said softly. "Later." There *would* be a later. And he was going to make up for lost time. Lost opportunities. Lost love. "Get us out of here."

OUTSIDE, JACK ENVELOPED THEM in a clear protective shield, then they worked together to amp their powers. The bezel on his watch started to turn, amping his powers until his entire body surged and pulsed with magic. He suggested that Sara hold her sunstones instead of just touching them.

She did so, clasping one small stud, in each fist. "I've never taken them off before." She felt naked, and oddly vulnerable.

Jack stood behind her. She loved the solid warmth of his body and his familiar smell as he loosely wrapped his arms around her waist. "One second—I want to clear the animals out of the area first. . . . Ready?"

Oh, Jack. She inhaled deeply. "You bet."

"Hit it with all the juice you have. One. Two. *Three!*"

Sara had never used as much power. It seemed to come from the soles of her feet and up through her body, all projected at the C-4.

The massive explosion three seconds later was worth the wait. Showers of debris and giant chunks of rock rained down forcefully on the shield. The entire face of the cliff collapsed in on itself, blown away as they watched.

"Cool!" Sara pressed closer to the invisible wall of the bubble, fascinated as the rocks crashed around them, bouncing harmlessly off the shield but tearing into the trees and shrubs outside the entrance to the cave. "A thing of beauty, really." She spun around and wound her arms around Jack's neck, running her fingers through his thick hair. He smelled of clean male, and her pheromones went into overdrive. "Maybe we can go to the Council tomorrow?"

His lips twitched. He shook his head.

She nibbled his chin. The man never seemed to shave. How fortunate that she loved his stubble, and God only knew, it made him look sexy as hell. "Tonight?" she asked hopefully.

"Sorry, sweetheart. I'll take a rain check on that offer. But they want us there—now."

THE FULL COUNCIL WAS present. Jack worked backward, starting with blowing the hell out of what they believed to be the Omnivatic's portal, then backtracked to their reactions upon returning from the Icehotel, their visit to the hospital, and their reasoning behind their conclusions.

"You're *convinced* Grant Baltzer is the Omnivatic?" Duncan Edge demanded, leaning back in his massive chair.

"Ninety-eight percent," Jack told him, aware of the unseen eyes behind the Head of Council watching their every move, analyzing their every word. He didn't bother sitting down. He and Sara both stood in front of the enormous desk. "The other two percent goes to his partner William Roe." He left out a few percentage points for Harry the boa.

"Your opinion, Sara?"

"Unfortunately, considering my relationship with Grant, I agree." She stuck her hands in the pockets of her red jacket, looking fresh and sexy and kick-ass in her jeans and yellow-laced red hiking boots.

Between them, Jack and Sara filled the Council in on what they knew.

"Want me to do the Sarulu bit?" Jack asked her softly, concerned by her pale cheeks and the haunted look in her eyes. Admitting Baltzer's guilt to the Council was hitting her hard, he knew. Knowing that someone she'd always believed loved her was capable of deception of this magnitude must be devastating.

His slid his fingers through hers. Her hand was as cold as ice as he tugged her against his side.

Shooting him a grateful look, she shook her head. "No. I'll do it."

Jack had never been more proud of her as she stood there, straight and elegant, and told the Council in measured tones about being attacked.

"Were you raped?" Edge asked baldly.

Jack took a step forward. "Easy—"

Sara reined him in. "It's okay. No, I wasn't."

"Yet the other women were."

"I don't know why them and not me. I zapped him with fire—but when my power didn't have any effect, I beat the crap out of him with a big stick. Maybe I woke up from the hypnotic state too soon?"

"And he called you by name?"

"He called me by name."

He, Jack noticed. Not the snake. Not it. *He.*

Sara's throat moved, but her gaze on the Head of Council was steady. "I believe Sarulu and Grant are one and the same."

"And therefore Omnivatic."

"Yes."

"The Aequitas Book of Answers revealed a message last night," Jack inserted. "'Erebus Novem two are one to infinity if not stopped.' I believe that the ninth member of the Erebus is the Omnivatic attempting to rule, and that Grant Baltzer is Novem. 'Two are one' could allude to him being Sarulu. And the rest is obvious." He hesitated. "There was another message a couple days ago: 'All that you seek is here.' The *Book* was alluding to Baltzer being the Omnivatic." Or else *Sara* was the one he sought, Jack thought.

The Head of Council steepled his fingers, watching Jack for several seconds. "Thank you for your service." Edge rose from behind his desk and put out his hand to Jack. "You've both done an exemplary job and confirmed the Council's suspicions. We'll take it from here."

"What?!" Sara cried.

An icy chill of premonition slicked Jack's body. "You're dismissing us?"

"Others will take over from here. Isn't that what you wanted, what you asked for when we first gave you this assignment?" He raised his hand to summon someone out of the darkness behind him. "Lark, escort Miss Temple to the secure location until the comet has passed."

Jack moved in front of Sara. "Whoa. Hold up. No one's taking Sara *anywhere*," he said dangerously. "What pertinent piece of the puzzle have you left out, you son of a bitch?"

"You've already put together the puzzle," Edge replied coolly.

"No. There's something missing. What is it? What's the key to making sense of this clusterfuck we're dealing with?" He stepped to the edge of the desk.

"Jack—" Sara grabbed his arm.

He shook her off, then braced both hands on the desk, crowding the other man's space. Fury pulsed behind his eyeballs as he said tightly, "What haven't you told us, Edge?"

Edge's eyes flickered for a nanosecond to Sara, then back to him. Jack's heart pounded harder. Something, then, to do with her. Something the Council had known all along and deliberately withheld.

"It's on a need—"

"*Bullshit.* We're far beyond need-to-know," Jack growled.

There was a squeak of patent leather against leather as Lark unfolded herself from her council chair behind Edge. She sauntered up to the desk and perched on the edge, her flossy leather bodysuit gleaming in the spotlight as she flicked back her black hair.

"You were asked to do a job." Edge telegraphed Lark a message Jack couldn't interpret. "You did the job. That's all there is to it."

"You've done more than you can possibly understand," Lark said smoothly. "Right now, Sara's a danger to all of us."

"This isn't a damned pissing contest, Edge. *All* of this has something to do with Sara. Doesn't it?"

He heard Sara's murmur of denial behind him, but Jack was a hundred percent focused on Duncan Edge. He reached over the desk and grabbed Edge by the front of the black-and-silver robe, bringing them nose to nose. "What the fuck are you hiding?"

Edge put a hand up to keep the rest of the Council at bay. "Sara's father was an Omnivatic."

Jack released his hold and stepped back. Chances were, no matter how much he wanted to hurt the son of a bitch, if he touched the Head of Council again, *he'd* be the one dead. "Impossible. They chose immortality. They *can't* breed."

"Jack's right." Sara came to stand beside him. "My father wasn't Omnivatic. I'd know. We were very close— if that were the case, he would've told me."

Edge shook his robe back into place in a flash of heat and silver. "The facts of your birth are irrefutable. Because of the rareness of your parentage, the first mixed-breed Aequitas-Omnivatic child in three thousand years, the Archon has kept an interested eye on you from birth."

Jack circled Sara's shoulders with one arm, tucking her tightly against his side. "Again. Impossible."

"An aberration. But clearly *not* impossible."

He didn't want to go into the *aberration* statement right then. "And you know this how?"

"Just as the Archon had an Aequitas in our Council, the Wizard Council has had someone in the Archon. Have for centuries." Edge's sharp gaze focused back on Jack. "We don't know if the Omnivatics think the Aequitas were using her to discover their weaknesses, or if they're trying to get to her to use her as a means to bring the Aequitas down from within. Either way, she's as much a liability as an asset to us now."

"Which is why she needs to come with me. The Wizard Council will protect her and you. We can't predict how the comet will impact her Omnivatic powers," Lark said simply.

Jack glared at Lark. "Protect her? With all due respect, Edge, they already took out the entire Archon, *and* the Aequitas member of *your* council. *Nobody* is getting within a fucking mile of her. Not you *or* the Omnivatics! I will protect Sara without the Wizard Council's help."

"Excuse me. I can speak for myself," Sara inserted furiously, breaking away from Jack to face Edge, Lark, and the rest of the Council. She rubbed absently at her temple, her face pale. "I'm not going *anywhere* without Jack."

"Fine. He can accompany you. This will all be over in five hours."

"First, tell us *why* the Omnivatics want Sara," Jack demanded. The Council was still holding back. And until he had all the facts, he wasn't going *anywhere*.

"He wants to—oh, God. He wants *mate* with me, doesn't he?" Sara's small voice was devoid of expression.

"No!" Jack was appalled, and a freezing chill ran up his spine. "Not just no, but fucking no." Yes. He knew the answer, and it was a resounding freaking *yes*. That's *exactly* what this whole thing had been about. Baltzer wanted Sara, and he wasn't going to stop until he had her. "To what purpose?" He heard the thread of revulsion in his own voice. "Omnivatics can't procreate."

"Fact is that Omnivatics *can* breed, given the right circumstances." Lark sent Edge a speaking look as he sat back in his chair.

"As your father did, Miss Temple, they have to give up their immortality," Edge said simply.

Lark drew a long black-lacquered nail over the polished surface of the desk over and over in an infinity symbol. "It's a bit more complicated than that. First, they must find and be accepted by their Lifemate; then they must choose mortality. If, and only if, they don't manage to kill their Lifemate during the mating process, and the mother is strong enough to survive the pregnancy and birth of the half Omnivatic growing inside her—*then* they can have a child." The dark curls slid over the patent leather as Lark cocked her head to one side and stared straight at Sara.

"If we're right about Grant," Sara said in a monotone, "then I've been betrayed by someone I trusted. And now you're telling me that my *father* was an evil man? An Omnivatic, like Grant? It's hard to wrap my mind around."

"Well, wrap it fast, lovey," Lark told her briskly. "The information you gave us confirmed our suspicions, and whatever is to be done must be completed in the five hours left to us."

"I understand. Grant *won't* give up being immortal. I know him. He wants something from me, but he won't risk his immortality to achieve it. He's vain, ambitious, and competitive as hell. Being an Omnivatic, knowing he's fooling everyone, gives him a thrill. Knowing things no one else does gives him power. Being in control gives him power. If you take me away somewhere, it's going to shoot his plan to hell. If you do that—then God only knows what his next move will be."

"She's right." Jack looked from Duncan to Lark to Sara. "Take her out of the equation now, and you've just shot your chance of neutralizing the Omnivatics' as a threat."

Lark looked at Duncan. "What do you think?"

"It's a risk, but I say we let them see it through." Duncan turned his gaze to Jack and Sara. "I don't like it, but all right. What's your next move?"

Sara started pacing. "We have to figure out what it is he wants from me. He's an immortal already. Sex?" She chewed her lip. "It must have something to do with sex."

Lark raised a pierced brow. "He already screws any woman who crosses his path."

"He's oversexed," Sara agreed. "He enjoys the chase, gets off being the hunter." She glanced at Jack. "Remember what Valentina said? He told the girls to *run*." She turned to Edge. "He wanted to hunt them like prey.

This isn't about sex for sex itself. It's about using it for power.

"He's watched me since I was a child. Oh, gross! It wasn't his father who was friends with my dad, was it? That was Grant all along. Grant watching me as I grew up—oh, God. *He* killed my parents, didn't he?"

"We believe so," Lark said, not able to cushion the blow.

Sara dropped into a chair. "He's been manipulating me my entire life. Shaping me, forming me to be what he wants."

Nobody said anything, and after a few moments she dragged in a deep breath and let it out slowly. "What does he *want* from me? How does the comet's appearance after all this time link with me and with Grant? What does the combination get for him?"

Sara being a half-breed changed the game. The Council hadn't come right out and said it, but Jack knew the score. Baltzer wanted Sara specifically. Otherwise, he would've killed her along with her parents.

She was the link between their immortality and their ability to create more Omnivatics. With her, they could unlock the secrets to gaining more numbers, and possibly even greater strength, enough to overwhelm the Aequitas and the wizarding world as it was. Enough to bring down the system that had protected blissfully ignorant humans for so long.

With sickening certainty, Jack realized the answer. "They want to use her as an experiment." All eyes turned to Jack. "It's the only thing that makes sense. They hope that the fact that she's half Omnivatic is the key to them being able to have children." He blew out a breath.

Jesus. He hated this. Hated Sara's involvement. Hated where his limited imagination was taking him.

"That's it, isn't it? Goddamn it. Baltzer wants to impregnate Sara in the hope that between them they will create an Omnivatic child."

~Nineteen~

*O*h, God." Sara stared at him wide-eyed, her face ashen. "*That's* what he wanted all along. That's it. Eeeuw! The son of a bitch! He couldn't risk wasting this opportunity. He had to make sure I was *fertile!*" She shuddered. "And I was. But he didn't want me to have that child."

Her eyes welled and she dashed the moisture away. "As if I'd ever let him put his hands on me, let alone any-freaking-thing else!" She rubbed her cheeks. "It's all tied in with the approach of the comet. It isn't a coincidence that Grant moved us to San Cristóbal, right near the cave. He must've been planning this for—holy crap. He waited thirty *years.*"

"He's waited three *thousand* years for this moment," Duncan Edge pointed out. "For an Omnivatic to rise in the ranks of the Erebus, he must amass power. What greater power than being the only member capable of fathering a child? The powerful magic and magnetic pull of the comet must activate something in an Omnivatic."

"The comet has passed before," Lark pointed out.

"and there's never been a child born to an Omnivatic other than Sara. And she's only half."

"True." Jack didn't feel any better about this than Edge and the Council. Worse. "So Ophidian's comet must—hell. That's it! We know he becomes more powerful with the advent of the comet; but what if the strength he derives from its passage makes him incredibly *potent*? For a brief time the infertility is gone, and he can impregnate—"

"Speculate the whys and wherefores later." Sara grabbed his hand in a death grip. She looked as though she wanted to vomit. Jack felt the same way. But for her . . . Jesus, for her it was so much worse.

"Edge. Will wizard magic work?"

"Let's find out, shall we?"

"What did you do?" Jack demanded. Because everything in the chamber looked exactly the same.

"Sent my people to the cave to see how far they can get in."

Jack felt a glimmer of relief. If Edge's people got as far as the portal and their magic, unlike his own, *worked*, Sara would be safe.

A few minutes later, a man materialized before Edge's desk. "I don't fucking get it. The cave is small, tiny really. But we couldn't do any magic, and only got as far as a solid rock wall a few hundred feet inside." He vanished.

Edge's eyes met Jack's. "You have your answer."

"Fucking shitty answer." Jack's voice was grim. "I have to go back to San Cristóbal, take another look at the portal we thought we blew up. There might be another entrance. I'll follow it, find the nest, and destroy it from the inside." And Baltzer with it. He'd reduce the twisted snake-dick to *very* small pieces.

"Your powers don't *work* in the portal, Jack," Sara reminded him through bloodless lips. "I'll have to go in with you—"

"Not just no, but hell to the tenth power, no."

"There is another way in." Sara stood, ignoring him. "If Grant wants me—for whatever reason—*he'll* have to take me inside his nest."

Jack jumped up. "No! There's no way you're going through some portal to God knows where."

Sara placed a gentle hand on his arm, and he took it tightly in his. "It's the only way, Jack. We've run out of time. We all know that. He'll take me to the nest. You can follow."

Jack gritted his teeth. "What if I *can't*? Are you thinking of that, Sara? The two of us couldn't proceed more than two hundred feet inside that fucking cave without hitting a wall. What if I *can't* get to you?"

Sara took a deep breath. "Then I'm on my own, and I'll have to kill him myself."

"I won't let you do it. There's got to be another way. We just have to find it." He turned to Duncan. "What about that team you were ready to use, huh? You were going to replace us. Do it!"

"We *can't*. Wizard magic, even Aequitas magic, doesn't work inside the portal, as we've proven. Not to mention that, even if we could breach his stronghold, Baltzer would trace us before any of us could get close enough to do any damage. None of us can get anywhere near it. Sara is our Hail Mary pass."

"Don't go there," Jack cautioned, his voice tight. "Do not fucking go there, Edge."

Duncan ignored the angry outburst. "Someone has to be *inside* the nest to destroy it, and Baltzer with it. That portal has to be closed for eternity." He looked at Sara, then pointedly at the monitor he'd summoned that showed the progress of Ophidian's comet as it approached the Earth. "Five hours before the natural disasters start. *Cataclysmic* events, Slater."

"I'm well aware of the ramifications as well as the time limit, Edge."

"If the portal is destroyed, what will happen when the comet passes?" Sara demanded.

Edge's eyes glinted. "The events won't be as cataclysmic. Bad, but not irreparable."

Sara sucked in a deep breath. "I'll do it."

Jack spun to face her. "What the fuck do you mean, you'll do it?!"

"It's the *only* way, and we all know it."

"We'll find *another* way."

Her eyes, soft brown velvet, held his. "In five hours, Jack?"

He took Sara's hands. "Don't do this. Please."

"I have to, Jack." Determination etched her stark features. "I'm the perfect weapon of mass destruction." Her lips twitched, but her eyes were very, very serious. "I'm half Omnivatic. My powers work there. Grant *wants* me inside his nest. We have no other options. I'm the only one who *can* do this."

Jack dropped his hands. "Come over here." He walked about twenty feet, taking Sara with him, because he was damned if he was letting her go, even to cross the room.

He summoned the psionic safe, then whispered the words; a second later the door popped open, emitting a spiral of acid green vapor. Jack removed the crystal dagger, then sent the safe away.

They returned to face the Council, still hand in hand. "I'm stating on record that I adamantly oppose what you're doing." Jack held the sparkling dagger out to Sara. "I'll rip that goddamned cave apart to find you. Take this."

Sara reached out, but before her fingers touched the dagger, she stiffened in surprise, "He's here—"

She vanished.

SARA WAS SURPRISED TO find herself not in the cave or some terrifying "nest," but in the hanging cage in Grant's suite at the hacienda. Haydn swelled through hidden speakers, some violin concerto number something that Grant favored.

She looked around. She was alone. For now.

She let out a shaky breath, then did her best to control the in-breath. For a moment, she was back in a meditation class she'd taken years ago, hearing the teacher's instructions: "Concentrate on the breath. Breathe in; pause. Breathe out; pause. In those spaces, you'll find your center, your balance." She hoped like hell he was right. She needed all the balance she could get.

Her life was going to depend on keeping her cool, no matter what happened.

Was Jack even now tracing her?

He could find her here, but that wasn't enough. The problem was, *she* had to be in the nest to kill Grant and close the portal.

She ran her fingers over the cool bars of the wrought-iron cage in which she was locked—magically repaired after Antonio had destroyed the room what felt like a lifetime ago. She swallowed hard as the cage swung several feet off the floor. It took every ounce of self-control not to use magic to turn the opulent, creepy room into a freaking bonfire.

Her lungs inflated uncomfortably as she dragged in another ragged breath. The teleportation used to steal her from the Council chambers wasn't normal wizard magic, and she felt slightly nauseated. The light sway of the cage, combined with the heavy spicy smell of the incense smoke hanging in the still air, didn't help. The room was unbearably, steamy hot. She needed no reminders that snakes liked heat.

Clearly the air-conditioning was off, and it felt as though the heat had been turned up to high as well. She stripped off the red linen jacket, glad now she'd put it back on for the trip to the Council. The color couldn't be missed. She tossed it on the floor of the cage with a jangle of bracelets. On second thought . . . Crouching, she squeezed the fabric through the bars until it dropped soundlessly to the carpet below. Even on the busy black-and-red oriental carpet, Jack would see it.

Standing, she quickly touched each earlobe to make sure the sunstones were with her. Satisfied that she would be able to amp her powers when necessary, Sara slid her fingers into her back pocket. Removing the thin leather cord with the crystallized snakeskin amulet that Incz had given her, she slipped it around her neck. Tucking the crystal into the neckline of her T-shirt, she gave it a pat for luck. She wished she'd been able to accept the crystal dagger from Jack before she'd been teleported.

"Where are you, you son of a bitch? Why did you teleport me here? Why not to your freaky nest?" As scared as she was to confront Grant, the anticipation of what was to come was far worse.

Stretching out both arms, she touched the bars on either side of her. Seven feet across. The arched "roof" was another arm's length overhead.

Where was he? *What* was he? Would he appear as Grant or Sarulu? She wasn't sure which terrified her more.

Crap, it was hot in here.

The music ended, and there was a brief pause before the piece started up again. Haydn had never been one of her favorites. She liked his work even less now. If nothing else, her location confirmed that Grant was the Omnivatic. Faced with all the evidence, it was impossible *not* to believe it. But she'd harbored a tiny grain of hope that the evidence had been wrongly interpreted. That Grant was just Grant. Her guardian. Her protector. A man who'd loved her like a favorite niece for years.

Knowing that she'd trusted him almost all her life, trusted and *loved* him, and that he'd deceived her from day one was devastating. The music was getting on her last, extremely stretched nerve. Magically she turned it off in mid-swell. The silence was such a relief she almost wept.

Even though the intricate bars surrounding her were only an inch in diameter, they were precisely spaced six inches apart. Thank God he hadn't attached the wrist and ankle straps hanging from the domed roof and pro-truding from the grid floor, because then she *would* be screaming her head off. She untucked her T-shirt and fanned her belly with the hem. *Hey, Jack? I'm melting here.* As open as her birdcage prison was, she was overwhelmed with an intense feeling of claustrophobia.

I still have the free will to teleport the hell out of here, she reminded herself, striving to contain her rising panic. The reality was, she was afraid to attempt any major magic. Turning off the stereo wasn't in the same league as a full-body teleport If she tried and wasn't able to use her full powers, she'd start babbling in terror. Sometimes ignorance was bliss.

Which brought her back to wondering why Jack's powers didn't work in the Omnivatic cave. They prob-ably wouldn't work in Grant's quarters either, now that she thought of it. And the only way Jack and the Wizard Council were going to be able to defeat the Omnivatics was if she went to the nest and helped them find a way in.

She was damned if she did, and damned if she didn't.

Alert for Grant's arrival, she took a deep breath of

hot, heavily perfumed air and surveyed the bedroom—
a room she'd seen only once after she'd made the original decorating selections a year ago. It hadn't improved
with time, she thought, disgusted and repelled. But the
destruction caused by Alberto wasn't evident now. Only a
wizard could have restored everything to its pristine state
this quickly.

How had he created and sustained such a perfect illusion for so long? An illusion perpetrated on her for most
of her life?

The fussy room, done in blood-red wallpaper and
ornate light fixtures, was filled with sex toys. The big
pieces—including the cage she was in and several large
machines she'd rather not investigate too closely—took
up a lot of floor space. The mammoth four-poster canopy bed, draped in red-and-gold silk and covered with
satin pillows, took up a large footprint as well. Now she
realized the bed had been converted to support a pulley
and strap system that didn't even bear thinking about.

Breathe in; pause. Breathe out; pause.

If she was this freaked out before anything actually
happened, what was she going to do when Grant dragged
her through that portal and into his nest?

The far wall held various ankle and leg straps, face
and body harnesses, and assorted paraphernalia to
imprison his victims. The faint sound of a footfall on the
carpet made her turn around too fast. The cage swayed.
She braced her feet and clung to the bars to maintain her
balance. She sucked in a startled breath when a dark head
appeared instead of Grant's golden one.

"Just where I left you," William said smugly. "Hello, baby." His topaz eyes gleamed with amusement.

Sara's fingers tightened on the bars as a ridiculous sense of relief washed through her. *William*. Not Grant. Thank God. Grant wouldn't let William do *anything* to her, and William knew it. Besides, they were in Grant's room where he could walk in at any moment. She hoped he would. Now would be good.

"Why am I here? Where's Grant?" Shit. Had William *killed* Grant?

In an instant, he was by her side. Lord. He'd just shimmered. Impossible. He seemed bigger and more imposing, and frankly more threatening, than he had over their lunch in Lima a yesterday ago.

The floor of the cage was just below his eye level, and he reached in through the bars and stroked a cold hand up her bare skin. The tattoo on his forearm almost looked as if it was slithering a few inches higher. Sara yanked her foot away. The cage swung to and fro for several seconds before he put a hand out to stop it. "Tsk, tsk. What can Grant do for you that I can't?" he asked smoothly, rubbing the pad of his thumb suggestively back and forth across his bottom lip.

The movement caught her attention. She'd seen that before—exactly the same slow motion, with the same hand. Grant. Grant did that when he was contemplating a victory over a competing hotelier. Her fingers tightened around the bars until her knuckles went white. "Did you bring me here, or did Grant?"

In a flicker of movement, his smirking expression

started to crinkle. No—Sara blinked sweat out of her eyes—his skin was buckling—oh, hell—*peeling*. His entire face was peeling off his skull in long strips, taking hair, flesh, and expression with it. No blood. No gore. Just strips of skin that crystallized as they dropped to the carpet. His clothing fell in a heap around his feet, leaving him naked. Naked and shedding his skin.

She backed up until her spine pressed against the bars behind her. *OhGodohGodohGod.* Disbelief and fascination kept her gaze glued to the transformation. Beneath the mess of William's shedding skin appeared the fair hair and pale blue eyes she'd known most of her life. Her stomach twisted with revulsion. Sweat ran down her temples and stung her eyes as a fresh-faced Grant emerged.

Every atom of her body urged her to teleport out of there. *Now.* Now, while he was in the process of his metamorphosis.

Erebus Novem two are one to infinity if not stopped.

Two are one to infinity.

William and Grant were one. He *was* the immortal Omnivatic.

JACK VAULTED OVER THE wide desk before Edge knew what hit him. Grabbing the Head of Council by the throat, he lifted the other man six inches off the floor, his viselike hold tightening around the other wizard's throat. "Bring her back, you bastard!"

Instantly, searing flames ate their way up Jack's arms and licked at his face. He was incensed enough, and scared enough for Sara, not to feel the heat. "Bring." He shook Edge. "Her." Shake. "Back."

Edge broke his hold, sending Jack crashing into the desk behind him. An explosive whoosh of flames soared high, then swirled around Edge's body in crackling orange, red, and blue sparks. "I'll give you a pass on that, Slater. One fucking pass, because I understand where you're coming from. Do that again, however, and I'll burn your ass to ash. Sara's disappearance had nothing to do with the Council."

Jack was on his feet, squinting against the intense heat. "Bullshit." When he went in to grab Duncan again, Edge turned up the flames. Jack's skin sizzled, and the moisture in his eyes dried painfully; he was forced to retreat.

"Admit it—you sent her through that fucking portal before she was ready. Before I had a chance to . . ." *Prepare her. Tell her I love her.* Not *say good-bye.*

Edge shook his head and waved off the other Council members, who were on their feet. He rubbed his throat where bruises were already beginning to develop, and said exactly what Jack didn't want to hear.

"The Omnivatic took her."

∽ Twenty ∽

"Why, Grant?" Sara demanded. It pissed her off that her voice shook a little. Yes, she was scared, but she was also livid that he'd betrayed, used, and damn well manipulated her for most of her life.

Suddenly she found herself free of the cage and standing beside him. In heels, she was eye to eye with him; in her hiking boots, she was a couple inches shorter.

Although his body was tanned and fit, she could've happily lived the rest of her life not seeing Grant naked. He, like Jack, kept himself in shape. She guessed that if one wanted to live an eternity, one had to maintain a healthy lifestyle.

She saw nothing of the Grant she knew in this man's eyes. The Grant who'd held her head over the toilet as she barfed up her first bottle of cheap wine. The Grant who'd given her dance lessons, and gone with her to choose the "prettiest, most expensive dress on Bond Street" before the prom. William had been her prom date. Her throat swelled shut and ached. Her whole history, her whole life, an illusion.

She couldn't help it; her eyes filled with tears, and all she could do was repeat, "Why?"

"Why William?" Grant trailed his finger down Sara's cheek. She jerked her head away, and he frowned. "Because I realized when you were sixteen that you would never consider me as a lover. I gave you someone you could be attracted to. Someone young and fun and wealthy. Someone you could relate to until the age closed."

"That wasn't the question."

Ignoring her, he kept going. "But the minute you met Slater, things between us changed."

If Jack hurried the hell up, he would find them in the house. And while he might not be able to enter Grant's suite, he'd be close enough for her to help him help her. Once Grant took her to another location, all bets would be off. Oh, damn. If Grant *didn't* take her, they'd never find—and destroy—the nest. Still, she wanted Jack to at least know where she was; even that much of a link would help her keep it together.

Hurry, Jack! "I love him."

"Yes, I know. Inconvenient." Grant touched her hair, a faint smile on his beautifully shaped mouth as his long, elegant fingers moved down to stroke the side of her face. Her flesh crawled. "It was hard enough getting rid of him the first time."

"You didn't 'get rid' of Jack, Grant." She forced a mocking note into her voice when what she wanted to do was surround him with a fireball until his skin turned black and his dangling penis burned to a crisp. "He left because he thought I'd aborted our baby."

Grant laughed, then tweaked her nose as though she were five years old. "Silly little Sara. Of course I did. None of the fights I caused in those last few months broke you apart—and really, I caused so many I lost track. But there you went, kissing and making up no matter how much I escalated your temper. Nauseating, really."

"How did you make us fight?" Come on, Jackson! Where the hell are you?

"Either I was there—invisible of course—or good old 'Harry' kept you company. Of course, being half Omnivatic, you sensed my presence. We're masked from wizards and Aequitas, but Omnivatics sense one another in the same way wizards do." His clear blue eyes sparkled with amusement. "Those headaches, baby doll. Indicating headaches every time I was near you and maintaining my cover one way or another."

Sara couldn't remember every argument she and Jack had had, but she did recall the ones since Jack had come to San Cristóbal. Harry had been in the room every time. And the headaches preceded every argument.

She swallowed her anger. She could probably do without any of Grant's answers. But she needed to buy time for Jack to find her. "You killed my baby?" Her throat closed with emotion. That loss had ripped out her heart and changed her forever.

"The fetus was the only way I could drive a permanent wedge between you and Slater. It worked perfectly. I had you back."

Her heart literally hurt at his casual dismissal of that

life-shattering event. "I wanted that baby, Grant. You stole my child from me. Miscarrying almost killed me."

"Nonsense, you were in perfect health. And it was a *fetus*," he repeated a little impatiently. "You told me you were uncertain about having a child with Slater. And, of course, you were correct. The child you bear will be *mine*. Mine, Sara. The first child ever born to an Omnivatic woman."

She'd confided in him that she was afraid to have children because of her erratic powers. But she'd also told him that she was going to work it out with Jack, because she wanted their baby desperately. She'd been scared, but happy. "You know that's impossible."

He looked pleased. "I see you've done your home-work, but there's a gap in your education, baby. No Omnivatic has ever bred with a *half-breed*. Your earlier pregnancy proved that you are fertile even though you're half Omnivatic. When the comet passes, it will make my sperm powerful enough to inseminate you. You *will* bear my children, Sara. I'll rule the Erebus, *and* the world."

Oh, is that all? Sara thought caustically. Grant was a megalomaniac, and a dangerously powerful one. One wouldn't know it to look at him. God, what irony— Grant looked like an angelic choirboy, while Jack looked like the devil incarnate.

No; it just seemed a prudent precaution, and it was easy to do. Every time you wanted to spread those little magical wings, I reminded you about poor Mommy and Daddy burning to cinders because you were too power-ful for your own good. Then every now and then, when you wanted to put your toe back in the magical water, I'd tweak your memory. Kill off some other poor fool as an example. Like Pavlov's dog, you eventually got the message that your powers weren't controllable."

"That was cruel." Hair freed from the cage, she stepped to the side, but he stayed with her. She swiped the back of her hand under her chin, where perspiration dripped on her shirt. Materializing a glass of ice water, she drank it down practically in one gulp, then held the ice-filled glass to her throat. "You killed my parents, didn't you?"

"Of course. Your father did his job—he produced you. They were redundant. I had my own plans for you from the day you were born. None of them included a loving relationship with Mommy and Daddy."

She didn't want to kill him quickly, Sara thought viciously. She wanted to roast him over a low flame for a very, very long time. She had to change the subject or she'd go for his throat now instead of later.

Breathe in; pause. Breathe out; pause. "Tell me more about William." William who was always charming and flirtatious, William who'd visited her at boarding school and taken her to the movies. William—she shuddered—who'd given her her first French kiss. Sara wiped the back of her hand over her mouth.

"Turns out my alter ego was convenient in business dealing as well. Good cop, bad cop. Being both was delightful fun."

"So William never existed?"

"Only when I needed him to."

Bile rose, acidic and bitter, in the back of Sara's throat. All the times Grant had pressured her to go out with William, especially when she'd been with Jack—it was all Grant. It had always been Grant. Their relationship, her entire life, was nothing but lies. Jack was the only truth she had.

"You're an Omnivatic. Why not just come right out and tell me?"

"Magic hasn't always been kind to you, my little Sara. I was merely trying to make you feel more comfortable and secure."

I freaking bet, asshole. "You lied to me."

"Only by omission, and for your own good."

Sara tried shoving the shocked haze out of her brain. She had to focus.

She forced her lips to tilt into a passable smile. "So now what? I assume you teleported me here for a reason instead of just inviting me." The ice in the glass had melted. She made the prop disappear.

Grant grinned and held out his hand. "Come with me. I want to show you something amazing."

Oh, she did not want to hold his hand. She ignored it, and his arm dropped. "Better than the Icehotel?"

"Is that where you two slipped off to?"

She fished her hankie out of her pocket and wiped away the sweat pooling at the base of her throat. "You wouldn't have enjoyed it. It was below freezing."

"I'm cold-blooded, baby. I like the tropical heat. I built this house here in San Cristóbal in 1623. Not a white man around but me. Lots of tasty villagers with pretty daughters." He threw his head back and laughed, delighted with himself. "I must say, I enjoyed modern civilization's denial of the 'legend' of Sarulu. For that matter, I'm impressed by how many of them survived and kept their wits enough to tell the tales."

As Grant led her toward his enormous walk-in closet, she dropped her hankie at the door.

Grant pulled her against him, tucking their joined hands against his naked, hairless body. "But I was always there for you, babe. I placed you in the best boarding school in the world. They took good care of you there."

"Boarding school wasn't family. Not like you, Grant," she said sweetly, wondering if he heard the sarcasm. "I know your father and mine were close friends, but that didn't mean *you* had to assume responsibility for me."

He brushed aside a strand of hair that had stuck to her cheek. Sara fought the impulse to flinch from his touch.

"There was no *father*. That was always me. I knew you were mine from the day you were born."

Gross. Her revulsion increased, even though he'd just confirmed what she'd told Jack and the Wizard Council earlier. "Then why on earth have you waited so long to tell me? You've always enjoyed younger women. I'm not exactly a spring chicken anymore." *Come on, tell me about the advent of Ophidian's comet. Tell me that you have to impregnate me as it travels overhead. Tell me all that, you miserable, lying sack of shit.*

The closet racks rotated on a circular hanging apparatus until a gap appeared at the far end of the room. He pressed the stop button, and after a moment the rack stopped, revealing a gap between a row of indistinguishable, ten-thousand-dollar dark business suits. A panel slid open in the wall hidden behind the clothing, exposing a set of stone stairs that disappeared downward in the dark.

A drift of dank, cold air slithered inside, mixing with the fragrance of cedar from the closet.

Her heart, already working overtime, sped up another few notches as she saw the stairs.

Show time.

THERE WAS NO TRACE. Jack couldn't follow her, because he couldn't Trace-teleport after her. "Where the hell did he take you, Sara?" Fear rode him with sharp claws.

"The hacienda? The rubble of the cave? The village?" *Think, damn it. Think. Where makes the most sense?*

EREBUS NOVEM TWO ARE ONE TO INFINITY IF NOT STOPPED.

He stood in the center of Sara's ultrafeminine all-white bedroom in San Cristóbal. The ceiling fan fluttered the drapes and the ruffles on the pillowcases. The air smelled delicately of lemon, ginger, and woman. *His* woman. He materialized both his Sig Sauer and the Ka-Bar knife. If magic didn't work in the cave, then goddamn it, brute force *would*.

He'd do a lightning-fast shimmer through the entire property, cross it off the list, then go directly to what was left of the cave. There had to be another entrance. He'd find it if he had to rip the hillside apart with his bare hands stone by fucking stone.

There was a light tap at the door, and it opened. "Sara, can I ask you—oh," Pia said, surprised to see him standing there armed to the teeth. "Jack."

"Obviously, you haven't seen her this evening." Damn it to hell. So she wasn't in the house. Fine; he'd teleport directly to the cave.

"No. I was—what's going on?"

"Baltzer's taken Sara. I'm afraid he's going to hurt her."

Pia blinked. "Grant? Hurt Sara? Why on earth would he—no, Jack, you're wrong. I saw him go to his suite about half an hour ago, and he was alo—Jack?!"

"THE TIMING HAD TO be optimal. I've waited more than three thousand years for today. This is my time. My destiny. You're about to witness history. You should be proud of your contribution to this momentous occasion, Sara."

How in the hell would Jack know where they'd gone if the panel closed behind them? Where *was* he? Shouldn't he have been here by now? She had to leave another clue.

Glancing around casually, her eyes fell on a hanging assortment of belts. She leaned over and ran her free hand over them, lifting several off their hooks and making appreciative sounds. The top belt had a distinctive pattern, and she waved the bundle at him. "Snakeskin, Grant? A relative, perhaps?"

He laughed, took the belts from her, and carelessly dropped them to the floor. The bulk of them fell in the doorway; perfect.

Grant turned his gaze on her. Sara felt the weight of his stare, hot, hard and heavy. "I've been biding my time. Waiting for *you*, Sara. You don't pick a peach until it's ripe. Now you're ready."

Yes. Ready to douse him with cheap brandy and flambé him, Sara thought. She locked her gaze on the pale blue chips of ice that were his eyes, but released his hand, stepping away from him. This time, he let go, confident that she was under his control.

"It's way too hot in here, Grant. I'm going to faint if I don't get some fresh air soon."

A change in the air, almost like static electricity, lifted the small hairs on her arms and neck, and made her jeans and T-shirt stick uncomfortably to her already overheated skin. His eyes were manic as he grabbed her hand again, pulling her after him through the opening.

"Think about it, baby," he said over his shoulder as they descended the steep, hand-cut stone steps. "The first Omnivatic birth, a full Omnivatic, in three thousand years! Aren't you proud and excited to be the woman making history?"

"It won't *be* a full Omnivatic, though, will it?" Sara pointed out. "I'm only half myself." Holy crap. Would she have *eggs?* The thought repulsed her even more.

"Our offspring will have enough Omnivatic blood to rule beside me for eternity."

God, he was pleased with himself. Filled with his own importance. "My father had to choose mortality to achieve that, and he only had one child," she told him, tripping down the narrow stairs much too fast as he refused to let go of her hand. The risers were several inches too deep, the treads several inches too short. "Are you going to choose mortality, Grant? I don't see why. You're a powerful Omnivatic. Who'd choose to be a puny mortal wizard when you'll eventually rule the world?"

There wasn't a mark on his body that she could see, Sara noticed. Thousands of years old, and he'd never been hurt? Never had a cut or a wound? That didn't bode well for her—or for Jack defeating him.

Grant laughed. "Between us, we will build my army in no time at all. Gestation takes one hundred days, and you shall have litters of anywhere from eighty to a hundred. I am viviparous. You don't understand this term? You will have *live* births, my dear. My children will arrive in this world alive and ready to serve. I shall quickly rise from Novem to Unum. With control of your womb, I'll not only rule the world, I'll rule all wizards, all Aequitas, all Omnivatics *and*, of course, all humans. I'll be invincible."

Somehow, some way, you'll be dead long before that happens. "So I'll be queen to your king?" *As Jack would say, Not just no, but hell no.*

He huffed out a laugh. "Right."

Lying sack of shit. "Excellent, because you know how much I love to shop, and I have *very* expensive taste. Can I have anything I want?"

"Sure, baby. Anything. Anything except Jack Slater."

Sara's heart did a double bump-thump of fear mixed with a liberal shot of anger. The stairs leveled out into what she realized was the back end of the crystal cave she and Jack had been in earlier. The C-4 they'd placed there was exactly where they'd left it. No sign of the massive explosion they'd witnessed earlier. Not even a scorch mark.

Grant must have set magical wards on it, which she hadn't detected because she had been so busy controlling her fear, and Jack hadn't noticed because it was Omnivatic magic.

The entire explosion had been nothing but an illusion.

One Jack would see immediately when he came back to look for her. He'd know this was where Grant would bring her.

It was marginally cooler in the cave. Sara carefully removed one of her gold bracelets, palming it until she could leave it somewhere for Jack to find.

Dusk must've fallen because the cave was dimmer than when she and Jack had been there setting the explosives earlier that day. Grant was yanking her along like a child's pull-toy. Okay. This place, Jack *could* find. Easily. He might not be capable of utilizing his powers in here, but he could enter with no problem. She hung back a little, ostensibly to get her bearings, and dropped the bracelet onto the sandy floor.

"I can't decide, did you mean it to come across as gothic with a hint of creepy or as early caveman chic?" They walked between walls embedded with crystal fragments.

"The crystal cave is merely a portal. You don't decorate a door, baby."

Sara winced and bent over, making a show of

massaging her ankle. "Hang on, I think I twisted something." *Come on, Jack.* "Give me a minute, Grant. These boots are too new, and they're hurting my feet." She undid the yellow laces and slid off one boot, sighing in relief. "That's better."

"Do you love me, Sara-mine?" This time the change was instantaneous, no shedding as he morphed. Sara let out a little scream of surprise as she straightened.

Jack stood there in his scruffy clothes and five-o'clock shadow. Stunned, she almost flung herself into his arms. Almost.

Grant turning from William to himself had been creepy enough, but changing to Jack shocked the hell out of Sara. God. All the times she'd been with Jack . . . had any of them been Grant? She shuddered, swallowing bile.

He turned her in his arms. "Kiss me like you mean it."

"Then be Grant. I don't want to kiss Jack."

"I think you do," he murmured against her mouth, his lips firm and familiar. Sara's heart thudded painfully. *Not Jack. Not Jack. Not Jack.* His skin sort of smelled like Jack's. His mouth almost tasted like Jack's. He stuck his tongue in her mouth. The sensation was . . . definitely, no way in hell Jack!

She shoved him away with both hands. He might look like Jack, but Sara's body knew it wasn't Jack she was kissing. She held her body stiff until, with a laugh, he let her go. He held out his hand.

The amulet she'd been wearing was draped across his palm. "Did you think this would deter me?" He smiled Jack's smile, but his eyes were flat and very much Grant.

"I love giving people the illusion that there's something that can stop me. *Nothing* can stop me from what I want, be it a nubile village girl to slake my sexual hunger or an athletic young woman who enjoys the chase. I'm unstoppable, Sara. What I want, I take."

"The 'athletic woman who enjoys the chase' didn't enjoy it at all, and you know it."

He brushed his thumb across her lower lip. "I enjoyed chasing you, baby. I *really* enjoyed chasing you. And didn't I give you the comforting illusion of safety by letting the chase happen in another woman's body? Didn't you feel good getting away? Didn't you feel triumphant and smug, thinking you'd won?"

"Go to hell, Grant. Cut to the real chase. Where are you taking me?"

"My home in the Pyrenees."

Sara forced a laugh. "We're in Venezuela. A long, long way from Spain." *Take all the time you want. Jack will figure this out and be right on your slimy ass. Then we can incinerate you together.* Sara was looking forward to it.

"This is a direct portal. Don't worry, we're almost there. Did you know that Omnivatics started breeding with the Basque people more than three thousand years ago?"

"Are you telling me that you're three thousand years old?" Sara asked incredulously.

"Give or take a decade or two. Returning is a link with our past," he continued in Jack's voice. "The nest is where I go to rejuvenate." Jack's body was also tanned all over. But his body had scars everywhere. The one on his shoulder caused by a kid at school throwing a psionic spear at him and him not dodging fast enough. The scar on his thumb where his father had hit him with a poker. Oh, damn.

This was not Jackson. Not Jack. Not Jack.

She kicked off the other boot; the sandy ground beneath her socks felt cool and cushiony.

"We've reached the portal," he said softly in Jack's voice. "Look."

The entire wall in front of them was a sheet of crystal as smooth as glass. She and Jack had come this far earlier that day, but the wall had appeared to be solid rock sprinkled with a few glittering crystals. No wonder they thought they'd come to a dead end.

It took a second for her to notice their reflections in the shiny surface: herself—and a giant iridescent anaconda. Sara's knees went weak. Oh, hell. The snake was taller than she was, and stood upright on its curled tail; its flat, triangular head, as large as her own, swiveled to look at her. Its rainbow-colored tongue flicked out, caressing her cheek.

Gogogogo! her mind screamed, but her feet refused to move. The snake, growing even larger, curled itself around her, pulling her into its coils. She sensed every muscle twitch, every bit of pressure, as the snake moved closer to the glass, taking her with it in its tight embrace.

"Sssssar

～ Twenty-one ～

Not waiting for an invitation, Jack kicked open the imposing double doors to Grant's suite. Inside was a regular freak fest complete with whips, chains, ball gags, cages, and spikes. Whatever Grant was into, Jack prayed he wasn't making Sara go along with it. His heart pounded harder, echoing in his head like the thumping rhythm of the aboriginal didgeridoo.

"Sara?" he yelled. "Sa-raa!"

No answer. The scent of dark wet cave swirled through the stink of incense, chilling his skin despite the oppressive heat. Underlying the cloying smell was the faint tang of lemon. *Yes!*

He noticed a heap of red under a monstrous cage. Recognizing Sara's jacket, Jack picked it up, then crushed it in his fist when he saw a pile of men's clothing nearby. Baltzer had taken off his clothes. . . .

No. Baltzer might be bare-ass naked, but Sara had dropped her jacket—just her jacket—intentionally. "Good girl. You leave me a trail of bread crumbs and I'll be right behind you."

Where were they?

Sara was smart. If she'd thought to leave the jacket, she'd leave something else. A splotch of yellow stood out against the red-and-black carpet across the room; Sara's hankie. As he bent to retrieve it, he looked through the open door it rested against. A huge closet. He leaned in and caught a glint of gold through the gaps between the perfectly hung suits on the suspended rotating rack. Jack walked through the wardrobe until he came to a space in the clothing where he saw a pile of belts wedged into a slight gap in the wall—a gap that looked a hell of a lot like a doorway.

Using the Ka-Bar knife as a lever, Jack forced the door open. Stairs. He materialized a Maglite and raced down the stone steps, looking for any sign Sara might have left behind—or anything that slithered.

The beam of his flashlight illuminated a speck of gold in the dirt of the cave floor up ahead. Jack ran toward it, scooping up a gold bracelet. He stuffed it into the front pocket of his jeans. "Sara-mine, I don't know where he's taking you, but you aren't alone," he muttered. The words came back in a mocking echo from the cave walls. All he heard over and over was the word *alone*.

He recognized the unusual crystal formations in the walls. Either he was in another cave that had exactly the same properties or this was a back entrance to the cave he and Sara had been in earlier.

He tried using Trace, not surprised when it didn't work. Not so much as a flicker. Fuck it. He hoped Sara's powers were still operational.

He picked up a small, bright red hiking boot with yellow laces, then its partner several feet ahead.

He could smell her in the confined space—smell her skin and smell her fear. "Hang on, sweetheart," he whispered, scanning the area for more clues. "Almost there."

What the hell—

There was the fucking C-4 they'd stuffed into the cracks in a rough semicircle overhead. Crap. The spectacular explosion had been nothing more than an illusion. Baltzer was damn good at them.

That was the bad news. The good news was that there was no blank rock face in front of him now. The wall flattened out into a plate of crystal that extended easily twenty feet to the roof and nearly as wide across. His reflection looked sunken and hollowed out in the flashlight's glow. Hell, it was probably more than just his reflection. It was how he felt inside. Without Sara, all of it was just a hollow imitation of living. He saw that now.

"I'm here, sweetheart." So near, and yet so far.

He peered closely at the mirror, looking for some seam, some spot that might indicate where they had gone. All that the Mag picked out was a single pair of footprints, nearly obliterated by a five-foot-wide swath of smooth earth. The track of a giant snake, he knew without a doubt.

Jack stared at his reflection in the mirror-smooth crystal. "None of it is going to matter if you don't save the girl, asshole. So get over it."

He jogged back a half dozen steps, then ran at the

mirror, intending to break through it. His shoulder exploded into radiant pain as he bounced off the crystal and catapulted sideways into the rough wall.

"Not that way." He looked around. "If not through the looking glass—then which way?"

Inside his head, a metronome ticked off the minutes.

❧ Twenty-two ❧

Sara's world went sheer white, then eclipsed to dense black. They passed through the crystal portal into a cathedral-size cavern filled with mammoth crystals, some fifty or sixty feet long and twenty feet in diameter. The enormous crystals jutted from the walls, ceiling, and floor. Most were as clear as glass, while others glowed an eerie opaque white. The entire chamber seemed to pulse in time with Sara's heartbeat.

"Beautiful, isn't it?" Grant/Jack asked, pausing just inside, his chest—*Jack's* chest—expanding with pride. Did he think that if he resumed Jack's form, she wouldn't be able to kill him? No, Sara realized; the thought would never cross Grant's mind. He considered himself invincible. But if necessary, she would use that arrogance to do just that. He wasn't Jack. She had to remember that.

As dramatic as the cavern was, it was the closed door behind them that held more interest for her. How was she going to The hair on the back of Sara's neck rose. Snakes. Every size and every color. They hung and swayed from the crystal beams thirty feet overhead. They slithered along the glittering floor by the thousands, making the floor undulate and move like a living thing.

Nobody could survive bites from multiple snakes. With a full-body shudder, she levitated three feet off the ground. Grant/Jack reached up and tugged on her hand. "Silly little Sara, nothing will hurt you here."

Except you. "Right. Not like you haven't lied to me before," Sara said flatly. "I'll just stay right—"

He tugged harder, and against her will, her feet touched the ground again. All her internal organs shrank up as several sinewy black snakes slithered across her sock-covered foot. She wished she hadn't left her damned ankle-high boots as clues for Jack to follow.

"Where are your shoes?" he asked with a puzzled frown.

"Let *go*." Yanking her hand out of his, she shot him a fulminating look.

He smirked. "Left them for Slater to find? How naive you are. Aequitas are incapable of entering an Omnivatic portal. You should know that."

"I must've missed that class." She'd missed all the classes.

She didn't know how to play Grant. For once in her life, she wished like hell she didn't feel compelled to ponder a decision. She wanted to be like Jack—a quick choice, and then live with it.

"My nest is half a million years old," he told her proudly, using Jack's face to smile.

Don't *do* that, Sara thought fiercely. "Did *you* make all these?" She indicated the glittering beams, the stalactites and the stalagmites that were so clear, so luminous they appeared extraterrestrial.

"Of course not—"

"Then it's not exactly a matter of pride, is it?" Was she capable of doing a good enough acting job to convince Grant that she was willing to go along with this?

Or should she show her disgust and fight him all the way?

Come on, Sara Jeannette. Decide. *Now.*

She wasn't a good actress.

Decision made.

"I can't stomach looking at you pretending to be Jack. Are you incapable of being the real you, Grant? William, Harry, Sarulu—who or what are you?"

He smiled Jack's smile. She resisted the urge to scratch that smile from his face with her fingernails.

"I'm whoever you can live with, Sara-mine." The use of Jack's special name for her was the last straw. He could try looking like Jack, sounding like Jack, smelling and tasting like Jack, but her heart knew differently. There was never going to be anyone like Jack Slater.

"It doesn't matter who you pretend to be. I'm not having sex with you. Ever," she told him flatly. "Get it, Snake-boy? No. Sex. You're going to have to do without, or find another half-breed to bear your snake-children. I'm not going to do it."

"Sara, you misunderstand me. I want to make you a goddess. Mother to the leaders of a new world order."

"Really?! You have a funny way of showing it."

He slid his fingers into her hair at her temples, the wrong side of too tight, making her wince. "You aren't thinking clearly." He tilted her face up so she was forced to look at him. Sara unfocused her eyes so Jack's face was a hazy blur. But his voice . . . "You're half Omnivatic. You can't change that. We are destined to be together. I will rule with you at my side. The Omnivatics will rise again."

Grant kissed her, crushing her lips hard against her teeth as he forced his tongue into her mouth. He tasted like seaweed. Bile rose up the back of her throat, and she instinctively bit down on his tongue. He backhanded her so hard she crashed to the floor, sliding on her hip and shoulder until her back struck a crystal stalagmite with enough force to make her teeth rattle. Snakes scattered in every direction. Shaking, Sara turned enough to break off a small chunk of C-4 before staggering to her feet. Her face was hot and throbbing, but she reached behind her and stuffed the quarter-size putty against the side of the crystal. A swipe of the back of her hand across her mouth left a streak of red blood.

"Stay the hell away from m-me." Her voice shook.

He reached out, and a second later she slammed into his body like a puppet on a string.

"Do not think that our past relationship gives you license to mess with me, little girl."

Lightning fast, he gripped her face with both hands, lifting her off her feet. "I can impregnate you conscious or unconscious, broken or unbroken. Makes no differ-ence to me. *Choose*."

"Put me down."

He lowered her until her socked feet touched the sandy ground that sparkled like diamond dust. "Do that again, and I'll break your spine."

It wasn't an idle threat. Her breath wheezed in and

out in sheer, unadulterated terror as she stood paralyzed, not knowing what he'd do next. There was a chance, a faint, *very* faint chance that Jack would swoop in in time to rescue her. But Sara knew that possibility was getting more minimal by the second. Even a powerful wizard couldn't break into Grant's nest without accessing the portal. A wizard without his powers had no chance at all. That was her grim reality.

Mere hours was all she had to figure out a way to kill Grant and get herself out of the cave. That was hardly any time at all. She tilted her wrist, then sucked in a horrified breath. Not hours. The hands on her watch had jumped forward in the process of traveling through the portal.

Twenty minutes.

Twenty miserly minutes before Ophidian's comet passed closest to Earth. Twenty minutes that would change the course of her life forever.

She was scared down to her marrow. She wasn't equipped to deal with *any* of this. She hated the feeling of helplessness that was preventing her from taking action. *Breathe. Focus. Look for a weapon.* The smooth touch of Grant's hand ran down her back, and she shuddered. It didn't matter if he looked like Jack. He sure as hell didn't feel like Jack.

"Show me the Grant I know," she begged. Having Jack do what Grant intended somehow made this worse.

"You like this form. I know you do, Sara.

"Then I want one thing in return."

"Just one thing?" Jack's familiar laugh made her throat ache. Sara knew unequivocally that she'd never see the real

Jack again. "You're far easier than I imagined. What is it?"

He slipped his hands around her wrists, pinning them behind her back. Too late, Sara realized what she should have seen all along. Grant didn't have a better side. His dark side was the only side he had.

"I want my baby back. Mine and Jack's baby."

He hissed at her.

There was almost a sense of relief knowing that she was on her own in this, a kind of finality that calmed her frayed nerves and shredded sense of self. She could go out guns blazing, but she'd do it alone. The reality was, she'd always been alone, she just hadn't known it. No one was going to save her. It was her against Grant. She weighed the odds, and the chances of her survival were nil.

But if she died, she'd make damn sure Grant died with her.

"Come now, as much as I enjoy your fighting, time is growing short. The comet is coming, and when it passes, I must be inside you. It is your destiny." He wrapped his arms around her. For a moment, just a moment, Sara let her head fall on Jack's broad chest. He squeezed her so hard she couldn't breathe, and his erection jabbed between her legs, hard and insistent. She wriggled and squirmed until she could get both arms between them, then shoved as hard as she could.

Then she braced herself to be knocked across the room again.

He shoved her aside. "I don't have time to play rough right now. But I'll entertain you later. There's no way out. A quick fuck, and you can spend the rest of your life—"

"There won't *be* a rest of my life," she cut in. "Once a child is born, if that's even possible, you'll have no use for me. None. You'll kill me."

His eyes glittered. "That's where you're wrong. I'll put a child in you every hundred days until I build my dynasty."

"I'd rather die."

He grabbed her chin and turned her to face him. Face *Jack*. "I can make you *wish* you were dead."

"I wished I was dead when you killed my baby, you sick fuck." She wanted to lash out and tell him nothing he could do to her now could hurt as badly as that had. But, of course, that was ridiculous—he could hurt her very badly indeed. He could hurt her so she begged him to kill her.

"You miserable coward. Can't you face me as who you are instead of who you'd like to be? Jack is everything you wish you were, Grant. He's—"

"I can be anything to you. I can be everything to you. You don't need Jack Slater. You need me." The impostor Jack leaned forward, his firm lips looking oh-so-kissable as if it were the real Jack who held her. But as their lips were about to touch, a long, thin, dark tongue darted out, the forked end flickering along her cheek in a mock caress that left a glistening trail. *OhGodohGodohGod.*

She wanted to vomit.

Golden eyes with elliptical pupils flashed. "Ccccease talking, woman." He'd morphed into Sarulu—man-size, but a snake with iridescent black skin. He pulled her to him, his scales rasping against her clothing, the pressure around her body unbearable as he wrapped her with his coils.

She tried the only thing she could think of.

"Grant, stop. You're crushing me."

The pressure eased slightly, and a long tongue, now thicker and multihued, reached out to stroke over her mouth, across her cheek, and down her neck, flicking and feathering a damp trail into her cleavage.

"Fear tastes good on you, Sssara."

She twisted her face away, refusing to meet those yellow eyes.

"Welcome to my nessst. Now you will sssee real power, the kind of power that will dominate the world. And you will be my gateway to that power. My offssspring will be invincccible."

"I'm not willing!"

"That'sss no way to greet your mate, my little Sssara."

She shoved, hard. The broad chest was now like a wall of iron, cool and smooth and totally unyielding.

"Go—" Hard to breathe. Lights danced before her eyes as the enormous snake grew and grew. Ten feet. Twenty feet. Thirty feet. More. He swung her twenty feet off the floor, squeezing the breath out of her body. The giant crystals overhead weaved and spun as he slithered across the glittering floor. "Go—to h-hell."

She called fire to him. Hot. Hotter. Supernova fire.

With a sibilant laugh, he daangled her upside down over an enormous black-draped bed, sunk deep within a circle of glittering ten-foot-high crystal shards. If he let her go over them, she'd be impaled before she had time to kiss her ass good-bye.

The flames danced over his glossy coils, amplifying

the colors. The heat made her eyes burn and her lungs stutter as she tried not to cough, but the fire had no impact on him. None at all.

The flames winked out.

And so did her hope.

It was all she had. Fire was her power to call. She'd given it everything she knew.

"We mussst be in sssnake form to rejuvenate, but fire issss a gift of the Omnivatic. Fire issss both desssstroyer and creator." His gold eyes flashed red. "Time to create, little Ssssara."

Struggling was useless. The snake twisted her this way and that as he slithered, making the cavern reel and shimmer. Her ears filled with the sibilant whispers of thousands of snakes as they converged on the bed from every nook and cranny.

Darkness crowded Sara's vision.

Her bravery had been a delusion of her own making.

Sarulu released her. For a moment, Sara hung suspended twenty feet off the bed; then she dropped like a stone.

His MAGIC DIDN'T WORK worth shit. He'd known it wouldn't, but fool that he was, Jack kept trying. He blasted the rock face: nothing. Feeling impotent, scared, and pissed off, he tried again, all the while searching the crystal mirror for a hinge, a handle, a fucking way in. "Hang on, sweetheart. Just hang on. I'm coming. You did a great job leaving me clues; I'm here. Just a few more. . ." Fuck. Who was he kidding? This might be the portal, but so far he was stymied. Would he be able to follow the lead she'd left him?

He took out the Sig, held the muzzle flush to the reflective surface, and pulled the trigger. The spent bullet—hotter than hell—dropped onto his booted foot. "Shit." He tried again; same damn result. Holstering the gun, he pulled out the big-ass Ka-Bar knife. Jack wasted precious seconds digging around the perimeter seeking a chink, a crack. The carbon-steel knife, factory-tested to a strength of HRC-61, was pretty much indestructible; yet all he got for his pains was a broken tip.

Sweat ran into his eyes, and he impatiently swiped his face with his sleeve. Explosives hadn't worked. A gun fired point-blank didn't work. A Ka-Bar didn't work.

Pounding the portal uselessly with his fist, Jack thumped his head on the mirrored surface, squeezing his eyes shut on a prayer. "Sara."

SARA'S FREEFALL HAD HER screaming all the way down. She hit the hard surface of the bed, then bounced as if it were a trampoline before landing flat on her back, which knocked what little air she had left out of her lungs; she lay there stunned.

Sarulu's pink-white mouth opened in a semblance of a smile as he hovered over her. His enormous triangular head dipped to confront her face to face. "Sssssaraaaa." For a second, she saw Grant's devious expression transposed over the reptiles and a sharp pain hit her between the brows.

She struggled up on her elbows, fighting to draw a sip

of air into her starving lungs. The crystal rim of the bed was covered with snakes, all of them staring unblinkingly at her. Sarulu's triple-forked tongue lashed around her throat. One fork held her still; another slithered beneath the neck of her T-shirt, inside the cups of her bra, and curled around her breasts. The third slid up between her legs.

"They know I'm here," she said unevenly as her lungs struggled to fill. "The Council will find you. But Jack will *kill* you."

"Exxxcellent. If we are to have an audienccce, you sss-hould be more presssentable."

Between one breath and the next, her hands and feet were spread wide, and tightly bound. Her clothes vanished, cool air washing over her sweat-damp skin. Sara screamed with shock and loathing. Terror pulsed inside her, black and absolute. Incapable of moving more than a few inches, she bucked and struggled, powerless to free herself.

Sarulu twisted her body, flipping her face-down like a freaking pancake on a griddle. Snakes slithered down the crystals en masse. They wriggled and writhed all over the black bed in a mass of flailing bodies, making it impossible to distinguish heads from tails.

OhGodohGodohGodohGod.

Through glazed eyes she watched them slither over her, her heart palpitating impossibly fast as they crawled over her wrists, her arms, her bare legs, through her hair. She noticed in a dulled part of her mind that the bed-covering wasn't lamé or silk but a giant swath of black, iridescent snakeskin that had crystallized into the jagged shards along the edges.

Sarulu's shape transmogrified again into a more man-like form with arms and legs; it's fingers and toes elongated, becoming thin, wriggling, taillike probes. She wanted to close her eyes. Even though her vision was impaired by the way she lying, she saw enough. Her heart couldn't pound any faster.

A dozen thin, slick tongues caressed her body from behind. One slid between her chest and the mattress to curve around her breasts, clamping down painfully on her nipples. A leathery tongue slithered down the crease of her ass. A rubbery wet forked tongue glided up her spine.

She gasped at the invasion, twisting and bucking. Her movement sent dozens of smaller snakes arching into the air before they landed on the sheet nearby. The larger, heavier ones clung to her tenaciously, their forked tongues darting out to taste her, their beady eyes dark and malevolent.

"Easssy, Sssara. You don't want to upsssset the oth-ersss."

They seemed pretty upset to her already as they writhed all over her, their tongues fluttering on every inch of her skin. The flick of a forked tongue inside the shell of her ear made her flesh crawl.

"Do you know that sssometimes when sssnakes mate, we form a tightly writhing ball of sssex? And tonight, my brothersss and sssisters will be part of our joining. And you, Sssara, will be the cccenter of it all."

She summoned a sheet of fire, sending it flaring around her body. The heat was intense, and she squeezed her eyes tightly shut at the flash of brilliant white light. High-pitched sibilant squeals and hisses surrounded her, but other than a few apparently charbroiled bodies, it was business as usual for the survivors. The smell of cooked snake assaulted her nostrils, and a low pall of brown smoke hindered visibility for a few moments before it began to dissipate.

The temperature suddenly dropped, shocking her. Sara welcomed the chance to get some brain cells collected so she could think. Think, damn it. Think. Twisting her head, she peered over her shoulder to see where Sarulu was. He'd reduced his size, maybe twenty feet long now. His powerful man-snake body, covered in shimmering black scales, loomed over her. He—it—was coiled between her spread legs.

No!

His dead-fish-colored smile, filled with needle-sharp teeth, widened, and his elliptical eyes glittered. A large green and brown snake as thick as her arm curled over and under her right thigh, pulling her gaze away from the giant snake hovering over her; when she looked back to her nemesis, she almost passed out with sheer terror.

The clawlike spurs at his sides sank into her hips to hold her steady, and Sara screamed with the excruciating red-hot pain. Black encroached on her vision. . . and she welcomed the darkness.

~ Twenty-three ~

Defeated, Jack slumped against the wall. There was nowhere else to go. No place to turn. No way—what the hell? His ass burned as if someone had stuck him with a red-hot poker. He sprang away from the rock and clamped his hand over his—

The crystal dagger. Jesus. How the fuck could he have forgotten?

He ripped it out of his pocket, neatly slicing through the fabric of his jeans. The dagger gleamed with a pure white light in his hands. "Help me save the girl," he instructed, more a prayer than a command. Taking the dagger in both hands, he aimed for the heart of the crystal portal, and sliced downward.

Jack didn't have time to think. One minute he was being pulled apart and bathed in blinding white light as the portal pressed him through to the other side; the next he was staring, horrified, through a ring of giant crystals at a distorted image of a naked Sara covered in snakes, with the biggest mother-fucking snake he'd ever seen wrapped around her, poised over the curve of her sweet bare ass.

With a roar of rage, he lunged forward, dagger fisted

in his hand. He shattered the crystal between them and kept going. Two-handed, Jack raised the dagger, plunging it hilt-deep into the giant snake's back, then braced his foot on a lower coil, ripping through the flesh with both hands. With a twist of its body and a hissing roar, Sarulu arched over him, tongues lashing, yellow eyes glittering.

Jack leapt high enough to grip the hilt of the dagger and sliced a few more feet down the thick hide, which oozed black, foul-smelling liquid. He jumped down to the bed, where snakes of every fucking size writhed and twisted around his boots. The faster he pulled snakes off Sara, the faster more crawled over her.

"Sara, run. Get out *now!*"

There was no answer, and his heart thundered at the thought that she might be . . . no, Grant needed Sara alive. To keep her that way, Jack had to kill the Omnivatic. Focusing on Sarulu, he kicked more eager snakes out of his way, spreading his feet on the springy mattress for balance. He gave a little bounce. "Come on, you motherfucker. It's just you and me now."

The giant snake reared, screaming as Jack slashed a thin black line along the outer corner of its eye. It reared back again, then lashed out with its triple tongue. Jack wrapped the fork on his left around and around and around his forearm, stretching the rubbery thing as far as he could, then lopped it off with the deadly blade of the crystal dagger.

The snake went ballistic. The sound it made was ear-splitting. Good. One down, two fucking tongues to go.

No, wait—Jack spotted something even more rewarding to lop off. He went in hard, fast and low, and grabbed the dick by one of its dicks. With a feral smile, he cut through the penis, the dagger like a hot knife slicing through butter. He went in for the other one.

His arms and the front of his shirt were covered in black blood, slick and vile-smelling. The snake tried to shake him off, him, Sarulu couldn't see Jack beneath him, its own body too large and cumbersome. Jack severed the second penis as neatly as he'd done the first.

He felt a soaring sense of victory as the giant snake fell backward, rapidly coiling around itself as protection. Damn thing must be at least two hundred feet long. Jack planned to carve it up into belts and shoe leather before he was done.

Black blood streamed from the gaping wounds, onto the already slick and slippery bed.

Sara was up on all fours, disoriented. Snakes crawled all over in an attempt to tie her down.

"Hell, woman. You still here? Go go go," Jack yelled, dodging a slashing tongue. He jumped for it, missed, waited; when Sarulu lashed at him again, he grabbed onto it and swung the dagger in a gleaming arc. The rubbery rainbow-colored tongue landed on the bed. Jack kicked it out of his way.

"Sara! Go! Get out—" Sarulu slashed at the side of his head, slicing into his cheek and knocking him into Sara, who was staggering to her feet. They went down in a tangle of arms and legs.

"Now, Ssslater, it'sss time for you to die." The three-thousand-year-old snake loomed over them, its fangs, gleaming and bared, the size of swords.

Somewhere in the mass of snakes, Sara's hand found Jack's. A stream of energy flooded into him, and he knew instantly that Sara was tapping into and amping his powers with her own Omnivatic powers. He pulled her flush against his side, his body shaking with the intensity of the power.

"Watch out!"

He whipped his head around just in time to see the giant snake lunge forward. Jack thrust his hand into the white cave of its mouth as far as it would go, then jerked his arm up hard and fast, thrusting the dagger through Sarulu's brain.

The vertical slits of the Omnivatic's eyes widened in shock, and the behemoth began to fall like a giant tree.

Jack grabbed Sara's hand, yanking her out of the way as the giant snake toppled across the bed. The weight crushed hundreds of other snakes, and broke the bed in two.

"Is he dead?" Sara asked hoarsely, her eyes huge.

"Hang on." He climbed a jagged section of the bed, then crawled up Sarulu's large body. For a moment he just stood there, staring down at the Omnivatic.

Then he plunged the dagger once more into its brain.

With a mighty roar of escaping gasses, the all-powerful Omnivatic deflated like a giant balloon, curling and coiling into a small empty skin.

Sara came up beside Jack, and laid a shaking hand on his arm. "Let me." A second later, the last of the Omnivatic went up in a spiral of black, stinking smoke. All that remained on the floor was a pile of ash.

With an elaborate sigh, she shook her head. "A

woman's work is never done." And zapped an incendiary fireball directly at the remains of the snake-covered bed. The noise was horrific, but undeniably satisfying. She dusted off her hands and shot him a grin.

Jack wrapped his arm around her shoulders. "Good job, sweetheart."

A BLINDING WHITE FLASH of light, and they were back in the cave. Sara came to a dead stop, grabbing his arm to stop him as well. "Wait! We have to destroy the portal for good this time."

She spun on her heel. Flames ate along her arms and danced on her fingers. Her naked body glowed in the fire's light. She was magnificent. With a giant whoosh, she let loose an enormous fireball from her fingertips that smashed against the crystal mirror, shattering it into a million glittering shards and sending a giant rumble through the cavern.

Jack grabbed hold of Sara and tucked her under him to protect her from the flying debris. The rumbling grew louder. The ground rolled beneath their feet, and rocks and bits of crystal rained down from above.

"Earthquake. Get us out of here!" he yelled.

As the cavern began to collapse, turning itself inside out in a spectacular display of glittering, sparkling crystal, they ran flat-out, taking the stone steps two at a time toward the square of light at the top. Grant's bedroom hadn't changed any, but for Sara, everything had changed.

"We need to get everybody out of here." She stumbled as the floor shifted beneath her feet in the roll of a full-fledged earthquake. Nearby, the cage swung violently from side to side and the chains on the walls rattled.

"Where?"

"Just focus, Jack. Get them out. This place is going to blow to hell."

He grabbed her hand, braced his feet, and held her steady against the pitch and roll. Together they reached out, found every person they could, and teleported them to the nearby village.

The grinding sound of mortar loosening and bricks falling in the walls around them snapped Sara to full attention. A giant crack rent the ceiling above with the sound of a shotgun, raining down plaster dust and sending the cage crashing to the floor.

"We've got to get out. Now," Jack yelled. He yanked her to his chest and wrapped himself around her, then teleported the two of them to the jungle's edge.

A deep, grinding rumble shook the walls of the hacienda, and they watched it collapse in upon itself, almost dissolving from the center out into a deep crevasse caused by the collapsed cave on which it was built. A wave of dust and air whooshed past them, coating the thick green foliage around them in powder white.

Overhead, a brilliant white streak of light arced across the night sky.

Oblivious to her naked state, Sara stared at him wide-eyed and triumphant. "There's the comet! We did it. Holy crap, Jack. That was too close, but we did it!"

He grinned. "Come here. Not nearly close enough." He pulled her to him.

"Wait just a sec. Let me get some clothes on." She glanced at the jungle behind them and shuddered. "I don't want the bugs to eat me alive."

He laughed. "*Now* you're worried about a little *insect* bite?"

"The only thing allowed to bite on me is you."

"Excellent." He grinned. "Then you don't need any clothes, do you?"

"Don't even think about it."

"You know what I want right now?"

She brushed his hair out of his face. "To be somewhere far, far away from jungles and snakes?"

He smiled. "Are you thinking what I'm thinking?"

Sara returned his sappy grin, and in an instant they were back in the cabin in Switzerland, shower-fresh and naked on the bed. Snow swirled in gentle white puffs outside the window, and with a snap of her fingers, Sara got the fire in the huge rock hearth roaring nicely.

"Is this what you meant?" she said with a grin that lit her beautiful eyes and went straight to his heart.

"Not exactly. I was thinking more like this." He pulled her against him, touching chin to toe, the heat of him seeping into her bones and making her melt inside. His lips were firm and sweet, the kiss perfect. "I love you, Sara-mine. I always have. I always will. Marry me?"

She ran a finger down his cheek, loving the way his freshly shaven skin felt. She looked up into his midnight blue eyes and felt him holding his breath. "I love you, Jack Slater. I love you to hell and back. You are my own. My heart."

A warm chuckled vibrated in his chest. "Is that a yes?"

"I want candles. Thank you." He gave her hundreds of pure white candles, their flames flickering gently with his movement as he rolled between her spread legs. Sara walked her soft feet up his thighs and climbed his ass, then crossed her ankles in the small of his back and wriggled to get more comfortable.

"Now?"

"I want soft music."

He gave her a track of mellow jazz, and her mouth hummed along his jaw.

"Now?"

"Champagne. And flowers, and sunshine gleaming on fresh-packed snow."

Jack dropped his head on her shoulder. "You're killing me, woman."

She laughed, rubbing his butt with her heel. "Tomorrow you start courting me."

"Deal. Now?"

She tilted her face and placed a sexy-as-hell kiss on his mouth. "Yes, that's a yes. I love you, Jack Slater. Just one thing. . ."

"Anything."

"Can we stick to *extremely* cold climates for a while? I think I've developed a serious snake problems.